WAR (

MW01537019

This page-turning sequel to Olivia's Hope is filled with drama and intrigue involving new and old friends. As we continue the well-loved story of Jenny and Seth, new characters and dangers arise to threaten the happiness of their family and friends. With secrets revealed and the past floating to the surface, don't miss the hair-pin plot twists in War Child.

—Kelsie Derbes

Although I am still testing the waters of fiction, Kevin Karella's second historical fiction novel, *War Child*, has me absolutely hooked. While this second novel introduces extremely interesting new characters, it also develops characters from his first exciting novel, *Olivia's Hope*; Example: Lincoln James becomes even more of an enigma to Seth despite new insights into Lincoln's past. Within these pages, be prepared for an adrenaline-inducing and emotionally-captivating ride that is so real you will be clamoring for more!

—Mike Botkin,
former Marine Infantryman/US Army Aviator

War Child is an incredible novel that pairs a story about finding true family & friendship with coming to terms with one's past. Then stir in a sweet romance and a page turning mystery as Celia struggles to lay the past to rest and live her life in the present. It is an inspiring tale that will leave a warm glow in your heart and a desperate need for the next book.

—Heather Flanagan, University Student

Emerging author Kevin Karella captured my interest with the most memorable Olivia's Hope ...

His second work in the Lincoln James Legacy series, War Child had me riveted as I attempted to sort out the characters and what their interactions would mean to the outcome of the story.

The words left me with vivid pictures of each character as they came to life.

I laughed, I cried, I was filled with passion when the "bad guys" repeatedly tried to destroy.

I felt compassion for the whole family when the twins were born and eagerly followed the emerging beautiful love story.

It's a complex tale with twists, turns and sub-plots that will keep the book firmly grasped in the hands of the reader.

—Linda Kuhns

From the first page to the last, Kevin's suite of character's captures and holds your attention. A powerful combination of adventure, mystery and relationship twists that kept me engaged. I'm ready for the next book!

—C. Perry

Action, Romance, Adventure, drama and at times Comedy too!

I read Olivia's Hope, Kevin's debut novel, when it first came out. It captured me from the very first page. It was so engaging, I felt as if I was part of the story. When it came to an end, it left me desperate for more.

War Child did not disappoint. The mysterious murders, the wonderful love story and the twists and turns keep you guessing. One of the main characters is much more than he seems on the surface. You are given only tantalizing glimpses of his past. A past the welds friendships together for a lifetime. But a past that even his family is mostly unaware of. You will love it.

Once again, impatiently waiting for next book.

—Kim McQuiston

LINCOLN JAMES
LEGACY

WAR CHILD

KEVIN KARELLA

Paperback: 979-8-9858370-0-1

Hardback: 979-8-9858370-1-8

Ebook: 979-8-9858370-2-5

DEDICATION

To the throngs of Olivia's Hope fans
that were so passionate for a sequel. Without them
I would not have had the courage to write the trilogy.

To my brothers in arms.
Warriors who love as hard as they fight.

Kevin Karella

"God has made a path for each of us, the happy man
is the one who finds it."

FORWARD

"Livin the Dream" is a common saying amongst Airline Pilots. At one time when Steak and Champaign was served in the First Class cabin and passengers wore suits to travel, Pilots were actually living the dream. The job today is pretty mundane, so it is pretty exciting when one of your fellow "button pushing monkeys" comes out with a book.

"Olivia's Hope" kept popping up on my facebook and instagram a few years back. The book cover was pretty feminine, in my opinion, and made me think of "girly romance novel." I purchased the book, and aspired to slog through a kissy face novel to support a fellow pilot.

Do NOT judge a book by it's cover - I was blown away. Olivia's Hope was filled with suspense, murder, intrigue - and some kissy face. Having a former career as an Army Aviator, I could tell right away that CPT Kevin Karella was a soldier. I called him up to chew him out for misrepresenting his novel with the cover. We ended up talking for a few hours.

During the conversation I found Kevin not only to be worldly, but he came across to me as a very passionate husband, a loving father and God fearing warrior that is wearing a full shield of armor. Having been a Best Selling Author myself, and having a history of helping books become bestsellers, I decided during that chat that I would push Kevin to aspire to become a bestselling author.

The Lincoln James Legacy book cover nailed it for me. Although I think this book stands alone, Guys, I'm going to enlist you to get your copy of Olivia's Hope as well. Read it in the privacy of your house or use a magazine cover to disguise it - but, get it today. Girls, not to worry, Legacy will make you all gushy and your hayfever will kick in a few times I promise.

I'm not sure if the cover for Olivia's Hope was a misstep or if Kevin is some kind of evil genius. His books are appealing to both men and women alike. I don't want to give away the sauce but Lincoln James Legacy is filled with flirting, knife fights, kissing, shoot outs, love, mysterious deaths, more kissing, military intrigue, jealousy, roughnecks…and a wedding (spoiler alert).

I was fortunate enough to get an advanced copy of Lincoln James Legacy. The book was so good that I am writing this Foreward in the hopes that I get a first look at his next book. Kevin has an adventure to tell and I am here to read it as it evolves. Humble as he is, I can tell you that CPT Kevin Karella is "Livin' the dream"

Donald Peters
Amazon #1 Bestselling Author, Aviator, Adventurer.
23 January 2022

PROLOGUE

The kidnapper stared across the filthy kitchen table at the semi-conscious woman. She was probably in her thirties, though hard living had taken its toll. Her head would lift occasionally, and the bloodshot, vacant eyes would slowly blink. A moment later, her head would loll back and forth before falling to rest on her folded arms as consciousness became more and more elusive. Her lank, brown hair flopped onto the table like an old, worn-out mop. At first it had been a bit of a struggle getting her to sit down in the old, dusty chair, but as the drugs kicked in and took effect, she became less belligerent, more compliant, and finally, there she was. She had absolutely no idea what kind of danger she was truly in.

The old house hadn't been inhabited in years and everything, including the old kitchen table, was covered in a thick layer of dust and filth. Dried and nearly mummified rat droppings littered the wooden plank floor and Formica kitchen counter. One of the mint-green cupboard doors hung crooked and slack on only one hinge. With all the windows boarded up long ago, there wasn't much danger of someone peeking in or accidentally stumbling upon this place. Considered by some as haunted, the once happy home had been abandoned and totally forgotten for years. It had been quite a while since the last visit. The fill from the cushions of the couch in the ancient parlor, stolen long ago by some raccoon or squirrel to build a nest.

I wouldn't want to live in that nest, the kidnapper thought dryly. Though not fresh, the memories were still there, still present. They somehow hung in the air as if suspended on the very spiderwebs that crisscrossed the rooms and doorways. They were also soaked into the painted panel walls and floor, even the furniture. The memories were the loudest, though, in the cold, dark, dank, basement. The smell of mold and rot permeated the structure, especially from the earthen floor of the root cellar in the back of the basement. The screaming, the crying, the digging, the cold, the fear. The blood.

The woman had passed out, a thin string of drool running down her chin dripping slowly onto the table. Her chemically induced stupor was born partly of her own high intake of alcohol and a little something extra that had been dropped into her last beer.

Hmm, her last beer.... Ever.... Period. *I wonder. Would she have had that Bud Light or something more...exotic. Probably, that is, if she would have known it was to be her last beer.* A thin smile spread across the face of her kidnapper.

She was rather pretty. Probably beautiful before the recent years of alcohol and cigarettes took their toll. Late nights and too much partying sure could age a person. One would think someone in the medical profession would be a little more careful with their health.

Of course, her current state wasn't so great. The shoulder length, soft brown curls that had been styled just so were now a mass of tangled hair. The carefully applied mascara streaked down her cheeks from the fits of crying that came with sad drunks, and her brown eyes appeared bloodshot whenever they fluttered open for a moment or two. Too bad she wasn't a happy drunk, the kidnapper mused. On second thought, it didn't really matter.

Her body wasn't bad either. She wore tight-fitting jeans, and western-cut, short-sleeved, snap-up shirt. The top three snaps were undone to show off her ample cleavage, and the bottom three were undone so she could tie the shirttails, revealing a fairly fit, flat tummy. Damn, the kidnapper observed. That takes some work.

Should I do this? The kidnapper carefully considered. *Could I do this?* Was probably more to the point. There was no real relationship. Nothing to be traced. An even better question was, *what did she ever do to me?* Nothing, really. The wrong place at the wrong time. Talked to the wrong person. Smiled at the wrong person. Trusted the wrong person. Had the wrong job. Chose the wrong target for her affections. Commiserated with the wrong person. Just bad luck is all. *Would it hurt her?* Does it matter either way? Not really.

Well, I guess it's time to get it done.

The bedraggled woman, again, briefly raised her head up off her arms, only this time, her red-rimmed, whisky-brown eyes rolled back in her head before it dropped back to the table with an audible smack.

The kidnapper pulled out a pair of latex gloves from a box on the table. First one, and then another, and slipped them on with practiced efficiency. One more moment to check if there was any real feeling inside. *Fear?* No. *Excitement?* Not really. Actually, nothing at all. *How unfortunate.* The combination of Ambien and the roofie in that last beer would have kept her from remembering anything if there had been any feeling of regret. The next step was straight forward. The latex-clad hand was simply placed over the mouth and nose and held there tightly for only a few minutes. No real struggle, just a twitch or two. Strange, the *killer* thought. That wasn't so hard. Not hard at all. Too bad… "Such a pity." the killer said aloud to the corpse. Now to move her. At least she wasn't too heavy.

CHAPTER ONE

Seth looked over at Jenny's pale, petite left hand. The only ring on it was her mother's opal. He knew how much it meant to her. It was the only physical thing she had left from her besides fading memories. Today though, Seth hoped to add another ring and another memory, if Jenny would agree. He'd thought a lot about it and had picked out the ring within a few days of getting out of the hospital. He'd had to have Link's help to go pick it up after it had been sized properly and now it rested in a red velvet box tucked into his inside jacket pocket. "Hey, babe," he'd said earlier that morning. "I've got to fly the airplane down to Dickinson to have a new radio installed. How do you feel? Would you like to come along?"

He had to talk real fast to get Doc Griffin to renew his flight medical. The biggest issue was to need nothing stronger than ibuprofen and Tylenol for pain management for his bullet wound. He refused to let anyone know just how much it really hurt. *Movie actors lie.* He thought to himself with a little chuckle. At the time though, he was so pumped up on adrenaline, he didn't even realize he'd been shot. It was only afterwards that the excruciating pain kicked in.

Barely thirty minutes into the flight, Seth glanced over at Jenny, already nodding off. He was sure that she had no idea that they were going in a big circle. Her strawberry blond hair and elvish nose reminded him of Tinkerbell the way her front locks drifted over her eyes as her head bobbed up and down. *Zing!* Another heart string just attached itself. *How can one man get so lucky? Twice.*

"Hey honey, I've got an idea. Let's see if we can spot your wild stallion when we are over the badlands." he suggested

"Oh, that would be so cool," she said, her eyes suddenly wide with excitement. "It seems like such a long time ago that we saw that beautiful stallion but really, it was only a few months ago." She said almost as an afterthought.

Both of our lives have changed, and soon it will change yet again, he thought as he was resting his hand on her belly. Suddenly there was a huge kick. It made him feel gooey inside. *That's one of my children. He* thought.

They weren't flying much more than a few minutes when Jenny started to nod off again. Try as she might, she just couldn't seem to keep her sky-blue eyes open. *Occasionally they were stormy blue depending on her mood,* Seth thought with a quiet little chuckle. The pregnancy took its toll on her energy reserves, and that made Seth smile even more, as his plan was coming together quite nicely. He positioned a certain hayfield outside of Jenny's window and pulled one of the engines to idle.

Jenny's head popped up, and she looked around. "What's wrong?" Brushing the hair from her eyes, her gaze darted from Seth to the controls and back to Seth.

"We seem to be having a little engine trouble," Seth said calmly. "I knew I should have bought more gas back there."

"What?" Jenny exclaimed. "We ran out of gas?"

"Yes, but just in that engine. Not to worry honey, we can fly just fine on the other one. That's why we fly a twin-engine, sweetie," he responded with a patronizing smile.

"Are you sure?" she asked, narrowing her eyes nearly to slits.

"Oh, yeah," he said in a big, confident voice. "As long as the other engine doesn't also run out of gas, we'll be just fine."

"Oh, okay." Her eyes then snapped wide open, and she asked with no small amount of alarm in her tone, "Wait, what happens if the other engine quits too?"

Seth looked at her for a brief second and then said with a little, nonchalant shrug, "Uh, we crash."

Seth waited another couple of moments for the idea to soak in before he pulled the other engine to idle. "Uh, oh," he says calmly. "It looks like we lost the other engine."

"I thought you said, 'Not to worry,'" Jenny snapped again as she looked anxiously around the airplane.

"Well, it's not my fault. I *thought* we had enough gas," he said lamely.

"Okay, what do we need to do? They teach you this, right? What to do in a crash."

"Yes, honey, we're going to be okay. I can still land safely if we can find a big field."

She stared at him with wide eyes. "Okay. A big field." She finally said. "Got it." but she continued to focus her expectant gaze directly at Seth.

Seth glanced out his window. "Jenny, I've got no big fields on my side. There's nowhere to land." he said with a tinge of desperation in his voice. "You've got to look out your window and see if you can find us a field on your side of the plane."

Jenny stared at him for only a half second in silent disbelief, then quickly peered out her door. "Seth, Seth!" She exclaimed, bouncing in her seat. "There's a *huge* field outside of my window. Can you land there?" she asked with a combination of fear and excitement as she pointed down at the earth below.

"I don't know, honey," Seth replied with concern. "What does it say?"

"What do you mean what does it say?" she asked incredulously. "It's a big field. What's it supposed to say?"

"Look down there again." As he said the words, he banked the airplane so she had a clear view of the biggest sign in the world cut into the hayfield. JENNY- PLEASE MARRY ME!

"What?" Was all she could say. She read it again. Nothing was making sense. The rush of the wind over the wings, the nearly floating sensation of the rapid descent combined with the blind terror of crashing was preventing the words from sinking in. While she was staring down at the sign just beneath them growing ever closer, suddenly both engines roared back to life and the airplane started to climb.

"Oh," Seth exclaimed as the G-forces pulled her back into the leather seat. "It looks like we had a little gas left over after all." She was filled with a sense of elation as she looked back at Seth. He was smiling like the Cheshire Cat, while holding out the most beautiful, red velvet box she'd ever seen.

Seth quickly glanced over the instruments and clicked on the autopilot before turning back to her. "Honey, I didn't get a chance to give you a ring, nor did I ask you properly, so I'm doing it right now."

"What are you talking about?" she asked, still clearly confused.

"Jennifer Michele McKenna, will you still marry me and make me the happiest man in the world?"

"But…I thought…" She looked outside the airplane again as Seth kept circling over the hay field. You mean we're not…" She glanced back at Seth.

"No, we're not."

"Wait. This was planned?" she accused, emotions warring within her. Relief they weren't going to crash, anger that he'd played such a dirty trick, so much love for him in her heart….

"Yes, but I love you," Seth said softly. "Will you please, take the box?"

She glared at him as she quickly reached for it. Before her fingers touched the velvety box, her hand began to shake, and her fingers trembled. Turning it over in her hand, she peered at it, unbelieving it could be real. She never expected anything like this at all.

"Open it." he suggested.

Lifting the lid, she gasped at the teardrop solitaire set so beautifully against the red velvet. "Oh, Seth, it's more beautiful than I could have ever imagined."

"Will you marry me?" Seth asked.

"Um, yes. Yes. Of course. But…but you know that. I love you, Seth. So much." Tears ran down her glowing cheeks even as she couldn't stop the smile from spreading across her lips, losing every hint of anger.

"I wanted you to know how much I love you." Seth said with shiny eyes of his own.

"Oh, Seth." She popped her seatbelt off and stepped out of her seat. Seth quickly glanced at the autopilot and slid his chair back as she tumbled into his lap.

In the middle of the kiss, she pushed back on his chest to look him in the eyes. "I can't believe you scared me half to death just to ask me to marry you."

He grinned his devilish grin. "I wanted to make sure you'd say yes."

She slugged him in the chest, and then kissed him again.

CHAPTER TWO

Celia's eyes snapped open as she threw her hands up in front of her, desperately trying to fight off the soldier that was attacking her.

"Mama!" she screamed.

A knife. The smell of warm blood.

Her hands flailed in the blackness, hitting nothing. Striking only air.

With her heart pounding violently in her chest, she reached over in the dark and frantically searched for the light switch. Her fingers found their mark, and light mercifully shattered the darkness. Breathing heavily, she clawed backward up against the headboard while desperately sweeping the room, her eyes wide. Her muscles tensed.

Where is he? Where's the soldier who was hurting me? she thought as stark fear filled her mind.

Taking quick, shallow breaths, she looked down at her own hands then continued the visual search until she was sure she was alone. She finally blinked, sweat stinging her eyes.

No soldier. In fact, the soldier hadn't been there for a long time, that is, except for his visits in her nightmares. Breathing deeply, she glanced around her room one last time. Yes, the soldier was truly gone. She flipped the sweat-soaked sheets and blankets off of her and took a deep, shaky breath. The aftermath of the adrenaline dump left her feeling nauseous. Easing forward and swinging her legs off the bed, she placed her bare feet on the cool, wooden plank floor. It felt good. Solid. *I am an adult.* She thought angrily, trying to take control back. *So why is it that I am still haunted by this soldier?* She said aloud, clenching her fists till her knuckles turned white. Hearing her own heart thump in her ears, she realized she was holding her breath. Letting it out slowly and rolling her shoulders she tried a different tack. She willed herself to drift back into the mind of that child. A child who lived through a long-forgotten war. She tried to bring the images back, only this time on her terms. But, as usual, they wouldn't cooperate no matter how hard she concentrated. Finally giving up, she realized that she was drenched from head to toe in perspiration. Yet again. Her nightmare continued to hunt and haunt the little girl she once was. And in so many ways, apparently, she *still* is.

Taking another shaky breath, Celia laid her arms across her bare knees and rested her forehead on them. She began to shake. Then, as always, the tears began to flow, followed by sobs that would quake through her entire body. Her muscles clenched as she desperately attempted to expel this demon, this terror from within. Then, as always, the adrenaline slowly gave way to the final part of her never-ending episode, she saw it again. Sometimes she felt it, sometimes she caught a scent, the vague scene would never stay long enough for her to understand, but it always seemed to calm her.

Sunshine, laughter, a flower, chocolate. *Oh, how I love chocolate.* The thought brought a smile to her face. *Maybe it's my coping mechanism,* she thought as her breathing and heartbeat gradually returned to normal.

Celia picked her head up off her forearms and shivered. She glanced over at the clock on her nightstand—five o'clock. She'd only been asleep for a couple of hours. *"What is wrong with me?"* she desperately asked the blank walls as she forced herself off the floor. Combing long fingers through her unruly, dark hair, she plodded into the bathroom and turned the shower all the way to hot. The mirror steamed up as she peeled off her sweat-soaked nightclothes and tossed them out of the bathroom onto an already overflowing hamper. As she turned to climb into the shower, she caught sight of something in the fog. Just a fleeting, almost teasing image of a shirt pocket and a little white flower. She caught her breath and desperately grabbed for it, but then it was gone like the mist, leaving her feeling empty.

I need a run. She shut off the shower without getting in and turned back to the bedroom. Quickly yanking the soaked sheets from the mattress, she wadded them up and dropped them on the growing pile of unwashed laundry. Then, pulling on her running clothes, she corralled her hair back into a ponytail and grabbed her Adidas. Slowly opening her bedroom door, she looked around. *Empty.* Leaving her door open, she glanced across the small flat to confirm the other bedroom door was still closed. *Okay, good.* She thought. From experience, she knew which floorboards creaked, so she quietly padded across the old wooden planks in her socks, stepping only in the safe places. Silently, she opened the outer door of the small apartment and went through the opening into the kitchen at Maria's Bar & Grill. After easing the door closed, she walked by memory through the pitch-dark kitchen and out into the bar itself. Quickly dragging an upside-down chair from a bar table, she sat down and put on her shoes. Glancing at her smart watch, she did some quick mental math. Next, she completed some stretches and a quick warmup before heading for the door under the dimly lit exit sign. It was still dark outside, but the streetlights along Main Street made her feel safe enough and the light of dawn would soon arrive.

Celia rated her nightmares on a scale of miles. *How many miles will it take for me to outrun this one?* She thought. *At least ten, maybe more.* That meant running all the way to Spring Lake Park, one lap around the lake, and back. Eleven miles. Looking at her watch once more, she mentally calculated her time with a seven minute per mile pace. Ninety minutes. *I'll be back by seven at the latest*, she thought, and pushed off into an easy warm up stride.

Running was about the only thing that helped her deal with these uninvited night visitors. She always felt better after she ran. It also gave her time to think. The nightmares come to an end, but they never finish. What happens? Why does everything become murky? Maybe the extra oxygen would help her figure out the ending that never ends. When she was a child, back in the war, the dreams were a nightly manifestation full of strange people and fleeting images of horror, but nothing ever seemed to be in focus. Things felt much better now that she and Maria were in America. They might still come several nights in a row, but then a week would go by without any visits at all.

Maria and Sophia had taught her how to protect herself, and how to take the fight to the enemy, but they could never teach her how to feel normal. *How is it possible that I am afraid of nothing that I can touch, yet I am terrified by what I cannot touch? What I cannot understand?* She wasn't alone in the world; she still had Maria. *So why did she feel alone and empty most of the time?* Devoid of joy or excitement? Maria was like her mother, her friend and a big sister all rolled into one. An aunt. Quickening her pace, she made the left turn onto Dakota parkway and headed north. Just as the rising sun was beginning to show itself above the eastern horizon.

As her pace quickened, her breathing dropped into a comfortable rhythm and her heart rate was just about right. She found herself thinking about her nightmares, wondering what was real and what wasn't. She loved chocolate, that's for sure. But specifically, Hershey's. Maybe it was because it was just comfort food. But why was Hershey's so special? A grin crossed her lips. Running had many attributes, one of them was that it allowed her to eat and drink anything she wanted. *But the little white flower? What was that?* She asked herself. The problem was that she felt dead inside. Or numb. Not sad, not happy. No passion. Just going through the motions. Anyone who approached her was quickly stiff-armed and held steadfastly at a distance. Safer that way. She believed she had a real family once, before the war. But were they ever real? Or the soldier? Maybe there wasn't a soldier either. Maybe it truly was just a terrible nightmare without reason. "It isn't real. It never was," she lied to herself out loud. It was more convincing that way.

Feeling better, she dropped her head, swung her arms a little harder, and pushed into the stiff northern headwind.

You are wrong, said the little girl inside her. *You are a* liar.

* * * * *

Victoria glanced down and checked the time on her cell phone as she waited in traffic. She hadn't worn a watch in years and silently marveled at how much she depended on the electronic contraption. For a small town, Williston was known for its wicked traffic. Not because of the locals, but because of the hustle and bustle of an oil boomtown. Crude oil tankers trying to refuel would sometimes stick out into the street, waiting in line to fill up their huge tanks, snarling traffic even worse.

Her reputation for being late wasn't fully deserved. She wasn't always late. And she wouldn't be late this time either. With morning rush hour in mind, she'd left with plenty of time to arrive at her favorite bookstore. Books on Broadway was an eclectic, cozy, hometown bookstore that was surprisingly similar to a general store. It had a little bit of everything, and if they didn't have it on the shelf, she could order it and have it in just a couple of days. Besides, it boasted the best little coffee shop in the back to go with the books. They had some sort of magical bakery that created the most heavenly coffee cake. Was it the books, the coffee or the coffee cake that was her favorite? That was one of those existential questions that required no answer, Victoria happily concluded with a smirk.

She was more than a little nervous, Victoria had to admit to herself. She hadn't spent much time with Abby, her niece, since she was just a child. Life got busy and time flew past and before she knew it, the little blonde toddler had suddenly graduated from nursing school and her first job was working at Trinity Hospital, right there in Williston. The location wasn't ideal, but the price was great, so Abby wound up renting the little apartment that happened to be above the bookstore.

Adding to her nervousness, Victoria hadn't seen her much at all since she arrived. In fact, with Abby's crazy schedule at Trinity, she was only able to meet in the early morning. Despite Victoria's distaste for all things that start with *early* and end with *morning*, she actually woke up before her alarm clock. *Now that's worth a headline.* She thought.

After leaving the main highway, the downtown traffic was still light at this time of the day. Broadway was particularly quiet, and there was a parking spot right in front of the store. As Victoria pushed through the glass door, she smiled broadly. One of her favorite books, Olivia's Hope, was displayed prominently on the front table. Looking toward the coffee shop, she could already see the top of a head in one of the booths, chatting with the owner.

"Chuck, how are you?" Victoria asked as she made her way past the overflowing bookshelves. Before he could answer, she continued. "What are you doing working the early shift? Aren't you supposed to be the big boss?"

"Yes, and when you're the boss, you must be equally proficient at making coffee, washing dirty cups *and* running a bookstore. Especially when one of your employees decides to get married and actually take time off for a honeymoon," he said with feigned exasperation.

"Some people are just so demanding," Victoria added dramatically.

"How are you, Victoria? I was just getting to know our wonderful new tenant."

Abby stood up, bumping the table and sloshing some of her coffee onto the lacquered wood. While giving Victoria a hug, she said, "Aunt Victoria, it's so good to see you. I just barely got down here myself." Dressed in black leggings and a long-sleeved t-shirt, Abby's long blonde hair was done up in a quick, messy bun on the top of her head, and black rimmed glasses adorned her blue eyes.

"Coffee?" Chuck asked in Victoria's direction.

"Oh yes," Victoria said a bit desperately. "Do you still have my white coffee?" she asked hopefully.

"It's already in the French press." he said grinning.

"You are amazing." Victoria laughed. Chuck glanced from one to the other, nodding his head. "You two look so much alike, are you sure you're not mother and daughter?"

It was true, Victoria and Abby looked so similar that most people automatically assumed they *were* mother and daughter, even when Abby was a child. After Chuck had left, Abby turned to Victoria.

"I am so sorry to make you get up this early," Abby gushed with a heartfelt apology as she scooted back into the booth.

"How are you doing? How's the new job going?" Victoria asked, taking the seat across from Abby.

"It's going well. I'm going through orientation mostly, meeting everyone and learning about the hospital. I would have never imagined coming to North Dakota, but since I've been here, I've met so many great people."

"I'm so glad you're here, and we are just going to have to *make* time to see each other," Victoria stated emphatically. "When can you come over for dinner?"

"Orientation has some crazy hours, plus the hospital is still short-staffed, so until I get a normal shift, I really won't know," she replied apologetically.

Chuck returned with Victoria's coffee and a healthy piece of heavenly coffee cake.

"Oh, Chuck," Victoria exclaimed with a feigned frown. "I didn't ask for coffee cake."

"You didn't have to because your eyes were silently pleading," he said with an air of drama.

Victoria burst into laughter, "You know me way too well." she conceded as she broke a morsel off and popped it into her mouth.

"Now, if you two lovely ladies will excuse me, it appears that I have a customer up front." With that, he made the slightest bow, and departed.

"So, what kind of stuff are you having to deal with at the hospital?" Victoria asked, taking a sip from her steaming mug.

"Well, a lot of the usual stuff in the ER like coughs, fevers, stitches and crazy injuries like broken fingers from a game of *touch* football." Abby held up air quote fingers as she said it. "But some things are really unusual unless you happen to live near an oil field, then you get to deal with such things as major broken bones, crushed hands and Hydrogen Sulfide poisoning which can kill you fairly quickly. One of our patients nearly died before he arrived at the hospital. Oh, and a few days ago, they brought in a guy that was killed by a load of drill pipe that fell on him," Abby concluded with a grimace and a sip of her coffee.

"Link said there had been a lot of crazy mishaps going on lately," Victoria stated. "He doesn't like it and believes that too many seemingly random events in a row are not random at all."

CHAPTER THREE

It was one of those lazy spring Sundays in Williston, North Dakota. Due to its location on the map near the Canadian border, Jenny discovered that just because it looked sunny and warm outside, it wasn't always the case.

Miss McKenna, soon to be Reagan, was in her favorite place in the entire cabin. The sunroom. Her five-foot nothing frame was dressed in her current favorite pregnant sunroom clothes, which consisted of a large, blue and red flannel shirt she stole from Seth's closet. She knew he liked it on her by the way he always grinned when he saw her in it. Plus, she loved the softness on her skin. The practical side was that its size was large and had plenty of room for her growing belly. It wasn't too long into her pregnancy that she had to give up her old denim cutoffs that Seth liked, but she found a new pair of blue denim shorts that had the same worn-out look, except they stretched. At first, they fit fine, but now she wore the waistband low on her tummy because of the ever-growing twins inside her. Now, at thirty-two weeks, the babies seemed to be growing exponentially in both size and activity.

Her bare feet were propped up on a long, soft brown leather ottoman that pulled double duty as a coffee table.

The built-in Bose sound system and speakers were playing smooth jazz, and the sun was setting low on the horizon. She looked up from the dog-eared pages of her baby book and gazed about the room, listening. She had heard something, or more like felt something. Almost a low rumble. An earthquake? She tucked a wayward strand of her strawberry-blonde hair behind her ear as she listened. Nothing. She went back to her book. Her left hand held the book while the fingers of her right hand drew absent minded, lazy circles around her pregnant belly.

The notes that Olivia had written in the margins, plus the letter she had written to the yet unborn baby was just amazing. *She's the reason I'm here.* The thought made her smile yet again, *babies.* Olivia was Seth's wife and Victoria's best friend. She couldn't conceive and had one of her eggs harvested for in vitro fertilization in her hope of having a child. *It still breaks my heart.* Victoria had explained that the accident was so bad that Seth and Link drove past the scene of fire trucks and ambulances without even realizing she was part of it. Eventually, Seth began a search for a surrogate to keep Olivia's hope alive. Nobody expected they would conceive twins and fall in love. She looked down at the book again and thumbed the same pages as Olivia had. It was because of that day that Jenny was here now. She could almost hear Olivia's voice as she read her notes once again. The notes were great, but it was the letter she wrote that always conjured up the feeling of closeness that she felt so strongly. It was almost as if they were going through the pregnancy together in some kind of crazy way. She had re-read the book at least ten times since she had discovered it on the bookshelf covered in dust. Looking up from the pages, she allowed her gaze to wander around the room until they settled on the man sitting across from her.

Seth sat in his favorite, but rather ugly, overstuffed chair. It used to reside upstairs in the living room, but when he realized that Jenny preferred the sunroom, he decided to move it downstairs. He had it set between the hot tub and the fireplace, creating an L with her couch. Jenny had gently suggested that he didn't need to move the chair down, and that it was probably just too heavy. She made the reasonable argument that maybe it would be a better idea to buy something new, but he insisted it wasn't a problem.

So much for hinting... Hmm, I wonder, does a man really not get it or do they simply ignore the hint? She briefly smiled but then her thoughts flickered into darkness for a moment. Although he no longer needed the wheelchair and had somehow talked Doc Griffin into giving him his flight medical back, he still used a cane sometimes and walked with a significant limp. When her brother, Chase, had shot him in that crazed, meth-induced rage not so long ago, she almost died of fear. Thank God for Link.

Seth couldn't stand up for any real length of time, but he was getting better and better every day, and that was all that mattered. She broke herself away from the grip of that terrible day and focused her eyes on the man sitting close, but not close enough.

The love of her life and the father of her's and Olivia's yet unborn children wore a plain white T-shirt and a pair of Levi's with a thirty-eight-inch inseam. She smiled again.

The mystery was exciting instead of terrifying, now that she stood on solid ground. It didn't matter if both babies were from Olivia or if there was one of each, her life was full and wonderful.

Seth sat adjacent to her, with the setting sun to his back and his bare feet resting on a throw pillow placed on the ottoman. His crystal blue eyes were busy reviewing a ream of spreadsheets from a folder that Susan, Reagan's office manager, had brought by earlier.

The sun beams seemed to glow through his somewhat unkempt tangle of curly, sandy hair that fell just short of a halo. Jenny loved how the sun brought out the reddish hue of his Irish ancestry.

It's time.

"Ahem." Jenny cleared her throat.

Nothing.

She tossed her book onto the ottoman with a loud slap.

No reaction.

She let out a big yawn and a nice, noisy stretch.

Still nothing. Not even an upward glance.

Music, she thought. Looking around, she found the remote control and changed the music to country. *Nothing.*

Okay, wise guy, how about rap?

Still nothing.

She shut off the music entirely and reached over and picked up her guitar that was always laying on the couch and strummed it.

It wasn't a fancy guitar, but it was special to her. It took six months of saving all of her tips as a waitress before she could finally afford to buy it from a local pawn shop back in Chicago.

She placed it across her pregnant belly and melodramatically wiggled it around a bit as if trying to find a position that was comfortable for her small frame.

Completely obtuse.

Come on, Seth.

Failing that, Jenny started strumming the instrument lazily in a jazzy blues rhythm. She chuckled as a little song formed in her head, so she went with it.

"His name is Seth, da dah dah dant," she teased.

"He's taaall and lanky, da dah dah dant,"
A few more giggles still with no reaction.
"He cheated death, da dah dah dant,"
"But nooooww he's cranky..." She laughed, but he
didn't react.

She moved her foot closer to his and used her recently
polished red toenails to tickle the bottoms of his feet. It
startled him out of his concentration and made him flinch,
which in turn made him wince as pain shot through his
wounded hip.

"Oh, Seth, I'm so sorry," Jenny said as she jumped up
and moved over to him. Sitting on the arm of his chair with
her bare leg cocked over the armrest, she put her hand on
the back of his neck and touched her forehead to his. "Are
you all right?" she asked, an almost imperceptible giggle
in her voice. She pulled back and stared into his twinkling
eyes and stroked her fingers through his hair.

"Are you kidding me?" Seth asked incredulously with
an impish grin. "If that's what it takes to get you to sit next
to me like this, you should have kicked me a lot sooner."

"I did not kick you," she retorted in mock offense. "I
was merely playing with you."

"Oh, yeah," he smirked. "You mean like this...?" Seth
trailed off as he pulled her to him for a kiss. She folded
herself into him, and he cradled her in his long arms. "So,
you think I'm cranky, huh?"

His kisses were soft and tender against her lips, then
trailed down her neck to the hollow of her throat, where
he nipped lightly at her skin, making her shiver. That's
what she wanted, she thought with a languid smile as she
wrapped her arms around his neck and tipped her head
back to give him better access.

Papers crinkled under her, and with a sigh she pulled back enough to raise herself back onto the arm of his chair. With one arm still around his neck, she looked down to assess the damage she had done to his spreadsheets. What she saw surprised her. On top of the spreadsheet was several sonogram images, nearly as good as photos, of the two little babies growing inside of her. They were growing fast and not so little anymore. The images showed how the two of them would roll around and sometimes be face to face, and other times one would have a foot in the other's face.

Jenny finally mustered up the courage and asked, "Seth, how do you feel about the two possibilities?"

Seth looked totally puzzled and asked, "Why do you call them possibilities?"

"No, not *them*," Jenny said. "The two possibilities are that they might be identical twins...or not."

Seth set down the folder with the spreadsheets and the glossy sonogram images on the ottoman and pulled her back into his lap. He put his hands on her tummy and said, "I am already in love with these two babies, and it doesn't matter to me if they are boys, or girls, or one of each. It also doesn't matter if they are identical twins or not." He frowned up at her. "But wait, does it matter to you?"

"No, not at all," she blurted.

"No matter what, if they are identical twins or individuals with yours and Olivia's DNA, they are still part of me, too."

She breathed in heavily as if an invisible weight had been lifted off her shoulders.

"Baby, I am crazy about you, and no matter which way they turn out," he said with a mischievous grin, "I have to tell you that I have no intention of stopping with just them."

Jenny giggled and then bit her lip a second before asking the next question. "Have you thought of any names yet?"

He shook his head. "No, I haven't. I've thought about it quite a bit, and I can't come up with anything that strikes me as the right names for boys or girls. Have you thought of any?"

"No, but if they are girls, I think Olivia has already named them," Jenny said cryptically.

"What do you mean?" asked Seth.

Just then, something caught Jenny's attention. She looked past Seth and murmured, "What the...?" As she scrambled to get off of Seth's lap, she stared behind him and out through the big sunroom windows. Then a giggle escaped her lips while holding one hand over her mouth and the other holding her belly. "Seth, I think we've got company."

Seth struggled to get out of his chair to see what she was looking at, but heard the rumbling before he could stand up fully and see. A rather large herd of cows and newborn calves came wandering through their garden, surrounding the Lover's Apple tree, softly mooing as they grazed on the unmowed lawn.

"I'd better call the Perrys and tell them we finally know the answer to the question 'where's the beef,'" Seth said with a chuckle as he looked around on the floor for his missing cell phone. Not finding it, he limped upstairs as Jenny ogled at a set of newborn twin calves trailing behind their mother. Jenny's hand drifted instinctively to her belly as she marveled at the sight.

Cheri and Dean Perry owned the Rockin' P Ranch that adjoined the back of Seth's land. The two neighboring parcels were separated by a four-strand, barbed-wire fence that ran the entire length of the property line. The fence was normally good at keeping the cows in their own pasture unless a herd of wild buffalo or even a big ol' moose decided to walk through it, and when that happened, it wouldn't hold anything. The Rockin' P wasn't a huge ranch, as far as cattle ranches go, but they did manage to raise about one hundred and fifty head of prime Black Angus cattle each year without buying additional hay to winter them over. Their prize bull, Amos, was nearly as big as buffalo and just under two thousand pounds, but with all those heifers, he never seemed to wander off.

A few minutes later, Seth came back into the sunroom, this time, with his cane. Jenny knew he hated using the thing. *He must be in a lot more pain than he is letting on. Is it just his ego, or is there something he doesn't trust about me? That he can't tell me what's really going on?* She mused some more before she finally shook the doubt from her mind as Seth dialed a number.

"Well, howdy neighbor," Seth said into his cell and paused for a moment. "Thank you, we're doing fine. You've got several thousand pounds of hamburger roaming around in our north forty, with some mighty good-looking veal tagging along behind."

"What?" Jenny yelled as she turned to Seth and slugged him in the arm. "How could you call those adorable little calves…veal?"

"No worries. Sounds good. Take your time. I'm sure Jenny will keep them entertained until you get here," he said teasingly while looking at Jenny. "She has a guitar and wants a cowboy hat, so it's nearly a done deal."

Jenny raised her eyebrows. "Oh, yeah?" She pulled back her fist for another shot at his big arm, but Seth made an abrupt attempt at dodging her light, little punch. He sidestepped wrong onto his wounded hip and started to tip over backwards, dropping his cell in the process. Jenny leapt forward and grabbed the big guy and tried to steady him, nearly taking them both to the floor.

"I'm so sorry," Jenny apologized with a giggle. "Did I hurt you? I had no idea how strong I was."

Now it was Seth's turn to blush a little. "No, no. It's okay. So maybe that *was* a bad idea. I should have just let you hit me. It wouldn't have hurt anyway," he complained with a wry chuckle and a little wince.

Jenny helped Seth hobble back upstairs and walked out the French doors onto the wraparound deck of the cabin. The view was better from there, plus they didn't have to worry about being stepped on by cows.

It wasn't long before they spotted Cheri Perry galloping her champagne quarter horse *Bucky* across the back pasture toward the house. Whether it was because of her time spent on the rodeo circuit barrel racing, or her Sioux Indian ancestry, she sat tall and easy in the saddle, as if it were second nature. Her big brown eyes and high cheekbones were framed by loads of wavy, shoulder length, brunette – almost black – hair pulled back loosely in a ponytail. She had her hair tucked underneath a sweat-stained, nut-brown, cowboy hat complete with a black leather strap tightened under her chin. Bucky, a cross between a buckskin and a champagne-colored quarter horse, was getting older and maybe slowing down a bit, but in his prime he was one of the best cutting horses in North Dakota and carried Cheri to more than one silver and pink champion belt buckle.

She slowed Bucky to a walk and looking over at Seth and Jenny yelled, "Sorry, neighbor!" Followed by an exasperated laugh. "Did you see what those buffalo did to our fence?" Without waiting for an answer, she added, "They demolished a fifty-foot-wide section." She reigned Bucky to a stop in front of the porch and patted him on the neck. Jenny reached her hand out to pet his nose. Bucky nickered and nuzzled into Jenny's hand. Jenny giggled again and looked in Seth's direction.

Seth just stared at her for a long second. "Um, gee, Cheri, is that the latest in cowgirl casuals you're wearing today?" He commented with a smartass grin.

Cheri laughed at the question and kind of looked herself over. "No." She laughed again. "I had court today."

Her day job was that of a deputy sheriff and chief investigator for Williams County, which meant she usually dressed in a collared shirt and jeans, with a western belt, some sort of blazer, boots and of course, her service weapon. But today she was dressed in white, button-down collared shirt, pearl stud earrings and pearl necklace plus black dress slacks with the legs tucked into her old, muddy Ariat work boots. It was quite a contrast. She still had her badge on a lanyard around her neck. "I didn't have time to change when you called, so I just saddled up as I was." She shrugged and flashed a big, white, toothy smile.

Cheri had been the first to respond to Link's 911 call when Jenny's brother, Chase, had shot Seth. She had been the one that put the handcuffs on her brother after Seth choked him unconscious in the ensuing fight. Link had to talk fast to keep him from killing Chase outright in the moment. Seth didn't even realize he'd been shot till after the fight was over.

Jenny looked up from petting Bucky's nose. "I wanted to thank you for getting Chase into a rehab program while in prison. I can only hope he can get the help he needs while he is in there."

"You're welcome," Cheri replied. "Drugs can make people do terrible things, but it doesn't mean they can't come out on the other side, stronger, hopefully better."

"Yes Ma'am," Jenny agreed. "I'm praying you are right."

Just then a calf started bawling for its mother. Looking around, Cheri laughed and said, "Bucky and I'll have these pesky critters rounded up and headed back to the Rockin' P in a jiffy."

"No worries," said Seth. "Just remember to drop off a side of beef when you have one to spare."

"Well, that reminds me," Cheri commented. "You two should come over this Saturday. We're firing up the big BBQ pit for Dean's birthday. And besides, we need some time to talk one of these days and decide what to do about the old Jorgenson place."

"What's the Jorgenson Place?" Jenny asked.

Seth turned to her and said, "The Jorgensons were the first homesteaders in the whole area, and their original home place is that old clapboard building that straddles both of our parcels where the property lines meet highway 85. You can see it from the highway."

"You mean that old building that looks like it would fall over in a stiff wind?" Jenny asked as she pointed in the general direction of the building.

"Yep, that's the one," Cheri replied. "Believe it or not, that was the nicest, fanciest home in the Dakota territories back when Teddy Roosevelt lived in these parts. In fact, he stayed with the Jorgensons when he first came through here. We really need to do something about it soon."

"What's the hurry now? It's been there for over a hundred years," Seth asked with a shrug of his shoulders.

"We've had our deputies catching teenagers hanging out there recently. One of them had made themselves a little love shack out of it."

"A what?" Jenny asked with raised eyebrows. "Seriously?"

Cheri's cell phone rang and made Bucky dance a little. She pulled it out of her pocket. "Oh, crap," she said as she looked at the number. "I'm sorry. I've got to take this. It's my boss. He probably wants an update on how the trial went today."

"Yeah, sure," Seth said. "No worries."

"Go for Perry," Cheri said bluntly into the phone. She leaned forward, propping her forearm on the big roping saddle horn while listening. Bucky pulled at the reins. She loosened them, and he started grazing while she listened. After several moments of silence and nodding her head, she exploded.

"Come on, Boss, I'm a Detective now. I'm not a traffic cop. Besides, I've already spent all day in court."

"Oh, that bad?"

"*How* many fatalities?" She asked with a grimace on her face.

"Yessir, I can be there in…" She looked at her watch. "Say, half an hour."

"Wilco. I'll keep you updated as soon as I learn anything new."

She hung up, took a deep breath and looked up. Her big brown eyes seemed confused. A cross between angry and sick.

"What's happened?" Seth asked.

"Whatever it is, it sounds pretty bad," Jenny added.

"Huge wreck on Highway 85 down by the bridge. So far there's seven fatalities with another fourteen badly burned and wounded inbound to Trinity or waiting on transport. The MEDEVAC helicopter is already enroute to the hospital with the worst victims and additional ambulances are just arriving at the scene. They have no clue yet how it all got started, and from what I just heard, the initial statements don't make any sense,"

A dark flicker crossed Seth's face and his blue eyes grew a bit deeper. "Uh, sounds like you better get going," Seth said distractedly. "Look, Cheri, uh, tell you what. I'll just close the front gate on our place so they can't get out on the highway, and you can come get the cows later."

"Oh, thank you, Seth. I greatly appreciate it. Or, who knows, we might get lucky and they'll come home all by themselves when it starts to get dark."

"If not, Dean can come over after he's done and herd them back with the four-wheeler."

She gave a quick wave, wheeled Bucky around and galloped back to the Rockin' P.

Jenny reached out and took Seth's hand. He lifted her hand to his lips and kissed it, then put his arms around her and they walked back into the cabin.

CHAPTER FOUR

Michelle Derbes knew she would eventually out-grow Williston, North Dakota, but for right now, in her journalistic career, an oil boom town where anything could happen was exactly where she needed to be. She was smart, attractive, and it didn't hurt that the camera seemed to accentuate all of her attributes. Adding to that, she was hungry and unafraid of hard work. Like many others in the oil fields, she was a transplant who came looking for fame and fortune. Atlanta would always be where she called home, but she'd been a small fish in a big pond. She needed to learn to be a big fish in a small pond first. She wanted to make a name for herself, get noticed, and that just didn't seem possible in Atlanta, LA, and certainly not New York. Her instincts were good, and she followed her gut. KFYR-FOX was the incubator of her career, along with her dual degrees in Law and Journalism.

Right now, she raced to the scene of a large, multi-car pile-up roughly fourteen miles south of town on Highway 85. Bill, her cameraman and occasional protector, was intently driving the large television broadcasting truck with both hands on the wheel.

"Hey, Bill?" Michelle's voice cracked. "I'm totally okay if you slow down a little on the curves." She gave a nervous laugh as she gripped the Jesus handle mounted above the passenger window. Her white-knuckled grip barely held her in place as they rounded through a particularly tight curve.

"I'm really not going all that fast," he replied in his own defense. "It doesn't take the curves very well because this POS van is in desperate need of new shocks. And besides, you've been unusually quiet over there until now, so maybe you needed some excitement to get the juices flowing." After he finished speaking, he paused for a quick second and risked a quick glance her way.

"It isn't that I enjoy seeing these big wrecks and accidents," Michelle replied. Her stomach did a little flip as she remembered the last bad wreck she covered. "I especially don't like seeing the carnage, but it's big news and someone is going to bring it to the public. It might as well be me." She set her jaw in determination.

If it is as big as it sounds, she thought, *we'll get a significant segment on the local FOX channel.* But if it is really big, there might even be a chance to get a segment on the national news channel. She allowed a brief smile at the mental image of Ainsley Earhart or Harris Faulkner saying, "Reporting from North Dakota, we have Michelle Derbes. Michelle, what can you tell us?"

She was torn by the excitement she felt as she began to see the flashing red and blue lights. *It's not the carnage, the murders, the robberies that gives me this thrill. This drug.* It was the chase of the story and the jazz she got from being on TV. There, she could make a difference. The more experience, the more she could hone her skills.

That was what brought her here. The excitement of a real modern-day boomtown where anyone could blend in. The chaos attracted every kind of person from fortune seekers to shysters and everything in between. When she first arrived in the Bakken, there was at least one fatal accident on Highway 85 between Williston and Watford City every single day. Of course, most of the accidents occurred after dark and on icy roads. Today, on the other hand, it was still daylight as they approached the scene. It was early summer, the roads were dry, and the pile-up occurred on flat ground. A tingle ran through her body, and then her nose twitched.

She broke from her internal thoughts as Bill started slowing the van.

"Look, there's Ireana," she shouted and opened her door to get out even before Bill brought the vehicle to a complete stop. In a hurry, she didn't release her seatbelt and nearly choked as it stopped her exit. Scrambling, she quickly hit the button, untangled herself from the mechanism and was past the front of the van before Bill turned on his flashers.

Ireana Longoria was a local cop in Williston. Michelle and Ireana weren't exactly drinking buddies, but they'd shared more than a few drinks over life stories at Maria's.

Ireana looked beat as Michelle approached her to get an update. After ninety seconds of rapid-fire information that Michelle mentally noted each item given to her, Michelle said, "Thank you so much, Ireana." She turned back toward the camera while yelling over her shoulder, "The next round of margaritas is on me," while she instinctively moved herself to position the accident slightly behind her.

Turning to Bill, she straightened her jacket and asked, "How do I look?"

With a smile and a wink, Bill said, "In three... two... one..."

"I'm Michelle Derbes, live.

"Oil field traffic combined with weekend travelers was heavy today on Highway 85 when a fourteen-car pileup occurred just a few miles south of Williston, North Dakota, near the Missouri River bridge. The crash happened just before 2:30 p.m. on dry roads and under clear skies. At least three people were believed to be killed when crude oil from a ruptured oil tanker spilled out over the scene of the accident and caught fire. Of particular concern to first responders is a semi-tractor pulling a flatbed trailer loaded with propane bottles that is also engulfed in the flames. With the driver among the deceased, authorities are attempting to contact the trucking company in order to ascertain if the propane tanks are full or empty.

"Of the fourteen vehicles involved, four were oil tankers and two motorhomes. As you can see behind me, the oil tanker caught fire and its flames engulfed several other vehicles, including the motorhomes pulling trailers full of motorcycles. According to local officials on the scene, besides the three confirmed fatalities there are fourteen casualties with critical burns and other life-threatening injuries. Area ambulances and medevac helicopters have already transported the most critically injured to Trinity Hospital in Williston, where doctors were put on alert for a mass casualty event. Police officers on scene informed me that one of the tankers is carrying Toluene, a highly flammable chemical that is used to clean oil wells.

"Sources also tell me that witnesses stated that the pickup that caused the wreck left the scene heading south at high speed after inexplicably breaking hard in front of a loaded oil tanker. The vehicle was described as a standard, white, four-door Dodge, four-by-four pickup but no one caught a company name or license plate. The only lead officials have at this time is that it sustained significant damage to the tailgate with blue paint from the semi-truck that hit it.

"I'm Michelle Derbes, KFYR-TV Channel 8.

"Back to you, Ken."

Before Bill had a chance to cut the take, the second tractor trailer with the propane bottles exploded in a massive fireball.

* * * * *

Coming down the home stretch of yet another run, Celia was feeling good and managed a little speed kick for the last hundred yards back to Maria's. Slowing to a walk for the last few yards, she began to circle the parking lot, stopping here and there to stretch and let her heart rate slow back to normal. The soldier was returning more and more, she begrudgingly admitted. Way too often lately. *But why?* She wondered. *Why now?* Somehow, running was no longer working either, the anxiety and fear refused to go back into the box, where she could keep it deep inside her soul. It was too big for the box and now the lid refused to even close enough to where she could once again put a big, fat, heavy lock on it.

After she had cooled down enough, she stepped inside the bar and headed in the direction of the kitchen. Pushing through the swinging doors, she left them flapping noisily behind her. Reaching automatically, her hand felt for the light switch in the room lit only by a few rays of the morning sun. As the lights popped on, she jumped a bit, when she realized someone was already in the kitchen.

"Oh, good morning, Maria. you scared me," she said, holding her hand against her chest.

Maria was leaning on a tall, stainless steel prep table with a heavy ceramic mug of steaming fresh coffee held between her two hands. "Good morning," she greeted Celia in a smokey, almost gravelly voice. Still in her pajamas and housecoat, Her Eastern European accent still hung heavily on each word. Both were accentuated by the early hour and the lack of sleep. Her raven black hair had traces of silver, but not nearly as much as the hardships in her life would merit. She still was a beauty to behold that belied the heart of a lioness and the fierceness of a badger.

"What are you doing up so early?" Celia asked. Her own natural accent had softened much more than Maria's.

"I've been up since five o'clock," Maria responded, watching Celia's face intently.

"Oh, I'm so sorry," Celia said nonchalantly. "Maybe you should try to go back to sleep?"

"I've been waking up around the same time for the last several days." Maria stated, still trying to lock eyes with Celia.

Celia ignored her comment and let it go without responding as she opened the fridge and stared at nothing.

"Sweetheart, why did you tell me you no longer have them?"

"Have them? " Celia asked innocently. "Have what?"

Maria tilted her head knowingly. "Nice try."

"Well, because," she said, tucking a loose wisp of hair behind her ear while searching for a reason. "Besides, it's... it's no big deal," Celia stated a little more defensively than she intended.

"I think it's time we had a talk about your nightmares."

"No," Celia said sternly as she slammed the refrigerator door."They are not real. They are only dreams."

"You need to understand a few things," Maria prodded.

"I don't want to understand. I want them to leave me alone. Why can't they just leave me alone?" Her voice grew shaky, and her hands began to tremble as an unwanted wave of adrenaline began to pump through her body. *I can't go on living this way.* She pleaded silently.

"You don't have any friends. You push everyone away. You have no life except bartending and running. I think you are running away from your past but wherever you go, no matter how fast, your past will ever be your shadow."

"It's my way." Celia replied stubbornly.

"But to understand is the only way forward," Maria coaxed. "Don't you have any questions?"

"No. I don't." Celia stated emphatically as she turned to walk out of the kitchen, but just as she made it to the door she spun around and shouted, "Well, yes, I do… but…" She backed up against the wall and crossed her arms over her chest and stared at Maria. Her chin began to shake. "I don't know, and I'm afraid. I don't want to be afraid. In fact, I hate being afraid and I'm angry with myself for being afraid." Tears stung her eyes as her vision misted over. Her legs buckled and she slowly slid down the wall to sit on the floor. *Why couldn't they just leave me alone?* Wrapping her arms around her folded knees, she clenched her teeth refusing to allow her emotions to take over. *How can they make me feel so helpless? What did I do so wrong?*

"Oh, my *duzo*, my sweetheart." Maria stepped around the prep table and eased herself down to the kitchen floor next to Celia. "My heart is breaking."

Celia stared out into infinity, her mind's eye trying desperately to focus. "After every nightmare, I always have these vague, dream-like memories that never become clear. I can't seem to figure out what or why. Sometimes the feeling seems good, but other times it feels very bad. It frightens me. What's more…" She paused, then looked at Maria as her eyes darkened. "It really makes me angry." She concluded with fisted hands and gritted teeth.

"There are reasons for both of those feelings," Maria said, wrapping her arm around Celia's shoulders.

"One of the soldiers reminds me of Link," Celia said distantly as she stared back at the wall, attempting to retrieve a memory.

"There is a good reason for that too," Maria replied earnestly.

"Then please, tell me what it means, Maria," she begged. "Please, help me."

"I never wanted to tell you but..." Maria confessed. "But perhaps the time has come."

Celia looked up at Maria and sniffed. "Is it true what they say?

"What are you talking about?"

"That Lincoln James is my father? Or... is he the soldier that attacks me in my dreams? Or... or both?"

"No, no, Celia. Not either." Maria responded.

"Have you seen how he stares at me?" She asked as her chin dropped back to her arms. Her eyes, once again, drifted into the dim memory.

Maria took Celia's face in her hands and turned her so she could look into her eyes. "*Duzo*, sweetheart. He is not your father, nor your attacker, he was your *rescuer*."

CHAPTER FIVE

"What? I don't believe you," Celia sniffed. "My nightmares seem to grow more and more real until sometimes I don't want to sleep." She dropped her head again.

"Don't let that monster who attacked you continue to win. He's dead! He cannot hurt you or anyone else, ever again. You must take your life back." Maria pleaded.

Celia's head popped up from resting on her arms. "What?" She wiped the scant evidence of a tear from her face with the back of her hand. "How do you know that?"

"Link found a soldier attacking you and he killed him. Then he scooped you up and brought you to live with me and Sophia."

Celia stared at Maria for a long moment, trying to take it all in. "No." She slowly shook her head. "That's *not* possible. If it were true, why would he treat me this way now?" she asked through gritted teeth, her anger building all over again.

"I'll tell you, but you must promise to listen," Maria said firmly, her gravelly voice almost stern.

Celia nodded and stayed quiet.

"Promise?" Maria insisted with a nudge.

"Yes," Celia agreed with a sigh.

Maria waited another moment before she began. "You see, back in our old country, Link did not normally wear a typical military uniform, and he wasn't wearing one the day he rescued you. He was wearing a flight suit. In the days and weeks after he brought you to me, he would come by and visit us, and you would sit on his lap and play with his face and laugh. One day when he was visiting, you sang him a little song and then asked. "*Mogao bi biti moj tata?*"

Celia looked at her and blinked a couple of times as she silently translated the words. *Would you be my daddy?* "I... asked him that?" She demanded sharply.

"Yes. *Duzo*, you did."

"Well, what did he say?"

"The big tough guy got choked up but finally yelled, 'Yes. Yes, I will be your daddy.'"

"You squealed with delight and said, 'Thank you, Daddy.'" Maria's eyes misted over as she dug up the treasured memory and re-lived it once again before the sadness reappeared on her face.

"But what happened? Why does he not talk to me?" Celia asked indignantly. "Why did he leave us?" Her anger fed the storm that had been building for a lifetime.

"Because of something very unfortunate," Maria confessed with a sigh.

"What do you mean? What did I do wrong? Why does he hate me now?"

"You did nothing wrong," Maria stated emphatically. "On the day he found you, he was wearing a flight suit. During later visits, he always wore his flight suit or civilian clothes."

"Where is this going?" Celia asked, her impatience growing.

"Do not talk to me that way, Celia," Maria said as her deep brown eyes flared.

"I'm sorry, *Tetka*." Celia said, forcing herself to calm down a bit. "Please, forgive me."

Maria patted her hand and continued. "One day he came by for a visit but this time he was wearing a military uniform. For the first time, he wasn't dressed in a flight suit or regular clothes. You screamed when you saw *the soldier* walking up to the gate and ran from him. After that, you would never go near him again. You even quit talking to me for a while. When we realized what was scaring you, he came back without it. But it was too late. He tried and tried, but it was no use. You were terrified of him. He had to let you go, and it broke his heart."

"I can't believe that. Then he must not care either," she said defensively as she recrossed her arms on her chest.

"*Duzo*," Maria responded kindly. "It is not your fault. He has never blamed you. He blamed himself for not realizing what the uniform might have meant to you. He loves you. In fact, *he* is the one who sponsored us to come to America. Link pulled every string he could reach in order to get us here. He is the only reason why we are in America now."

Celia stared at Maria silently, blinking, as if she was staring through her, into the distance, trying to make sense of it all.

"Your nightmares are your past," Maria continued. "They are not your present but even now, you are allowing them to steal your future."

"Why have you never told me this before?" Celia suddenly snapped.

Maria pulled away slightly and folded her own arms over her bent knees. "Now it's my turn to confess. Honestly, when you were younger, you were not ready. As you grew older, and the bad memories began to fade, I had hoped that you would heal inside. With enough time, you would never have to know the rest of the story. The real story. I wanted to believe that with time, your nightmares would go away forever. I am so sorry, Celia. I would have never hidden it from you this long if I'd known that it wouldn't go away and be forgotten."

Celia nodded imperceptibly.

"*Duzo*, sweetheart. I have watched you push everyone away. You don't trust anyone, you keep everyone at a distance, so they never can get close to you. I understand why, but Link is someone you can trust. Someone you should trust. He, if anyone, deserves your trust."

Celia's mind raced as she tried to take it all in. The foggy, wavy, dream-like images flashed across her mind, going faster and faster before Maria finally broke into her thoughts.

"Do you know how old you are?"

"Of course."

"*I* don't even know how old you are, or even what your real birthday is," Maria said cautiously.

"What do you mean? We celebrate it every year," Celia retorted, refusing to allow the words to sink in.

Maria held her breath for a moment then blurted out, "When Link found you, you told him a lot of terrible things, but you didn't *know* your birthday."

"Then how *did* you find out when my birthday was?" Celia asked even though she knew she wouldn't like the answer.

"We never did, because, despite everything Link and I tried, we could never find out any more about your parents, other than what you told Link at the time. We didn't even know what village you were taken from."

"Then what do we use as my birthday now?" Celia asked quietly.

"We used the day that Link brought you to me. That is the day we celebrate your birthday. And we guessed you were somewhere between six and eight, although we were never sure. You had been through so much already, we never pushed it."

Celia's heart thrummed in her chest. The radical shift of emotions was nearly unbearable. "But... how can this be?" she begged.

Maria sat quietly as Celia tried to process it all. After a while, she reached over and took Maria's hand in hers and kissed it. "*Tetka*, Auntie, do *you know* what happened to my family?"

"I only know what Link told me when you first arrived. And what he told me is what you told him all those years ago. You would not speak of it to anyone else but him. Maybe because he was the one who rescued you. After you stopped talking to Link, you never spoke of it again."

"What did I say?" Celia asked. "What can you tell me? I've forgotten everything."

"Maybe it's time for you to ask him." Maria suggested softly.

"I can't." Came the instant reply. The idea sent a panic through her entire being.

"You must." Maria paused. "And please, don't push him away, For your sake, and for his."

Celia threw up her arms. "What am I supposed to do, *Tetka*? Walk up to him and say 'Hey, Mister Link. What can you tell me about my family? What part of my nightmares are real and which parts aren't?'" She jumped up off the floor and began to pace. "I cannot even begin to get my head around this." Her accent grew thicker with her frustration.

"You should maybe call him," Maria said. "Now then, help me up," She asked. "My old bones do not do so well sitting on this cold floor."

* * * * *

The newest employee of Reagan Oil Field Services glanced furtively behind him. Licking his dry lips, he scanned his audience as they popped off all manner of wisecracks.

Jesse James was a quick-witted, wiry, twenty-five-year-old with curly blonde hair, ice blue eyes and broad shoulders. Known for his charm, he had a smile that tended to turn up more on one side than the other, giving him an easy, lopsided grin. Despite the look, he tended to be a bit more on the serious side but was also part maverick with a mischievous streak that would show up unexpectedly. A character trait that was often linked directly to his DNA.

Licking his lips again, Jesse took a deep breath and popped the latches on the brand-new drone helicopter case that rested on the back of the flatbed work truck.

His new boss and a dozen other Reagan employees, including his dad, Lincoln James, were watching him intently. Jesse's heart was beating rapidly with 'first-day jitters and the occasional smart-ass comment from the crowd wasn't helping.

The DJI Phantom 4 Pro was the best and most expensive drone in its market. Much more expensive than the cheap drones he was used to flying for recreation. Reagan had purchased the drone for help in surveying job sites from the air, as well as monitoring their progress on the pipeline work. Until now, the company had been using their own twin engine King Air turboprop aircraft, but Seth and Link were the only pilots, and they weren't always available. And besides, the drone had far cheaper operating costs. They'd had the drone for over a month, but until now, there was no one who knew how to fly it.

Jesse rapidly completed assembling the drone with slightly shaking hands. *No pressure.* He thought. *It's just your new boss and your dad looking over your shoulder.*

"I thought you never flew this kind before?" Seth, his new boss, asked.

"I haven't," Jesse confirmed.

"Then how did you assemble it so easily without reading the instructions?"

"Last night I watched every YouTube video I could find," Jesse confessed with a bit of a blush.

"So what you're saying is that you wanted to be prepared," Seth observed.

"Yes, sir," Jesse agreed.

"Works for me. Nothing like setting a precedent early." Seth grinned. "Now, the question is, can you fly my brand-new machine without crashing it?"

Jesse just smiled and thought, *I sure hope so.*

"No pressure," Seth said. "Just thousands of dollars."

Jesse picked up the controller and the flying machine and carried them both a few yards from the trucks. He set the drone down and assessed the wind direction. Backing up a few yards, he took one last glance at his boss. Seth nodded his head and said, "Let's do it."

Jesse took a deep breath and hit the Go Fly button. As he worked the controls, the mini aircraft came up to a hover at about four feet in the air and did a complete 360-degree turn. Link and Seth were looking over Jesse's shoulder to see the camera video during the entire turn. There came a bunch of whistles and hoots from the Reagan roustabouts watching from the backs of the thier work trucks.

"That's a pretty good hover, son. You'd make a great helicopter pilot," Link whispered in Jesse's ear.

"Ah, dad. This is probably way easier," Jesse admitted, but the obviously proud comment from his father made him grin.

At that, Jesse moved the flight controls, and the drone started to climb into the air and fly in the direction of the current work area.

Link leaned over to Seth. "I can't believe how good the video is on that thing."

The video was truly spectacular as they could see details in the terrain as well as all the tiny flags marking the natural gas pipeline that they would be working near for the next couple of weeks.

"What's that?" Seth asked, pointing at something on the screen.

Link looked at the video screen. "Holy cow, that's a bull moose catching an afternoon nap down in the wood line at the bottom of the hill."

All three men looked in the direction of the Woodline, but from their vantage point, they couldn't have possibly seen the big animal.

Seth let out a low whistle. "I'd sure like to invite him home for dinner next hunting season."

Link grinned. "Oh man, you could feed an army with that one."

"Hey, guys," Jesse announced. "We've got a bogey on the far side of this section line. It looks like a white pickup."

"What are they doing there?" Link asked.

"Jesse, fly over there and see if you can get a better look at that truck," Seth requested, his eyes narrowed. "There shouldn't be anyone in that area.".

"Roger that, boss," Jesse responded with a grin as the drone heeled over and headed toward the truck. It wasn't long before they could clearly see a man standing next to the truck.

"Can you zoom in on that guy?" Seth asked.

"Sure," Jesse replied. "Watch this."

As Jesse zoomed in, they could see the man had a pair of binoculars to his eyes and was looking back at them.

"Get a shot of the name on the side of the truck," Link commanded.

As Jesse flew the drone toward its target, the man with the binoculars suddenly made a dash back to the truck, sending rocks and dirt flying as he sped out of the area.

"Did you make out the name on that truck?" Link asked.

"No, sir," Jesse admitted. "But we've got the video recording. Maybe we can take a closer look at it later."

"I doubt we got close enough to read the sign. The only glimpse I had, there appeared to be some sort of boomerang logo," Seth added.

"Follow that truck," Link commanded

"Uh, Dad," Jesse said nervously.

"What?" Link responded

"The battery didn't get fully charged and it's going to need to come back soon before it dies."

"Damn," Link said under his breath.

"Who could be trying to horn in on our project?" Seth asked, looking at Link.

"That's what I'd like to know," Link stated as he narrowed his eyes in thought. "Kody," he yelled. Kody was one of the longtime Reagan hands.

"Yes, sir," Kody yelled as he jumped off the flatbed and walked over to them.

"I want you to cut back out on the highway and find out how that Joker got onto that tract of land up on the hill over there."

"On it, Boss," Kody said as he turned toward his truck.

He pulled open his truck door just as Seth hollered, "Uh, Kody?"

Kody turned back. "Yeah, Boss?"

"Take your brother with you. And, if you happen to actually catch up with this guy, just ID him. No broken bones, okay?"

"In fact, no bruises either," Link added.

Kody and Jeff shared a smile and said in unison, "Roger that, Boss."

CHAPTER SIX

For Jenny and Victoria, the afternoon drive through downtown Williston was unusually quiet, and even a bit eerie. In fact, it was completely devoid of the big tractor-trailer trucks, service rigs, and the normal rush of oilfield traffic that they normally encountered. Just a few cars here and there with nothing to slow them down.

"Where is everyone?" Jenny asked in wonder as she looked around. "The streets are practically empty."

"Link said this morning over coffee that there is a Bakken-wide safety stand-down today."

"What is a safety stand-down?" Jenny asked. "And how does it make all the people disappear like in some sci-fi movie?"

"Apparently, there has been a rash of accidents and incidents lately. Bakken wide. Two of which were fatal. So today, every company associated with the oil field is holding meetings about ratcheting up the safety."

"Seth didn't mention anyone at Reagan getting hurt," Jenny offered.

"No, none at Reagan. Thank God," Victoria said with relief.

"Link said it's been kind of strange. That they have been freak accidents. The kind that you can't pin down to a specific cause."

"What do you mean?"

"Well, if the accidents were all from carelessness, it would give you a place to start. But these are random. Some could be chalked up to carelessness, but others are freak equipment failures that just don't normally happen. The insurance companies are really freaking out and they are driving the safety stand-down."

"So that's why," she said softly.

"Why what?" Victoria asked.

"Seth said that Link has been a little moody and brooding lately," Jenny concluded.

"Yeah," Victoria agreed. "He doesn't like it and feels that unless they can figure out what they have in common, a safety stand-down won't help at all."

Victoria found a spot right in front of Doctor Griffin's office—a rarity—and they headed right in, nearly fifteen minutes early.

Lilly, who held two positions at the clinic as both Doctor Griffin's Nurse and his wife, looked up, wide-eyed as if in shock. "Well, as I live and breathe," she said in a mock southern accent. "Is there something wrong with my watch, or are you actually early?" She let out a chuckle as she stepped out of the office into the reception area and greeted them warmly with a hug for each of them. "Jenny, Victoria… How are you? How have you been?"

"Fine," Victoria and Jenny said in unison as if they'd been practicing. The two women looked at each other and burst out laughing.

"It may be possible that we're spending too much time together," Victoria confessed.

"Let me see that ring," Lilly gushed.

Jenny held out her left hand and blushed as Lilly made a big deal out of it.

"Any luck keeping those two men of yours out of trouble?" Lilly asked with a bit of a twinkle in her eye.

"If there wasn't a blue moon out last night, then no," Victoria said with a laugh. "And come to think of it, maybe not even then." She gave an exaggerated look of frustration as she animatedly threw her hands in the air. "The more time they spend together, the more they are alike as well."

"Lord knows that's the truth," Lilly agreed. She pointed toward the hard plastic chairs in the small waiting area. "You two take a seat, and I'll be with you in just a quick minute."

Victoria and Jenny selected the same pair of seats that they sat in during the first baby checkup with Doctor Griffin. The blue and pink pastel colors on the walls were broken up by framed medical posters, some of them showing the dangers of drinking and smoking during pregnancy, and others showing the different stages of pregnancy. The ever-present smell of antiseptic was mixed with the aroma of fresh coffee from the thermos style, pumper coffee carafe labeled Bakkens' Best Coffee.

Jenny looked around the room, remembering her very first appointment. Suddenly, she leaned her forehead toward Victoria conspiratorially and whispered, "The only thing I don't like about coming to these checkups is dealing with Brooke." She nearly hissed the name of Doctor Griffin's nursing assistant. "I really don't understand why she seems to dislike me so much. Am I special, or does she hate everyone the same?" Jenny asked, then without skipping a beat, "You know, she really doesn't need to be in the *helping people* industry with that attitude."

"Oh, honey. If it makes you feel any better, it's just you," Victoria shared in a whisper of her own, but with an added giggle. "Lilly told me that Brooke had been chasing after Seth for a couple of years after Olivia passed away, but he never took notice. In fact, he couldn't even remember her name. Then you showed up and caught his attention," she finished the comment with an impish grin, pointing to Jenny's belly. "She even dyed her brunette hair to a strawberry blonde."

"*Sooo*, I am special after all," Jenny said with a sarcastic chuckle of her own. "Well, lucky me."

Lilly returned a few minutes later with a clipboard in her hand and her reading glasses dangling from a bejeweled lanyard around her neck. "Let's see here," she said as she put her glasses on, looking first through her glasses and then over the top of them. "It's been a long time since I had to read this myself." Lilly turned down the corridor and said, "Follow me, please," over her shoulder as she once again passed through the swinging doorway.

"Where's Brooke today?" Victoria asked as they followed Lilly down the hall.

Lilly looked up from the form. "Brooke?" she asked a bit absentmindedly. "Oh yeah, Brooke. She decided to go to Mexico for her annual vacation. The day she got back, she called and said she was offered a position at Trinity Hospital. I didn't even know she had applied."

"So, kind of sudden," Jenny offered.

"Well, she did say they pay a lot better than we could. So, it's really hard to blame her."

"Well, good for her," Jenny said a bit too enthusiastically, which garnered a brief look from Lilly over her glasses.

Victoria shot Jenny a sideward glance and agreed. "Yeah, good for her."

"Not good for us though. Do you know how hard it is to find clinical help in this crazy boomtown? Anyone that is good is already taken, so we've already started advertising out of state."

"Seth has connections in Chicago. Maybe Ty could help in the search. After all, he found me," Jenny said with a grin.

"I believe you were kind of expensive and a lot more important," Lilly said, matter-of-factly. She turned aside and ushered them into the same exam room in which Jenny had first seen Doctor Griffin.

"Take a seat, dear," she said as she pointed to a black vinyl chair next to a small desk. Jenny put her purse down on the desk and quickly removed her light blue windbreaker and sat down with an excited smile. *Yay, no more Brooke?* she thought, a grin spreading across her face.

"Victoria, would you like me to bring in another chair?" Lilly asked.

"Oh, no thank you. If it's alright with you, I'll just sit on the exam table, and when Jenny needs it, we'll swap."

"Works for me," Lilly said as she turned to Jenny. She sat on a little round black vinyl stool on wheels, pulled herself over to the desk, and opened the top left drawer. After rummaging around for a quick second, she finally pulled out a blood pressure cuff and turned her attention back to Jenny. With the cuff in place on Jenny's arm, Lilly pulled the stethoscope off her shoulder and placed the cold end on Jenny's arm. "So," Lilly said, "do you want to know if they are boys or girls yet?"

"Or maybe one of each," Victoria piped in.

"You never know until you know for sure," Lilly offered hopefully.

"Umm, yeah… about that…"

Jenny looked from one to the other. "As both of you already know, during the last ultrasound Seth and I agreed to wait to find out the sexes after they are born." She sighed.

Lilly looked at Victoria and then over in the opposite corner where the ultrasound machine stood. She looked back at Jenny and said, "Hmm. Seth isn't here, and we could…

you know… do another ultrasound and accidentally see." She gave a conspiratorial grin. "The whole town is wondering. They are just dying to know," Lilly pleaded.

"Oh, no. Seth would kill me if I did that. And besides, I am excited to wait for the surprise," Jenny said with more conviction than she felt.

"Well, your blood pressure is good," Lilly said as she wrote the numbers down on the chart. "Now, let's get you on the scale."

Jenny attempted to hop up from her chair but failed. What she actually managed was more of a wobble. When she finally got to her feet, she walked over and stepped up on the scale.

Lilly looked over her glasses and adjusted the counterweights on the scale. "Hmm." She wrote down the number and referenced a chart pasted on the clipboard.

"Is everything all right?" Jenny asked, holding her breath.

"Well, yes," Lilly said while running her fingers down a line of the chart. She stopped and wrote down a number then looked up. "According to this chart, your weight gain with twins is right on the money."

Jenny let out her breath and said, "Whew, I never thought I'd think that gaining weight was a good thing, but I'm elated now."

"Okay, it's time to swap positions," Lilly said to Victoria.

"Yes, ma'am," said Victoria as she slipped off the table. Jenny walked over and took her seat on the exam table.

"So, Jenny. Have you and Seth picked out any names yet?" Lilly asked while surreptitiously glancing at Victoria.

"Well yes…and no."

"That's interesting," Victoria mused. "You're naming them Yes and No?"

"Okay, Victoria. You've been spending way too much time around Link," Lilly said.

"I agree," Jenny chimed in. "That was totally a 'Link smartass-ism.'"

"Okay, okay. I'm sorry," Victoria feigned. "I'll never channel Link again."

After they all had a good laugh, Lilly dove back in. "Lilly is always a good middle name if one of them is a girl."

"So is Victoria," Victoria stated.

"Well, the truth is, we have decided *who* gets to name them, but we haven't decided on any names yet. Or at least, Seth hasn't, but I've got some ideas of my own. Or should I say, Olivia's ideas. I get to name the first born, and Seth gets to name the second. Without knowing boys or girls yet, there are way too many *what-ifs* involved."

After taking measurements of her belly and adding them to Jenny's chart, Lilly said, "Everything looks great so far. I've got to get back out front, but Doc Griffin will be in to see you shortly." After another quick hug for each of them, Lilly disappeared through the doorway.

"Ahem." Victoria cleared her throat as she stared into the corner of the room. Jenny looked up to see what she was staring at. It was the ultrasound machine.

"Are you sure you don't want to know?" Victoria asked slyly.

"Are you kidding?" Jenny asked. "Of course, I want to know, but Seth and I agreed to wait, and I'm not going against that."

"Okay, okay. And you're right, you know."

"About what?" Jenny asked.

"About sticking to your guns and not breaking your agreement with Seth. It shows integrity and faithfulness. What's more, it's the right decision, even though I really want to know in the worst way." Victoria finished her comment with a bit of a whine.

The two looked toward the door when they heard the now familiar double-knock of Doc Griffin. Both women said, "Come in," in perfect unison and then burst into laughter.

Doc Griffin poked his head in. "Okay, what did I miss this time?"

"Oh, nothing, Doc," Victoria waved away. "Just girl stuff."

"Well, that's what I'm here for." He grinned. "So, how are you feeling Jenny?" he asked as he reviewed her chart and the new sets of numbers that Lilly had recorded.

"I'm feeling fine," Jenny answered. "I'm glad the morning sickness didn't last long, and my appetite keeps growing."

"You're spot on for the size of the babies," he offered without looking up from the clipboard. "However, I'd like to see you gain a little more weight. Having twins can take quite a toll on your body. Especially on a smaller frame." He placed the chart on the desk. "Let's take a look."

After finishing a quick exam, including listening to both of the babies' heartbeats, he asked, "Are you experiencing any significant swelling in your legs or feet?"

"No, not that I'm aware of," Jenny answered.

"Good. Both babies appear to be preparing for birth. They have both moved into the head-down position. It looks like they might be getting ready for a race to the finish line."

"But I'm only thirty-three weeks," Jenny exclaimed in a shocked tone.

"Most twins come sometime after thirty-four weeks, so if I were you, I'd pack your overnight bag in the next week or two," he advised with a smile.

CHAPTER SEVEN

"**A**re you all right?" Victoria asked. "You haven't said a word since we left Doc Griffin's office."

"Umm, yeah, sure," came the half-hearted reply. And then nothing. Just silence from the eight-month pregnant girl sitting in the passenger seat. It was obvious that something was going on. Something was bothering her. Victoria was sure that if she could just get Jenny talking, then it would come out.

After waiting a long moment for Jenny to say something, anything, Victoria tried a different tact. "Say, do you need anything from the grocery store?"

"Uh, yeah," she responded from somewhere a million miles away. "I could pick up some things."

"Okay, great. Link said they'd be finishing up their project in Montana today and would be home early. I'd like to pick up some ribeye steaks before he gets home."

More silence. Just a nod.

They entered the store, and each grabbed a cart and went in separate directions to complete their lists.

Victoria saw Jenny twenty minutes later pushing her cart through the diaper aisle, but her cart was still empty.

"Are you okay?" Victoria asked.

Jenny looked up and said, "Sure, why do you ask?"

"Oh, I don't know. But hey, there's nothing in your cart and you seem like you're on a different planet, that's all."

Jenny looked down into her cart and then looked around as if to see where she was. "Oh, Victoria. Every time I reach a new phase of my pregnancy, I think, *Wow, now it's getting real.* I just got used to this last phase, and then another one starts today. When Doc Griffin told me to pack my overnight bag, it just got a whole lot more absolute or certain." She turned to look directly at Victoria with shiny, scared eyes. "I can't do this. I don't think I am ready," she said with a shudder. "Oh, God, Victoria, I'm suddenly terrified, and I can't even think straight."

In one fluid motion, Victoria stepped over to Jenny and wrapped her arms around her as Jenny's silent tears started to flow.

"I don't want to be scared but suddenly I'm terrified."

Victoria just held her for a few minutes right there in the diaper aisle. She remembered the first time she'd comforted Jenny. It was in the bathroom of the Williston Brewery, and she thought, *how ironic,* when earlier Jenny was crying because she thought she *wasn't* pregnant.

It was after dark by the time they finally left the grocery store. As Victoria drove up the road to the Cabin, she looked across to Jenny. She was quiet. Jenny still seemed to be in some sort of catatonic state. *No, that's not it.* Victoria realized. It was much more complicated. More like resolute, in the face of fear. Fear of the unknown. Fear of failure. Jenny's jaw was set. Her eyes stared straight forward without looking left or right. Wait a second. *Determination,* Victoria thought. That is what she was seeing. Resolute determination. She breathed out a sigh of relief and allowed herself a little smile. *She's going to be okay.* Victoria thought. *Especially in light of what's headed her way in just a few minutes.*

Victoria pulled into Seth and Jenny's driveway at 'The Cabin' and put the truck into Park. She looked over at Jenny and asked a question that she already knew the answer to, even if Jenny didn't. "Are you going to be okay?"

Jenny opened the truck door and stepped out onto the running board and then down to the ground without saying anything. She picked up her bag containing some eggs and milk and hung it on her right arm at the elbow. Reaching back in, she grabbed her purse that was sitting on top of the drink holder nestled between the two front seats and only then looked directly at Victoria.

"Jenny?"

Jenny closed her eyes for a moment and when she opened them up again, Victoria saw what she needed to see. Her bright eyes, glistening in the dome light, and wearing a determined smile.

"The answer is yes," Jenny replied. "I'm going to be just fine. And thank you for coming with me today. I really needed it."

"You are more loved than you know. But it will become clearer soon enough," Victoria said with a knowing smirk.

"What does that mean?" Jenny asked with her eyes narrowed.

"Do you need a hand with your groceries?" Victoria deflected.

"Uh, no. I think I can handle this big ol' bag of food," she replied with a smart-ass grin as she animated the heavy weight of the groceries. Then, with a dismissive wave of her free hand, she said "Good night."

"Okay, take care," Victoria said as Jenny closed the truck door.

She waved at Victoria as she stepped around the big bumper and walked in front of the truck. She turned away and headed up the few quick stairs to the kitchen's French door. Holding her grocery bag in one hand, she got the keys from her purse and unlocked it, turned the handle, and hit the door with her hip to swing it open.

Reaching for the light switch in the dark, she realized that she was not alone. She could hear breathing, and her blood ran cold. Dropping her bag of groceries, she started to turn and run when someone blocked her escape, grabbing her by the arms. Screaming, she desperately tried to break away and run.

"Jenny, it's me, Victoria," she yelled as she held Jenny's arms. "It's okay. I've got you."

All the lights came on suddenly and there was a raucous, "*Surprise!*"

Jenny's eyes darted around the room. Gulping air, she took in the scene. The entire house was filled with people and food. Pink and blue balloons were hung everywhere with a large sign hung across the room "CONGRATULATIONS".

"What?" Jenny's hand went to her chest. "I thought…"

"I'm so sorry, Jenny," Victoria apologized. "We were only trying to give you a surprise baby shower."

Jenny breathed a sigh of relief, but no words came out yet. The faces were all a mixture of embarrassment and glee. Apologies drifted from all sides as she looked around and then down at her feet. Still trembling from the adrenaline, she realized she had stomped on her groceries trying to get away. The carton of eggs was smashed and oozing whites and yoke all over the floor and her shoes. Celia pushed through the crowd with a damp bar towel to wipe up the mess. She handed a second towel to Jenny to clean the mess off of herself. Jenny attempted to bend over to wipe her shoes off with little success. Someone grabbed the wet towel from her hand and said, "Honey, let me do that for you." Jenny recognized the voice, but it took a moment to realize who it was.

"Peggy?" Jenny asked in surprise. Peggy was Jenny's friend and mentor back when she lived in Chicago and worked as a waitress.

"Hello, honey." Peggy said beaming as she held out her arms for a hug. "I'd ask how you're doing, but I think I already got the picture."

Jenny threw herself into Peggy's arms, bouncing on her tiptoes in excitement. "Oh, Peggy! I'm so happy to see you! How'd you get here?"

"Well, I got a call at the diner from some guy named Seth asking me if I could come to your baby shower, and if I could, he'd have a plane ticket waiting for me. Did you know he bought me a first-class ticket?" Peggy gushed. "I've never been treated so nice in my life."

"Wait, where's Seth?" she said as she pulled away from Peggy and looked around. "I've got to thank him." She looked around expectantly.

"He and Link are running late," Victoria offered. "I'm so sorry that they're not here yet. Link just called and told me to expect them in a half hour or so."

Maria reached for Jenny's hand and guided her into the kitchen, through throngs of friends and family, and into the living room with Victoria following behind. There was food and desserts of every kind stacked on the large kitchen island.

"Where did all this food come from?" Jenny asked anyone who might be listening.

"Seth called Maria and asked if she could cater the shower because everyone was so busy," Victoria answered.

"And I happily said yes," Maria piped in. "We closed the bar for the evening, but it turned out not to be much of a loss." Maria threw her hands in the air. "Over half my customers are right here anyway."

* * * * *

As the crowd mingled, laughed and joked, Jesse wandered into the kitchen in search of another beer. The built-in speakers were playing some easy jazz, but with the noise of conversation, it was barely audible. A bottle of Jameson was displayed in a place of honor, with two shot glasses. One upright and one tipped on its side. It was somewhat of a memorial to his older brother Jason, a Marine who'd been killed in Afghanistan. It caused an involuntary flashback of a Christmas tree created years ago by his brother, from nothing but Jameson bottles. It brought a smile instead of sadness. *I guess it all depends upon the circumstances.* He thought to himself.

Shaking himself back to the present, the search for beer continued. He spotted additional, still-covered food trays stacked neatly on the granite kitchen island. With his own penchant for cooking and his curiosity peaking, he decided to investigate. Setting his empty beer bottle down next to the commercial sized gas stove, he began to lift the lid. Suddenly he heard a terse, *"Hands off,"* as a hand came from behind and slapped his own away from the unopened yet mysterious food.

"Those trays are for later," came the heavily accented scolding.

Jesse spun around like a little kid getting caught with his hand in the cookie jar. Shocked at the firm rebuke, at first he couldn't speak. He looked down at his hand, then back up into the beautiful emerald eyes of his assailant. Quickly shifting his stance, he gave her his famous Jesse James smile.

"I'm sorry." He blushed a little. "I was just wondering what was in there," he explained, giving his best defense followed by his infamous lopsided grin. It would normally melt the heart of an ice cube, but it didn't seem to have the desired effect on this one. Without responding, she turned back to the tray and snapped the lid back on. Her green eyes suddenly locked on to his empty beer bottle like a laser. She snatched it from the counter and threw it in the trash. Tossing a single glance, or maybe a glare, at Jesse, she hoisted up a heavy tray of hors d'oeuvres and disappeared into the family room full of hungry guests.

"Wow," Jesse exclaimed under his breath. "What was that?"

CHAPTER EIGHT

S kipping the long waiting line as usual, Link nodded to the bouncer guarding the entrance and opened the door for Victoria as they walked into Maria's. The bar and grill was dimly lit and constantly busy, but Maria always made it clear that they were *never* too busy for Lincoln James to get a reservation. Maria was known for her bone-in, smoked ribeye steaks and twice baked potatoes. Her motto was, *If you're going to stick to meat and potatoes, make it the best meat and potatoes.* The building itself had started out in life a hundred years earlier as a mill. When Maria turned the old, abandoned building into a bar, she worked hard to retain much of its history. The exposed beams, dark shiplap walls, and the heavy wood plank floors were brought back to life during the restoration.

Holding Victoria's hand, Link guided them through the crowd to their favorite table near the small dance floor. It was nothing special, just a standard four-top with a lit candle placed in the center next to a simple handwritten sign stating in block letters. RESERVED FOR LINK.

"Oh, what an extravagance it is being married to someone so popular," Victoria chided.

Link smiled and pulled out her chair. "Nothing is too good for you, my queen."

Link sat down across from her and reached out his hand where it was met halfway by hers. She had long fingers with fire red nails that Link was particularly fond of.

"What a crazy week," Victoria commented. "What do you think caused that pile up on 85?"

"I don't know and I sure don't like it," Link said. "And," he paused for a moment while gathering his thoughts. " just how does that happen with sunshine and dry roads?"

"It doesn't make sense." Victoria agreed.

"Damn right it doesn't." Link stated angrily as he slapped his hand down on the table.

"So, how did Jesse do on his first day at Reagan?" Victoria asked, changing the subject.

"Really well, actually," Link said. "I was a little nervous about it at first but he totally rose to the occasion. He's his own man now."

"He is Lincoln James' son," Victoria declared. "I have no doubt that this is going to work out. Just watch. He's going to make you proud."

"I'm already proud," Link stated matter-of-factly. He began to stand as Maria approached their table.

"Link, Victoria, it's so nice to see you." Maria greeted them in her warm, smokey voice as she came out of the kitchen. "Welcome." She kissed Victoria on each cheek before turning to Link and giving him the same treatment. Victoria knew that it was a European thing, but it did take some getting used to.

"How is everyone?" Maria asked.

"We're all good," Link replied, sitting back down.

"Seth & Jenny? Still doing well I hope?" She asked.

"Jenny's doing great," Victoria said with a grin. "Though she was exhausted after the scare we gave her at the baby shower."

"I think my job is harder now that he's back to work," Link complained. "Keeping that boy out of trouble is a full-time job all by itself, especially in light of the fact that he's also my boss."

The trio chuckled.

"Now, what can I get for you to drink?" Maria asked.

Link opened his mouth to speak, but Maria cut him off. "I already know what you want. The question was for the lady."

"You do?" Link asked in surprise.

"Blue Moon, with two slices of orange," she declared with a *I told you so* tilt to her head.

"Am I really that predictable?" Link asked, looking at Victoria.

"Yes," both Maria and Victoria stated in unison before all three burst out laughing all over again.

"Hey, no fair. I'm getting ganged up on here."

"And you, Victoria?" Maria asked, wiping a tear from her eye.

"Um, how about a Moscow Mule," she said. "Can you make them?"

"I can't, but I'm sure Celia or Jake can," Maria said, pointing toward the bar. "Would you like any starters from the kitchen?

"How are your divine bacon-wrapped jalapeño poppers this evening?" Victoria asked.

"Sent straight from heaven about an hour ago," Maria responded with a smile. "I'll be right back with your order."

Link and Victoria both glanced over to the bar. Celia had already poured and placed a tall Blue Moon on a tray with two slices of fresh orange on the rim.

"Ah, to be known and loved," Link said with uncharacteristic melancholy.

What is it with those two? Victoria wondered for the thousandth time.

She watched him closely as his eyes lingered on Celia. There, just for a fleeting moment, something flickered across his face, almost a sadness. But then as quickly as it appeared, he set his jaw and looked away.

In fact, every time they came into the restaurant, Victoria watched Link as he looked over at the bar where Celia was usually busy serving drinks. This time though, Celia was staring back while handing a drink to a patron who was still too far away to reach it. Link quickly wrenched his eyes back to Victoria and cleared his throat. "Mrs. James, would you care to dance while we await our liquid libations?"

"Why yes, I would," she said as they both stood up.

The three-piece band was doing a cover of "Cruisin'" by Smokey Robinson.

As they danced, Victoria's mind began to ponder. She knew that Link and Maria had been friends since his time doing *projects* in some war. Strangely, Link skillfully avoided her questions when she would poke around at the edges, so she had no way of really knowing what the actual connection was. One thing was sure, theirs was a very strong friendship, undoubtedly forged in the fires of hell. Victoria bit her lip. She had heard rumors whispered around town that Celia was somehow Link's daughter, some love child but he never mentioned it. It was well before she met him, so it didn't matter in that sense, but she wanted to know because it was part of him. Part of the past of the man that she was madly in love with. *So how do I ask the question?* Victoria asked herself. It wasn't as if she could just say, hey, Link, are the rumors true? Is Celia really your child? Maria would surely know, but there was no way she'd go behind

Link's back and ask her. Victoria discreetly peered at Celia over Link's shoulder, to see, once again, if there was any noticeable resemblance. She was tall, five foot-nine or so, and athletically built just as Link was, but that was as far as the similarities went.

The song ended, tearing her from her thoughts. They returned to their table, and just as they sat down, Maria approached. Her expression changed as she nervously twisted the bar towel she held in her hands. The sudden reversal gave Victoria a bit of alarm.

"What is it, Maria?" Victoria asked. "Are you okay?"

"Link, she knows now," Maria blurted in a hoarse whisper.

Maria's comment made Victoria's heart skip a beat. She glanced between Link and Maria.

"Who? About what?" he asked with more than a little apprehension in his voice.

"Celia," Maria answered. "About you."

Link flashed a worried look at Victoria and then at Maria as he slowly shook his head.

Maria looked from one to the other, then sat down at their table, her eyes nervous. "Victoria doesn't know?" asked Maria, obviously in surprise.

"No," Link said. At first he seemed angry and then his face just dropped.

"Why, Link?" Maria asked softly. "She loves you. She needs to understand."

"That's just it," he snapped. "She won't understand. She won't understand about me, or who I was. About then. She didn't even know me then."

Victoria listened to the discourse and decided to keep her mouth shut. She didn't know exactly where this was going, but instinct told her if she chimed in, it would shatter

65

the possibility that she would learn some very important things about her husband's past.

"You've got to tell her," Maria insisted.

"Then you tell her," Link snapped as he abruptly stood up and marched for the exit.

Victoria held her breath as she and Maria watched him go. After what seemed like an eternity, Victoria gently touched Maria's shaking hands. "Tell me what?" she whispered.

At first Maria simply stared in the direction of the door without answering. The bar towel in her hand was now torn, and the sadness on her face told of a breaking heart.

"Is Celia Link's daughter?" Victoria finally blurted out.

"No," Maria snapped as if the question was totally absurd. "Celia just asked me the same thing." Maria paused for a moment as if in thought. "Where does that stupid question come from anyway?" Her abruptness took Victoria off guard.

Victoria pulled her hand back and bit her lip for a moment before deciding to plunge forward. "Well, maybe it's the way he looks at her every time we come in here, as if she's either an ex-lover—and I find that hard to believe given the age difference—or she's his daughter."

There, I finally put it out there, Victoria thought as her heart hammered in her chest. She held her breath, waiting for the answer.

"Well, both are wrong," Maria answered with a voice that was more gravelly than usual. There was a hint of mist in her dark eyes, but the look was no longer sad, it was something else. Wishful.

Victoria put her hand back on Maria's. "I'm so sorry if I have offended you, Maria. I know that you and Link are close. I know that something in the past has welded a friendship between the two of you that nothing can ever break." She paused for a moment and then decided to thrust forward. "But sometimes I feel like an outsider looking in when the two of you talk, or even share a look. An unspoken memory."

Maria glanced toward the doorway once again before turning to Victoria and, leaning in, spoke in a low whisper. "You know Link is very private about his past. The poor man had his heart accidentally ripped out by an innocent child that he dearly loved. I only know the parts that I was part of, even so, there is a lot that I'm unaware of." Maria took a breath. "So, as far as feeling like an outsider looking in? When it comes to Link, I've been there too." She admitted with an empathetic nod. "Link truly believes he is protecting us all by keeping certain *secrets* hidden away."

It occurred to Victoria that, where Link fits in, Maria was a kindred spirit. "I'm sorry. Please go on."

"Okay, here goes," Maria said with trepidation. "He did say that I could tell you, right?" she confirmed with a cocked head and raised eyebrows.

Victoria looked over toward the door again and said, "Yes, he did." Her heartbeat rapidly, and her mouth suddenly went dry.

"Link accidently rescued Celia when she was just a little girl."

"How do you accidentally rescue someone?" Victoria asked.

"Link and his secret Dagger group that he doesn't talk about, went to this hotel compound used to hold female prisoners. The mission or 'Project' as Link prefers to call them, was to locate a high value target for a snatch and grab. In fact, I heard it was a general that was responsible for shelling and sniping innocent civilians. Anyway, when the Dagger team landed within the compound, Link and his men spread out and started searching, clearing the hotel room by room. Link entered a room and found the target with his pants down on top of a small child. He was attacking her on a filthy bed."

Victoria sucked in a deep breath and shook her head in disbelief. "Oh, no."

"Link lost it. He pulled his knife out and grabbed him from behind. As he plunged the knife into the rapist, he looked down at the terrified little girl. Not wanting the blood to spill on her, he rolled the body off the bed and dumped it in a corner."

"Was the little girl Celia?" Victoria asked, her heart in her throat. Her eyes narrowed with anger as the mental picture began to form in her mind.

"Yes...it was," she confirmed. "Link said she was so scared that when he went back to her, she scampered backwards on the bed, up against the wall. Terrified."

"Oh, that poor little girl." Victoria breathed.

"He should have just left her," Maria stated matter-of-factly. "He should have carried on the mission. She wasn't the purpose of the raid. But that's not Link. Dagger command was really pissed at him for killing the general. "

"But that's not Link." Victoria agreed with a hint of pride. Her jaw was tight as she envisioned the atrocity on tbe innocent child.

"That's right. To Link it didn't matter who he was. He was evil." Maria said. "Link wanted to scoop her up and take her out of there, but she was so terrified, even of him, her rescuer. So, instead of trying to pick her up right away, he unslung his rifle and eased it down on the floor. She just watched him, unblinking. Sitting down on the edge of the bed, he smiled at her. Her face was filthy with grime and tears. Her wavy dark hair was a tangled mess as if it hadn't been brushed in months, and her big green eyes were wild and frightened. Link slowly pulled out a chocolate bar from his cargo pocket and smelled it. Then he turned it over in his hand. He looked back at her and then looked down at the candy bar. After turning it over, he opened the wrapper and carefully peeled back the foil." She paused again and looked at Victoria. "You know the kind that has lots of little squares?"

"Yes, yes I do," Victoria said impatiently, waving her hand for Maria to continue.

"Well…" She paused, obviously enjoying this part of the story, "He broke off one of the little rectangles and ate it, acting like it tasted real good, but still said nothing."

"I can totally see Link doing that," Victoria interjected.

"The dirty-faced little girl was looking down at the rest of the chocolate bar he held in his hand and then up to Link's face, back and forth. Link said it almost killed him. She slowly moved off of the wall ever so slightly.

"Link ate a second little piece and made an even bigger show of it. Finally, he held out the rest of the chocolate to her. She only hesitated for a second before she moved close enough, took it, and gobbled it up." Maria paused again. "She was such a mess. She still had chocolate all over her face when I first met her. After she finished the rest, he held out his arms, and she came to him. Link wrapped her up in a smelly blanket and brought her out to his helicopter. He handed her to his door gunner and flew her to my place on the coast."

"Why you?" asked Victoria. "How did you two know each other?" She had waited a long time to ask these questions.

"Sophia and I were part of the underground. I had a small bar there in Split. It wasn't much, just a hole in the wall really. About the size of one of those small yellow school buses. We organized guerilla style raids against the enemy, and we happened to be a small part of one of

Link's bigger projects. The general's people caught one of our fighters and soon found out about us. His henchmen laid a trap. Many of us were killed and the rest captured." Maria paused and took a deep breath, sadness in her eyes. "It was a devastating blow to our fight.

"Two days later, Link and his team came in and rescued us. If it weren't for him, I'd be dead now, after torture and who knows what else. If it weren't for Link, there would be many more good people murdered. The next time I saw him, he came into the bar. When I tried to thank him, all he would say is, 'It's no big deal.'"

"Oh, that is so like Link," Victoria said. "Now I understand your loyalty and the friendship between you. But why would he want to keep me from knowing this?"

"I don't know. But maybe it's because he's afraid of how others, especially you, will look at him, treat him differently."

"But wait, what happened with Celia?" Victoria asked, nearly holding her breath. "Why don't they talk?"

"Oh, they used to talk a lot. Link would come over and visit whenever he was in Split. She would run to him and leap into his arms when she saw him coming through the gate. Then he would sit down on our little garden bench and let her search his shirt pockets for a chocolate bar. He would always pick a little white flower and tuck the stem into the wrapper. At first it was already sticking out of his pocket but after a while, he would button the pocket, so she had to work a bit harder to get it. It was their game. While she would gobble up the chocolate, he would tuck the little white flower into her wavy hair. It was almost as if the sun would only shine in her life when Link came around. We had no idea how long that terrible war would go on. Sophie and I could teach her how to survive, how to fight, and we tried to make a home for her, but no one could compete with Link."

Victoria smiled.

"Link would call her *Moj mali mišu*." Maria chuckled and looked like she was again, halfway across the globe watching the two of them sitting on the bench in the warm sunshine. Her eyes focused inward on the distant memory as she became quiet.

"What does that mean?" Victoria asked, interrupting her thoughts.

"What?" Maria asked, looking up at Victoria. "Oh, yes. It means My Little Mouse.

"Why did he call her that?" Victoria asked with a chuckle.

"It's a lovely term of endearment, but he probably called her that because of the way she ate her chocolate." She chuckled again.

"How do you say it again?" Victoria giggled as she asked the question.

"*Moj mali mišu…*"

"Moj Molly Miss you." Victoria mimicked and laughed again, this time at her poor attempt.

"Close enough," Maria beamed. "And one beautiful day, this little girl asked Link a question that he didn't understand, and while she was sitting on his lap squishing his face into funny shapes, he asked me what it meant."

"What did she ask?" Victoria asked, barely able to contain herself.

"*Bi li bio moj tata*," Maria said with a sad smile.

"What does that mean?" Victoria asked anxiously. "Is it something bad?"

"No, not at all. It means, *Would you be my daddy?*" Maria said the words slowly, as if tasting each one again.

Victoria gasped as her hand went to her mouth, a lump in her throat.

Maria continued. "Link looked up at me for a long moment, just blinking. I think he was digesting what it truly meant. After a long second, he looked back down to Little Mouse. It was as if the reality of the idea was beginning to register.

"Suddenly, he jumped up off the bench while holding Celia out at arm's length over his head and whooped. '*Da, da, hoću, moj preslatki mali mišu.*' which means, *Yes, yes I will, my adorable little mouse.* And he picked her up over his head and spun her around as she shrieked and giggled in the sunshine. Then he pulled her down to his chest and hugged her like he'd never let her go. After a while, Celia laid her head on his shoulder and snuggled into him. '*Moj Tata.*' *My Daddy.* And fell asleep, safe and sound, her little mouth slightly open and softly snoring. Link looked like he had already taken up residence in heaven itself."

Victoria's eyes were brimming with tears and her lower lip quivered as she asked the next question. "So, what happened? Why don't they talk at all anymore? I can't take this. My heart is breaking."

"It can be so difficult with a man like Link," Maria observed.

"Why would Link want to keep this a secret from me?" Victoria wondered out loud. "Maria…" Victoria looked at her across the table. "Were you and Link lovers?" Her words were direct but soft and not accusing.

Maria sighed and shook her head. "No, Victoria. It was never like that. It might have been…under different circumstances." Maria took a deep breath. "But you see, my husband was killed in the war. They murdered him even before we realized there *was* a war."

"I am so sorry," Victoria said. "I had no idea."

"That's when I fled to the coast and became involved in the underground."

"I still don't understand why Link would keep this from me."

"I do not know the answer, but here is my guess. Link is a very good man with an amazing heart, but he was also very good at his job. The aftermath of the atrocities that he personally witnessed scarred him deeply, which, in turn, caused him to use his skills to avenge so many innocents." Maria paused for a moment and then looked Victoria in the eye. "He made them pay dearly, but it didn't heal his wounds."

"I've seen a few of the scars," Victoria admitted.

"I believe Link desperately needed some form of hope, of light, when Celia tumbled into his life. When he lost Celia, I think he attempted to lock everything away, somewhere deep, dark and impregnable."

"My little bar was the only way I had of making money during the war. It was big enough though, and we made the best of it. I remember one night, Link was there getting drunk on my homemade plum brandy. We called it Slivovitz. Our version of moonshine.

"He was so angry and so drunk he could barely keep the stool under his butt." Maria allowed herself a little chuckle in the middle of the dark story. "You see, getting drunk on plumb schnapps is easy, it's the next morning you must be concerned about."

"I've seen Link tipsy and happy, but I've never seen him hammered," Victoria divulged.

"He would slam his fist down on the bar and yell the way a drunk, hurting man will, slurring his words and sometimes forgetting his point. 'This isn't...uh... This isn't World War Two. It's not even 1938.' He would seethe in his drunken rage. 'These aren't Nazis in Poland or Imperial

Japanese Soldiers in Nan King. But they are still committing the same horrible, disgusting crimes.' He'd stop and look at me a moment through blurry eyes and sway a little. 'Only, these people have been living next door to one another for the last fifty years. What the hell?' he would ask the empty glass in front of him."

"Why, Maria? Why would they do this? How could they do this?' He would beg for an answer, a reason, a meaning, anything."

"I had no answers for this man that I admired, so, the only thing I *could* do was just keep pouring and let him roar. I truly believed that he needed to let some of this caustic poison out of his heart because if he didn't, it would explode in some other manner, in some unpredictable direction. I poured schnapps and prayed that this would somehow flush some of those demons from his soul...." Maria trailed off as she stared at the entrance to the bar.

Victoria turned around and saw what Maria was looking at. Link was right under the exit sign when Victoria caught sight of him. The dim greenish light didn't help the way he already looked. His face appeared drawn and his jaw tight. The bright blue eyes had become sullen and brooding, with an occasional bolt of lightning and flash of anger. It was the look of a man who had lost control.

Link strode purposefully toward the two women, narrowly missing a bar patron crossing his path. He arrived at their table but did not sit or speak. Instead, he gripped the back of a chair, white knuckled, and stared at the lit candle in the center of the table.

"You look like a cornered mountain lion," Maria observed.

"Do you have any idea how many people love you?" Victoria asked. She realized that it wasn't anger in his eyes, it was uncertainty as Link looked from one to the other without speaking. Both Victoria and Maria placed a hand on each of his.

"Lincoln. You must sit." Maria's smoky voice was calm, gentle but commanding.

Link pulled the chair out noisily and dropped into it but still appeared on the edge with arms fastened across his chest.

"Maria. How did you do that?" Victoria asked with a feigned shocked look in an attempt to break the icy surface of Link's demeanor.

"Do what?" Maria asked.

"Get him to do what you say? You simply must tell me your secret."

"Easy there, Ladies," Link cautioned with a reluctant smile.

CHAPTER NINE

"Wow, what a view," Jesse said as he and Seth leaned against the safety rail of the highest point on the oil rig.

Breathing hard from the climb, Seth's face was flushed. "I can't believe just how out of shape I've become after sitting on my butt for the last several weeks."

"How's your hip?" Jesse asked, "I heard about you getting shot."

"It's still not fully healed where the bullet went in, but despite Jenny's concerns, I can't take another minute sitting at home or even at the office."

"Dad said that you saved his life that day."

"It was really the other way around," Seth countered. "If your dad hadn't acted when he did, I am sure you and I wouldn't be having this conversation right now."

"Not the way he tells it," Jesse assured.

"Yeah, well that's typical Link."

Seth continued with quote fingers as Jessie joined in unison, "*It was nothing special.*"

"Yeah, that's dad all right."

The famous North Dakota wind was blowing hard enough to make even the heavy drilling derrick sway back and forth, giving Jesse a zing up and down his spine.

"Can you feel it?" Seth asked.

"Feel what?" Jesse asked nonchalantly as he unconsciously gripped the handrail.

"The movement," Seth replied.

"Uh, it's... well, barely, but it's enough to make me feel a little funny," Jesse confessed, feeling the heat rise in his cheeks.

Seth released a little chuckle, remembering his first time this high on a rig. "You get used to it after a while. We're a little over ten stories up. Each stick of drill pipe is about thirty feet long, and we set three sticks at a time."

"It feels a lot higher than that," Jesse admitted.

"When the rig starts tripping pipe out of the hole, roughnecks stack pipe up here in the monkey boards. There is such a commotion that, after a while, they don't even notice the movement, and neither will you."

Jesse said nothing but his look was doubtful.

Holding his head real still for a moment, he gauged the movement's effect on his equilibrium. "I guess we'll have to wait and see."

"I've got to admit that after only a few days on the job, you've done really well. So far..." Seth acknowledged, then added, "That is, for a green hat." He turned toward Jesse.

"It's been great being around my dad again," Jesse confided. "We haven't had a lot of time together since he and my mom went their separate ways."

"Why'd they split up?"

"I don't know, really. I guess the military kept him gone too much. Beyond that, it's anyone's guess."

"Link never talks much about his past," Seth commented. "Even after all this time with him working for Reagan, I still don't know much about him."

"Join the club."

"Why didn't you stay with your dad?"

"I don't know." He paused as he gazed out on the rugged ridge tops. "I guess because my mom had less rules than Dad, and I was a kid that thought I liked less rules."

"I guess we all like the path of least resistance," Seth observed. "Are you settled into your new apartment?"

"Yeah. I was pretty lucky that they rented it to me. It seems that Reagan as my employer and being the kid of Lincoln James carries a little weight around here."

Seth smiled. "I tell you what. You reap what you sow, and when the chips are down and your back is against the wall, that's when you really see what you've been sowing."

"I didn't know you were a philosopher," Jesse poked.

Ignoring the jab Seth asked. "Can I ask a personal question?"

"Sure, go ahead."

"Why didn't you join the military like your older brothers?" Seth asked without taking his eyes off the mountains in the distance.

Jesse considered Seth's question for a moment without speaking. He was Lincoln James youngest son, and he was just now forging a relationship, as an adult, with his father.

"The proverbial Prodigal Son, I guess," Jesse admitted. "At least where my father is concerned

"I know it's stupid, but I've always regretted not joining the Marines when Jason did." Seth confessed. "I'll never forget the day he left for boot camp. And now, a part of me wonders if I had joined and been with him, somehow, he wouldn't have been killed. We always had each other's back."

"I don't know," Jesse said in regard to Seth's question. "I thought about it a lot. In fact, I had originally intended to go into the Marines as well, but instead, I decided to follow my own path."

"You know your dad is proud of you," Seth said quietly.

"Yeah, I know. Admittedly, I was a bit nervous," Jesse gave a wry chuckle. "Coming to work for you and Dad seemed like a lot to live up to. I almost didn't come, but I am glad I did."

"I gotta admit that I was nervous too," Seth retorted. "Being Link's kid and all, I wasn't sure how I'd deal with it if you turned out to be a lazy dirtbag."

"Are you kidding me?" Jesse said as he looked sideways. "Dad would send me down the road himself if I didn't give it my all, and you know it." He finished the last sentence with a hint of pride in his voice.

"Well, your seemingly innate ability to fly our new drone really saved your butt. The aerial videos have been great and a whole lot cheaper than a helicopter or the airplane. Even your dad reluctantly acknowledges that, and he flies them both. And I suppose it doesn't hurt that you've completed any other task that I needed done, which, I hate to admit out loud, has made you a valuable part of the team."

"I noticed Jameson at your house during the baby shower," Jesse commented.

"There will always be a bottle of Jameson Irish Whiskey in my house in memory of Jason James and the true cost of Freedom," Seth replied stoically.

Both men grew quiet as they stared out over the pre-dawn sky and the expanse of the North Dakota badlands.

After a bit more silence, Seth cleared his throat. "You know, when I first started working with your brother, before he left for the Marines, you were just a kid. Now look at you. All grown up."

"I know Dad thinks of you as another son," Jesse confided.

"I know, and I really appreciate it. I'll never forget the day he saved my life. I see it over and over again in my mind, but I can't wrap my head around it."

"I know what you mean," Jesse replied.

"What did your dad do before he came to work for Reagan?" Seth asked, skirting around the edges.

"I don't really know exactly," Jesse replied. "Honestly, all I know is that he was a pilot for the military, and he was gone a lot. Sometimes he would disappear after a late-night phone call, and it might be weeks or even months before we would hear from him."

"That must have been hard."

"Yeah, it was. The thing is, when I'd ask him what he was doing while he was gone, he'd always reply, '*Nothing special*,' and drop the subject."

"Yep. That's him all right," Seth agreed. "He says the exact same thing to me."

They both chuckled then, Jesse with a mischievous smirk said, "Well, I guess you are the red-headed stepchild in the family." Jesse was already dodging when Seth's giant hand reached out to grab him, but the sudden move made Seth wince.

"Did Kody ever find out how that white pickup got onto the jobsite the other day?" Jesse asked.

"Yeah," Seth replied with a frown. "He found a gate about a mile away with the lock cut off."

"Sounds like the guy came prepared."

"Sure was," Seth agreed. "It was even a hardened lock, but Kody said the guy must've used some sort of a battery powered grinder to cut it off."

Seth's phone vibrated in the pocket of his heavy work shirt, startling him and breaking him out of their conversation. It wouldn't normally have signal this deep into the badlands, but he was somewhere near the top of the brand-new oil drilling rig purchased by GEA, allowing the rare reception. Global Endeavor Alliance was an up-and-coming competitor in the dog-eat-dog world of oil exploration. Even though it was fully assembled, it wasn't commissioned yet. But in three more days, everything would change and there would be a team of men scrambling all over it like ants. It was a chilly morning, and the perfectly round orb of the sun was only halfway above the horizon of the rocky peaks of the North Dakota badlands without a cloud in the morning sky.

His cell quit vibrating as he struggled a bit, pulling off his work glove. A Reagan crane was setting the oil tanks down below that would hold the crude oil when it eventually came out of the ground. Before he could reach inside his jacket, it started vibrating again rather impatiently. "All right, all right," Seth said to no one, finally reaching his right hand inside his jacket and pulling out his phone. He looked at the number and then looked at the time. Too early in the morning for casual phone calls. Something is wrong. The first call was Victoria, now it's Jenny.

"Hi, babe," Seth answered with concern in his voice.

"Seth, where are you?" Jenny's voice came over the crackled and almost digitized cell signal. Even with a poor reception, he could hear the panic in her voice.

"What's wrong, Jenny?"

"What's wrong? I'm in an ambulance on the way to the hospital, that's what's wrong!" Jenny shouted. "I think I'm in labor, Seth! Victoria and I have been calling both you and Link, and nobody is answering their phones." It sounded like anger, but Seth knew she was scared. Suddenly, he was too. He immediately started climbing back down the first ladder, precariously holding on with one hand as he held his cell in the other.

"But aren't you too early?" Seth argued. "I know Doc Griffin said they would most likely come early, but he didn't mean this early, did he?" He fought back the panic in his own voice as he clamored down the endless ladder to the ground below.

"He said both babies were already in position, but I didn't think they would come this soon either," she hollered over the cell.

"Wait." Seth stopped climbing down. "Has your water broken?"

"No, not yet."

"They can't be coming now," Seth countered. "Besides, Doc Griffin is still in Denver for that weekend symposium." As if that was a good reason why she couldn't be in labor.

"You tell that to these babies!" Jenny shouted. Then he heard her voice change from anger to scared. "Something is wrong, Seth. I can tell. I feel excruciating, stabbing pains..."

That was all he heard before the line went dead. He stopped on the stairs and quickly looked at his phone.

"Damn! Lost the signal." His stomach was lurching, and his jaw muscles were knotting up. It wasn't possible to descend the drill rig fast enough, especially with his hip, but he set his mind to action and the pain would have to take a back seat. Just as he cleared the last set of steps and hit the rig floor, he saw the bald guy.

"Link!" he yelled. Link was sitting in his truck and holding his cell phone out the driver's window and waving it around in the air like he was trying to catch something. He looked up at Seth's shout, started the truck, then leaned over and opened the passenger door just in time for Seth to slide in and slam the door, yelling, "Go, man! Go! I'll fill you in on the way." Seth was breathing heavily and looking for his seat belt as Link punched the accelerator, spitting gravel, and headed for the highway.

* * * * *

Mr. Erickson swiveled in his high-back leather chair and looked out through the floor to ceiling window of his opulently appointed office. "Oh, how I hate this God forsaken place," he complained to the world beyond the glass. With disgust, he caught the hint of a smudge on his $1400 Italian Santoni Shoes. He grabbed a monogrammed handkerchief from the pocket of his Brioni suit jacket and gave the offending smudge a quick buff, then tossed the linen cloth into the trash can.

Jack Martin, Chief of Operations, entered the office without knocking. He was a different kind of man: The kind that has a deep scar on his cheek from a knife fight and a couple of bullet holes collected while wearing camo and a beret. Casually tossing a file folder onto the coffee table, he dropped audibly into the soft leather sofa sitting opposite from Mr. Erickson's desk.

"The new numbers are in, and you are definitely going to like them," Jack said, forgoing any preamble.

Without turning around from the window, Mr. Erickson replied, "What could you possibly tell me that will break me out of the gloom that this backwoods hellhole called North Dakota has put me in?"

"How about this…" Jack Martin grinned as he picked up the file from the coffee table and tossed it onto Mr. Erickson's desk. It slid for just a bit, coming to rest tidily, in the middle of the workspace.

"With today's price for Bakken crude oil, we just hit $1.2 million a day in gross production. That means, with our friends down south paying all the bills, we are clearing over a half a million dollars a day, each. And that, my friend, goes straight to our accounts in the Caymans.

Mr. Erickson swiveled his chair around at the news and grinned, showing his typical British teeth. "Now then." Mr. Erickson paused to open the file. "That news makes the thought of another six months away from our beloved London, almost bearable."

"In six months, we'll be having a pint in Piccadilly," Jack said. "And all this will be just a bad dream with a happy ending."

CHAPTER TEN

"**S**eth..." Jenny yelled into her cell. "Seth!" she shouted louder as she jammed her cell harder into her ear, trying to hear him. Tears of anger, tears of frustration, tears of fear. She looked at the face of her cell and realized she'd lost him.

"Jenny, I need your attention," Donna, the ambulance paramedic, said. "You're dehydrated, and we need to start an IV right away. You'll need all the help you can get if these babies are coming early."

Gripping the phone tightly, her knuckles turning white, she began to pray. "Please God, let them be okay!"

Donna held her hand. "Jenny, it's going to be okay. You've been through tougher times. Be strong." The ambulance sped over the rough road, jostling them all the way to Trinity Hospital.

* * * * *

Victoria was driving right behind the ambulance that carried Jenny. Lincoln and Victoria James had practically adopted Jenny as one of their own, and fear gripped Victoria's heart. To them, there was no difference between her and any of their other grown children. Right now, it was her soon-to-be-born grandbabies that had her driving like a crazy woman. She kept redialing, alternating between Seth and Link's cells, but with no luck. Finally, she gave it a break and dialed Susan's cell instead. Susan was Reagan Oilfield Services office manager and unofficial office mom. She picked up on the third ring.

"Reagan Oil Field Services," came the sweet, southern drawl.

"Oh Susan, I'm so glad you answered," Victoria said through her mobile earpiece.

"Oh, no. What's wrong now?" Susan asked. She had been on the receiving end of more than one phone call that changed all of their lives.

"We think Jenny's in labor," she said as calmly and cheerfully as she could. As Jenny came closer to term, Victoria had been spending more time at the Cabin. Especially when Link and Seth were working far out of town.

"It's too early, isn't it?" Susan asked, unable to keep the tension out of her question.

"Yes, it is early, but I'm praying it's not too early," was all Victoria could get out before she paused to gather her thoughts and swallow images that she just couldn't allow to surface.

"What can I do to help?" Susan asked. "What do you need?"

"Have you heard from Seth or Link lately?"

"No, not since they left for the job site early this morning. You know they're in the badlands, right? So, there is little or no cell coverage out there."

"That's what I'm worried about," Victoria said. "If either one calls in, please let them know that Jenny is at Trinity. Her contractions were sporadic, and she was in extreme pain when the ambulance finally showed up at the Cabin."

"Will do," Susan agreed.

Victoria had been following close behind the ambulance during the call. She was using it like a spearhead through the traffic and hadn't realized how close she was until they were near to the hospital and the ambulance hit the brakes to make a quick left turn into Trinity's parking lot. The driver shut off the lights and siren just as they pulled into the emergency bay. Victoria hit the brakes hard to avoid hitting them and quickly peeled off to find a spot in the visitor parking lot. She pulled in too quickly and was violently jostled as she hit the curb. Her big truck tires bounced hard and rolled over to the other side of the concrete stop. Wasting no time, she jumped out of her pickup, slammed the door, and ran to the entrance without even locking it up.

She approached the automatic opening door in such a rush that she was forced to come to a complete stop to keep from hitting the glass. "Come on, come on." She frowned with impatience and willed the door to open faster. Finally clearing the entrance more than slightly annoyed, she immediately began firing questions at the poor nurse manning the ER nursing station long before she arrived in front of her desk.

"Aunt Victoria, is that you? What's wrong?" Abby said as she quickly walked around the counter to greet her.

Although a transplant from Washington State, the blue-eyed, blonde naturally fit into the large Scandinavian population found in North Dakota. Even in her scrubs though, she still looked like a fifteen-year-old with her hair braided in pigtails. As the tidal wave of oil workers streamed into North Dakota, it caused a massive increase in the need for medical services, and when Victoria mentioned that Abby was graduating, the hospital focused their recruiting staff like a laser.

Because the hospital was short staffed, she was manning the ER desk and clearly feeling a bit overwhelmed. The last few days with the big pileup had given her more ER experience than in the previous years in nursing school and clinicals all put together.

"Abby, thank God you're here," Victoria said, nearly out of breath. "I won't have to talk you into helping me. Do you know what room they put Jenny in?"

"ER-104." She pointed toward the correct door. "I'm running the front desk so I can't come with you right now. Let me know if there is anything I can do to help," Abby said as Victoria made a beeline for the door with ER-104 on it.

"Who is the doctor on duty?" Victoria asked without looking back.

"Doctor Scott just went in moments ago," Came Abby's reply. Doctor Scott was a former Navy Seal and currently the ER doctor on duty.

Just as Victoria's hand was reaching for the door, she heard her name called out.

"Hey, Victoria?" She turned toward the voice. Cheri was just coming down the hall from the direction of the ICU.

"Oh, how are you, Cheri? What are you doing here?"

"I'm interviewing the victims from that huge pileup we had a few days ago. Some of them are just now regaining consciousness. An elderly couple didn't make it. They passed before I was able to take their statements."

"Listen, Jenny's in labor, and I've got to get in there."

"Where's Seth?" Cheri asked.

"Somewhere in the badlands. We can't get a hold of him or Link. I've left messages for both of them."

"Let me sneak in with you. I just saw Jenny the other day when our cows rampaged through their yard."

"What?" Victoria asked as she paused with the door half open.

"I'll fill you in later," she said as they walked through the door.

It wasn't the same room as before when Jenny was in the ER, but it had all the same equipment in it. As Victoria and Cheri eased the door closed, Doctor Scott was approaching Jenny's bed.

"Hello, Doctor Scott," the nursing assistant gushed as she was busily putting a patient ID bracelet on Jenny's wrist.

The look on Jenny's face was of utter shock and disbelief.

Doctor Scott glanced over. "You must be Brooke. Welcome to Trinity. I had heard that we had poached you from Doctor Griffin," he said pleasantly.

Victoria looked up in disbelief. It *was* Brooke. She had cut her hair into a new choppy bob and dyed it a deep sort of brunette with almost imperceptible reddish tinges, but it was Brooke all right. Now she understood the look on Jenny's face. The poor girl had thought she was rid of Brooke.

"Why thank you, Doctor Scott. It is such an honor to be working with such a talented and handsome physician."

The room went silent.

"Imagine my surprise when I returned from Mexico, and the hospital had an opening."

"Oh... How was Mexico?" Doctor Scott asked distractedly as he reviewed Jenny's chart.

"It was fantastic, but definitely not long enough," she said with a gush. "But…" She dropped her chin a little and turned her head sideways to look at the Doctor. "It would have been much more fun if I had better…*company*." She batted her eyes, not even trying to disguise the flirtatious comment.

"Yep," Victoria said under her breath. "That's definitely Brooke. Just what Jenny needs."

Cheri looked over at Victoria and leaned in. "What did you say?"

"Oh, nothing," Victoria said. Then she leaned in and whispered conspiratorially, "I'll tell you all about it later."

Doctor Scott managed to avoid replying to her hint by saying, "We are so glad you had your application in already. We were all shocked when Danielle Robertson took off with just a scribbled note. We had no idea how miserable she was here. She didn't even say goodbye. We're going to miss her, but we are glad to have you here."

Victoria watched as a nearly imperceptible smile flickered across Brooke's face and then was gone.

"Yeah, I heard that the only place she could find to rent was a little trailer. That's just got to be hard," Brooke offered.

"So, Jenny, it's been a little while since I've seen you," Doctor Scott said, bringing the conversation back to the patient in the room. "Despite the circumstances, you look so much better than you did last time."

"I'd say it's good to see you too, but I'm really scared," Jenny confessed.

"Tell me what's going on? What are you feeling?" a visibly tired Doctor Scott inquired. The entire hospital staff had been on duty for over thirty hours.

Jenny looked up from the gurney toward Victoria and Cheri with grateful eyes. She held out her hand toward Victoria as she spoke. "Well, I'm feeling really sharp, stabbing pains that I've never felt before. Sometimes it feels hard to breathe and even my heart hurts."

"Hmm. Remind me please of how far along you are." Doctor Scott gently touched Jenny's belly. It wasn't that large but on her small frame it seemed huge.

"Almost thirty-four weeks," she said.

"That's a bit ahead of schedule, even for twins. Is the pain constant or is it cyclical?"

"It never goes away, but it gets more intense sometimes."

He took his stethoscope from around his neck and put it on her belly, seemingly listening to it and her at the same time. "Hmm, I see. When was the last time you saw Doctor Griffin?"

"Two days ago."

"Oh well, that's good. What did he tell you?" Doctor Scott asked while raising his right eyebrow.

"He said that both babies were in position and to expect an early delivery as most twins do deliver early and they seem to be preparing already."

"I see." Doctor Scott lightly massaged parts of her distended belly. He suddenly cocked his head a little and retraced the path of his fingers. And then again....

"But I don't think he thought it would be this early," she blurted. "Because he went to Denver for a few days for some sort of stupid symposium." The last few words tumbled out with tears in them.

"Did you ever feel like your water broke? Or have you felt anything that might be contractions?"

"No. Not Really. In fact, not at all. Just this intense pain that I've never felt before," she said, taking a deep breath, she bit her lower lip to keep it from shaking.

"Okay, well, let's see what we have here." He moved to the end of the table to finish the exam, then stood up, snapped off his gloves, and moved his hand back to her belly. "It seems that you are only dilated two or three centimeters. Jenny, I really don't believe you're in labor just yet. Let's figure out what's really going on."

"Is that bad?" Jenny asked with a worried look on her face.

"We don't know anything yet, but we will. I know it's hard, Jenny, but try to relax and we'll get some help in here to find out why you're feeling this kind of pain.

"Brooke? Can you please call upstairs to the NICU and ask Ivy to come down with her magic twin finder ultrasound machine? From what I think I am feeling, these twins aren't finished giving their mom a hard time."

"Yes, Doctor Scott. *Anything* for Jenny," Brooke mumbled under her breath.

Victoria gave Cheri a quick nudge with her elbow and a look that spoke volumes.

Just as Brooke reached the door, Doctor Scott called, "Oh, wait. Also ask Abby to wake up Doctor Frey and see if she can come in and give me a hand. She's resting in the on-call room."

"Yes, Doctor," Brooke replied again. Her tone changed and became icy and devoid of any sweetness whatsoever.

CHAPTER ELEVEN

"Who is Doctor Frey?" Jenny asked, wincing a bit and holding her breath for a moment. "I've never met her."

"Doctor Frey is a semi-retired doctor and an old friend of mine. She spends most of her time with Doctors Without Borders. Fortunately for us, she has just returned from an assignment on the Venezuelan-Columbian border."

"Her life sounds so exciting," Victoria commented, trying to distract Jenny from focusing on the pain.

"If you asked her right now, I'd bet she'd disagree. I called asking for help when we had the pileup and although she was dead tired, she readily agreed," Doctor Scott replied as he moved his stethoscope tenderly around Jenny's belly.

"Is that the new German doctor?" Cheri asked. "She was doing rounds when I was interviewing the crash victims."

"Yeah," Doctor Scott replied. Then he let out a little chuckle. "She's originally from Germany, but Babs has been living here for nearly twenty years. The funny thing is, when she gets really tired, her accent becomes super thick." He paused to listen for another moment. "And right now, she's totally exhausted."

She came through the door in whirlwind fashion. Her shoulder length brown hair was pulled back into an effortless ponytail.

"*Was ist los? Herr Doctor*," she asked in German.

Everyone in the room snapped around and looked at her with a funny expression.

"What?" Doctor Frey looked back and forth from one to the other and then it dawned on her. "Oh, I'm so sorry," she said, beginning to blush. I must be more tired than I thought. "I mean, what's going on?"

"No worries," Doctor Scott grinned and answered in German, "*Alle ist klar.*"

"Let me make introductions," Doctor Scott suggested. "Jenny, this is Doctor Babs Frey and Babs, this is Jenny. Not only is Babs a real doctor, but she's also played one on TV too."

"What does 'all is claw' mean?" Jenny asked them. "Is it something bad?"

Doctor Frey laughed and said, "It's fine, it's fine. It's German for 'all is well.'"

"What about the TV doctor thing?" Jenny asked.

"Oh that. Well, that was just for a little while," she said as she let out a little laugh.

"Well, I can see why you were on TV," Cheri said, stating the obvious. "In fact, if I looked as good as you after a day and a half on duty, I'd be ecstatic." Jenny heard a little envy in Cheri's tone. "Your smile lights up the room even when you're exhausted."

"It always helps ven you love your work as much as I do," Doctor Frey replied.

"Maybe there is a medical beauty secret that only doctors know," Victoria whispered loudly to Cheri.

"Yeah... Maybe we need to take her into interrogation and find out what it is," Cheri chimed in.

"Thank you so much," Doctor Frey replied in her heavy accent. "You have no idea how happy your lies make me feel."

Cheri's cell buzzed in her purse. Looking at it, she cocked her head a little. "Folks, I'd love to stay, but something has come up. I've got to finish these interviews and then, *maybe* get some sleep of my own," Cheri said as she eased out the door.

"Now, what have we here?" Doctor Frey asked. "Not another car crash, I hope."

Victoria and Cheri's attempt at humor nearly went unnoticed in Jenny's mind. *Oh God, please help my babies.* She silently prayed. *I know you haven't brought them this far just to let them down now.*

"No, thank God," Doctor Scott sighed. "Not another car crash." He proceeded to fill her in on Jenny's situation thus far.

"Have you ordered an ultrasound?" Doctor Frey asked without looking up, intently examining Jenny's belly with her hands.

"Ivy's on the way, now," he replied

"Excellent. Now, let me take a look at you, sweetheart." After a moment, she looked up. "Oh, you poor thing," she said to Jenny as she continued her examination. Pulling her stethoscope off her shoulder. She placed it against Jenny's tummy, moving it from place to place as she listened intently. "Hmmm."

Jenny was silently watching every move. She was waiting anxiously when another stabbing pain ripped through her abdomen as she let out a guttural scream.

"Ah, I see," said Doctor Frey as she pressed back against something sticking out of Jenny's abdomen like some kind of alien.

"What is it?" asked Victoria. "What's wrong?"

"Well, I'm thinking that one of the twins is being a shtinker," Doctor Frey said matter-of-factly. The pain slowly subsided, giving Jenny a chance to breathe.

"A what?" Jenny asked. "How do you mean?"

"You see, it appears to me that one of them has turned sideways and is blocking both of them from coming out. That is probably the reason for the intense, stabbing pain. I can feel a foot here," she said, indicating a bump pressing toward the outside of her left rib cage. "And here on the other side feels like the head of the same baby. Of course, the ultrasound will tell us for sure."

* * * * *

Seth looked down at his watch for the sixth time in as many minutes. "Damn." Link didn't hear him over the loud whine of the truck's all-terrain tires, but his face said it all. Seth stared at the speedometer in front of Link. The needle was north of ninety, but it was still going to be well over an hour to get back to Williston. To Jenny.

"Buddy, I'm reading your mind. If the roads weren't so rutted by all these oil tankers, I'd take it to the floor, but you arriving dead at the hospital won't help anybody," Link said in a raised voice to overcome the whine of the tires. "Plus, it would really piss off the redhead."

It was so strange. For three years after losing his wife and the love of his life, Olivia, in a terrible car crash four years ago, Seth felt he'd never love again, never feel again, never care again. He had been perfectly content to remain mired in the misery of his past. Of the loss of Olivia. Then, less than a year ago, he was jerked out of the dark, miserable past and slammed full blast back into the present. Jenny not only came into his life like a lighthouse to a lost sailor, but she was also carrying his twin babies, one or more of which could be from Olivia's frozen egg.

"Seth?" Link said, interrupting his thoughts.

"Yeah?"

"Don't you think it's kind of strange that we're seeing such a large uptick in random accidents and incidents lately?"

"What do you mean?" Seth asked as he continued to stare out the window.

"Oh, I don't know. Like the accident over at Barnes Gas & Oil. How could the vent on the separator get jammed open and flood the whole area with hydrogen sulphide gas?"

"I suppose carelessness on the part of the Barnes roustabouts. Some of them are pretty green."

"That could have gotten a lot of people killed," Link said emphatically. "Just lucky that it didn't."

Seth nodded his head but had a hard time concentrating on the conversation. He just kept thinking about Jenny. And the babies. And Olivia. And Jenny.

"What about the load of drill pipe breaking loose off that flatbed over at the pipe yard? Those bands just don't give out. Especially after being shipped all the way from Michigan, just to let go while it's been parked."

"Just an accident," Seth responded with a shrug.

"Tell that to the widow of the guy that was underneath it when it popped. Or the other three guys with broken arms and legs. One of them lost all his teeth."

"What are you getting at, Link?" Seth asked, finally trying to focus on what Link was saying.

"I don't know, but the rate of accidents seems to be spiking for no reason. I'm telling you, my spidey sense is tingling. I've got a gut feeling. Or, what about the big pile up on Highway 85 the other day? The witnesses said that it was caused by some unidentified white four-door oilfield truck."

"That could be one of a thousand work trucks out here," Seth said incredulously.

They said that the driver deliberately hit the brakes right in front of that tanker. After the accident, and the road was completely jammed, the guy drove off and disappeared. What do you think is really happening?"

Seth turned back toward the window. He had bigger things to worry about right this second than car wrecks and accidents caused by carelessness in the field.

Seth was still lost deep in his thoughts when Link suddenly braked hard and started to pull over. "What the hell?" Seth exclaimed as a knee jerk reaction.

* * * * *

Link looked over, smiled, and nodded his head toward something off in the distance. "I think I may have found you a faster chariot," he said. Seth followed Link's stare till his gaze fell upon a medevac helicopter just off the road on an oil pad. The rotor blades were still turning, and it looked like they were hot refueling. Link only slightly slowed the Reagan truck as he turned the wheel. The tires left the pavement and dropped onto the rutted gravel road with the rear end of the truck fishtailing, but Link kept it well under control. "Yeehaw," Link hollered as the truck bounced

"That's the Trinity Hospital medevac helicopter. If you can bum a ride, he'll get you there in less than twenty minutes," Link stated without taking his eyes off the road. Another sixty seconds and they were pulling through the gate of the oil pad, leaving a trail of dust behind them.

Seth had his door open and was already out of the truck before Link could bring it to a full stop. He had already disappeared into the murky, whirling dust before Link put the truck in park.

As the brown cloud settled, Link could see Seth already standing on the toe of the helicopter skid, talking to Neil Murphy, the pilot. A few nods and a jerk from Neil's head, motioning to the passenger door was all Link needed to know the plan was in motion. Seth was in and buckling up as Neil lifted the sleek helicopter off the ground, rolled to the right and started climbing. "Atta boy," Link said aloud. Then he put the truck in drive and, after a quick check of traffic, pulled back onto the highway and pushed the accelerator to the floor.

* * * * *

Victoria stepped out into the hall to call Link. Just as she pulled her cell from her purse, the elevator dinged and finally opened up to reveal a nurse in scrubs with blonde hair, blue eyes, glasses and a smile that could warm the coldest heart.

"Hi, Ivy," Victoria burst out. "I heard you were coming down to see Jenny."

As Ivy drew closer Victoria let out a low whistle. "Is this the new Ultrasound machine that Reagan sponsored for the hospital?"

"Yes," Ivy gushed. "On this cart," she said dramatically, "is the latest technology in 3D ultrasound and the images of the babies it creates are amazing. In fact, they are just like taking a photo."

"You sound like a commercial." Victoria chuckled. "Is it really that much better?"

"Oh yeah. The machine I was using when we discovered Jenny was actually pregnant with twins wasn't nearly as good as this."

Ivy knocked at Jenny's door, then opened it as she pulled her cart into the room. "Well, hello there, Jenny, it's been a little while since we last saw you, but you look so much better this time."

"Oh, Ivy! I am so glad to see you!" Jenny said, reaching out her arms for a hug.

Looking around the room, Doctor Scott muttered, "It's almost like old Home week."

"So, Doctors, what have we got?' Ivy asked, looking up at her nephew and Doctor Frey.

They quickly filled Ivy in on what they thought might be happening. It wasn't long before the ultrasound machine was set up and ready to go. "Okay, Jenny. Do you remember how this works?" she asked.

Jenny nodded.

"Now, let's see what in the world is going on here."

Unlike last time, Ivy left the monitor so everyone in the room could see the results. The graphics were stunning as each baby came into view.

"Look at that," Victoria gushed. "You can even see their hair."

"Well, would you look at that?" Doctor Scott breathed. "It doesn't take a doctor to see what's happening here. One of the babies, this one…" He paused as he pointed, "… is in perfect position, head down. But the other one has maneuvered down toward the birth canal and has turned right side up and crossed legs, blocking the only way out."

"Exactly," Doctor Frey said in her thick accent. "A shtinker."

She turned to Jenny and said, "Sweetheart, you are definitely not in labor right now, and that's very good. It gives us a little time. We need to turn that little one so it's positioned properly."

"How do you do that?" Jenny asked. "Does it take long?"

"Well, the procedure is called an external cephalic version or ECV. It's a non-surgical procedure. First, we'll give you some medicine in your IV that helps relax your tummy muscles, and then we make the baby uncomfortable by taking my hand and pushing in on the little head so that it moves away from the pressure. Sometimes they move easily and sometimes they don't. I must warn you that it won't be any fun for you. It's quite physical. However, what we need to do right now is get a lot of fluids in you before we start. So whatever you do, don't go into labor yet," Doctor Frey said emphatically, but with a reassuring pat to Jenny's hand.

CHAPTER TWELVE

After lifting off, Neil Murphy banked the helicopter back toward Williston. They quickly climbed to fifteen hundred feet and accelerated to cruise speed through the mountains, sometimes following the highway and sometimes taking shortcuts across lower peaks.

"I sure am glad you happened to be at that oil gathering facility," Seth said into his microphone. "But where is your medic?" He gestured toward the back of the helicopter.

"Today was your lucky day," Neil responded. "To answer your question, I was out doing a maintenance test flight, so I didn't need a medic. I decided to come down here and check out the facility and make sure they have the right adapters for refueling the helicopter. We've flown several injured employees from this group in the past. Just last week, one of their engineers had a heart attack, and we were able to get him back to Trinity Hospital. Between the quick response and short flight time, plus my awesome medic, we saved the guy's life. The head of the company met us at the Hospital and caught up to us in the cafeteria. He was so grateful, he told me that if I ever needed to refuel while on a medical mission, I could land at any of their facilities in the badlands and they would refuel us gratis."

"Reagan has done quite a bit of work for them as well," Seth said, looking at his watch again. "They've always paid on time and seem to be a real stand-up company."

"Was that Link James with you driving the white pickup?" Neil asked.

"Yeah, it was. Do you know him?"

"Well, you might say we've crossed paths a time or two back in the old days," Neil offered. "It all started out in flight school. We were both in green flight. There was something special about him, even back then. Did you know that he won every award you can possibly win in flight school? At graduation it was almost embarrassing the number of times he had to go up and receive another award."

"Wow, I can't imagine it not going to his head," Seth surmised.

"Oh, it didn't. You'd never know what lies beneath the surface of that man. He's a good guy to have on your side. Especially when it counts."

"Really. You knew him back then?" Seth asked with a smile. "Link doesn't talk much about his past. In fact, he's worked at Reagan for several years now, and we still don't know much about it."

"Well, there might be a reason for that," Neil said as he raised an eyebrow.

"What can you tell me?"

"What do you already know about him?" Neil's question seemed to deflect but Seth pushed forward.

"Not much. I don't even think his wife knows much about his past."

That made Neil chuckle. "I don't doubt that."

"What I do know is that a few months ago, I was tied to a chair in my own kitchen," Seth explained. "I was being beaten and pistol-whipped by my future brother-in-law who is a drug addict that was looking for money. Link appeared out of nowhere, and just walked right into the kitchen and stood there. The guy screamed at him and stuck this gun right in Link's face. The next thing I know, Link is holding the guy's gun like a professional and the guy is lying on the floor unconscious. Link checked his pulse and muttered. '*He'll live.*' Then quickly came over and cut me loose. I asked him how he learned all that and he said something about it being nothing special."

That made Neil laugh out loud. "Yep. That's Link all right."

"Oh, and another thing. When I was in the hospital, Doctor Scott seemed to know him as well, but he didn't call him Link, he called him Jiff."

"I forgot they'd worked together," Neil said more to himself than to Seth.

"They did?" Seth asked "Where were they? What were they doing?"

"It seems to me they were both on a *little project* based out of Trieste, Italy…"

"Okay, but why did he call Link, Jiff?"

As Neil paused for several seconds, Seth's heartbeat increased. *Come on man, give me something…*

"Oh, that?" Neil said thoughtfully.

Was that a question or a statement? Seth asked himself.

Neil grinned as if remembering something and then chuckled. After an agonizing moment he said, "Well, what I've heard is only a rumor, so you'd have to ask Link about that directly.

"That's the problem," Seth exclaimed in frustration. "He doesn't talk about it."

"Look," Neil said, "I probably shouldn't have told you what I have. That group kept itself deep under the radar for a reason." Neil then added almost as an afterthought, "It's kind of funny how many people from the old days are drawn to this boom town. Lots of jobs, a certain amount of anonymity with new people showing up every day and sometimes, best of all, a new beginning."

"Speaking of the old days, what do you know about Maria? How does Link know her?" Seth asked, pushing in a different direction.

"Maria? She and Link go all the way back to the Balkan wars. Those were some terrible years during the war. It's a miracle that either one of them made it out of there alive." Neil's voice suddenly cut off, and he got real quiet.

"Maybe the frenetic pace around here, which seems to always be verging on chaos, seems to make many of us feel a bit more normal," Neil added softly. "You know, almost like home." As if breaking out of his inner thoughts he said, "Seth, you ask way too many questions. Right now, you'd better tighten your seatbelt. We'll be landing in a few minutes, and it looks like we're going to have a nasty crosswind today, and the approach is going to be a bit bumpy. You can thank our kind Canadian neighbors for all the wind they send down from up north."

Seth grinned to himself and thought, *I just increased my knowledge of Link ten-fold.* Then he tightened his seatbelt as his thoughts returned to Jenny and the twins.

As Neil brought the heavy helicopter in for a landing, Seth could see a medical team waiting. As they landed, Doctor Scott immediately moved toward him, instinctively ducking under the spinning rotor blades. Seth stepped out of the helicopter and waved goodbye to Neil. Just as Seth turned back, Doctor Scott leaned his head in toward Seth and yelled over the loud thump of the rotor blades, "Where are you hurt? Is it your bullet wound?"

Seth didn't understand the question, and really didn't understand why Doctor Scott was looking him over so intently. "Me?" Seth yelled, pointing to himself with his thumb. "Doc, I'm not hurt at all. I'm fine," he yelled back over the deafening roar of the turbine engine.

"Then what the hell is going on?" Doctor Scott yelled with irritation.

"I'm sorry about the confusion Doc, I just hitched a ride into town," Seth said, pointing towards Neil.

Grinning ear to ear, Neil looked back at the two of them and made a salute toward Doctor Scott. Then he waved his gloved hand as if brushing them away from his helicopter. Taking the hint, both men backed away from the helicopter and out from under the spinning rotor blades. Talking was now impossible, so both men just watched as the helicopter first got light on the skids, became airborne, then effortlessly turned and flew away to the north. As the roar of the rotor wash and noise began to die away, Seth started to yell toward Doctor Scott, "Jenny…" and then realized he didn't have to yell anymore. Starting again, this time in a normal voice he said, "Jenny, is she okay? How are the twins? Is she in labor? I saw you out here when we landed…" He sucked in a harsh breath. "What's wrong with her?"

"Yes, she's here," Doctor Scott replied. "And I've already seen her."

"Is she alright? Are the babies okay? Has she had them yet?" he asked with a mixture of fear and excitement and more than a little desperation in his eyes.

"Yes, yes. She is doing fine." Doctor Scott replied. "And the babies are doing fine too. "She already had them?" Seth asked in shock.

"No, no. She hasn't even gone into labor yet."

"Yes, she did. Jenny called me from the ambulance. She was really hurting."

"That's true, but it wasn't labor pain that was hurting her. One of the twins turned sideways and was pushing hard on her insides, causing some significant pain. We're dealing with that right now. The other issue is that the baby is now blocking the birth canal and making it impossible for the babies to be born."

"What do we do, Doc?"

"Well, for now I've told her that under no circumstances is she to go into labor until we can get the baby to turn head down again."

Seth stopped in his tracks and reaching his long arm out, he grabbed Doctor Scott's shoulder and spun him around to face him. "Oh no. Doc. Please tell me that you didn't tell her *not* to do something."

"Why not?" he asked with raised eyebrows.

"Well, Doc, to tell you the truth, the last time I told her not to do something under any circumstances, she got mad and did it anyway and the whole thing ended up with her and her car in a snowbank."

"Okay, well we'll be sure to keep her away from snowbanks for a while," Doctor Scott stated facetiously.

"But, Doc, you don't understand Jenny," Seth said anxiously. "She can't help it."

"I think she'll be fine, Seth," Doctor Scott stated firmly, using a calming tone. "For now, she needs lots of rest, and we need to get her fully hydrated. We've started an IV to build up her fluids. That will make the procedure go at least a little easier."

"How long will it take?" Seth asked cautiously.

"Several hours at least. Overnight would be ideal. For now, we've got her resting."

* * * * *

The hospital room was quiet except for the gentle beeping of the IV machine and the occasional exercise of the automatic blood pressure cuff. The lights were dimmed low so the glow from the two fetal heart monitors seemed a bit bright.

Once the medication had taken effect and the stabbing pain had subsided, Jenny was so exhausted she couldn't keep her eyes open. After she fell asleep, Doctor Frey and Victoria quietly stepped out of the room just as Seth and Doctor Scott came down the hall.

"Shh," Victoria said while holding her index finger to her lips. "She's sleeping right now."

Seth looked from Victoria to Doctor Frey.

"Oh, Seth. This is Doctor Frey," Doctor Scott said as an introduction. "She is helping out here at the hospital after the big pileup on highway 85."

"Speaking of which, I need to make my rounds and check on the rest of the patients," said Doctor Scott.

"I'll go with you," said Doctor Frey.

The two turned to walk down the hallway.

"Can I at least see her?" Seth asked, as he started toward Jenny's door without waiting for an answer.

"Sure, but just a quick peek," Doctor Frey whispered. Then she held her finger to her lips.

"Like anyone could stop you," Victoria pointed out.

Seth smiled and cracked open the door just enough to see inside. There was his sweet Jenny, asleep. The impact of seeing her there released a raw flood of emotion that nearly staggered him. He wanted to go to her, to hold her hand, to caress her face, but knew she was going to need the rest. He swallowed hard and reluctantly allowed the door to quietly close again. He paused for a moment and then turned to look at Victoria. Seth blinked hard and could feel the lump in his throat and the sting in his eyes.

"Oh, Seth, Jenny's going to be fine," Victoria assured. "All three of them are going to be fine,"

Seth didn't respond at first, he just pushed the door back open a crack. "I know you're right. It's just…"

"I know…" Victoria said as she looped her arm through Seth's. "Let's go down to the cafeteria for a bite to eat and get you a large cup of coffee. They've got a new coffee bar down there that carries that new brand that you and Link are all fired up about." Then she added, "You know, you look like hell. I'll bet you could use a double shot of espresso right now."

Her comment served its purpose and brought a flicker of a smile to Seth's face. "Black Rifle coffee?"

"You got it," she said as they walked toward the elevator. Victoria suddenly stopped mid stride, turned to Seth, and asked, "Wait, where's Link?"

Seth grinned again and started to fill her in on all the action from getting the call to the helicopter ride and arriving at the hospital. They were both still laughing as they pushed through the doors to the cafeteria.

"The look on Doctor Scott's face was priceless when the only patient that climbed out of the helicopter was me."

"You're lucky he didn't break something just to make the trip worth it," Victoria warned.

Ignoring her comment Seth said, "Oh, I can already smell the coffee."

"You could smell a good cup of coffee from a hundred miles away," Victoria chided, and they both laughed again. "Like a shark smelling blood."

Seth opened the door for Victoria and then followed her into the cafeteria. There were a couple dozen tables full of patrons dressed in various colors of scrubs eating and talking animatedly about one thing or another. The area was light and cheery for it being late in the day. As they made their way through the maze of diners, Victoria noticed Brooke sitting alone at a four-top table against the wall. *Big shock that she's dining alone,* she thought. Brooke was wearing a magenta set of scrubs with her brunette bob a bit of a mess. Her back was to them, and she was leaning forward in her chair with elbows propped up on the table as she sipped on a tall cup of coffee. It seemed as if she was intently watching a muted rerun of Jeopardy on the flat screen TV mounted to the wall. A few green beans and a bit of mashed potatoes along with a fork and a used napkin littered the heavy cafeteria bone china plate that was pushed to the side.

"Hello, Brooke," Victoria greeted with an obligatory smile as they passed Brooke's table.

At first, Brooke appeared to be annoyed by the intrusion and started to look away, but then, upon seeing Seth, she set down her coffee and quickly looked up at them both and with a plastic smile of her own said, "Hello, Victoria. Hello, Seth. It's so nice to see you." Her voice was sticky sweet.

Go back to acting class, Brooke, Victoria thought. *Nobody's buying it.*

"It's good to see you too," Seth replied automatically.

"I sure hope everything works out for Jenny and those sweet little babies," Brooke replied, continuing the tone.

"Thanks," Seth said sincerely. "Doc says she's going to be fine. And the babies too."

"I am so glad," replied Brooke. She glanced at her watch. "Oh, look at the time. I've got to be back on shift soon." Without missing a beat, she snatched her coffee from off of the table and spilled some brown liquid onto her scrubs. This caused an angry mutter under her breath, but she never once broke her smile as she grabbed a napkin and dabbed at the stain.

Brooke, life wouldn't have to be that hard... if you weren't such a jerk, Victoria thought as she and Seth made their way to the barista.

After ordering their coffees, Seth and Victoria found a recently abandoned table against the opposite wall from Brooke. The table was cleared of dishes but there were still a few crumbs scattered about that Victoria swept up with her hand and tossed in a nearby trash can before she sat down. Out of the corner of her eye, she could see Brooke staring at them. She was leaning back into her chair with one leg crossed over the other. Her elevated foot bobbed up and down in agitation. She angrily stripped off the protective cardboard ring from around the to-go coffee cup and carelessly discarded it to the side and went back to watching the muted TV.

"So, when *does your* shift start, Brooke?" Victoria asked under her breath.

"I met someone who knew Link back in the *old days*," Seth said with a smug look on his face.

"Oh, Really," Victoria said as she turned her gaze from Brooke back to Seth. "Do tell."

"Have you ever noticed that Link collects people? And..." Seth paused for effect, "...those people have a fierce loyalty to him?" Seth asked.

"What do you mean?"

"Well, think about it. There's Maria and Celia, then there's Sophia, the waitress at Teddy's Restaurant down in Bismarck."

"And then there's Moose over at Zorbas," Victoria added. "And even Doctor Scott seemed to know him from before. I've asked him questions about it, but he dodges them with expertise."

"Yeah, well the helicopter pilot said Link was part of some group that always stayed under the radar."

"Did he say why Doctor Scott called Link by the name of Jiff?" Victoria wondered out loud.

111

"He definitely knew about it, but he wouldn't say any more."

"This is really interesting and more than a little fun, but I don't think it's a good idea for us to be spying on my husband."

CHAPTER THIRTEEN

"Coooffeeee," Cheri Perry declared loudly as she passed Brooke in the doorway. She shuffled into the cafeteria looking like something the cat dragged in. Dark circles had formed around her eyes, attempting to take up permanent residence.

"What's going on, Cheri?" Victoria asked as Seth pulled a chair over for her to sit down.

"Unfortunately, a lot has happened in the short time since I've seen you all last."

"No offense, neighbor, but you look rode hard and put away wet," Seth commented.

The remark made Cheri laugh. "No offense taken. I feel even worse." A tired smile was left behind.

Just then, Rose, the barista brought their two coffees and placed them on the table while rattling off the order.

"One large white coffee mocha and one Bakken crude with a double shot of espresso."

"Oh, can I *please* get one of those too?" Cheri begged Rose with a bit of desperation.

Laughing, she replied, "Sure, which one would you like? The white coffee or the crude with extra espresso?"

"Definitely the Bakken Crude please. But maybe with three shots?" There was dire need in her voice.

Seth peered at Cheri for a moment. "Uh, I'm a professional coffee drinker, Cheri, and I'm not sure I could handle three shots."

"Okay, fine. Make it two shots. I've got to get some sleep sooner or later."

"Do you need room for cream or sugar?" the barista inquired.

"No, sweetheart. Bring it to me straight up. In fact, can you just give me an IV?"

Seth smiled. "I knew there was a reason why I liked you." He slid his coffee over in front of Cheri. "Here, take mine. I can wait for yours to arrive."

"Oh, no," she said graciously. "Thank you, but I can wait."

"Uh, sweetie, you look like you need it way more than me," Seth said with a raised eyebrow and a smartass grin. "So, take it."

"I wouldn't argue with the man," Victoria advised. "I confess, I've never seen him offer anyone his precious coffee before. And I mean *anyone.*"

They all laughed.

"Okay. Okay. You can quit twisting my arm now," Cheri chuckled as she grabbed the coffee and deftly removed the lid with a practiced flip of thumb and forefinger. "I happily accept." The heavy, pungent smell quickly permeated the air around them as she blew on the hot liquid and took a sip. Letting out a little moan of pure joy, she briefly closed her eyes as the richness eased down her throat. She opened her eyes again and looked at Seth. "How's Jenny?"

"She's doing fine," Seth answered with a sigh of relief. "A little trouble with the babies, but the doctors have it under control."

"What's got you running yourself into the ground? Your herd stampeding again?" Seth asked.

"No. I'm so sorry about leaving my cows at your place the other night." Cheri replied. "It seems like a week ago."

"No worries," Seth replied. "Not only do I not have to mow for a while. I don't even have to use fertilizer for the next month or so."

The trio chuckled.

"So, what's up?" Victoria re-directed the conversation back to Cheri.

Cheri took a deep breath. "Rough night in Williston."

"Oh?" Victoria said as she cocked her head.

"In fact, it's been a rough week, what with the mysterious pile up on 85 and now a murder."

"Murder?" Victoria asked.

"Who?" Seth chimed in.

"A local twenty-five-year-old female who worked as a security guard for GEA. At first blush, the working theory was that she was robbed and murdered in her home, but she was still in her uniform when the body was found, which was several hours past her shift."

"We do a lot of work for GEA. What was her name?" Seth asked with more concern.

"Natalie Hotah," Cheri answered. "Did you know her?"

"No, I don't think so. The name doesn't sound familiar, but GEA has acquired quite a few new oil leases. So, who knows? We may or may not have crossed paths," he finished with a shrug. "Poor girl."

"From the initial marks on her body, she put up a hell of a fight. Her last name, *Hotah*, do you know what it means?" Cheri asked.

"No, what does it mean?" Seth and Victoria asked in unison.

It means, *Strong*, in Sioux, and it sure looks like she lived up to it," Cheri granted with a sad smile.

"Was she sexually assaulted?" Victoria asked with a look that didn't really want to know.

"No, according to the coroner, there was no initial indication of rape."

"That's at least a small relief, given the circumstances," Victoria breathed.

"Who found her?" Seth inquired.

"Her roommate found the body when she returned home from her own shift as a waitress over at Don Pedros. The poor girl was nearly catatonic. We had to call her folks to come get her." Cheri paused in thought, her jaw set. "The whole thing just breaks my heart, and now I'm pissed."

"Cheri, what caused you to change your mind?"

"Well…" Cheri hesitated a moment, took another sip of coffee, hastily looked around the room and then said, "Yeah. Just now."

"What do you mean?" Seth asked while Cheri was in mid-sip of her coffee. "What changed your mind?"

She put the cup down and looked up at the two of them. She hesitated again, then leaned in and lowered her voice. "I just stopped by the morgue to pick up the initial findings and time of death, and that's when it got weird. According to the pathologist's estimated time of death, she was still on duty when she was killed. On top of that, there was dirt and hydrocarbon residue all over her uniform, as if she was rolling around in it."

"That means that she was probably killed at work and her body was dumped at her apartment just to make it look like…uh…" Seth paused looking for the right phrase.

"Like a random home invasion?" Cheri finished the thought for him. "What it actually means to me is that I went from tens of thousands of possible suspects to a much smaller pool. You see, the shift she was pulling last night was on GEA's oil pad, but it's actually on a federal land oil lease. If I can reasonably confirm that she was killed at work, that means I can get help from the FBI. And right now, we are stretched so thin we could really use the help and resources."

Seth looked up and noticed that Rose was standing near with his coffee in her shaking hand. Her face was pale, and she stared at them without speaking.

"Are you okay?" Seth asked as he jumped up to take the coffee from her before it ended up on the floor.

Her lip started to quiver when she spoke. "Um, I accidentally overheard you talking about Natalie and Anna. Natalie was my cousin."

Cheri quickly stood up. "I am so sorry. Are you okay? Do you need to sit down?"

"No, I'm fine," Rose replied stoically. "At least I will be. I think I just need to go home."

Cheri quickly pulled a business card from her pocket and handed it to her. "Rose, give me a call if you need anything or hear anything. Anything at all?"

"All right," she replied. Rose nodded her head and attempted a feeble smile, then turned and swiftly walked away. She had only made it a few feet when she began to sob, stopped, and turned back toward Cheri. She wrung her shaking hands and wiped the tears from her cheek. "Natalie was getting really scared at work lately." She spoke in a quavering voice. "Does that help?"

"Who was she scared of?" Cheri asked gently.

"Umm, that's it. She didn't say. Just that crazy things were happening. Um, I'm sorry, I've really got to call my mom," she said as her sobs returned.

"Go ahead, Rose. It's okay," Cheri said as they watched Rose break into a run and head for the door.

"Oh, that poor girl," Victoria said. "My heart is breaking all over again."

Cheri set her jaw. "A murder is like throwing a giant rock into a pool of water. The splash continues to cast ripples throughout the entire community."

They returned to their seats as Victoria took a deep breath and made an attempt to change the subject. "What's the update on the pile up on 85?"

"That's another puzzle," Cheri said with exasperation. "It appears to have been caused deliberately by a white, four-door, oil field pickup. Probably a Dodge Ram. But unfortunately, I don't have any license plate or name on the truck."

"And white four-door trucks are the most popular oil-field truck in the Bakken. Not exactly narrowing that down," Seth suggested.

"So, really nothing to go on?" Victoria added.

"Not quite nothing. One witness, a passenger in one of the motor homes, thought there was a blank white magnetic sign covering the driver's door, but it didn't cover all of the logo. She thought she saw the bottom of an L or an E."

"Did she get a look at the driver?" Seth asked.

"The only thing she could tell us about the driver was that it was a male, white and maybe balding or at least really thin hair. And that he was wearing sunglasses. She said that after he jammed on the brakes and caused the crude oil tanker to jack-knife, he briefly looked back and then sped off."

Cheri's cell phone rang. She reached into the inside pocket of her jacket, retrieved the device, and looked at the caller ID. "Uh oh." She reluctantly answered. "Go for Perry."

While listening, she grabbed her jacket. "Uh huh." Another pause. "In other words, there is no doubt she was killed while on duty."

Victoria & Seth both stared at Cheri as they listened to one side of the conversation.

"Sure, while you're at it, can you get me Special Agent Bravis Brown's number over at the FBI in Fargo?" She waved goodbye to Seth and Victoria and headed for the door. "Yes, thanks. They've got resources we'll never have and desperately need."

"When you get his number, text it to me right away, okay? Thanks." And she clicked off.

Victoria's cell rang moments later. The name associated with the number said, *My Love.* She smiled a genuine smile of her own and answered.

"Hello, my love."

"Howdy, gorgeous. I just got into cell coverage. How's Jenny? Did Seth arrive all right? I'm starving."

Victoria chuckled at the rapid-fire questions. "To answer your first question, yes. Jenny's doing fine. She is not in labor but one of the babies has turned sideways and is being a pill. Oh, she's just got to be related to you."

"Very funny, Mrs. James," Link responded.

"All things considered. She's doing great."

"Okay, that's good to hear. What about Seth?"

"To answer question number two. Did Seth arrive all right?" She repeated the question looking straight at Seth. "I'll say he arrived all right. In style too, from what I hear. I'll let him tell you all about it when you get here. We're in the hospital cafeteria, and they have a meat loaf special."

"That'll work. I could eat a whole one all by myself."

"How long till you get here?"

"Well let's see…" He paused for a brief moment. "If I don't get stopped for speeding, I'll be there in just over thirty minutes."

"So don't get stopped," Victoria said emphatically.

"Well, if I do, you'll probably have to come bail me out with the speeds that I'm hitting."

"Lincoln James," Victoria stated his name in staccato. "Everyone is fine, there is no need to rush."

"Yes, there is," he complained. "I'm missing out on all the excitement."

"This coming from the Mystery Man," she said teasingly. "All I ask is that you get here without killing yourself on the way."

"Yes, Mrs. James, ma'am. Will do," he replied like a willful child.

"Link, please be careful. I love you. Tell you what, big guy. I'll have a steaming cup of hot coffee waiting for you when you get here."

"You know me so well. That's why I love you too, honey. See you in a few." And then the line went dead.

Victoria pulled her cell away from her ear and said, "That man drives me crazy sometimes."

"I hear ya," Seth said, grinning.

"It's a good thing I'm so crazy *about* him."

Then, in a rare moment of truth without any smartass comments, Seth swallowed hard and said, "That's the way I feel about Jenny."

CHAPTER FOURTEEN

The antiseptic smell permeated everything. The hospital room was rather dark with only the dimmed, soft light above Jenny's headboard and those of the machines. Some lights were steady, and others gently blinked in time with the quiet beeping. She noticed the IV drip bag attached to the vein in Jenny's arm was nearly empty. Jenny's eyes were closed, and her breathing was a slow, steady, constant rhythm. Looking down, she stared at the massive diamond engagement ring on Jenny's finger. *Mrs. Seth Reagan. I can hardly wait.* She thought with a deep sigh of her own.

Suddenly the door opened, flooding the room with light from the hallway as Abby quietly slipped into the room.

"Oh, hey, Brooke," Abby whispered. "I didn't know you were in here."

"Hey, Abby," Brooke replied, moving away from the bed.

"What are you doing here?" Abby asked curiously.

"Oh, nothing," Brooke said casually as she looked toward Abby and then back at Jenny.

"Aren't you supposed to be on your lunch?" Abby asked.

"Yeah, I had a few minutes left on my break and decided to sit in here with Jenny. Isn't she just the sweetest thing?"

"She sure is," Abby agreed. "She's been through a lot though."

"Poor dear," Brooke added. "I sure hope she doesn't go into labor anytime soon. That would be awful with that baby twisted up inside her. It might even kill her."

"Don't even say that," Abby chided, then quickly changed the subject. "Can you do me a favor?"

"What do you need?" Brooke inquired.

"I need to change Jenny's IV Bag, but Mrs. Simonson, down the hall in room 204, just called. She needs help going to the toilet. Can you go and help her? Please?" Abby nearly begged.

"Sure thing," Brook said as she stepped past Abby into the hallway. "Anything you need, you just ask. I think you're about the only nice person in this whole hospital. Maybe in this town," she said with a genuine smile. "I'm on my way." She smiled again as she fingered the empty syringe in the pocket of her scrubs.

* * * * *

Jenny woke with a start and cried out in pain. The biggest cramp she had ever felt in her life contorted her insides, starting from her lower back and plowing mercilessly straight through her abdomen. All she could do was grit her teeth and grab the side rails of her hospital bed. The pain wracked her body with rolling convulsions, and her mind raced into a blinding light. After what seemed a lifetime, the pain subsided momentarily, allowing her to think again. She fumbled around the blanket on her bed, desperately looking for her call button.

Mercifully, she finally felt the controller in the semi darkness, but it kept sliding out of her trembling fingers. She managed to grip it with both hands and pushed the button with all her might. Not wanting to wait for someone, she called out, "Please! Somebody, help me!" She screamed uncontrollably when another blinding bolt surged through her body, and she collapsed back onto the bed in agony.

Abby burst through the door, hit the light switch and rushed straight to Jenny. "I'm here. I'm here, Jenny. You're okay. You're going to be fine," she said in her most convincing and comforting voice. But when Abby looked down at her bed, she saw blood...

* * * * *

Link had found his way to the hospital cafeteria just by following the smell of coffee. He and Seth were already deep in conversation, their table cluttered with dirty plates and silverware, half empty coffee cups and left-over crumbs. Just as Seth was finishing up his story about landing on the hospital helipad, the loudspeaker emitted a high-pitched squeal for a split second. Then a staccato digitized female voice broke the silence.

"ATTENTION: CODE BLUE ON LEVEL TWO." And then it went silent. Several of the scrub-clad diners in the cafeteria stood up and made their way to the door. They didn't run, but they made it out of the cafeteria in under thirty seconds. Link leaned over to one of the diners nearby that didn't leave and said, "Uh, pardon me."

"Yes, sir?" the man replied after swallowing a mouthful of apple pie.

"Hey uh...Dan," Link said after reading the guy's hospital ID badge clipped to the pocket of his scrubs. "What was that all about?" he asked. "Is code blue, what I think it is?" Dan wiped his mouth on a paper napkin and replied, "Yup, in this hospital, when they call a code blue it generally means that someone had a heart attack, or they think a heart attack is imminent or stopped breathing and there's a specific team that convenes." He punctuated his sentence with a shrug of his shoulders and forked a final morsel of pie into his mouth. Before he could swallow, the loudspeaker squealed again.

"ATTENTION: RAPID RESPONSE TEAM REQUIRED ON LEVEL TWO."

"Oh, that's me," Dan said as he jumped up.

"Sorry to bother you again but what's a rapid response team for?" Link quickly asked.

"It means significant trauma or heavy blood loss. Probably another car accident. I hope it's not blood loss, because we are out of most blood types. We're basically down to plasma," he said as he wadded up his napkin, tossed it onto the table and headed for the door at a brisk pace.

"Just what this town needs is another car accident," Seth observed. His thoughts went dark as he relived the memory of Olivia's accident and then Jenny's. The reaction was visceral, and it made him shudder.

"I'm just glad that Link is already here," Victoria chimed in, pointing her thumb at her husband sitting next to her. "Otherwise, I'd be freaking out thinking it was for him as fast as he was driving."

"Hey now, I just wanted to get next to you as fast as I could."

Seth chuckled a bit and let his chin settle in the palms of his hands as he rested his elbows on the table.

"ATTENTION: CODE PINK ON LEVEL TWO."

This time a jolt went through Seth. He looked around at the rest of them sitting at the table and knew they were all thinking the same thing. Seth jumped up and quickly walked toward the door to catch one of the medical personnel heading toward the door. "Hey man, what's that mean?" The guy looked up but didn't say anything as he exited the door. Seth blocked the next one from leaving with his big frame and asked the same question.

The guy ignored Seth and went to step around him, but Seth grabbed him by the shirt and nearly lifted him up off the floor. Link jumped to the guy's aide. "Easy buddy. He's not the enemy." The next one was a young woman about Jenny's age. She stopped and said, "Look, you guys, Code Pink means that there is something really wrong in either pediatrics or obstetrics. We don't have any newborns here right now, so it has to be obstetrics."

"Obstetrics? You mean like having a baby?" Seth asked, trying to tamp down the panic rising in his throat.

"Yeah, like having a baby," was all she said as she ducked under his arm and headed out the door.

Link grabbed Seth's arm.

Seth jerked back.

"Whoa, buddy. Probably nothing, but let's go up and check on her anyway. I'm coming with."

Link hit the button for the elevator, but it seemed to be stuck on the second floor. Seth looked around and found the door marked stairs. He took the steps three at a time and was stepping out onto the second floor in seconds. Link was right behind him. As they ran down the hall to Jenny's room, they saw a scramble of people pushing a gurney the other way. They ran into Jenny's room and Seth went into full panic.

"No, no, no! It can't be happening. Not now. Not to her. Not to them! God, please no," he pleaded as he dropped to his knees and stared at all the blood.

Abby came through the door. "Seth." He jumped up and spun around.

"Yes. That's me," he said, wiping some tears from his cheek with his shirtsleeves. "What's happening to Jenny? Where did they take her?" he pleaded desperately for answers.

Victoria came through the door next and took in the scene.

"We don't know exactly what happened, but she's hemorrhaging, and her water broke. She is in heavy labor, but she isn't dilating yet. They've taken her into surgery for an emergency C-section. They've already given her an epidural, and she's asking for you and won't take no for an answer."

"Let's go. Take me to her," Seth said, breathing heavily as if he just ran a marathon.

"First, I need you to wash up and put these scrubs on." She handed him a folded set of magenta scrubs. "There's soap and washcloths in the bathroom. Go in and get cleaned up and changed. I'll be waiting to take you into the OR."

Without a word, Seth took the clothes and disappeared into the bathroom.

CHAPTER FIFTEEN

Jenny gripped Seth's hand tight and stared into his eyes. He was her rock, and right now she needed him to be solid enough to keep her from being washed away in a flood of emotion and stark, cold fear. The baby's heart monitors were beeping loudly, and one was much slower than the other. The surgical team seemed to appear out of nowhere as they rolled her into the operating room. One of the nurses on the team had already put a green hospital hair cap over Jenny's head. Another was draping her for the emergency cesarean section so she couldn't see her belly. Jenny looked down, one last time before they put up the curtain between her and her babies. The anesthesiologist had already given her an epidural in her spine, so now she couldn't feel anything, and she couldn't see anything. As they moved her bed into the room, her IV got caught on the door handle and nearly yanked it out of her hand. She could tell Seth was freaked out as well but was holding his own. His jaw was set, and the muscles on the side of his temples were throbbing in and out as he looked back and forth from Jenny to the procedure unfolding. With his left hand, he held hers, and with his right, he gently stroked her cheek and forehead. At least he thought it was gentle.

Jenny involuntarily pulled back a bit from his gentle strokes.
"What's happening?" she asked Seth. "I can't see anything, and I can't feel anything either."

"They are putting iodine all over your belly," he said
matter-of-factly. Trying to keep his own emotions at bay.

"Please tell me everything they're doing?" she pleaded.
Her lower lip was shaking, and she had a silent tear trick-
ling down her cheek. The doctors and nurses were talking
in a staccato.

"Really?" Seth asked, with a furrowed brow. "Are you
sure you want me to tell you everything they are doing?"

"Yes," she said, squeezing his hand even harder.

"Okay," Seth said, still a bit unsure. "They are cutting
a line in your lower belly."

"They are?" she asked, the surprise evident in her voice.
"I can't feel it at all."

"Yes, and now they are moving things around and cutting a little more...

"Okay. okay. That's enough. Don't tell me anymore of
that stuff," she said. "I regret asking."

Seth smiled a quick smile and looked down at her. She
was so pale, and perspiration was building all over her face
and upper lip.

Seth suddenly gripped her hand tightly as the doctor
lifted their first baby out of her tummy and into the light.
It was a little girl with blonde hair and screaming her head
off. The surgeon quickly handed the child off to an await-
ing nurse without even cutting the umbilical cord and
reached for the second. Seth's heart stopped. It was another
little girl, but with dark hair. Only, she wasn't screaming.
She didn't seem to be breathing, and she was totally blue.
Seth's world came crashing down, and he looked up and
begged, "Please, God. Please save my little girl." The surgeon
unwrapped the cord from around her neck, and a neonatal

team whisked her into a corner while the surgeons went back to work on Jenny.

"Doctor, the patient's blood pressure is dropping," the anesthesiologist called out in a calm but urgent tone of voice.

Jenny turned ghostly, and then her hand went limp in Seth's.

"Jenny. Jenny!" Seth yelled as he shook her lifeless hand as her heart monitor stopped beeping and went to a solid tone. "*Jenny!*" he screamed.

"That's enough. Get him out of here," Doctor Scott directed the surgical staff with a military command tone.

"No. I'm not leaving," Seth shouted.

"Seth, knock it off. You can't help her right now, and you're keeping us from doing what we need to do. Please leave and I promise you, I'll come out as soon as I can and tell you what I can."

"Jenny!" he cried as he held out his hand toward her as they physically pushed him out the door. He didn't fight them anymore.

Link and Victoria were there when he came out of the OR. Seth staggered through the double doors like a drunk or a madman, rubbing the stinging tears away from his face with the back of his hand. Breathing rapidly, his anger boiling over, he turned and punched his fist through the white hospital wall, creating a hole as sheetrock dust filled the air. Just as he drew back for another punch, Link caught his arm and spun him around.

He put his face right into Seth's. "Get hold of yourself, Seth. You are not doing her any good like this." Link's voice was probably the only thing that had a chance of getting through.

Seth pulled away and grabbed his own head with both hands, clenching every muscle in his body, in a desperate but futile attempt at stifling his primordial scream. He backed away from Link until he hit the wall. Then he broke, as he slid down the wall to the floor. Link squatted in front of him and waited. After a few moments Seth got to his feet. And without a word, he turned away from Link and started walking down the hall, away from the growing crowd. Susan was coming the opposite direction and tried to stop him, but he just held up his hands in front of him and said, "Please, just leave me alone," and continued walking.

"Let him go," came Link's voice. "Just let him be for a while."

Seth didn't remember coming into the small hospital chapel. His mind was numb. No, it wasn't. It was actually screaming in his head. He desperately wanted it to be numb. Sitting in the second row, he rested his forehead on the back of the wooden pew in front of him and just sat there for a while. His eyes stung, his body ached, and his hands would not stop shaking until he clasped them together to try to make them stop. He finally slid off the seat and onto his knees.

"God, I know I haven't really talked to you since Olivia died. It's like my hope died with her, and my faith was crushed. It's just that I was so mad and angry and…and hurt." Seth stopped while his body was wracked with another set of sobs. "But you didn't give up on me, even though I had. You brought Jenny into my life. And now there's three. God, I can't lose them again. Please, God. Please save them. Give me the faith that I need to survive this. Give me Hope that you will see me through. I'm begging you. I will do anything."

Seth looked up at the sound of the chapel door opening.

"She's going to be okay," were the first words out of Doctor Scott's mouth as he stood in the doorway. "Jenny is stable for now, and if we can find blood in her type, she'll be just fine."

"Thank you, Jesus," Seth prayed under his breath as he leapt to his feet and strode toward Doctor Scott and bear hugged him. "Can I see her?"

"No, Seth. Not yet. But you will as soon as she recovers at least a little."

"How long will that take?"

There was a large crowd building outside the chapel as Doctor Scott and Seth exited into the hallway.

"What did you say about needing blood?" Seth asked.

"The good news right now is that we were able to stop most of the bleeding. Jenny is strong, but she lost a lot of blood."

"So, what's the problem with getting blood?" Link demanded a little harshly from the hallway.

"She is AB negative, and the hospital blood bank doesn't have any of that specific type left after the big pileup. We gave her plasma to keep her blood volume up, but it's only a temporary fix. What we desperately need is to get whole blood, some AB negative or at least O negative, which is the universal donor."

"But what about the babies?" Victoria asked the question that Seth was afraid to.

"What? They didn't tell you?" Doctor Scott asked, looking from one to the next.

"No," Seth replied in a shaky voice. Another bolt of fear went straight through his heart.

"I'm told they are both doing fine," Doctor Scott said with a smile. "Ivy took them both up to the NICU an hour ago. It's my pleasure to inform you that you are the father of a beautiful pair of lively fraternal twin girls. One appears to be blonde and with an attitude, the other a brunette with somewhat less of an attitude."

Seth's legs nearly buckled under the reversal of fear to elation in his heart. He finally cleared the massive lump in his throat and said, "Thank you, Jesus." Not under his breath this time, but loud and clear even with a quavering, breathless voice.

"You can go up and see *them* now if you like."

"But wait, can I see Jenny first?" Seth asked expectantly.

"No way, Seth. I'm sorry, buddy, not right now," Doctor Scott said apologetically but firmly. "She is in recovery and still very weak." The doctor paused for a second and looked at the dive watch on his left wrist, a hold over from his years as a SEAL. "We'll move her over to the ICU in a few hours, and you can see her then. Right now, you need to go meet your daughters." He pointed in the direction of the elevator. "Third floor. Left turn. Can't miss it."

Seth nodded his head without a word, shifted his weight forward and quickly moved toward the elevator. He hit the up button and immediately looked up at the indicator light. As he waited impatiently, he noticed the sign for the stairs next to the elevator and abruptly turned and disappeared into the stairwell.

* * * * *

As Link watched the door closing mechanism shut the fire door behind Seth, he turned to Doctor Scott. "So, what in the hell happened?" he asked, pointing down the hall toward the room that Jenny had been in. "What went wrong?" Link paused and took a deep breath. "First, we're told that she's not even in labor, and the next thing we know there's all these code blues and code pinks?"

"Listen, Jiff," Doctor Scott grabbed him by the elbow and motioned into an alcove with a couple of cushioned waiting room chairs and a small coffee table between them. "I don't know what went wrong yet, but something is off.

Way off. I don't know what yet, but I sent some blood samples down to the lab for testing."

"What's your gut saying?" Link asked.

"Well, it's crazy. It's almost as if Jenny received a massive overdose of Pitocin."

"What the hell is Pitocin?" Link asked through gritted teeth.

"It's a drug used to induce labor."

"What? I thought we didn't want her in labor?" Link asked.

"Exactly," was all Doctor Scott gave for an answer, but Link saw the look on his face. That look said more than words ever could.

"But who? Why?" he asked incredulously.

"I don't know, Jiff, but something is wrong here. Very wrong. But right now, our primary concern is to get Jenny well."

Link started to leave the little waiting area when Doctor Scott pulled him back in again. He looked at Link thoughtfully and said, "Jiff?"

"Yeah? What is it?"

"Do you have anyone who can sit with Jenny in her room? You know, just as a precaution?"

"I got a redheaded momma grizzly. Have you ever noticed the western style leather purse she carries?"

"Not really," Doctor Scott admitted.

"Yeah, I don't notice that stuff either," Link admitted with a chuckle of his own. "However, that purse contains, among other things, of course, the cutest little, pink-gripped Czech CZ-75 nine-millimeter pistol you ever laid eyes on." Link said with a wink. "Santa thought momma grizzly was a good little girl."

Doctor Scotts eyebrows shot up, and he cocked his head a bit and said in a low tone, "Nice."

"Now, what are we going to do about the blood?" Link asked, abruptly changing the subject as they stepped out into the hallway.

"We're calling all the other hospitals in the state to see if we can find a supply of the right blood type."

"Hey Doc, I've got O negative," Link said. "That's the universal donor type, right?"

Doctor Scott looked at him hard for a minute, as if he was considering his words. And when he spoke, he dropped his chin and extended his forehead toward Link and with a soft, quiet voice. "Jiff, weren't you in the sandbox when all those Sarin gas canisters were blown?"

"Yeah, so what? That was a while ago," Link defended. "You know that I'm healthy as a horse."

"No, Link. Don't even think about it."

"But Doc…"

"We have no idea what the consequences might be. You know you can never safely give blood again… *Ever* again."

"Okay, okay." Link raised his hands and gave in. "I get it."

"Good," Doctor Scott replied with raised eyebrows and a satisfied look on his face. He turned to walk away.

"Hey, Doc. Isn't my blood better than Jenny being dead?" Link asked, using a different approach, trying to outflank the former Navy SEAL's argument.

"All right, if it comes to that. We can use yours only as an absolute last resort."

"Good," Link replied with his own satisfied grin. "I win. Which way to the leach?"

"Because we are short staffed, Abby is filling in as our *leach* today. Go give your blood to her, and we'll use it if we *need* to. We are waiting to hear from Bismarck, Fargo and even Billings to see if they even have any. The problem with that is it will be at least three to four hours before that blood reaches us, and that's in a perfect scenario."

As Abby applied the bright pink tourniquet to Link's arm, she nodded. "Nice veins. Sure makes my job easier." She began applying an alcohol swab to the area surrounding one of Link's larger veins that were standing out nicely now that the tourniquet was taking effect.

"If you've got any trainees that need practice, you can send 'em my way," Link offered. "Doc Scott wants my blood labeled with my name, and to let him know. It'll only be used for Jenny in case of emergency."

"Not a problem," Abby said with a slight frown as she pulled the needle out of Link's arm with practiced efficiency and pushed down hard on the puncture with a gloved thumb and a piece of gauze. "Hold pressure here," she commanded as she pulled Link's own index finger over and placed it on the gauze. Once he was holding it tightly on his own, she reached over and selected a Band-Aid from the stainless-steel cart to put over the wound. It said, *Yaba Daba Do.*

"Awe," Link said with a whine in his voice. "I was kind of hoping for *The Little Mermaid.*"

"Too bad," came the instant retort, followed by a grin.

While he'd been sitting there, he had an idea and went off to find Doctor Scott who was grabbing a coffee in the cafeteria. He got in line behind him. "Hey, Adam, I was thinking."

"Uh-oh," was all he said.

Ignoring his comment, Link continued. "Trinity has a public affairs officer, right?"

"Yeah. Of course. Most hospitals do these days."

"Who is Trinity's?" Link asked. Then placed his order with the barista.

"She's one of the best. Her name is Kelley Rankin, but it's the weekend and she won't be in until Monday. Where are you going with this? We don't have a PR problem."

"I was just thinking… Why don't we put out a call for blood donations over the radio?"

Doctor Scott nodded. "Not a horrible idea." He dug the phone out of his pocket, flipped through it to find a number, and held the phone so Link could see it.

Link pressed the digits, hit send and Ms Rankin picked up on the third ring. He quickly introduced himself and why he was calling and then asked, "Can you have them put out an emergency announcement over the local radio stations that the hospital needs type AB negative or type O negative blood? There's got to be some folks out there with that kind of blood."

She said she would, and he grinned.

"Thank you so much," Link said. "I greatly appreciate you answering the phone on your day off."

Link dropped his cell back into his shirt pocket and said with a big, satisfied grin, "Done and done."

"There is one problem," Doctor Scott warned. "Williston is a boom town and the permanent, local population that gives blood is pretty small. As I said before, we already used up a large amount of that group with the last wreck. There are people willing to sell plasma, but often they are addicted to drugs, are needle users, and know they have bad blood. Anyone unknown to us must be screened for HIV, etcetera."

"Oh, ye of little faith," Link chided. "Just wait. You'll see."

CHAPTER SIXTEEN

Seth took the stairs two and three at a time arriving at the third floor landing, and shoving the heavy fire door open with too much force. The noise of the door crashing into the hard, rubber stopper made him wince. His heart beating loudly in his chest, he strode down the wide corridor toward the double doors with the initials NICU above.

He stopped in front of those doors.

Swallowing hard, he slowly pushed through, and his feet stopped, as if another, invisible door got in his way. His heart hammered in his chest as he took the next two steps, then he placed his hand on the large window and peered through the glass…

The scene was a cacophony of beeping machines and voices chattering noisily as several nurses worked in a seamless, coordinated rhythm. The words themselves were unintelligible, but the determination was obvious. In the center of all the activity were two newly arrived little beings, both nestled into a single incubator. There was a label stuck to the side with BETTY scrawled with a large black magic marker. Another incubator pushed to the side appeared to

137

be recently abandoned. Stuck to it was another label with VERONICA scrawled on it with similar handwriting.

Seth placed his other hand flat onto the glass as if holding out his arms to embrace his children. So close, yet so far away. For a day already filled with a roller coaster of emotions, the reality of his children struck him like a hammer blow to his chest and physically rocked him. Swallowing hard, he realized, *Those are my children. My little girls.* The lump in his throat would not give way. *Olivia, honey, just look at them. They are so beautiful.*

It wasn't long before Ivy looked up and saw him at the window and gave him a wink and a huge smile. He almost didn't recognize her with the sterile scrub hat and mask she was wearing. She held up one finger, pulled her mask down for a moment and mouthed the words, "Give me one minute."

Seth nodded his head as she finished taping a little tube down to the arm of one of his little girls, the brunette. As soon as she was done, she turned toward the door. Peeling off her latex gloves, she tossed them in the trash and exited the room.

"How are they?" asked Seth, his voice quavering right along with his stomach.

"Your two daughters are doing fine," Ivy replied. "They were both calm when we brought them in, but as soon as we separated them into the incubators, they both became agitated. As soon as we put them back together, they calmed down. There is definitely something to be said for the relationship between twins."

"What's with the labels?" Seth asked with a confused look on his face. "Has Jenny already named them?"

"No, she was too weak to even speak, but she did smile. What labels are you talking about?" Ivy asked as she scanned the NICU and then looked back at Seth.

"The ones with Betty and Veronica scrawled on them." He pointed.

Ivy looked back through the glass to where he was pointing and blushed a little. "Oh, I am so sorry, Seth. The names are from Betty and Veronica, the characters from the Archie's comic books. Without knowing their names and as one was blonde and the other brunette it was our way of quickly identifying which one we were discussing. I apologize. I'll get those removed immediately."

"No, no, no," Seth said as he looked from Ivy and then back to his little girls. "It's fine. Those won't be their real names," he said with a chuckle, "but you may have just given them nicknames without even realizing it."

"Are you sure?" Ivy asked.

"Yes, ma'am. I am sure. But are you *sure* they are doing okay?" The intensity in his voice was matched by the tightness in his throat. "It was pretty scary in the OR."

"Well, we have examined them both, and so far they seem to be perfectly developed. It's up to the doctor, but I doubt they will need a very long stay in the NICU."

"Thank you, Jesus," Seth prayed for the third time today, with such emotion as he tried desperately to swallow the lump in his throat. The relief flowed through him like a torrential river as he leaned heavily against the viewing window, hoping he wouldn't embarrass himself by passing out.

"How's Jenny?" Ivy asked tentatively. "We haven't heard anything yet."

"Right now, she's in recovery, but they won't let me see her. Doc says she's stable, but she needs whole blood to stay that way. They've got people searching the whole state for her type." He couldn't take his eyes off his babies, his daughters. Then the strangest feeling came over him as he pictured both Olivia and Jenny, smiling. *Our* daughters...

Ivy reached out and put her hand on his arm in a reassuring grip. "Are you okay? Do you need to sit down?" Ivy asked.

"No, no. I'm fine," Seth said as the heat rose in his cheeks.

"Seth, I've seen Jenny go through a lot. I was there when she was in the accident. In fact, I feel like I've known those two little girls for their whole life, even though I haven't held them until today. Jenny is really strong, and I'm sure she'll come through this as well. After all, she has a lot of work to do. She's not finished, the ride has only begun. Right now, you should concentrate on what you can do, like meeting your new little girls."

Seth turned toward Ivy, his eyes wide. "What do you mean?"

"Well, do you want to hold them?"

"Me? Now?" He stared at Ivy and then down at his big hands. "Uhm, yes. Yes, I do. But I don't want to hurt them."

Ivy laughed at that and said, "Don't worry. You won't. But first we'll have to find some fresh scrubs that will fit you," she said as she sized him up. "I'm not sure if that's even possible up here."

"It won't be the first time I've looked ridiculous in a set of scrubs that were too small," he said, allowing himself a little chuckle.

* * * * *

"What do you mean no one showed up?" Link barked at Kelley Rankin an hour later. She had come directly from her son's basketball game and was still dressed in her Basketball Mom regalia, complete with her son's jersey number painted on her forehead. A transplant from Texas, she had a reputation as a fixer. A person that could turn any ship around and this situation was no different.

"What can I say, very few showed up even after swamping the airways with pleas, and no one showed up with the right blood type."

Link looked at Doctor Scott. "Well, it looks like it's time."

"Not yet, Link," Doctor Scott replied. "We still have a little time."

"Time for what?" Kelley asked.

"Link's blood is O negative, but it's an unknown quality.

"He looks healthy to me."

"It's because he served a combat tour during which he had a few too many near death adventures with weapons of mass destruction. We've already drawn his blood, but we don't want to use it unless it's the last resort."

"How frustrating," Kelley agreed.

"I have an idea," Kelley said as she looked toward the nurse manning the station. "Can you access the hospital employees' records and see if anyone has AB negative or O negative blood type?"

"I don't have access," she reluctantly replied, "but I can try calling downstairs to admin. They may be able to help."

"Great. At least there's a chance." Kelley sighed. "Maybe we can find someone here."

Doctor Scott tapped his fingers with impatience while the nurse made the call. "Guys, keep in mind that she needs at least two units of blood to make it through the night. She lost approximately three in the OR."

The nurse set the phone down after a few minutes and was beaming. "We've got two employees at the hospital with that blood type but only one is on duty right now. The other is on vacation."

"Well, who is it?" Kelley asked.

"It's the new CNA, Brooke."

"Where is she now?" Link asked.

"I don't know. I think she's on her coffee break. She really seems to care about Jenny. In fact, Abby mentioned that she spent her lunch break in Jenny's room watching over her. But that was before everything went crazy. She might be down in the cafeteria by now."

Without another word, Doctor Scott reached over the nurses' station desk and grabbed the phone receiver and punched a button labeled PA. "Brooke, please report to the second-floor nursing station. Brooke, please report to the second-floor nursing station." And hung up the phone. The group as a whole started looking toward the elevator for any sight of movement.

After no more than ten seconds, Link let out a breath of air that he'd been holding. "Okay, I've had enough of this waiting. I'm going down to the cafeteria to see if she's there." He quickly strode to the elevator and punched the down button as if it had done something wrong. As the elevator bell chimed and the doors opened, there stood Brooke, looking a little bewildered. Maybe even scared.

"Oh, Brooke," Link said with relief. "Just the person we were looking for. Doctor Scott has something to talk to you about."

"Why me?" Brooke said with what almost sounded like fear. "I swear I don't know anything. I didn't do anything wrong." Her eyes were wide as she looked at the throng of people waiting for her.

Doctor Scott jumped in. "Brooke, I have a huge favor to ask of you, and it's totally okay if you say no."

Link nudged Kelly and whispered strongly, "No, it's not."

Brooke's eyes brightened, and her tone changed dramatically as she replied, "Doctor Scott, you know I'd do anything for you."

"Good," he replied with a sigh of relief. He then took both her hands in his and he looked into her eyes and said, "Jenny Reagan needs type AB negative or O negative blood if she is going to live through the night. Abby said you spent your lunch break sitting with her, so she must be just as important to you as she is to the rest of us. AB negative is so rare that you are the only one here that has the right blood type. Are you willing to donate a unit?"

Brooke's gaze went from soft to stunned. She almost looked as if she were going to faint. Her eyes went darting around the room, but just when Doctor Scott was reaching to catch her in a faint, she caught herself and settled down.

"Uh, Doctor Scott," she said while looking around at the group. "I am so sorry, I'd love to help Jenny, but I can't donate blood. I'm not allowed."

"Why not?" Doctor Scott asked in surprise.

"Well, because I got myself a little ol' tattoo at the county fair last year, and I read that I'm not allowed to give blood after that."

"The waiting period is only twelve months after a tattoo, so that means you are now eligible to donate blood again."

"Oh, right," Brooke conceded weakly.

"Isn't that great?" Doctor Scott exclaimed.

"Oh, my. Really?"

"Yes," The group assembled in front of her said in unison.

"I see. Well then... I guess so...."

* * * * *

When Jenny first awoke, she pried open her eyes one at a time. They felt so heavy. The lights in the room were dimmed so nothing would come into focus. She lay there, trying to think of what happened. Her left hand had an

IV attached so tightly that she couldn't move it much. She slowly managed to move her right hand down to her tummy. No babies, just bandages.

What happened? She tried desperately to recall through the thickly floating fog. Fighting back panic, she tried to yell but only a hoarse whisper came out. "Hello?"

"Jenny." She heard Victoria's voice. "How are you feeling?" She stepped up to Jenny's bed, pressed the call button, and then took a hold of Jenny's hand. "I'm so glad you're awake. You're going to cause me a heart attack!"

Jenny tried to manage a smile but then remembered. "What happened? I feel so weak."

"You lost a lot of blood, and we are working on getting you some more."

"Where are my babies?"

Just then an ICU nurse came rushing into the room. "We sure are happy to see your blue eyes, sweetheart. How are you feeling? Are you hungry at all?"

Victoria stepped to the foot of Jenny's bed to allow the nurse to talk to Jenny.

"I want to know where my babies are," Jenny said fiercely, fearing the worst.

"Oh, honey. Those two babies are doing just fine. They're both strong, healthy and already getting into mischief up in the NICU from what I hear. It's you that we've all been worrying about."

That brought a smile, followed by tears of joy streaming down her face. "I want to see them," she said desperately. "Where is Seth?"

Victoria said, "He's been splitting his time between you and the twins. He's with them upstairs right now."

"Can I see *him*, then?" her voice trailed off with a dry croak.

"Let me step out into the hallway and call him. I'll be right back." Victoria was already pulling her cell phone out of her purse before she hit the door.

Jenny heard Victoria's voice as the door to the hallway closed. "Seth, she's awake."

"You seem to be doing well, Jenny," the nurse assured her. "Doctor Scott will be by in a few minutes to check on you as well."

"I feel so weak," Jenny said again. Her mouth was dry, and she couldn't seem to even lift her head to look around.

"That's normal when you lose a lot of blood. We had one donor step forward, and that saved your life."

"Who was it?" asked Jenny.

"You'll have to ask the doctor." The nurse positioned the call button back on the bed next to Jenny. "Honey, if you need anything, just push the button."

As the nurse left the room, Jenny momentarily saw Victoria in the hallway talking animatedly to Debbie and Barb, the church ladies that stayed with her when she was pinned in the wreck. The day she found out she was carrying twins. A few more hot tears of joy made their way down Jenny's cheeks as a lump formed in her throat. *I'm a mother... my babies are doing just fine...*

"Jenny?" Victoria's voice broke into her thoughts. She had opened the door just wide enough to poke her head through. "There's a couple of ladies that would like to say hello. Can I sneak them in for a few minutes, that is, if you feel up to it?"

All she could manage at first was a nod and a half smile. Victoria flashed her a smile of her own and opened the door wide as she led the ladies into the room.

"Sweetheart, how are you feeling?" Barb asked with concern in her voice and worry on her brow as she approached Jenny's bed.

"I'm feeling a little weak, but they said that that is to be expected. What are you doing here?" she asked with her best attempt at a smile.

Debbie replied, "Barb heard on the radio that the hospital was needing blood donors, so we came down to donate, but neither of us have the type that you need."

"We're so sorry," Barb added with a heartfelt shake of her head.

"Would it be all right if we prayed for you and the babies?"

"Yes, please," Jenny readily agreed as she attempted to sit up a bit.

"No, Jenny, just lie still. No need to sit up."

"Dear Lord," Barb began, "we thank you for Jenny and her precious babies. We thank you for bringing her not only to our community but into our lives. We know that you have a purpose for them in your Kingdom. We ask that you send the right blood donor to help her regain her strength so she can take care of those precious gifts. We know that there is nothing impossible for you, and that you will always finish the good work that you started. In the name of Jesus, we pray. Amen."

Debbie beamed, "Jenny, we'd love to see you in church."

"I would love to. I want to, too." She smiled weakly. "And it might be a hard sell, but I'm going to try to talk Seth into coming with me as well."

"Talk me into what?" Seth asked as he pushed through the door. He wore a smile a mile wide.

A nurse right behind Seth was squawking like a wet hen. "There are entirely too many of you in here," she spluttered as she pushed Seth's body out of the way. "Jenny needs her rest, and she cannot get any with all of you jabbering in her ear."

"Uh oh, ladies. We're busted," Victoria deadpanned. "We'd better clear out and let Seth talk to this beautiful girl...and mommy." She grinned at Jenny.

Jenny burst into happy tears saying, "I'm a mom. I'm really a mom."

"Of two beautiful twin daughters, I might add," Seth said, still grinning wide.

"I can't wait to see them," she said as exhaustion weighed her down.

"You will soon," the nurse declared as she herded the other three ladies out the door.

As the door closed, Seth sat on Jenny's bed and held her pale hand in his. "So, what's this thing you are going to talk me into?" Seth asked while holding her hand against his cheek.

Jenny cleared her throat while she looked up at Seth apprehensively. "I know we haven't talked about it, but given the circumstances over the last few months, I would like to start going to church." She paused, looking into his blue eyes, searching for a reaction.

After a bit of silence, Seth asked. "And what is it that you want to talk *me* into?"

Jenny tensed a little. "Seth." She held his hand with both of hers. Then she breathed deeply and held it in. "I would really like us to go to church as a family."

Seth said nothing as he stared back at her. She felt like a scared rabbit, waiting for his response. She searched his eyes, his face, looking for his reaction.

"Okay," he said matter-of-factly. "I'm in."

"Okay?" she asked almost in disbelief. "I'm in?"

"Yeah, okay," he said again with a grin. "Were you expecting a different answer?"

"No. Well...yes. Well, I didn't know what to expect. We've never talked about it before. And I was really worried about what you would think and how you would react." As she spoke, her pale face began to blush.

"You know, it hasn't been boring since I met you. Jenny McKenna, soon to be Jenny Reagan."

She held his big hand to her lips and kissed it.

"Honey…" Seth's voice took on a serious tone. "I've got to admit that when Olivia died, I was very angry with God. I felt like He had stolen her from me." Seth gazed into her eyes. "I had no desire to go to church or even talk to Him for a long time. But, because I was so afraid that I would lose you too, I had a very good talk with Him while you were in surgery." He paused again. "Um, so yeah. I'm in," he said, bringing back his big grin. "All in."

CHAPTER SEVENTEEN

"How are we doing with public donors?" Link asked Kelley as he blew into her office without a knock as he rubbed the back of his neck. The impatience in his voice could be heard by a deaf person. He came to an abrupt halt and with a loud slap, dropped both hands onto her desk, palms down.

"Has anyone else showed up yet?" He asked with so much suppressed impatience, he was ready to explode.

Kelley looked at Link a moment before speaking. "Link, the way the blood vessels in your temples are popping, you are going to give yourself a heart attack or a brain bleed."

"Answer the damn question," Link growled.

She took a deep breath and let it out as she spoke. "Look, we did have a few more show up to donate blood, but, unfortunately, none of them have been a match," Kelley explained. "You've got to understand we just went through a desperate blood drive."

Taking a deep breath for himself he began slowly and deliberately. "Do you not understand what is at stake here?"

She fixed him with a basilisk stare. "Link, I've done all I can." She paused. "What else is there?"

"I don't know," he snapped. "Are you sure you hit all the radio stations in the area?" Link asked, grasping at straws as he began pacing back and forth like a caged lion.

"Yes, Link. I'm sure. I know you're worried sick, but trust me, we are doing all we can." She let out a long-suffering sigh that made him stop moving and turn toward her.

"I'm trying not to badger you, but there must be something we haven't thought of yet."

"I've also got ads out for local Pandora listeners as well as a copy going into the morning newspaper, but that won't do a lot of good for Jenny now."

Link started to pace back and forth again then suddenly spun around and asked, "What *exactly* did you put in the radio announcement?"

Kelley furrowed her brows at him. "The verbiage I used was," she paused to looked down at a document on her desk, "'Trinity Hospital is in need of blood donors due to the recent accidents depleting our blood bank.'"

"That's it?" he exclaimed, throwing his hands in the air. "That's all you said?"

Kelley looked at him in surprise. "What do you mean, '*that's it*?'" she asked as she stood up. "I am good at my job, Mr. James." Her eyes narrowed as the color rose in her cheeks. "What else should I have said?" The last few words dripped with outrage.

Without noticing her growing anger, Link plowed on. "Listen, we need to be more specific." Link started to pace again before snapping his fingers. "Here's what I want you to do. Re-run the announcements just as you did before, but this time I want you to specifically state that it is Jenny Reagan that needs lifesaving AB negative or O negative blood."

"Mr. James, I'm terribly sorry, but I don't work for you, and I highly doubt that it will make much of a difference."

Continuing to ignore her defiance, Link smiled and said, "It'll make *all* the difference in the world."

"But I don't see how..."

"You'll see," Link said

"Okay then," she said dubiously as she reached for her cell phone. "I'll make it happen, and I sure hope you're right."

"Trust me," Link said with a grin then headed for the doorway. He rested his hand on the jamb for a moment and turned back to her. "Ya know, I'm glad that you calmed down," Link said almost as an afterthought. "You need to be careful about getting all worked up. That kind of reaction can lead to a heart attack." Then he was out the door.

"Mr. James," Kelley hollered after him, "I didn't think you even noticed."

He pulled out his cell phone and hit a number on his favorites list. After two rings he said, "Susan. It's Link. Here's what I need you to do. Call everyone on the payroll and tell them what's going on. Tell them we need everyone who can donate blood, to come down now."

"Yes, sir," Susan replied. "I'm O positive if that helps."

"It won't do any good for Jenny, but it sure will help someone else," Link stated. "Oh, and Susan?"

"Yes?"

"Tell 'em it's not an order, but that I'd greatly appreciate it."

"You got it, Boss," Susan replied, but the line had already gone dead.

* * * * *

A young man stepped up to the front of the growing line of oilfield workers and said, "I've got O negative blood."

151

"Great," Kelley shouted above the noise as she reached for another form. "Are you sure you are O negative?"

"Yes, ma'am."

"Okay, this is fantastic," she exclaimed. "Tell you what, in order to expedite this, let me help you fill out your paperwork and get you in the lab ASAP."

"Works for me," he said with a shrug.

"Last name please?"

"James."

"First name?"

"Jesse."

"I'm sorry. What did you say?" Kelley asked.

"Yes, I said my name is Jesse James," he replied with a lop-sided grin.

"Are you serious?"

"Yes, ma'am, I am. My folks named all of us boys starting with a J."

"Oh, your parents must have had a good time naming you," she said almost under her breath as she wrote his name down on the form.

"Well, I don't know for sure, but you can ask my Dad yourself.

"What?"

"Yeah, He's the bald guy standing right over there," he said, pointing.

"Who? Where?" she asked, looking around.

"He's standing right there. His name is Lincoln James."

Kelley looked in the direction that he was pointing and then snapped back and asked rather rhetorically, "Wait a minute. Are you Link's kid?"

"Yes, ma'am," he said with an even bigger grin, getting a kick out of her reaction.

"Well, well, Mr. James, please follow me," she said as she took the clipboard and headed toward the door that said *LAB*.

Link caught Jesse's eye and mouthed the words, "Thank you, son," not attempting to yell over the crowd. Jesse smiled at his dad and followed Kelley into the lab.

He sat down in the phlebotomist chair and rotated the special arm over in front of him.

"It looks like you've done this before," Abby said kindly as she prepared her workstation. "Most people are pretty nervous about having blood drawn."

"Me? Not so much," Jesse commented nonchalantly. "I give blood a lot. I've got big veins and often let the newest trainees take my blood. It's not that I'm that altruistic, it's just that I have a sweet tooth, so I'm only here for the cookie or the chocolate."

Abby sat down in front of him and went to work trying to clean the crude oil smudges off his arm with alcohol wipes.

"What's this stuff made of?" Abby asked. "Super glue?"

Jesse chuckled. She had a clean scent with just a light hint of perfume. It might have been the fragrance of her soap. *Whatever it is*, Jesse thought, *it smells great, and it contrasts sharply with my own current personal aroma.*

"So, I've been wondering..."

"Yes?"

"Why don't you wear one of those white nurse's hats?"

"You're kidding, right?" she asked.

"No," Jesse stated with a simple shrug.

"Where, exactly, have you seen a nurse wearing the nurse's cap lately?"

"I don't know." He paused for a moment. "In the movies, I guess. I try hard not to spend too much time in an actual hospital. I'm told it's really not healthy."

"Really?" she asked, looking him in the eye. "It's not considered wise to deeply offend someone who is preparing to stick a needle in your arm. We haven't worn nurses' hats in a long time. Not even in this century."

"Well, why not?"

"Because some really smart nurses a long time ago voted that it wasn't necessary to wear them anymore. And besides, we rarely even use the nursing uniform anymore, because we mostly wear scrubs."

"Oh, too bad. I thought they looked kind of hot in the movies. Maybe you could bring them back, only this time, get colors to match your scrubs."

"Could you be any more demeaning?" Abby asked just as she was about to stick the large needle into his arm.

"I wasn't *trying* to be demeaning. I guess I was trying to say that you look pretty enough that you should be in the movies."

He thought he saw the corner of her mouth turn up in what might have been a smile, but then turned into an angry frown.

"I am sorry to say that wearing a nursing cap because it *looked hot* was definitely not its purpose."

"So..." Jesse paused for a moment, trying to think of another tactic. Then he gave his best boyish grin. "So, do you come here often?"

Abby did not appear overly impressed. In fact, she seemed impervious to his blue eyes. "Uh, yeah," she said almost as a question followed by a definite "*duh*" sound.

Continuing to probe the perimeter, he asked, "Do you live around here?"

"I just moved here."

"Really, me too," Jesse replied. "I got here a few days ago. Where'd you come from?"

"Washington," she stated with a sigh at the end.

"State or DC?"

Showing more signs of getting tired of this line of questioning she said, "State," rather curtly.

"I have family in Washington, too. Only by marriage though."

"Oh, really?" she asked in a tone that was unmistakably sarcastic.

"Sure, I do. I even have a cousin, or rather some sort of a step cousin that lives there. She's probably about your age. I think she was at my dad's wedding in Alaska. I don't remember if I actually met her, but Victoria talks about her a lot."

Abby's head snapped up from watching the blood bag slowly fill. "Alaska? Victoria?" she repeated, but this time without the sarcasm.

That got her attention, Jesse thought as he continued. "In fact, it just so happens that her name is Abby, too." He pointed to her name badge with his free hand.

Abby looked up at him, adjusted her glasses, and then looked over to his blood donor form and asked, "Who, um, exactly is your dad?"

"Lincoln James. He's been around here for a while."

"As in my Aunt Victoria's husband?"

"No way," Jesse blurted. "So that makes us what? Some sort of relatives, right?"

"Cousins, I think," said Abby with a bit of a giggle as she removed the needle from his arm. "Press down here."

"Somehow, getting your phone number for a date just seems wrong now."

"It would not have worked out anyway." she replied as she placed the bandaid on the wound. " I already have a boyfriend."

"Oh yeah? Where is he?"

"Idaho. He's finishing medical school."

Just then, Kelley stuck her head in the door. "Abby, quick. We've got a female AB negative donor out here, as soon as you're ready."

155

"That's fantastic, um…" She looked over at Jesse and then back to Kelley. "We're just finishing up. Bring her right in and put her in the other chair next to Jesse. What's her name? Is she already on the donor list?"

"No, she's a first-time donor, and we've already filled out all the paperwork."

"Great, bring her in and I'll get her started right away."

"Tell you what, *cousin*," Abby declared. "Since you're new here too, a couple of us nurses are going out to Maria's after work…"

Just then the door to the lab pushed open and a head popped through. "Is this where I go for blood donation?" Her accented voice caught Jesse's attention first. He withdrew his gaze from Abby and stared at the newcomer.

"If you'd like, we could meet for a beer," Abby finished as Jesse was gazing at this gorgeous creature.

"Uh, yeah, that sounds good. What's your phone number?" he asked while still looking at the girl—woman—that just walked in.

She was dressed plainly in worn Levi's, nothing fancy, no holes, no bling butt. White converse sneakers, no socks, and a white T-shirt with a left front pocket that was mostly covered up by her long, brunette hair.

How does someone look so good without trying? Jesse asked himself.

"Come on in," Abby greeted warmly. "Sit right here, please." She pointed to the chair next to Jesse. The girl glanced at Jesse but only fleetingly, handed Abby a clipboard with her paperwork filled out, and sat down.

"Thank you…uh…" She paused briefly to look at the form on the clipboard. "Celia. Thank you for volunteering to give blood. I understand this is your first time, so don't be too nervous."

"I am not nervous." As she replied, a pair of simple silver bangles tinkled near her wrist as a slightly shaking hand reached up and tucked the long hair behind her left ear, exposing a simple silver post earring.

Jesse watched as Abby started looking in drawers, then looked over her workstation, then checked the other drawers.

"Whatcha looking for?" Jesse asked.

"Um, I use special needles for first time donors, but I can't find any here," Abby replied. "Celia, I'm so sorry to make you wait. I need to grab some more supplies, so I'll be right back. Is that okay?"

"Not a problem," Celia answered and quickly tried to smile and said, "I mean, yes."

Wow, what a gorgeous smile. Why do you hide it? Jesse wondered.

Jesse smiled his most disarming smile, but Celia didn't take notice. Instead, she appeared to be concentrating on her smart watch as it started to beep an alarm. Jesse peered over and saw that she was watching the heartbeat symbol flashing.

So, you're not nervous, huh? Jesse thought with a quiet chuckle. At that rate, the poor girl is going to keel over right here.

He surveyed her face again. "Hey, don't I know you?"

Celia didn't respond.

"Yeah, now I know. Didn't I see you at Jenny's baby shower at the Cabin?

Still no response.

"Come on, wasn't it you that helped Jenny clean up the mess of egg yolks and stuff off the floor?"

Her gaze swiveled his way, almost imperceptibly before she looked away again.

"Yeah, I knew it. You work at Maria's, right?"

She finally glanced over. "Yes, I do."

"Yeah, and it was you that got mad at me for snooping in the kitchen?"

Celia looked directly at him for the first time. Recognition passed across her face. Even with her naturally olive skin, he could see a blush moving up her cheeks.

"I…I am so sorry about that," she stammered and looked away. "I should not have slapped your hand."

Jesse noticed that, as her nervousness grew, her accent increased dramatically, rolling her *r*'s even harder than before. "Hey, no worries. I probably had it coming," he replied, trying to set her at ease.

The smart watch began to beep even louder.

"Um, you might want to relax a little," he offered.

She licked her lips and tried to stifle the sound coming from her wrist by covering it with her other hand.

Jesse hopped up and grabbed a dixie cup from the dispenser, filled it with water and held it out to her. At first, she looked up at him with wariness in her eyes, but then took the cup from his hand and emptied it. "Thank you."

"Would you like a refill?" he asked.

"Yes, I would." She looked up at him and added, "Please."

He took the cup from her, refilled it, and gave it back to her.

Jesse was accustomed to most women throwing themselves at him. This one was a bit different. *No, this one was a lot different. Is that good or bad?*

"So, what do you do for fun?" he asked, trying to lighten the mood a little.

"I don't. I owe everything to Maria. I work and I run. Nothing else." Her voice had dropped back into her previous flat staccato.

"Are you kidding me?" Jesse asked. "Isn't that like being an indentured servant?"

"No," she replied curtly. "Maria has been like a mother to me. Better than a mother. I do it because I love her and where she goes, I will go, and whatever she needs I will find. I don't need anything else."

Wow, hit a hot button. That was some serious emotion there.

Slightly shifting the topic, he asked, "So you like to run, huh? Who do you like to run with? A boyfriend?"

"No one. I run alone," she stated without any hint of passion or inflection.

"Is it safe for you to run alone?" Jesse asked, then pushed on before she could answer. "Don't get me wrong, Williston's a nice town and all, but with all the oil workers here, it could be dangerous. You know, nothing but roughnecks and roustabouts around here," he trailed off with a shrug of his shoulders.

This time she actually chuckled. "I'm not stupid. I do not run in foolish places, but if it comes down to it, I am certainly capable of taking care of myself." Her heavy accent relaxed a little.

The confidence in her voice was authentic, not false bravado nor pretense. *Who is this girl?* "Well, just the same, maybe I should go running with you?" he probed.

She offered up a patronizing, and nearly condescending, smile. The same smile that an adult might give a little kid wanting to go *hike* up Mount Everest.

Abby pushed open the door with her hip as she entered the lab with an armload of miscellaneous supplies. Jesse stepped over and opened the door fully for her. "Thank you, Jesse," she said as she dropped the plastic covered items onto the stainless-steel cart.

Celia turned to Abby and said, "I am ready," then turned to Jesse almost as an afterthought and said, "You couldn't keep up anyway."

"Couldn't keep up?" Jesse mimicked. "You mean on a run? I'm just afraid I'd have to slow down for *you*."

He saw it suddenly flash across her face. It looked something like... *Challenge accepted.*

"Fine. Seven o'clock Sunday morning," she said, returning to her staccato cadence. Looking him up and down, she continued with a certain amount of derision in her voice, "That is, if you can get out of bed that early."

"Sweetheart, I was born early," Jesse said arrogantly. It wasn't until the last words escaped his lips that he realized how stupid they sounded, but he bulldozed forward anyway. "Where do we meet?"

"Spring Lake Park. At the old mill water wheel if you can find it." She glowered.

"I'll be there, sweetheart." Without another word, he reached over, jerked open the door, and exited with the last word.

Exactly what just happened? he thought as he strode down the hallway toward the door.

CHAPTER EIGHTEEN

A quick knock sounded on Jenny's hospital room door, catching Seth's attention. But before he could respond, Link walked in with Victoria right behind him. He had a very satisfied look on his face and just a bit of swagger in his step.

"We've got good news on the blood donor front," Link said with a big grin.

"What is it?" asked Seth. He was sitting in a chair next to Jenny. "Can they use your blood after all?" Seth asked the question with a touch of desperation. Seth looked at Jenny as he took her hand in his. She briefly opened her eyes and then closed them again.

"Well, in a manner of speaking, yes," Link stated, his thumbs hooked in his belt loops.

Victoria elbowed Link.

"Really?" Seth's desperation melted into relief.

"Yup, two units of whole blood," Link said.

"It's on the way up as we speak," Victoria added before Link could make another comment.

Seth looked back at Jenny as she opened her eyes and gave a wan smile. She looked pale and frail but happy all at the same time.

"Why are both of you grinning like you have a secret?" she asked with a little crackle in her voice.

"What secret are you referring to?" Link asked, impersonating an innocent child.

"I may be weak and half-conscious, but I can still tell that you are smiling big for a reason." As she tried to sit up, Seth jumped to his feet to help her sit up and quickly stuffed pillows behind her. He touched her cheek, and she smiled but closed her eyes again.

Victoria walked around to the other side of Jenny's bed and took Jenny's hand. "You see, Honey, it's Link's blood, but it's not Link's blood."

"What do you mean?" Seth asked as Link cocked a hip and leaned against the wall, looking delighted. Victoria smiled over at Link.

"Go ahead, tell 'em," Link said. Again, like a little kid.

"Well, it appears that Link and his son Jesse have the same blood type."

"He's down at the lab right now," Link blurted out, obviously unable to contain himself any longer. The pride in his voice was unmistakable.

"We'll have you up and holding your babies in no time," Victoria beamed.

"But wait? You said two units of whole blood. Jesse can't give two, can he? Are we still using yours?" asked Seth, both hopeful and bewildered.

"Nope, we also have a unit of whole blood type AB negative," Link said

"Whose?"

"Celia," Victoria chimed in.

"Maria's Celia?" Seth asked.

"No. My Celia." Link said under his breath, causing Victoria to look up at him knowingly.

"What? Wait, I don't understand either," Jenny said, barely keeping her eyes open for the moment.

As Jenny spoke, Seth watched Victoria as she looked down at the hospital tray table. It had a water pitcher, a pink plastic drinking mug with a straw, some leftover green Jell-O and some ice cubes in a small, clear juice cup. Next to the array lay two sheets of paper, side by side, face down. The sheets were onion skin parchment and had scallops on the edges.

"Are those documents what I think they are?" Victoria asked. Her question caused Link to push away from the wall and peer in the direction Victoria was pointing.

"Yes," Seth replied. "That is, if you are thinking that those might be birth certificates." He wore a big smile of his own as he looked back at Jenny. He reached out and tenderly stroked her cheek.

"Well, what do they say?" Link said, impatiently.

"We don't know," the two new parents said in unison. Jenny mustered enough strength for another smile.

"What do you mean you don't know what they say?" Link snorted. "Are you telling me you haven't decided yet?"

"No, no. We've definitely decided. It's just that we agreed that Jenny had the privilege to name the first born, and I got to name the second. We both filled out the girls' birth certificates and we were just about to show each other when we were rudely interrupted," Seth replied with a grin and a nod in Link's direction.

"Well, I can help you flip those over if you need me to," Link offered as he reached for the two sheets of parchment.

"No, it's okay," Seth shouted but it was too late. Link had already scooped them up and was staring at the names written in very different handwriting. He smiled as he read. Seth watched his eyes move across the papers from one to the other. He looked up at Seth and Jenny, then over to Victoria, but no words came out. Misty-eyed, he swallowed hard.

Link is speechless, Seth thought. Victoria was already looking over Link's shoulder and silently reading them for herself. She looked up at Link and then back to Seth and Jenny. Her blue eyes too, had taken on a brilliant shine.

Jenny looked at Seth for a moment and then spoke. "Link, would you please read our daughters names aloud?" Her voice cracked again as she leaned her head on Seth's arm.

Link sniffed and quickly wiped his eyes. "Stupid allergies."

"Go on, honey," Victoria prodded "Read them."

"I..." Link paused and coughed. "I proudly..." He stopped once more and sniffed for a second time. Took a deep breath, held both certificates side by side and started to speak clearly. "I proudly present the beautiful princesses, Faith Olivia Reagan and Hope Jennifer Reagan." He paused for a moment. "I am *so* going to spoil these kids totally rotten." He laughed again and wiped away the incriminating evidence of a tear.

Seth looked at Jenny in surprise as they blurted out together, "I love those names." A massive lump formed in Seth's throat. *How is it possible to turn such pain into so much joy?* Even the thought of Olivia brought thoughts of pride and joy. *My darling Olivia, I pray that you are truly dancing in heaven.*

"But wait. Who's who?" Victoria asked.

"The first born was Betty," Seth said. "The second was Veronica."

"Betty and Veronica?" Jenny asked, a bit bewildered.

"Oh yeah, honey, I forgot to tell you. When the first baby born was our little blonde and the second was our tiny brunette, at least for now, the NICU needed a quick way to refer to them both, so they assigned them temporary names. Betty and Veronica."

* * * * *

With both Jesse and Celia's blood now coursing through her body, Jenny was beginning to feel much better. She could sit up in bed by herself, and the ICU nurse had removed all monitoring devices and oxygen tubes from her body before moving her out of ICU and into a lovely room painted in pink and blue pastels of the maternity ward. Except for the IV drip still giving her fluids, she felt free. It was a double room that could be separated by a curtain, but the other bed had recently been emptied. Jenny looked at the clock on the wall of her hospital room, trying desperately to will the time to go faster. The anticipation was killing her. She stared at the door for what seemed like an eternity, then down at her own small, pale hands. They were shaking a little and her heart seemed to be beating crazy fast. So fast, in fact, that she could feel it thump in her chest, right next to the deep, unimaginable ache. The wait was killing her. At any moment, her two babies would be coming through that door, and she would get to meet them and hold them for the first time.

Faith and Hope. Jenny thought of Olivia's letter. *Faith and Hope.* She started to tear up but quickly wiped the droplet from her cheek and peered at the clock, giving it a glare.

A loud knock on the door caused her head to snap back from the clock, and she blurted out, "Come in. Come in!"

Before the second *come in* was out of her mouth, the door opened. Craning her neck to see, Jenny's first glimpse was the backside of Ivy in her scrubs, pulling a large cart with Seth pushing from the other end. Just before the door closed, Link and Victoria slid in behind them. On the cart was an incubator with a small bed enclosed by clear, hard plastic. Name tapes were stuck to the sides. In black magic marker, one had Veronica, 5.1 pounds and the other, Betty, 5.6 pounds. Betty's tape end was rolling up as if it had been pulled from somewhere else and re-applied to Veronica's bed.

Barely able to contain herself, Jenny reached out and begged, "Please give me my babies?"

"Absolutely," Ivy answered. "But before that happens, let me catch you up on what these two have been up to."

"Yes, please," Jenny said while staring at her two brand new babies through the plastic.

"Faith is holding her temperature and Hope is trying to catch up. Your precious Faith is already acting like a big sister. The temperature in the incubator is controlled to keep your baby's body temperature where it should be. We can care for babies through these holes in the sides of the incubator until they are strong enough to spend time out in the open. We still need to keep them warm. We've turned up the temperature here in your room to accommodate them spending time outside their little plastic bubble."

"What do you mean when you said Faith was already acting like a big sister?"

"Well, as you know, Hope was struggling. She couldn't maintain her temperature; she was having difficulty breathing and an irregular heartbeat. Faith, on the other hand, just seemed to be royally pissed off, but other than screaming her head off, she was doing fine. When we put Faith in with Hope, Faith settled down and put her arm around Hope. Hope's breathing became rhythmic and normal, her temperature began to stabilize, and they both developed an appetite."

"That's my girls," Link quipped.

"What?" Seth started to argue, but then saw Link wipe his eyes with his sleeve. "I guess you can claim partial credit."

"I don't care who wants the credit," Jenny exclaimed in exasperation. "I just want to hold my babies,"

"Coming right up," Ivy said as she opened the incubator and gently lifted out Hope first and brought her to Jenny. Almost immediately, Faith started yelling, but as soon as both babies were snuggled into Momma's arms, they quieted down. "Aren't they wonderful?" Jenny cooed, looking from one child to the other. "This is even better than I could have ever imagined." The touch and smell of her newborn daughters struck her with the raw emotion that only a mother could know. It flowed through her being like music, filling every remaining void in her life before welling up in her eyes and spilling freely down her cheeks. She breathed deeply, filling her lungs as a surge of renewed strength invigorated her, bringing the tears to an end, replaced by something else. Pure, unadulterated joy. She couldn't help herself. She giggled as she nuzzled Faith and Hope. *Thank you, Jesus,* she whispered.

Victoria moved to her side and gently stroked Jenny's hair. Jenny looked up at Victoria and then at the rest of the room and laughed out loud. Hers was the only dry eye to be found at the moment.

"Will you just look at yourselves?" she said to the crowd around her, but she was looking directly at Link.

"Shut up," Link demanded like a child. "It's just allergies." His voice held no conviction as he wiped his eyes with his sleeve. Jenny looked at Seth who seemed to be struggling for words, any words at the moment. He looked at her and swallowed hard. His big hand rested on her arm, but no words came out. Jenny smiled; the look in his eyes said all that was necessary.

Silence fell over the room for a long moment as she soaked in everything.

"Jenny," Ivy whispered as she stood at the foot of Jenny's bed, "right now, this very instant, our Olivia is thanking Jesus and dancing for joy in heaven."

"Aww," the sound, escaping from her very soul as she pictured Olivia dancing in her mind. Her lips began to quiver.

"And, honey," Victoria said, "your momma is so proud of you."

That did it. Jenny lost it all over again, taking the entire room with her.

Jenny closed her eyes for just a moment, but then struggled to drag them back open.

"Are you okay?" Ivy asked, giving her a quick once over. "Are you in pain?"

Jenny smiled again as her eyelids involuntarily began to droop. "Yeah, I'm fine," she replied. "No pain. I'm just feeling a little tired is all."

"Hey, Jenny. How about giving Uncle Link and Aunt Victoria a chance to get to know these two little miracles?" Link asked as he walked over to Jenny's bed, holding out his arms.

Jenny smiled. "Probably not a good idea to argue with uncle Link."

"Yes!" Link chortled. "Did everyone take note of that? Great advice," he said as he hoisted the five-pound little Hope from her mama's arms.

"Please don't encourage this type of behavior," Victoria begged as she lifted Faith and cradled the blonde little girl in her arms. "Is that a touch of red in her hair?" she asked, looking closer.

"I do believe it is," Jenny sighed with satisfaction.

Seth watched them for a moment and then turned back to Jenny. "Honey, are you sure you're okay?"

"Yes. I am totally fine," Jenny said as she tried to sit up a little straighter. "Seth, I want to start a tradition today."

"Okay?" Seth said, looking a bit bewildered. "Like what?"

"Victoria, did you get a chance to swing by the cabin and pick up that item for me?" Jenny asked.

"I certainly did." Victoria reached into her purse and pulled out a dog-eared book and handed it to her.

She opened the book and found a crisply folded piece of stationary and opened it too. She cleared her throat before beginning.

> *"My darling girls, Faith and Hope, every year on your birthday, we will read this letter together. It is from your other mommy, so you will always know how much you are loved by her."* She cleared her throat once again and began to read.
>
> *"To my hope and my love.*
>
> *"I don't know when you will finally arrive, only God knows, and I trust in that. But, when you do get here, you will find yourself surrounded by love, steeped in Faith and Hope. While I wait for you, I am preparing a wonderful garden for you. I dream of you, playing in the warm spring sunshine with flowers and our family apple tree blooming all around you. There is even a robin's nest in a tree for us to wonder at.*
>
> *"I pray for you every single day. Mommy and Daddy are working very hard to help you find your way home, although you have already found your way into our hearts.*
>
>

"Love always, Mommy.

"From the desk of Olivia Reagan."

CHAPTER NINETEEN

"**I** guess this is as good a time as any to bring this up." Seth said, tossing the comment into the room like a grenade.

"Uh, Seth," Link intoned, "Trust me, that's the wrong way to bring up any subject. It puts everyone on their guard."

"Well, here goes anyway." Seth forged ahead. "Jenny, I think we need to hire an au pair."

"No, we don't," came an instant, firm reply.

"See," Link chimed in, "I told you."

"I agree with Jenny," Victoria stated, coming to Jenny's rescue. "I can help her with the twins whenever Seth is off working."

"Are you going to live with us?" Seth asked with a touch of sarcasm. "When can you move in?"

Link jumped back in. "How is it going to work with not one but two midnight fussy, colicky babies? And..." he paused for a moment, "...it may have been a long time ago, but if I remember right, it's hard enough to catch a little nap when one is sleeping but I can imagine that one will be asleep and the other will want to eat or be changed? You'd have to move in with them full time to give her the kind of help she's going to need."

"Honey, you're completely exhausted as it is," Seth said. "Don't forget you have a good deal of healing to do as well. It will take you quite a while to get fully on your feet."

"With an au pair, you can get more rest and actually heal faster," Link added.

"Yeah, and it still doesn't stop Victoria from helping as much as she wants," Seth interjected.

Victoria's eyes narrowed a bit. "Did you two characters rehearse this before you got here?"

Link shrugged. "We, the accused, can neither confirm nor deny whatever it is that you may..."

"...or may not..." Seth piped in.

"...yeah, or may not be attempting to imply."

"Yeah, what he just said," Seth concluded, jabbing a thumb in Link's direction.

Jenny looked at Victoria for support.

"I really hate to admit it, but they just unloaded a lot of good points," Victoria conceded.

"So, what do we have to do to find an au pair?" Victoria asked. "Look in the yellow pages?"

"Funny you should ask," Seth said with a grin that had canary feathers all over it. "Link, would you be so kind as to open the door and invite her in?"

"But of course."

"Are you kidding me?" Victoria asked.

"We put Ty to work doing all the research and background checks," Seth said proudly.

"But we don't know enough about her," Victoria stated.

"We know more about her than we knew about Jenny when she arrived," Link said, clearly sitting at the table for Seth's defense.

"That's different," Victoria countered.

"Oh, just let her in," Jenny said with exasperation. "I can't believe you did this without us discussing it first."

Link opened the door and stood ramrod straight.

"May I present, Miss Taylor Hansen. Early Childhood Development major at North Dakota State, great cook, and all-around nice person who loves babies."

Taylor stepped nervously inside and was instantly surrounded. Standing there, in the middle of Jenny's hospital room was a five-foot five-inch brunette with a cute bob. Dressed as if she was going to a very important interview, wearing black slacks, a white top and black heels. Her studious brown eyes were covered with a pair of wire rimmed glasses, very little makeup, and for jewelry, only a pair of small pearl studs.

"When can you start?" Jenny asked with narrowed eyes and without preamble.

With a nod from Link, Taylor cleared her throat. "Ma'am, I'll be done with the spring semester in a few days so from what Mr. Reagan tells me, that should be about the time that you expect to take the babies home. I'll get credit for working with you all and the twins for next semester as well. That is, if you decide to keep me. I will be writing papers and such, but I don't think it will interfere with caring for the girls. In fact, if it's okay, I'd like to start coming by in the evenings and get to know them and get to know you better too, Miss Jenny."

Jenny's furrowed brow relaxed. At first, she tossed a glare in Seth and Link's direction, then sighed a sigh of resignation and said, "Thank you."

"No fight is too great, and nothing is too good for my daughters," Seth stated. "We all won today."

"Speaking of daughters," Victoria said, looking straight at Link. "Don't you think it's time to go back to Maria's?"

Link jammed his hands deep in his pockets, rolled his shoulders forward and sucked in a deep breath before speaking. "Mrs. James, I *do* believe it is."

* * * * *

Celia looked up from opening a bottle of bud light. *He's here, he's really here.* She thought. Her hand began to tremble as she watched Link and Victoria come through the front door. She had to place the bottle on the bar before she spilled it. Last time, when Link had left in a hurry, she thought she'd lost her chance, but here he was again. She watched as Maria greeted them before they all sat down, ignoring the drink requests down the bar while opening a bottle of Blue Moon and mixing a Moscow Mule. Their usual.

Celia had answered the phone when Victoria had just called for reservations a few minutes ago. She was the one that grabbed the 'Reserved for Link' card from the kitchen and placed it on their customary table. It was strange—she had placed that card on that same table so many times before, but this time it felt different. She had held it in her hands for a time, flipping the card before reading it yet again. *RESERVED FOR LINK. Could he be the answer to my questions? To my nightmares?*

All these years he's been giving me the space so I wouldn't be afraid of him, waiting patiently. Her thoughts continued to tumble out, unabated. *He never gave up on me. He's the one responsible for bringing me to America. After all this time, I now understand why he always looked after me. He's probably the only reason why I'm even alive today. What must he think of me?*

Maria looked up and made eye contact with Celia, waving her over. Celia bit her lip as she placed the drinks on a tray and walked around the end of the bar. Gone was the stoic look and self confidence that she carried on the outside for the rest of the world to see. Replaced now with a combination of nerves and fear, but also hope.

Instead of confidently balancing the tray over her head with one hand as she normally did, she now held it in front of her with two shaking hands. As Celia approached, Link pulled out a chair for her. Without a word, she placed the tray carefully on the table and sat down. She didn't take her eyes off of him, and they just peered at one another. Link swallowed hard, and his jaw was set firm as if he was holding back some great tidal wave of emotion.

"I'm so sorry," Celia burst out with tear-brimmed eyes. "I'm so sorry for what I did to you."

"You're sorry?" Link asked, his eyes wide. "*Misu*, you have done nothing to be sorry for. I'm the one who so stupidly frightened you. No, I terrified you. Though I never meant to hurt you in a million years." He reached for her hand.

She nodded knowingly and sucked in a shaky breath. "Um, I vaguely remember some things. They get all mixed up, and I don't know what is real and what is merely torment from my nightmares."

"You were such a young, innocent girl," Link said, brushing a wisp of hair from her green eyes. You were my little mouse."

Celia laughed and cried at the same time.

As they talked, Maria pulled something out of her pocket and held it in both hands. "I've saved this for so long, I was afraid I'd lost it." She sniffed. "I always prayed that one day you two would be able to have this conversation."

It was an old, stained, color photograph with rounded corners and one edge slightly rolled. She set it down and slid it, face up onto the table between them. Link and Celia both cocked their heads and looked down at it together.

"Is that me?" Celia asked. her heart beating wildly in her chest.

"Yes. Yes, it is," Maria confirmed. "And that guy, still with some hair, who's lap you are sitting on, is Link."

It pictured a much younger Link, sitting on an old bench wearing a flight suit. A small girl with a little white flower in her dark unruly hair was sitting on his lap while tugging a Hershey's chocolate bar out of his zippered pocket. *Little Mouse & Tata* was scrawled on the back of the photo.

Suddenly, Celia could see the flower, but it was not in her hair but tucked into Link's pocket. "It *was* you," she blurted. Her eyes, sparkled and shiny, as the flood of emotions began to flow through her, "You brought me the little white flowers. I remember now. You would have it sticking out of a pocket and that's how I knew where the chocolate bar would be." *and then you would put it in my hair...*

Link beamed and nodded his head. Unable to speak words but the tenderness glowed in his shiny eyes.

"That was *the* day," Maria said.

"What day?" Celia asked, sniffing, looking from Link to Maria.

The flicker in Link's eyes told the story.

"That was the day you asked Link to be your Daddy," Maria said.

Link wiped his nose on a paper napkin "You would gobble down that chocolate bar like there was no tomorrow," he said, his focus obviously locked more onto the picture in his mind than the one in front of them. "I loved to see your sweet little face all covered with chocolate." He smiled at Celia. "You were a very messy eater."

Celia reached for Link's hand and brought it to her cheek. "*Bi li i dalje moj tata?*"

"*Nikad nizam prestao.*" He stood up and kissed the top of her head. Then pulled her up out of the chair and wrapped his arms around her.

Afraid to break the moment, Victoria whispered to Maria, "What did they say?"

"Would you still be my daddy? And he said, "I never stopped."

* * * * *

It was dark, and a light rain began as they left Maria's. On the drive home, Link was quiet. The only sound was the windshield wipers intermittently sweeping away the rain drops, clearing Link's vision. Victoria watched him operate the truck in full autopilot as he sped up then slowed or stopped for lights before continuing. She was trying to imagine what was going through his mind, or more likely, his heart. He wasn't sad or angry. He wasn't jumping for joy either, but what? She reached over and gently stroked his arm. *Deep contemplation of memories that were locked in a box and long buried?* she supposed. *And now, with the locks busted off, those memories are suddenly laid bare in the sunlight once again.* Memories filled with joy and pain, but perhaps, no longer in equal measure.

"This was quite an amazing night," Victoria said casually, finally breaking the silence.

Link briefly glanced at her without saying anything before turning back to the road.

"You, Mr. James, have your daughter back," Victoria said as she slid her fingers between his.

She was rewarded by the slightest of smiles.

"Do you want to talk about it?"

Link glanced at her again. "No," he said, his jaw set briefly. Then after a short while of continued silence, he spoke again. "Well, maybe yes, but are you sure you want to hear it?"

"Lincoln James, if you've lived through it, then I want to hear it. The good, the bad and the ugly. I want to help." Victoria's voice told of both anger and steadfast love. *Please talk to me my love…* She begged silently.

Link glanced at her again, as if he considered her words. Then, he started talking in a very detached voice.

"Celia told me it was early in the morning when the soldiers came to their home. One of them was a sixteen-year-old neighbor boy who lived just down the road. He went to school with her fourteen-year-old brother, Luka. These soldiers busted down the door and came into their home, yelling and screaming at the whole family, but she didn't understand what was happening. Luka jumped out of the window of their old house and ran through the small family vineyard for the safety of the forest. But the bastard neighbor boy, older and faster, chased him down and slit his throat right next to the pig sty and left him there. The other soldiers were laughing and slapping him on the back for a job well done as her family was forced to watch.

"Her young mind could not understand what was happening to them. Then the soldiers shot her father right in front of them and herded her mother, her, and her older sister back into the house and into her parents' bedroom, laughing."

Link paused so long that she wondered if he decided the story was too hard to tell.

"They were taken to a resort hotel compound. She told me soldiers visited often. Her mother and sister were eventually murdered there at the compound and dumped, with a lot of others, in the river. Celia said she saw it from the window, and that she couldn't wait to join them."

Victoria looked out the window and realized they had passed their turn off, but Link just continued to drive, fully on autopilot. The rain was heavier now, and the wipers moved faster to keep the windshield clear.

"My group was assigned a project to find the general responsible for shelling innocent civilians. Intelligence had him at that compound. We went in with several helicopters and took the compound. While we were searching room by room, I opened a door and saw our target on top of this terrified little girl, and I just lost it. I grabbed him from behind and pulled him off of her, sticking my knife where it would do the most good. Afterwards, I looked at this poor, half starved little girl on this filthy bed."

Link paused and glanced at Victoria as if silently asking, Are you sure? before continuing. "She was so scared and, as I approached her, she scampered backwards against the wall. I sat quietly with her for a couple of minutes when I remembered I had a chocolate bar in the cargo pocket of my flight suit. I offered her some chocolate, and she eventually trusted me enough to let me pick her up. I wrapped her in a dirty blanket and brought her out to my helicopter and flew her to safety. She was sitting with my crew chief when we started taking some small arms fire. A bullet hole opened up in the belly of the helicopter, and I was suddenly so afraid that she might be hit, but she wasn't. I finally got her to Maria's place on the coast where she would be safe." Link paused again.

"She didn't know how old she was or even what her birthday was. Maria and I, we guessed around seven, maybe as old as nine. Maria decided to pick the day that I found her as her birthday." Link let loose an unexpected chuckle. "Later on, it made it very difficult for her to immigrate. We had to get real creative with the paperwork, but I called in a few favors and it all worked out."

Victoria put out her hand and tenderly touched Link's cheek.

"Now she's grown up but still fighting a war that has been over for a long time," Link said, his jaw set and tight, once again.

She sensed that this was as desperately needed for him as much as it was for Celia. And for the first time, Victoria felt that she might be able to say something without interrupting. "This is a good start toward healing for her. And for you, my love. She's got her *Tata* back."

"God answers prayers," Link said softly. It was dark so she couldn't see his face clearly, but Victoria heard the crack in his voice.

"But," Victoria began, an impish smirk on her lips, "you've got to admit something else."

"Admit what?" Link asked, brows knitted, suddenly on guard.

"Whenever you used the term Tata in the past, you weren't thinking of you," she said, testing to see if he'd laugh at her joke.

He did.

"If God can help *you*, my love, he certainly can help her as well," Victoria said as she slid her hand back inside the safety of his.

CHAPTER TWENTY

Look what just walked in, Brooke thought. It was Saturday night and Brooke was working on her second beer of the evening at Maria's Restaurant & Bar when Jesse James came strolling into the place. Brooke was seated in her favorite perch at the bar where she could see everyone who came through the door. She wasn't expecting to see anything worth going after tonight, so she wasn't really decked out for 'hunting'. *But how circumstances can change. Well, at least I'm wearing my new sexy jeans*, Brooke thought. They were tight and followed all of her curves perfectly. She knew most guys couldn't get enough of all those accidental rips and tears. *They better look, cost me a hundred bucks.* Her secret weapon though, was the one hole she had torn herself. It was high on her hip so guys could get a peek of her tattoo and... other possibilities. A wolfish smile spread across her face. *Yes, the possibilities.* Luckily, the top she had thrown on was a teal V-neck lantern shirt. During the day, she could get away with it looking somewhat modest, but with the right adjustment, it could turn into pure heat. She took a long pull on her beer as she considered the night's change in potential.

"Hmm, so, this is the newest, most eligible bachelor in the Bakken that everyone is talking about?" she said to the grizzled drunk seated next to her. "I can see why." She took a swig without taking her sights off of him as he made his way through the crowd. He wore a well fitting, black T-shirt that showed off his biceps, work boots, and rock revival jeans that fit way too good.

She unconsciously fanned herself.

Honey blond hair snuck out from under his ball cap, giving her a glimpse of the soft curls hidden beneath, and something inside her pulsed when she noticed the two-day old stubble. *My, oh my.*

Celia and a part-timer named Jacob were both working behind the bar. The green-eyed transplant's beautiful olive skin, long, dark hair and eastern European accent kept most of the male patrons begging for her attention. At first, Brooke viewed her allure as competition. But after a while, she realized Celia never gave an inch. Ever. She acted like she was too good for anyone in this town and anything they might consider fun.

"Are you ready for another one?" Celia asked over the noisy crowd.

Brooke tore her gaze from her new primary target and looked at Celia. "I'll tell you what; when I'm ready for another, I'll be sure and let you know." She let her disdain drip off each word.

Brooke took a swig of her beer and looked back at Celia smugly, but something had changed. Celia looked like a deer in the headlights. Her eyes were totally frozen, locked onto something. She looked in the direction of Celia's gaze and her eyes narrowed. *She's staring at Jesse, too.* But then, Celia spun to her left and quickly stepped over to Jake and whispered something in his ear. He nodded and headed down to Celia's end of the bar and she to his. *Interesting,*

Brooke thought. *Good taste, but totally out of her league and she knows it. Poor girl.*

It was a busy night at Maria's, so it was something short of a miracle that there were still a couple of seats left available anywhere at the long, dark wood bar. The band hadn't started yet, so the noise was only of patrons having conversations up and down the line of stools. Others were sitting and standing at the tall tables scattered randomly about the old wooden plank floor.

There was one empty stool next to Brooke, and the other vacancy was only three stools away. She quickly tugged down at the front of her shirt for maximum cleavage, ran her tongue across her white teeth then swiveled toward Jesse on her barstool and flashed him all her wattage while pointing to the empty chair. He didn't seem to notice her as he neared the bar. Thinking quickly, she pulled the scrunchy from her ponytail and tossed her hair and let it tumble down her shoulders, hoping that would get his attention. Somehow, his crystal blue eyes, fringed in the longest eyelashes she'd ever seen, would not lock onto her.

What is wrong with him?

As he approached the only other empty stool, he raised his hand to catch the bartender's attention and took a seat. Glancing to his left, he nodded and touched the brim of his hat as a way of saying hello to his seat neighbor. Tiffany was a couple years younger than Brooke and a triple threat. She was brunette, built and beautiful, and tonight she was definitely dressed for the hunt in her trusty Little Black Dress.

"Hello there, stranger," Tiffany greeted Jesse with a dazzling smile, showing off her expensive dentistry. "What's your name?"

Ammatuer, Brooke brooded.

"Jesse."

"Jesse? That's a nice name. Jesse what?" she asked with just the slightest slur in her voice as she tossed her mane. *She's pulling out all the stops.*

"You wouldn't believe me even if I told you," he answered, grinning as he rested his elbows on the bar.

"Sure, I would," she countered as she traced the top of her MGD with the tip of her finger. "Why wouldn't I?"

"Because most people don't."

"Try me," she insisted as she began peeling off the label of her sweating beer bottle.

"Okay then. My name is Jesse James."

"No. You're kidding me, right?"

"See, I told you that you wouldn't believe me." He gave a knowing smile and glanced around the bar.

He has the nicest dimple when he smiles.

Jacob stepped up, interrupting the conversation, inclined his head and asked, "What'll it be?"

Jesse was still looking around the room when he heard the question and quickly turned back toward the bartender.

"Corona," Jesse replied. That was always his knee jerk order wherever he went. As he looked at the bottles of alcohol on the top shelf behind the bartender, suddenly his eyes brightened and added, "Oh, and a shot of that Cincoro Tequila please." He turned on his seat and started scanning the crowd again.

"Blanco or the Anejo?" Jacob asked, causing him to turn back around.

"Uh, blanco, *por favor*," Jesse answered with an exaggerated Mexican accent.

"Salt and Lime?"

"Uh, no. Wait. Actually, yes, but just lime in the Corona."

"Gotcha," Jacob replied. "Coming right up."

Brooke quickly raised her hand, calling in a sing-song voice, "Hey, Jake."

Jacob looked in her direction. "Oh, Brooke. Are you ready for another one now? I heard what you said to Celia."

"Oh, I was just teasing," she said as she leaned forward on her elbows. She knew the move would show off her ample cleavage for anyone to see who might be looking down the bar. "Uhm, I'll have what he's having."

Jake looked in the direction she was pointing "On the prowl again, huh."

"Maybe," she replied slyly.

"Coming right up."

Brooke watched Jake as he brought her drink order. He glanced at Tiffany sitting next to Jesse as he passed them by. Placing the Corona and the shot of Cincoro on the bar in front of Brooke, he leaned in and said. "Not a chance, Sweetheart."

Brooke ignored Jake but instead, watched intently as Jesse picked up the Cincoro and took a sip of the clear liquid instead of shooting it like regular tequila. He pulled the tequila away from his lips and held that shot glass out as if to examine it more closely. Then took another stronger sip and set it down on the bar and picked up his Corona. After deftly stuffing the thick slice of lime down the narrow neck of the beer bottle, he took a pull on it then set it down on the bar next to the shot glass with a satisfied look. Meanwhile, Tiffany was talking a mile a minute, trying to capture his attention.

Good luck, Brooke thought, staring at the back of Tiffany's deep brunette hair. *Your little naked-shoulder black dress won't be enough. Not for him.* She glowered. *Just keep talking. You're digging yourself a nice little hole.* She mused.

Jesse continued to scan the crowd every few minutes and then turned back to face Tiffany as she continued to talk.

He's definitely looking for someone else, Tiff. It could be me? Brooke supposed. He'd nod his head from time to time but really didn't say much. *I'm not worried,* Brooke told herself. That was until something that Tiffany said made him laugh right in the middle of taking a swig from his beer. He slammed his beer back down on the bar, trying not to spew the contents of his mouth. In doing so, he accidentally spilled beer on himself and Tiffany, plus spilling *her* drink to boot. Laughing, Tiffany seized the moment and grabbed a bar towel from Jake and proceeded to dab at the beer on Jesse's well-defined chest. He apologized profusely for spilling Tiffany's drink and ordered her another from Jake, for which she also requested a Cincoro, rocks.

In an instant, a switch flipped inside Brooke as she watched the scene unfold. Something went numb inside. Or maybe, it just went back to *her* normal. She stood up, straightened her top and bundled her hair back into the scrunchy. Reaching for her glass, she downed her tequila, paid her bar tab, and headed for the door, leaving the Corona half empty. As she passed by Jesse, she brushed him, hoping. He glanced at her, holding his gaze for just a moment before he answered his ringing cell phone. She slowed her walk toward the door even more and glanced back, delivering her best, ravishing smile, but Tiffany put her hand on his arm, bringing his attention off of Brooke and back to her as he spoke on the phone.

Bad move, Tiff. Bad move.

Hanging up and laughing at whatever she said, he shook his head and reached for his beer. Standing up, he finished it off with one long pull and placed the empty back on the bar. Jesse held up his hand in a wave and in one fluid motion, he turned and headed for the door.

After Brooke exited the bar, she stepped into the shadows, hoping that Jesse had followed her out. Jesse went right past her, heading for his truck with long, booted strides.

She was just stepping off to catch up to him when Tiffany came running past in her heels.

"Hey, Jesse. Wait up," Tiffany called across the parking lot.

"*Well, Tiff. Aren't you just a little unsteady in those heels?*" Brooke thought. *You really shouldn't drink so much. It's downright unhealthy.*

Jesse had the truck door closed and the diesel engine started before Tiffany reached the pickup.

"What's the hurry?" she said with a pout on her lips. When he just looked at her and smiled, she motioned for him to roll down his window.

Jesse complied but shook his head. "Look, uh, Tiffany, it was nice meeting you tonight, but I've got an early start in the morning, and I need to have my head in the game tomorrow."

Take the hint, Tiff.

"No way, Jesse. You don't have to leave so soon…" she said with a bit of a whine. Then cracking a sly smile, she added, "That is, unless you want to go someplace where we can be alone?" She licked her lips. "In fact, it just so happens that my place is not too far from here." Tiffany reached out and grabbed the metal side view mirror mount to stabilize herself as she spoke.

"No, I can't. Not tonight," Jesse begged off. "You should go home too. You've already had enough to drink."

She held onto the open window with her left hand and stepped up onto his running board and leaned in. "Are you sure I can't talk you out of leaving? There must be something I can show you or do for you that would change your mind?" She reached her right hand behind his neck and pulled him in for a kiss.

He jerked his head back. "No, Tiffany. Knock it off."

Brooke smiled. *Atta boy, Jesse.*

He grabbed her wrist and pulled it back and away from him. She dug in her black polished nails as he pulled her hand away, leaving a stinging line of four scratches on the back of his neck. Grabbing her left hand firmly, he peeled it off the truck window and checked the back of his neck. When he pulled his hand away, there was a little blood on his fingers.

"Oops," she said with a drunken giggle. "Mr. Jesse James, I do believe I've left my mark on you after all."

"Go home, Tiffany. Get some sleep," he snapped. He rolled up the power window and put the truck in drive. She turned and watched him driving out of the parking lot, once again answering his cell phone.

"Looks like you didn't have any luck tonight," Brooke said, feeling rather satisfied.

"Oh, hey. Yeah." Tiffany stumbled a little. "No, but if he didn't have to work early in the morning, he'd be in my bed right now," she said with the confidence that comes from alcohol. "Isn't he just gorgeous?"

"Yeah, I suppose. Hey, I've got a six pack of Bud and a half bottle of Jack. What do you say we go drink it somewhere and commiserate?"

"Well," she said, throwing her hands up. "I guess that sounds like a decent plan B. Besides, these shoes are killing me."

CHAPTER TWENTY-ONE

J esse arrived in the parking lot at Spring Lake Park, Sunday morning at six-thirty. A full thirty minutes earlier than planned. Surprised by how many people were already there, he marveled at all the early risers. Across from the water wheel was a fenced dog park already teeming with dogs running and playing, and their owners sitting on park benches, busily chatting with one another and sipping on steaming cups of coffee. He chuckled to himself as he reached for his Stanley thermos. Carefully unscrewing the cap just enough, he refilled his Styrofoam cup. The intense smell of his Black Rifle Coffee was wonderful and exactly what his sleep-deprived body needed at this very moment.

His mind drifted to the real reason he was here at this time of the morning. Jesse had always been a confident athlete and an excellent runner but the words, *I work and I run, nothing else,* kept echoing in his mind. The brand-new, top-of-the-line Brooks running shoes he wore were meant to hedge his bet. First, he needed to take control of the situation, and the best way was to be here first. This girl was like no other female he'd ever met. Most girls he tended to run across seemed silly to him and, at times, a bit shallow. They nearly always came on to him first, and with his happy-go-lucky life, he'd never wanted to slow down enough to find out if they had any real substance. The thought that Celia was something new and unexpected was the understatement of the year. He hadn't had a moment of mental peace since the day he met her in Abby's lab. Or was it when she slapped his hand at the baby shower? He didn't know. Celia's comments kept buzzing through his head like a chainsaw. She was different, that's for sure. Maybe it was her accent that caught his attention. He cleared his throat and took another sip of coffee. *Why exactly did I agree to this?* He had no real answer but the corners of his mouth turned up. There was just something about her that was completely captivating.

Realizing he didn't know what kind of car she drove, he found himself scrutinizing every vehicle that pulled into the small parking lot. The place was beginning to fill up. He got out of his truck to read a large wooden sign depicting the layout of the park. It showed that one flat lap around the lake itself was one mile, but if the dirt trail up the hill to the lookout and back again was added, it was a mile and a half per lap. He recognized some of the runners that ran past him. Some of them were on their third or fourth laps and going strong. *I work and I run. That's all I do.* Her words echoed again, *I'm not worried.* It had been a while since he'd run five miles, but he'd always been in good shape. Working on the oil rigs was hard work, but it wasn't the same as running. At ten minutes till, a cute little two-tone green smart car began to slow and put its blinker on to pull into the parking lot. *That looks like something she'd drive.* He chuckled to himself. As he watched, a young blonde got out and started doing stretches.

He went back to sit in his truck. Jesse looked at his cellphone again. It was six fifty-eight. He watched and he waited. *Maybe she's going to be a no show?* Was it wishful thinking? He saw another runner complete his fifth or sixth lap and was still going strong. *Maybe this wasn't such a good idea.* The thought slowly began to creep into his mind. Suddenly there was a sharp rap on his side window loud enough to make him jump. He looked out of the window to see Celia running in place looking at her smart watch. She was wearing a Minnesota Vikings ball cap, black & red yoga pants or leggings, Jesse didn't actually know what you called them, and a bright red tank top. Jesse couldn't help noticing that everything fit perfectly, but it didn't seem like she was showing off.

Jesse jumped out of his truck. "I didn't think you were going to show," he said as he took off his hoodie. His tank top came up with it, exposing his toned abs and obliques for a brief moment. *She didn't even look.*

Tossing his sweatshirt onto the front seat of his truck, he closed the door and locked it with his remote. She was already sweating and breathing heavily, as if she'd been running for a while.

"I didn't think *you* were going to show up," she said, staring off over the lake and still running in place.

"Well, here I am," he said, holding out his hands with his palms up.

"Why aren't you warmed up yet?" she asked, finally looking at him.

"Naw, I don't need to warm up. I'm good to go."

"Oh, really? Do you actually run much?" she asked with an impish lift to her eyebrow.

"I run enough and by the looks of it, you've already warmed up."

"Yes, I've already run four miles."

"How? I didn't see you drive in."

"I didn't drive, I ran."

"From where?" he asked as his jaw dropped.

"Maria's. I live in an apartment in the back of the bar."

"Well, if you've already run four miles, then I promise to take it easy on you," he said with bravado he didn't feel.

"Okay, thank you," she said without sincerity. "Let's go." And she was off and running down the asphalt trail.

Jesse checked his cell, pushed the timer, and took off after her. She was running hard, but he was able to catch her within a minute or so. She was obviously strong, and her long legs took large, mile-eating steps. Even through the leggings, he could see the powerful muscles working. *And what a gluteus maximus.* He grinned. They continued to run without talking. Jesse easily matching her stride, their feet hitting the ground at the same time. Their rhythms in sync.

The big sign was now in sight and that meant the first mile was nearly done. He glanced at his phone—eight minutes. Wow, not a bad pace, he thought. *I got this.* His confidence was building. Coming up on the second lap, Jesse's breathing was locked to the pace, and he could feel his heart rate was right where it should be. He looked down at his timer and saw 15:33. She had picked up the pace on that last lap and hadn't said a word. By the third lap she was running a solid seven-minute mile and showing no signs of slowing. I can do this all day, he told himself.

The fourth lap was similar, but Jesse noticed a stitch in his side. As soon as he slowed even a little, she started to pull away. He leaned into his stride and caught back up. *How far are we going to run?* He couldn't ask her, so he kept right on. Rounding the lake for the fifth time, he was really starting to hurt. As they approached the sign, she started to leave the path that they were on, heading toward the parking lot.

"Thank you, Jesus," he said under his labored breath. He became elated when she approached his truck and began to slow. *She's starting her cool down period. Hallelujah.* This girl was in incredible shape, and he knew he was lucky to finish with his pride still very much intact. As she passed his truck though, he caught her glancing at him with what appeared to be a smirk nicely framed on her lovely face. Then, without warning, she snapped her head forward and began to pick up speed again.

What the... was all that came to his mind. He glanced ahead, in the direction she was running and groaned. Celia was aimed for the dirt trail that went straight up to the lookout point on the hill above. "Here goes nothing," Jesse said aloud. Once again, he leaned into his stride and hit the hill with everything he had left in the gas tank. His lungs began to burn fiercely, and his quads were on fire. He willed his legs to keep moving and concentrated on what was in front of him. Her butt. That caused him to smile a little. *Remember, it's ninety percent mental.* He reminded himself. Digging deep, he kept pushing up the hill, but she was gradually beginning to pull away from him. *I can't let that happen.* He gritted his teeth harder. Now she was more than twenty feet ahead and still pulling away. Jesse threw his arms forward with all his might, willing his muscles to obey his brain, or maybe it was his pride. Whatever it was, he was driving harder than he'd ever had before but thankfully the top of the hill was within sight. *Oh, thank God.* Was all he could think of. Celia looked back at him for the first time since they hit the hill, this time he thought she looked a little surprised. She was beginning to slow as she neared the top. Gasping for air, he pushed on to the top. She waited a few moments for him to catch up, while running in place and looking at her smart watch.

"Are you okay?" she asked. There was a tiny bit of concern in her voice but none of it showed in her face.

"Of course," he wheezed. "I tripped on something back there, that's all."

"Okay," she said. "Let's take a shortcut back down."

"Only if you need to," he said as he gulped air.

She smirked again and said, "Thank you so much," without even trying to make it sound believable, and took off cross-country. Down the hill she went, running through the tall grass and leaping over fallen trees. She was like a gazelle. If he wasn't near death, he could have truly admired the beauty of her leaping over logs, dodging low hanging branches and tiptoeing through a gopher village like hopscotch. *Was she even breathing hard? She's not human.* It was everything Jesse could do to throw his legs in front of him, trying to keep up with her and not crash and burn. He could see the bottom of the hill now, where the running path skirted the edge of the hill. Elation filled his senses. Suddenly, his left foot caught on something. *"Oh, shit!"* was all that came out of his mouth before he hit the ground. His momentum carried him back to his feet momentarily before crashing back down and tumbling face first through a thistle patch. He tried to gain his feet again as he neared the path where Celia stood. She leaped aside just as he tumbled onto the asphalt running path, crashing headlong into the large stones that lined it.

He lay still for a moment, trying to gain his senses. His head, resting on a big rock like a pillow, throbbed like a bass drum between his ears. He could feel Celia was next to him before he was able to open his eyes.

"Are you okay?" she asked as she kneeled on the ground by his side. Her smart watch beeping crazily.

When he finally dragged open his eyelids, the world began tumbling, and his eyes would not lock in on anything. It seemed as if they couldn't synchronize. One looked one way and the other in a different direction entirely. He closed his eyes tightly, letting out an involuntary groan.

He felt the warmth of her hand on his cheek. His second attempt fared better. Slowly, as he blinked and concentrated, he could finally make out her beautiful, worried face above him.

"Wow," was all he could say as her misty green eyes gradually came into focus."

"Are you okay?" she asked again. "Is there anything broken?"

He smiled up at her. "Oh, I'm fine." He tensed his muscles in an attempt to sit up, but spasms of pain shot throughout his body, causing him to give up on the idea temporarily.

"Lie still for a moment," she commanded.

"Good idea," he gasped, holding his breath.

He took stock of his body by trying little movements in his arms, legs, back and neck. Everything hurt, but there didn't seem to be anything broken that he could tell.

"It's good that I only hit my head," he said as he attempted a grin but only managed a grimace. "That's the hardest part of my body."

"I am so sorry," Celia confessed. "It is all my fault." She gently placed her hand on his arm.

"Exactly how do you figure that?" Jesse asked.

"You were doing so much better than I ever thought you would, and I was trying to make you quit."

"How is that your fault?" Jesse asked incredulously.

"But..."

"No, it's not your fault. I was being stupid, trying to keep up with you."

"I never meant for you to get hurt. I just wanted to make you quit. Why didn't you quit?"

"Me? Quit? Not in my DNA," Jesse said, trying to muster up some dignity as he tried to sit up once again.

"I should have never taken you down the hill like that. You could have been killed, and I don't even know your name," she lamented, her accent heavy.

"What?" Jesse asked as he thought about it. "Really? I know *your* name. It's Celia."

"I know *my* name as well, but what is yours?" she asked directly.

"Uh, I hit my head pretty hard, so, let me think about it for a second." He played it up. "Oh yeah, It's Jesse. My name is Jesse."

"Then be still, Jesse, and let me see if you have anything broken." She went to work checking his arms and legs first, then feeling along his chest.

"What is it you do when you are not chasing people around the lake?" she asked.

"I'm a roustabout for Reagan," Jesse said. "I just got here."

Her eyes narrowed a bit. "Yeah, like you said. Running around Williston with a bunch of oil field roustabouts might be a little dangerous." She punctuated the last word with a little punch to his arm. Her eyes showed a little lightning, but not the dangerous type. He hoped.

"Busted," Jesse confessed. "I did say that, didn't I?"

She smiled again and continued the triage, checking for wounds. "I was so shocked that you kept up for five laps. Then I decided that I would lose you on the steep climb." She paused for a moment and pulled an extraordinarily large thistle burr from his shirt. "When I was topping the hill, I couldn't believe it when I heard you breathing close behind me. When I looked, you were right there."

"You are amazing, Celia. Do you realize that?" He managed a little painful chuckle. It was the first real smile he'd seen from her, ever.

BEEP BEEP BEEP

Celia suddenly stopped what she was doing. "Why are you bothering with me?" Celia asked, staring down, intently into his eyes. A decidedly rare view beneath her tough outer shell.

"What do you mean?" Jesse answered her question with an honest question of his own.

"Why aren't you out running around with that pretty nurse? Or…or any of the other girls from the bar last night?"

"The bar? What nurse?" He had no idea what she was talking about. He didn't think Tiffany was a nurse…

"The one that took our blood at the hospital," she replied.

"Who, Abby?" Jesse laughed hard enough to hurt. "She's my cousin. It's a long story, but before that day, I hadn't seen her in like…ten years.

"Oh."

"Wait, come to think of it, I thought you never noticed me in the bar last night, but you did, didn't you?"

Celia blushed. "Here, let me help you." She started pulling the round, spiny thistle burrs from his face, arms and hands, each one leaving a tiny spot of blood where it had attached itself.

"You have a very gentle touch," he said.

Suddenly, the smile on her face dropped and shifted to concern. "Jesse. I need to check the back of your head."

"No, I think it's fine."

"Jesse," she said a little more forcefully. "There is a pool of blood forming between the rocks under your head."

She pulled him up to the sitting position and leaned him against a larger boulder. Jesse felt a warm trickle down his back when she removed her hand from his head, it was covered in blood. "Jesse, give me the keys so I can go get your truck. You need to go to the hospital." Her stronger accent returned.

Struggling to pull the key fob out of his pocket, he looked into her eyes. The concern on her beautiful face and furrowed brow made Jesse swallow hard. She took the key fob from his hand and quickly turned to run back to the parking lot. As he turned painfully to watch her go, he smiled to himself. *She is beautiful, intriguing, has a wonderful accent and a shell as hard as granite. Too bad it took a busted head to crack it open. Naw, I'd do it again in a heartbeat.* He thought as he steadied himself.

CHAPTER TWENTY-TWO

Cheri Perry drove through town in the pre-dawn light. *Did I go to sleep last night and wake up in Chicago or maybe Detroit?* It was butt-ugly Monday morning, and she had yet another murder? Williston might have one murder a year. Heck, the whole Williams County only averaged one murder a year yet, now they had two murders within a week of each other. As she drove toward Spring Lake Park overlook, the sun was just coming above the horizon in the eastern sky. The overlook had some of the best scenery anywhere in the county, with three-hundred-degree views of the Missouri River. It was also a favorite spot for local teenagers to go *parking*. Her cell phone rang as she drove through the park entrance at the bottom of the hill. She looked down to see who it was as she pressed the button.

"Hey, Boss. Yeah, I'm just pulling through the gate now." She ducked her head a bit to see the top of the hill through the upper portion of her windshield. Yeah, I'm at the bottom of the hill, but I can see the mobile crime lab lights lit up like a Christmas tree."

She hung up her cell and took a deep breath and weaved her way between news vans and patrol cars. She pulled up to the roadblock holding them all back. It consisted of red

& white traffic barricades, trees, and yellow crime scene tape. This part was never easy so she always took a moment to steel herself before getting out of the vehicle. As she exited the truck, she noticed the old, bent cottonwood tree that the locals all called the Sentinel. She smiled briefly, knowing that her name was part of the tree. She and her boyfriend carved their names inside of a heart when they were the ripe old age of eight or nine. When she looked up, she saw the Forensic Crime Scene Investigator, Belem Ureta, waving her in.

She took a deep breath, calmed her mind, and asked, "What've you got for me, Belle?" Belem, or Belle as many called her, wasn't a North Dakota native but was born and raised in California. Her straight black hair, huge smile, Latina attitude and copious tattoos, made her a standout in any local crowd. It was her work ethic, skills and vast array of knowledge that made her a favorite within law enforcement.

Belle looked down at her notebook, took a deep breath of her own, and started reading. "White female, brunette, early twenties, still in her LBD, complete with jewelry and watch, but bare feet and only one loose shoe, red strappy heel, so far."

"Got a name?" Cheri asked.

"Not yet. No wallet or purse, but we haven't moved the body yet."

"I don't suppose you found a cell phone."

"No, at least not yet."

"Have you had a chance to run her prints?"

"Yep. Prints are already sent off. Just waiting to see if we get a hit."

"We've got several tire tracks over here, but two different sets appear to have driven very close to the edge where the body was dumped. Hopefully, we'll get something there as well." Cheri stepped closer to the area that was blocked off. The techs had plaster of Paris poured in the tracks, waiting for it to dry enough to remove.

"Where is vic?"

"Still down the hill." Belle pointed down an embankment at the edge of the parking lot. Cheri noticed that there was a gap in the split rail fence to allow access to the frisbee golf hole number 9. The rising sun wasn't high enough to shine any real light down the hill, so Cheri donned latex gloves, pulled out her flashlight, and started carefully working her way down to the body. Belle followed her and continued the update.

"My team has secured all the park trash cans in the area with large construction bags to preserve any evidence we might find."

"Any preliminary cause of death?"

"No, not yet. But there appears to be some petechiae around the eyes, suggesting suffocation."

"Any sign of a struggle?" Cheri asked, shining the bright LED flashlight around the body, taking a close look at the head and neck.

"Not on the body, but we found skin under the nails of her right hand, so I bagged them."

"What about signs of sexual assault?"

"None that I've seen so far, but we'll know for sure after the autopsy."

"Got a time of death for her?"

"More than twenty-four hours for sure. Beyond that, we'll know—

"Yeah, I get it." Cheri cut her off. "We'll know more after the autopsy."

"I can sure smell the alcohol on her," Cheri observed. "When you run the tox screen, let me know how loaded she was when she died, will you? From the way she was dressed, someone definitely would remember seeing her."

Cheri continued shining her flashlight all around the victim. "What a young, beautiful girl. Who would want to do this?"

"Some sick son of a bitch," Belle said, almost under her breath.

"Who found her?" Cheri asked.

"Couple of kids out fooling around. The patrolman has them in the back of his unit."

Cheri heard a commotion above her and looked up to see two fire & rescue guys bringing down a stretcher and a body bag. "Okay. Thanks, Belle. I'll let you guys get on with your work. Let me know if you find any purse, wallet or ID after removing the body."

"You got it, Cheri."

Cheri waved and climbed back up the hill to the parking area. The sun was now halfway up the eastern sky, and the North Dakota wind was starting to blow. She looked down at the lake where wild geese and ducks were starting to honk and make noise as the wind blew up some morning whitecaps on the water. She allowed her eyes to linger a moment longer, thinking of the dichotomy of the situation. The sereness of the lake and a murder scene.

"Detective?"

She turned to see a patrolman walking her way. "Hey, Dustin, how are you? How's your wife and the new baby doing?"

"Oh, we're all doing good. That is, if you don't count not getting any sleep lately." He grinned.

"Little boy, right?" she asked. "What did you end up naming him?"

"Oliver," he said proudly. "Little Daniel is super proud to be a big brother now, too."

She didn't want to spoil the smile on his face, but there was a reason they were all there this morning. "What do you know so far about these witnesses?"

"Well, 911 received a call about 1:30 this morning. The kids were doing some extracurricular parking activities when the male witness, a Ron Kavan, age seventeen, stepped out of the vehicle, apparently to take a leak, when he found the body."

"Who's the female witness?"

"Name's Michelle Frost, age sixteen."

"How'd he manage to see the body in the hip-deep grass?" Cheri asked suspiciously.

"Apparently the vehicle headlights reflecting off her bracelet caught his attention. If not for that, I doubt he'd have seen the body at all."

"Good a reason as any to wear bling," Cheri supposed. "Wait. Did he pee on my crime scene?"

"No, ma'am." Dustin chuckled at her reaction. "According to him, he never got that far."

"Well, that's good."

"I've got them both in the back of my unit, waiting on the parents, if you want to talk to them."

"Yeah, thanks Dustin. I do need to talk to them."

She and Dustin walked over to the black and white. Cheri opened the back door and looked in. What she saw was a bedraggled girl with tear-stained mascara streaking down her face huddled in a police blanket. The boy was a clean-cut type that looked like he played football.

"Hi, my name is Detective Perry, and I am investigating the murder of that poor girl down there."

Cheri looked at them carefully. "Haven't I seen you two before?"

They both silently shook their heads no.

"Yes, I have. In fact, weren't you the two I kicked out of Jorgenson's old barn the other night?"

"We weren't doing anything. I swear," Ron blurted out.

"Honest," Michelle chimed in. "Please don't tell our parents."

"Yeah, please don't tell our parents," Ron agreed.

"Okay, enough about that." She looked right at Ron. "Wasn't it a school night? Why weren't you home in bed?"

"Teacher in-service day. We don't have school," Michelle blurted.

"What exactly happened?" Cheri asked the blunt question.

"Well, we went to the movies and then we drove up here. You know, just to talk and stuff."

"And...?" Cheri prompted.

"Like I told the other officer. I got out to use the bathroom and I saw something gold reflecting off the headlights. I started down the hill to see what it was when I saw it was a woman. I freaked out and scrambled back up the hill and called 911."

"Did you recognize her? Have you seen her before?"

"No, never," Ron said.

"Michelle, did you look at her?"

"No, only from the top of the hill. It was horrible." Her chin started to quiver, and tears ran down her face.

"Okay, just try to relax. About what time did you get here?"

"I don't know."

"Okay, what movie did you see?"

"*Unbroken*," they said in unison.

"That was a good movie, wasn't it?" she asked, trying to put them at ease.

They both nodded their heads.

"Okay, that was probably close to two hours with all the previews and commercials so what showing did you see?"

"Uh, the nine o'clock showing," Michelle blurted out.

"So that means the movie would have gotten out by about eleven or so."

They nodded.

"Did you happen to come straight here?"

"No, we stopped at the Dairy Queen first."

"What did you order?"

"Just fries and a soda to share," Michelle offered.

"I didn't have much money left after the movies," Ron said apologetically.

"Did you go in or use the drive-through?"

"Drive through," Ron volunteered.

Did you come straight here? Or did you go anywhere else first?"

"Straight here," Michelle said.

"Okay, so, max another thirty minutes at DQ plus fifteen minutes to drive out here," she said as she did the mental math. "So, you probably showed up here between eleven forty-five and midnight."

"They nodded."

"Was anyone else here when you arrived?"

"No."

Just then Dustin returned. "Cheri, Michelle's parents just arrived and are willing to take both of them. I told them his car couldn't be moved until the crime scene was cleared."

"Thanks, Dustin," Cheri said and turned back to the kids and handed them both one of her cards. "You need to go home now and get some rest. When you wake up, if you remember anything else, no matter how small, I want you to give me a call. Okay?"

"Yes, ma'am," they both agreed as they took her offered cards.

When Cheri turned away, she saw Belle frantically waving at her. She waved back and headed toward the mobile crime lab.

"We've got a possible name," Belle stated.

"Fingerprints back already?"

"Nope."

"Then who and how?" Cheri asked.

"When we moved the body, this credit card fell out of her bra." She held a clear evidence bag in a gloved hand.

"What's the name on the card?"

Holding the bag up to eye level she read. " Tiffany L Johnston."

"Prints on the card?" Cheri asked?

"Yep, and we've already pulled them, and they belong to the victim."

"Thanks, Belle. Good work." She took the credit card from Belle's outstretched hand. "Now, let's see what we can find out about Tiffany L Johnston."

CHAPTER TWENTY-THREE

"Hello. Special Agent Brown here."

Bravis Brown was a former Marine and still carried himself as if he never left active service. Even though he was pushing forty, his close cropped, but not quite hard-core marine haircut and his athletic build belied his retirement.

To that end, he trained daily at CrossFit and took special care of what he held most dear. His wife and triplet daughters. After leaving the Corps, he went back to college to study law. His keen sense of justice and gut instincts made him a natural fit at the FBI.

"Bravis, this is Deputy Sheriff Cheri Perry up in Williams County. We met at a forensic symposium in Fargo last year."

"Yes, Cheri. I do remember you." Bravis replied. "I saw a few messages from you but we've been swamped. My apologies for not getting back to you. How are things up in Williston?"

"Well, that's why I'm calling. We've had two murders up here in the last couple of days. One of them I can prove happened on a federal oil lease, so that's why I'm calling you."

"What about the other one?"

"I'm not sure if the other is related, but I'm guessing it is because we don't average more than one murder per year in Williams County."

"Tell you what. Send me all the preliminaries on the federal, and I'll get a case opened up on that one. Can you give me the victim's name so I can give the file a name and case number?"

"The victim's name is Natalie Hotah. Twenty-five years old. Security guard."

"Okay, and who owns the federal lease?"

"The company's name is Global Endeavor Alliance. They go by GEA around here. They were a late starter here in the Bakken, but I believe they are owned out of Great Britain."

"Britain? Global Endeavor Alliance," he repeated it back. "Okay, sounds interesting already. Got it. Send me everything you can. I'm going to run this up the flagpole, and I'll be in touch."

"Thanks a lot, Bravis. I greatly appreciate it."

"No problem. Talk to you soon."

"Bye." She hung up and dialed Belem over at the lab, but before she could get an answer, Ireana Longoria approached her in the hallway.

"Hey, Cheri, keeping busy?" Ireana asked with a sardonic tone.

"I haven't had any real sleep-in days," Cheri replied. "I better give my husband Dean a picture of me so he can remember what I look like."

"We got an update on the Spring Lake Park victim, Tiffany Johnston."

"Talk to me."

"We confirmed her identity by her fingerprints and driver's license photo. As a bonus, we located her car in the parking lot of Maria's. Apparently, it's been there for a day or two."

"Excellent. Where's the car now?"

"On its way back to the crime lab. The tow truck just picked it up a half hour ago."

"At Maria's, huh? Did anyone talk to Maria yet?"

"Yes, but only to let her know we were picking up the car."

"Okay, thanks. I'll head on over and see her after I talk to the lab. Good work, Ireana. I'll catch up with you later." Cheri tried calling the lab again but with still no answer, she decided to head on over.

"Belem," Cheri hollered in a sing-song voice as she entered the main door of the crime lab. "I come seeking knowledge." After turning the corner, she said, "Please tell me what you have so far. I need something solid."

Cheri dropped her notebook on the stainless-steel counter with an exhausted sigh. She looked over just in time to realize that Belle was on the phone. She mouthed the words, "Sorry," and raised her hands in apology then patiently waited for her to complete her conversation.

"Uh-hu," Belem said. "Got it. Thanks, I owe you one." She hung up the phone and quickly wrote down a few notes. "Hi, Cheri." She got up from her desk, grabbed her notes and came over to the counter opposite Cheri.

"Who do you want to talk about first? Natalie Hotah or Tiffany Johnston?" Belem asked as she reviewed her scribbles.

"Let's start with Natalie. She was the first victim."

"Okay, Natalie Hotah was killed by a combination of blunt force trauma and strangulation, but only after a big fight ensued. Lots of offensive and defensive bruises on her arms, knuckles, shins and back. That girl did some damage and did not go down without a fight."

"The poor girl," Cheri intoned with more than a little anger simmering beneath the surface. "She was fighting for her life."

"From what I can see, I guarantee that whoever she went toe to toe with will have a lot of bruises too. Maybe that will help find your suspect."

"Okay, that's a start. At least it gives me something to go on."

"Finally, she appears to have been bludgeoned from behind and then killed with manual strangulation. In other words, we found huge bruises around her throat and massive petechiae around the eyes. Oh, we also found a good bit of skin and what appears to be some cornea tissue under her fingernails."

"She poked someone in the eye," Cheri said with just a little satisfaction. "That's got to hurt. What did the tox screen say?"

"No drugs or alcohol in her system."

"Hmm." Cheri scribbled notes in her own notebook. When she finished, she looked up at Belem. "Thanks, as always, for the thorough workup."

Belem smiled wearily. "Someone's got to stick up for the victims. I can't change the fact that they *are* victims, but I take great satisfaction in finding justice for them."

"Good attitude, my friend," Cheri said. "No, great attitude. What did you find out about all the dirt and grime covering her uniform?"

"It matched samples we took from around the guard shack, so the time of death and the dirt and grime definitely placed her there when she was killed."

"Okay, that just became an FBI case." She wrote one more note, took another deep breath and asked, "What about victim number two?"

Belem looked down at her notebook and flipped a couple of pages before stopping to scan the sheet.

"Tiffany Johnston, age twenty-five. Actual cause of death was suffocation. Her tox report came back with a treasure trove of information. At the time of death, she had a blood alcohol level of .16, over double of legally drunk, plus some sort of cocktail of Rohypnol and Ambien."

"Good Lord," Cheri exclaimed. "She'd be nearly comatose with all that in her system. Unlike Natalie, she wouldn't have been able to put up any kind of fight."

"We also found skin with ample DNA under her fingernails. You find me a suspect, and I'll tell you if it's your murderer," Belle stated matter-of-factly.

"Where does one get Ambien and Rohypnol?" Cheri wondered out loud.

"Rohypnol is illegal in the United States, but it is still legal in Mexico and Europe. It has twenty times the power of Valium and takes less than fifteen minutes to take effect. Really, the Ambien would have been overkill, if you wanted to make a very compliant victim. She could still talk and even possibly walk, but she'd never remember what happened. But they killed her anyway." Belle finished with disgust.

"Hence, its reputation as a date rape drug," Cheri commented. "Wait, was she sexually assaulted?"

"No."

"Okay, anything else that will help me find her killer?"

"We did find something very odd," Belem said as she scanned more of her notes.

"What was that?"

"We found green paint flakes and rat dung on her clothing. And not just any paint flakes, old paint flakes that still contain lead, which means it hasn't been painted since the seventies. The rat dung was old as well. Nearly mummified, or rather dehydrated, which generally indicates there has been no food in the building to attract rats recently."

"So, if we find an old house with rat poop and old green paint on the walls then we find out where she was killed," Cheri said thoughtfully. "That'll be quite the crime scene."

"Cheri," Belem said. "We may have two killers on our hands instead of just one. If you look at them side by side, the MOs are completely different."

"My thoughts exactly," Cheri agreed. "I'm heading over to Maria's to see what I can find out there. Would you send all of your notes to Special Agent Bravis Brown? Here's his card, with his email address. He's expecting them."

Belem took the card from her. "Sure thing."

"Thank you," she called over her shoulder as she made her exit.

* * * * *

"Hello, Cheri, how are you?" Maria called in surprise from behind the bar as the deputy walked through the front door. It was just after eleven o'clock, still early for a bar & grill. The bar was still officially closed, and Maria was busy plugging in numbers on a laptop. Celia was at the other end of the bar calling out numbers for the weekly liquor inventory. She had on jeans and a red tank top. Her long hair appeared damp from a recent shower, and she wore a nice post-run glow.

"I'm doing well, Maria. Thank you," Cheri responded warmly, but then let out a sigh.

"What brings my favorite deputy sheriff into a bar this early in the morning? A rough night on the job?"

"No. Well, yes. More like a rough early Monday morning already," she answered a bit evasively.

"The grill is already heated up for the lunch crowd, would you like me to fix you something to eat?" Maria offered.

"No, but thank you."

"How would you like some hot coffee? It's freshly brewed," she offered again.

"Okay. You talked me into it," Cheri said with a chuckle. "I would love a cup."

Maria turned around to grab the coffee carafe and poured hot black coffee into two, heavy, bone white cups that had Maria's logo on them.

"So," Maria stated as she set the two cups down on the bar. "What brings you to my place besides some excellent and free coffee?" She took a sip from her cup.

"I need to talk to you about Saturday night," Cheri opened, then took a sip from her own mug as she watched Maria.

"Don't tell me it's about that abandoned car they picked up earlier," Maria said while putting her own mug on the bar. Her smokey, gravely, Eastern European accent was stronger than usual.

"Well, as a matter of fact, it *is* about that car."

"What's the story?" she asked. "And why does an abandoned vehicle involve an investigator like you?"

"Because it belonged to a twenty-five-year-old female named Tiffany Johnston," Cheri explained as she placed an enlarged drivers' license photo on the bar in front of Maria and paused for a moment.

Maria looked down at the photo. "Belonged?" Maria asked. "Who owns it now?"

"Maria, we found Ms. Johnston's body early this morning dumped on top of the hill at Spring Lake Park."

"*Govno*," Maria exclaimed in her native Croatian language. "What happened?"

"She was drugged and then murdered sometime late Saturday night or early Sunday morning. Do you remember her being in here?" Cheri asked.

"Celia, you and Jacob were working behind the bar that night. Do you remember if she was in here?"

Celia walked over and looked at the photo. "Yeah, sure," Celia said. "She was sitting alone at the bar for about an hour just sipping on a beer."

"Do you remember what she was wearing?" Cheri asked.

"Yeah," Celia said with sadness in her voice. Her eyes looked into the distance as she recalled the memory. "The girl was dressed to the nines. I can't believe someone killed her. She was a real regular in here."

"What do you mean?" Cheri asked. She quickly grabbed her notebook and pen out of her purse.

"You know," Celia said. "She had on the little black dress, fit her real good too, hair all done up and red, red, red lipstick." Celia paused for just a second before adding. "Yeah, that girl was definitely on the hunt."

"Was she with anyone? Or at least did she leave with anyone?" Cheri asked.

"She was alone for at least an hour, but then later on, that good looking new guy with Reagan came in and sat down next to her."

"Do you know his name?" Cheri asked.

"Yeah." She smiled a bit dreamily. "His name is Jesse James. You don't think he had anything to do with it, do you?"

"Who would name their son Jesse James?" Cheri asked rhetorically as she scribbled the information.

"That would be Lincoln James," Maria volunteered.

CHAPTER TWENTY-FOUR

"Wait, he's one of Link's son's?" Celia asked in surprise.

"Yes," Maria confirmed, still watching Celia. "He is."

"It never occurred to me before," Celia commented. Her eyes narrowed a bit. "Link is just Link. I never think of him as *Lincoln James*," she said in a haughty accent complete with finger quotes.

"He's Link's youngest boy," Maria added.

"Why haven't I seen him around here before now?" Celia wondered out loud.

"He just got here not long ago," Maria said "He and Link haven't spent much time together since they lost his brother, Jason. He was a Marine killed in Afghanistan. We always keep a special bottle of Jameson on hand for Link. Especially in October.

"Well, he's the talk of the town in single female circles," Celia confided. "Not that I pay much attention to that sort of thing."

"Why is everyone talking about him?" Cheri asked.

"When you see him, you won't have to ask that question," Celia replied. "You know, now that I think of it, he does have Link's walk and confidence, just like his brothers. Except the hair," Celia mused. "Unlike Link, he has amazing, curly hair."

"Oh?" Maria asked as she cocked her head. "What's got into you?"

Celia turned a nice shade of red. "Not for me, of course. He's a player and everyone knows it, but he's still nice to look at."

"You backpedal nicely," Maria observed while looking even more closely at her.

"Okay, ladies. Snap out of it," Cheri interrupted. "Was he meeting Tiffany here?"

"No, I got the distinct impression that he was meeting someone else," Celia replied.

"What makes you say that?" Cheri asked.

"Well, every few minutes, he would scan the crowd, look over at the door and then pull out his cell phone and thumb through it before putting it away again," Celia explained.

"Were you serving him?" Cheri asked

"No, Jake was."

"And you still happened to notice all this?"

"I wasn't watching him but I happen to notice things when I would look down the bar." Celia said lamely.

Maria studied Celia carefully.

"Was he drinking heavily?" Cheri asked.

"No, not really," Celia answered. "He just had one Corona and a shot of Cincoro."

"What's Cincoro?" Cheri asked.

"It's that new top-shelf sipping tequila," Maria interjected. "It looks like it might compete with Patron."

"Okay, but you weren't watching him." Cheri paused, looking at Celia. "Was he celebrating something?"

"No, I don't think so." Celia stated. "But it seemed like he was surprised that we even had it."

"Did Jesse and Tiffany leave together?" Cheri inquired.

"No, not really. Jesse got a call on his cell. After he hung up, he said he had to go, paid Jake with a credit card and headed for the door..." Celia trailed off, looking down at the bar for a moment.

Cheri snapped her fingers. "Hey, Earth to Celia. Are you okay?"

"Cheri, you don't think that he had anything to do with it, do you?"

"What about Tiffany?" Cheri asked. "When did she leave?"

"Come to think of it, she paid her tab as fast as she could and stepped out of the door maybe a minute or two after Jesse."

"Do you remember anything else?" Cheri asked.

"Yeah, there was another girl at the bar trying to get Jesse's attention, but I don't think he was really looking, if you know what I mean. Cause there were definitely multiple offers on the table."

"Who was the other girl?" Cheri asked.

"Brooke something-or-another. She's a local. She's here a lot and lately, she's been bragging about getting a new job at the hospital."

"Hmm, I just might know who that is," Cheri commented while taking her notes. "Maria, do you have any surveillance cameras overlooking the parking lot?"

"Sure, but they are only designed to watch the area around the door. There isn't much of the parking lot in view."

"Can I send my tech over later today to get a copy of whatever you have?"

"Sure, no problem," Maria replied.

"Thanks guys," Cheri said. "I now have tripled the amount of information I had." She closed her notepad and tossed it and the pen into her purse.

"You don't think Jesse had anything to do with Tiffany's murder, do you?" Celia asked, this time with something bordering on distress in her voice.

"Celia, that's the third time you've asked me that," Cheri observed. "There must be more of a reason."

Celia was quiet.

"Celia, *Duzo*, what are you not telling us?" Maria coaxed.

"Nothing, except..." She trailed off without looking up.

"Except what?" This time Cheri engaged her interrogation voice.

"Um..." She looked from one inquisitor to the other, dropped her gaze back to the old wooden bar and mumbled, "I kind of went running with him Sunday morning."

"You did?" Maria asked. "Why didn't you tell me?"

"Celia, did he do anything to you?" Cheri asked slowly and carefully. "Did he try to hurt you in any way or say anything that you can recall?"

"No, not at all. It was me that actually kind of hurt him. He seemed so sweet," she said and then blurted out the whole scenario as if a dam burst.

"His head just needed a couple of butterfly strips, but his clothes, shoes and socks were so full of those spiny burrs he didn't want to put them back on again. He asked me if I would retrieve the set of work clothes in his truck, so he could wear them home instead. He dropped me off afterwards."

"Why didn't you tell me about this?" Maria asked.

"I didn't think it was a big deal."

"Celia, did he take his old clothes with him when he left the hospital?"

"No, I think he threw them in the trash."

"Okay, great," Cheri said as she pulled her cell out. "Celia, I don't know what we are dealing with here, so you need to stay away from that guy until we figure this thing out."

Celia nodded without saying a word.

"Celia, I mean it," Cheri cautioned. "Prison is filled with good looking murderers and charming rapists. Do not go near him. Don't even answer your cell if he calls you."

"Okay," Celia said without commitment in her voice.

"Celia, *Duzo*. I can't imagine any son of Lincoln James being a murderer, but until we know more, promise me you will not go near him."

"I won't."

"And Cheri's right. Don't talk to him either," Maria insisted.

She heaved a heavy sigh. "Yes, Maria, I promise."

"Thank you both. Gotta go," Cheri said as she hit the speed dial on her cell. "Maria, can I get this coffee in a go cup?"

"Just take the mug."

"Okay, thanks." Cheri said over her shoulder as she neared the exit.

"Belem? Hey, it's me. I need you to get down to the hospital ER and see if you can locate some clothes that may have been dumped in the trash sometime yesterday..."

Cheri sat in her vehicle for a long moment without starting the engine. "How should I handle this?" She asked herself. Giving herself some much needed time to think. Time to assimilate the trove of information she just received. "The son of Lincoln James, huh?" Then a funny thought broke through the dimness of the moment. *Wait, isn't that what you call Jameson?* As she started the engine she mumbled, "If he is my killer, this is going to get very interesting if not just a little bit dangerous."

* * * * *

Monday morning came way too early. Jesse's brain awoke painfully to the beeping of his cell phone alarm. *Something hurts*, he thought without opening his eyes. *No, correction, everything hurts.* Lying on his side with a flat pillow doubled over under his head, he slowly cracked open an eyelid. Even that hurt. He blinked, attempting to focus on his cell phone. It was on the nightstand a mere eighteen inches away, but he couldn't seem to muster the power to reach for it. *Am I hung over?* He concentrated for a moment without moving. *I don't remember drinking last night.* The beeping slowly ratcheted up louder and louder. Jesse made the mental decision to reach over and shut it off, but his muscles would not budge. He was acutely aware of something wrong. Just rolling onto his back caused him to wince. When he tried to sit up, an intense explosion detonated in his body. The angry muscles in his legs, arms and abdomen shrieked maniacally as he lost momentum and flopped back down on his back, breathing heavily.

"Oh yeah. Now I remember." Gritting his teeth, he grabbed the cell phone and dropped it onto his chest while feebly fumbling to find the proper button to shut off the alarm. His stomach muscles were on fire, and his head throbbed from the rocks the day before. He gingerly touched the back of his head and found the wound. Uttering the groan of Atlas lifting the world, he rolled onto his belly and slid out of bed until his knees hit the floor. Flopping his head back down on the bed, he started to laugh because crying would probably hurt worse.

Oh Lord, what have I done to myself? His muscles were in full-on rebellion. The more he laughed, the more it hurt. He lay in that silly position for another few minutes, trying to regulate his breathing. He thought of Celia and smiled. Reaching for his cell, he clumsily punched in her number and hit send. It rang only once and went to voicemail. He looked at the phone as if it had personally offended him. Redialing the number, he thought of the day before. He thought of Celia. Again, it rang once and went to voicemail. The pang of disappointment was palpable even through the physical pain he was in.

Four ibuprofen and a very hot shower is all I need. And coffee. Pushing up with his hands on the bed, he slowly struggled to his feet.

* * * * *

"You're late," Jesse's foreman yelled across the jobsite. "Where the hell have you been?"

"I know, and I'm sorry, Dave. Won't happen again."

"Just because your Link's kid does not give you the luxury of his work schedule."

"No, Dave. That's not it at all. You are right to be mad and trust me, it won't happen again."

"Did you age like fifty years over the weekend?" Dave asked a little more gently as Jesse hobbled over.

The other Reagan roustabouts were already busy trenching for a new crude oil pipeline across the Bakken oil fields of North Dakota. This particular pipeline would remove the need for over one hundred crude oil tanker trucks. The reduction was desperately needed due to the congestion on the crowded highways, and Reagan was nearing its completion. It was just after noon and the day was a hot one, especially for spring on the northern prairie. The crew had just finished a quick lunch break and was getting restarted. The new line was being dug in and constructed parallel to an existing natural gas pipeline owned by the same company. Dave Short had just cranked up the big yellow excavator they were using for the primary trencher. The existing gas line had been located and marked by a series of little yellow flags planted across the field. The plan called for a twenty-foot separation of the two lines. Jesse, wearing his green hat, telling the world and any co-workers that he was a new guy, was given the task of shovel operator. Or, as his dad, Link, preferred to call it, a hickory handled backhoe.

"Boss, I am so sore, I could barely get out of bed this morning."

"What are you so sore from?"

"I took on a challenge to run against a girl that royally kicked my butt and everything else on my body."

"Who? What girl?"

"Celia, the bartender at Maria's."

"No way," Dave said. "I heard that she doesn't date anyone."

"It wasn't a date; it was just a run in Spring Lake Park."

"Yeah? Was it worth it?" Dave asked. "Cause you look like crap."

"Sure was," Jesse said adamantly as he hobbled alongside Dave's deliberately long strides.

Dave climbed up into the giant excavator and cranked it up. Jesse could feel the vibration in his feet as the heavy piece of equipment rumbled into position to continue digging. The job of the hickory backhoe operator was to guide the excavator and ensure there was the proper distance from the gas line. After confirming the necessary twenty feet, he signaled to the operator that he was good to start the next section. The big yellow digger let out a burst of black smoke from its exhaust, and the powerful shovel sank deep into the soil. Jesse glanced over to watch the rest of the crew placing pipe in the trench they had dug earlier in the day.

Suddenly there was a loud hiss. Jesse snapped his head around just in time to see a plume of natural gas erupt from the ground with enough force and pressure to blow a big hole in the ground, exposing the torn thirty inch gas pipe.

The gas was jetting out without restriction. Jesse waved his hands frantically for Dave to shut down the tractor engine before it caught the gas on fire. Dave saw the eruption right in front of him and cut off the fuel to the engine before leaping clear of the big excavator as it began to tip into the hole. The rest of the Reagan crew working a football field away were rapidly shutting down their heavy equipment and jumping into vehicles to escape the area. Jesse and Dave ran as fast as they could, desperate to clear the impending blast when the rumble foretold the explosion that rocked the very earth beneath their feet. As the land quaked and rolled beneath them, the blast hit them from the back and lifted them off their feet, sending them careening through the air for what seemed like an eternity, before impacting the ground.

He thought he was laying on his back, but he really wasn't sure. Blackness was all around him. The only thing he could hear was this crazy buzzing in his ears. He tried to shake his head but couldn't move. In fact, he couldn't move or feel anything at all. And he couldn't breathe. *Am I dead?*

Suddenly he sucked in a lungful of searingly hot, dusty air that caused him to cough violently. After his first breath, vision returned, and he continued coughing, trying to clear his lungs. Jesse instinctively tried to roll onto his side, but it felt like he was being weighed down. The coughing subsided, but then the feeling in his body was back and it was back with a vengeance. His face was hot, and his body felt like it had been crushed under a steam roller. He tried to sit up and realized Dave was lying on top of him. They had landed in a pile behind a dirt berm. The sandy loam hung heavy in the air. Jesse could tell he was breathing.

"Dave," Jesse yelled as he shook him. "Dave, wake up!" Jesse shook him harder.

Dave began to stir, transitioning into his own coughing fit. Jesse rolled him off and spun around to try to help Dave into a sitting position, but he wasn't ready, and he lay back down, struggling just to breathe.

Jesse pulled his fire retardant overshirt off and yanked his T-shirt up and over his mouth and nose, attempting to filter out some of the dust, and rolled onto his back again and tried to lay still. The scent of burnt hair hung in the air as he took his initial real look around.

The first thing that occurred to him was that he could see something bright in the sky behind the berm. The buzzing in his ears was replaced by the deafening roar from the flames shooting up into the air. Leaving Dave, he crawled up the earthen berm where he could see a massive fire tornado blasting its way into the sky. He could feel the heat on his face as the air seemed to sear his throat even more with his head above the protection of the dirt.

He slid back down the soft earth and tried to get his head around what had happened. After laying still for a moment, he realized that it must have been the berm that saved them from the blast of the fireball, and the mandatory fire-retardant clothing had done the rest. He looked at Dave and shouted, "I can't believe we're alive."

Dave just smiled and dug into his shirt pocket for his cigarettes and lighter. With only three of them left in the pack and all were broken, he grabbed a hold of the longest piece, stuck it in his mouth and lit it up.

"Are you crazy, lighting up a cigarette in an oilfield?" Jesse laughed as he slapped him on the shoulder.

"Yeah, I hear these things can kill ya," Dave said, smiling after exhaling a plume of smoke of his own.

Just then, the incredible roar of the gas fire began to lessen. Both men scrambled back up to the top of the berm to survey the scorched landscape.

"It looks like the fire is going out," Jesse stated in surprise.

"Yeah, it's probably the automatic shutoff valves in the pipeline. When they sense a sudden reduction in pressure, they close."

"That's good," Jesse said as he stared at the slowly dying flames. "Why'd it take so long to shut off?"

"The nearest valves are probably a couple miles away in either direction. With a thirty-inch pipeline, there was a lot of gas to burn off in between."

They sat there in silence for a few minutes. The back of Dave's hair was singed, and he had a cut above his eye. His face was covered in dirt and blood, but he still was smiling.

"Are you okay?" Jesse asked, "You look like shit."

"Yeah, I'm okay," Dave said in his easy drawl. "I guess God ain't done with me yet." He looked up at Jesse, blew out a smoke ring and smiled. Then he raised an eyebrow and pointed at Jesse. "And besides, I wouldn't be talking smack until you looked in the mirror."

CHAPTER TWENTY-FIVE

Seth looked up at the sound of a knock at the door. Link stepped into Jenny's hospital room as he dropped his cell phone into his back pocket. Seth was sitting by Jenny's bed, and Victoria was on the other side of the room in the so-called sleeping chair. Link's face was red, and the blood vessels at the side of his bald head were popping in and out like a blinking neon sign.

"What was that about?" Seth asked.

Link ignored Seth's question and instead walked over to Jenny's bed. "How are you feeling, sweetie?" The smile was fake and Seth knew it.

Jenny smiled. "It seems like someone gave me a new lease on life. I no longer feel like there is a ton of weight holding me down anymore. The Doc said the new blood would make a huge difference, but I had no idea how much better it would be."

"Link, what was the phone call?" Seth asked again. "Was it about work?"

Link turned toward Seth and said, "Thank God, nobody got hurt. That being said, it seems that we had a major explosion on the pipeline project this morning."

Seth stood up. "What happened?"

"Jesse and Dave accidently dug into the gas line we were parallel to."

Seth started to speak, but Link raised his hand to stop him. "Take it easy, Seth. Number one; no one was hurt. Number two; the excavator is totaled. Number three; Dave said the dig was good. They were twenty feet away from the marker flags. Jesse confirmed it. I got a call into 811 to find out more."

Seth dropped back down in his seat. "When do we get to drive down a smooth patch of highway?" Seth asked in exasperation. "It seems like one way or another, we've been fighting uphill in every direction."

"Dave is the one that called to give me the report. He said that Jesse was called down to the police station for an interview. I'm guessing that this is going to get a lot of attention. That tract of land we were on is federal and the watershed is controlled by the Army Corps of Engineers."

* * * * *

"Good afternoon, Mr. James," Cheri said as she opened the door to the interview room. The air in the little room was filled with the smell of burnt hair and from the looks on Jesse, she knew where it was coming from. "My name is Deputy Sheriff Perry. I am a detective and I'd like to thank you for volunteering to come talk to us."

He looked tired and totally disheveled. "No problem." Jesse chuckled. "As soon as we are done here, I'm heading home for a shower though."

"*He's very nonchalant,*" Cheri observed as she stood at the door smiling. She had her notebook in one hand and two cups of coffee in the other, with her index finger looped through both handles. One red cup and one blue. She set them both down and slid the red one over to Jesse.

"Coffee?" She asked. "I hope it's not too strong for you."

"Thanks," Jesse said as he took a sip. "It's good, and besides, I'm not sure there is such a thing as too strong."

So, this is definitely Link's kid.

"First things first," Cheri began. "Are you okay? Do you need any medical attention?"

"No, of course not," Jesse stated. "I'm guessing that this is about the explosion?"

"No, not exactly. But I heard the whole Reagan crew was extremely lucky. What can you tell me about it?"

"Yeah, it was kind of crazy, all right," Jesse responded. "But all-in-all it could have been much worse."

As Jesse ran through the incident, she scribbled notes in her notebook. At the end of the notes, she wrote BRAVIS with a question mark. It was on federal land, so he'd be the one to look into it. She let out a low whistle and moved her attention back to Jesse. "It's really lucky your whole crew wasn't killed."

"You're telling me," Jesse agreed as he took another slug of coffee.

She took another note. "Uh, pardon me, Deputy," Jesse said as he turned his head sideways and leaned in to see what she was writing.

"Yes," Cheri said, dropping the notebook face down in her lap.

"Uh, if this isn't about the explosion, then what do you want to talk to me about?" he asked, before draining his cup.

Without answering his question directly, she launched into her subtle interrogation tone of voice. "Mr. James…"

"You can call me Jesse."

"Okay, thank you," she responded kindly. "Jesse, can you tell me where you were Saturday night?"

"Sure, I went to Maria's for a beer. I'd planned on meeting someone, but they didn't show."

"I see, did anyone see you there? Or did you wind up meeting anyone else?"

"In a way, I guess," he stated

He's awfully relaxed for being in an interrogation room. Cheri thought.

"Who did you meet?"

"Well, I sat next to a girl at the bar. I think her name was Tiffany."

"Tiffany Johnston?" Cheri asked.

"I never caught her last name." Jesse shrugged. "What's this all about?"

Cheri watched him closely as she delivered the news. "Someone murdered Tiffany Saturday night."

"What?" Jesse gasped in a quick breath as if she'd sucked all the air out of the room with her comment. Jesse's casual pose in the chair changed and he sat up straight. "I can't believe someone murdered her. She was just a silly girl. Who would want to do such a thing?"

"It's my job to figure that out," Cheri said rather matter-of-factly. "What else do you remember about that night?"

"Nothing… Deputy," Jesse offered as his eyes narrowed just a bit. "Like I told you, I just went to Maria's for a beer."

Now that's more like what I expected.

"Oh, did you drive there?" Cheri asked, changing up her tactics.

"Yes, of course."

"Great. What were you driving?"

"My Reagan company truck."

"Do you have that same truck with you now?"

"Sure, it's parked on the street out front." He said with a jerk of his thumb behind him.

"Mr. James, do you mind if we take a look at your truck?"

"Of course not," Jesse stated. "Go ahead. I've got nothing to hide."

"Of course not," Cheri repeated, then stood up. "How was your coffee?" Cheri asked with a smile.

"It was good," he replied, tilting the empty cup.

"Would you care for a refill?"

"Sure, if you are going to get one for yourself as well."

"Great, I'll be right back."

She scooped up both cups and left the room for a quick minute before returning, this time with a green cup and a blue cup. She slid the green cup over to Jesse.

"What happened to the red one?" Jesse asked.

"I noticed it had a chip in the handle, so I got you a new one," she answered smoothly. "So, tell me, did you talk to the victim much while you were at the bar?"

"Yes. Or actually no. She did most of the talking."

"Were you there to meet her?"

"No. I already told you I've never met her before that night."

"Did you leave with her?"

"No," Jesse replied but his eyes narrowed a bit more. "Where is this going?"

"Nowhere, Mr. James. We are just attempting to establish the facts concerning our victim. Mr. James, I can't help noticing some scratches on the back and side of your neck. Did that happen during the explosion?"

Jesse put his hand up to his neck and felt them. "Oh, those? No. Actually, Tiffany gave those to me when she tried to kiss me." The moment the words came out of his mouth, he knew it didn't sound good.

"I see," was all the deputy said as she scribbled in her notebook.

"Look, do I need a lawyer?" Jesse asked as he stood up and walked behind his chair.

"I don't know, Mr. James. Do you?" The deputy said as she stood as well.

Just then her cell phone chimed. She picked it up and Jesse watched her read the text message. Putting the cell phone away, she said, "Mr. James, just hang tight and relax. I'll be right back." Moving rather quickly, she exited the door of the interview room. When the door fully closed, he heard the unmistakable sound of a heavy lock sliding into place.

* * * * *

"What do you have for me, Belle?"

"I've got a lot. Are you ready for a download?"

"Go," Cheri said as she whipped out her notebook and pen.

"Okay, number one. We took a look at Mr. James' truck and found a small shoe print in the mud on the running boards that looks like a match to our vic's.

"Number two. We found Tiffany's fingerprints on the side mirror and the driver's door.

"Number three. Mr. James' DNA matches the skin cells and dried blood we took from under the victim's fingernails."

"Wow, great work, Belem. It looks like we've got our murderer."

"There is one more item that doesn't make that much sense?" Belem ended her comment more as a question than a remark.

"Uh oh. What's that?"

"Remember you asked me to go over to the ER and get Mr. James clothes?"

"Yeah. Don't tell me you couldn't find them."

"No, I found them all right. They had blood smears all over the place that all turned out to belong to Mr. James."

"And?" Cheri asked. "What is the part that doesn't make sense?"

"Well, I found some tissue on the toe of his right shoe. Under the microscope, it looks like human tissue in a state of significant decomp."

"How old?"

"Best guess right now? At least a week, maybe more."

"Belle, do we have a serial killer on our hands?" Cheri wondered out loud.

"It's way too early for me to tell, but it looks like we can link him to no less than two dead bodies.

"But who is the second dead body?" Cheri asked. "Do you have enough material for a DNA analysis?"

"Just enough, and I've already put it through CODIS. Just waiting to see if we get a hit."

"Belem, you are amazing. What is your favorite poison? Because after this, I owe you a bottle, or maybe just a shot, if you have expensive tastes."

* * * *

Cheri threw the slide on the door lock and opened the heavy metal door. Jesse was sitting in his chair and looked up. Just as she entered the room a man in a suit followed her in and closed the door.

"I am so sorry that it took so long, Mr. James," Cheri said, her light affable tone had returned. "I have just a couple of follow up questions for you. This is my colleague from the FBI, Agent Brown."

Jesse nodded but didn't speak.

"Mr. James, are you familiar with Global Endeavor Alliance?" Agent Brown asked casually.

"Yeah, of course. Reagan does a lot of work for them."

"Do you have access to their facilities?"

"I suppose so… When we have ongoing jobs with them."

"Where did you go last night after you left Maria's?" Cheri asked. "Any place interesting?" She raised an eyebrow.

Jesse glanced from Agent Brown back to Cheri. "Look, I had nothing to do with that explosion, except nearly being blown up," he stated as he placed his palms flat on the table and began to stand.

Here it comes… Cheri thought as she prepared for what was next.

Agent Brown leaned in. "Mr. James…"

Jesse cut him off. "Agent Brown, I don't like where these questions are going. In fact, I think I better get a lawyer." The words came out of Jesse's mouth slowly and deliberately.

"From where I'm standing, that's probably a good idea." Cheri responded, her voice changing from easy gong to all business. "Mr. James, please stand up and turn around."

"What?" Exclaimed Jesse. His face went flush and eyes went wild as he stood glancing from one to the other and then to the door.

"You heard me. Turn around and place your hands behind your back."

He was only turned halfway when she fastened the first cuff onto his left hand.

As she placed the cuffs on the other, she could feel his pulse beating rapidly in his wrists. *Lincoln James kid or not, I gotcha, you murdering son of a bitch.*

"Jesse James, you are under arrest for suspicion of the murder of Tiffany L. Johnston. You have the right to remain silent…"

After a uniformed officer led Jesse away to a holding cell, Cheri turned to Bravis. "So, what do you think?"

"Well, if it wasn't for all the evidence you have against him, I'd say he's not your guy." Bravis stated. "But my gut is fairly sure that he is not *my* guy."

CHAPTER TWENTY-SIX

"Okay. Slow down, son. Say that one more time," Link said slowly into his cellphone. He was jamming the speaker into his ear to hear better because he knew he must've heard Jesse wrong. His heartbeat involuntarily picked up, and his knuckles were turning white where he gripped the device.

"It's all a big mistake, Dad, but I've just been arrested for murder."

"I know your world is tumbling right now, son, but you've got to listen to me."

"But, Dad, I had nothing to do with it."

"I believe you. Where are you?"

"I'm in the jail on Main Street." His voice cracked.

"Listen, I have no doubt it's a big mistake. I don't know what's going on, but the first thing is to get you a lawyer and we will figure this out together. In the meantime, just hang tight, don't talk to anyone, and I mean *no one*. And son, don't worry. I've got your back."

"Thank you, Dad." The stress in his voice was palpable. "I swear, I didn't do anything."

"I believe you, son. We'll figure this thing out together," Link said using a softer tone. "And remember, don't talk to *anyone.*"

"Don't worry, Dad, I won't."

* * * * *

Cheri set down her cup of coffee and picked up her vibrating cell. The name on the screen showed Belem. Clicking the button she said, "Go for Perry, Belle. What have you got for me?"

"Hi, Cheri. I've got a couple of things for you."

"What's that? I need some good news."

"CODIS got hit on the DNA."

"Excellent. What's the name?"

"I gotta warn you, it's kind of weird. The DNA belongs to Danielle Robertson. Twenty-nine years old."

"Any record?"

"Yeah, she was busted for felony DUI as a minor." Belem said. "Apparently crashing your parents SUV into the neighbor's barn while smashed out of your gourd isn't a good thing to do at seventeen. That's why her DNA was in CODIS."

"The name sounds kind of familiar. Is she listed as a missing person?"

"Yes ma'am. Her parents filed a missing person's report just a few weeks ago. The officer that followed up on it left some decent notes.

"Super, Belle. Have you pulled them yet?"

"That's a silly question," Belem chided.

"Sorry. *Mea culpa, madame,*" Cheri apologized.

Belem chuckled. "No worries. The possible vic worked as a CNA for Trinity Hospital. The Trinity folks said she quit unexpectedly a few weeks ago. Left a note that she'd met someone online and left. She was renting a trailer, and, according to the notes, it looked like she left in a big hurry. Nobody has heard from her since."

"Okay, so we have a missing person that no one was really looking for, and her DNA shows up on a shoe. But what you're telling me is that she might've gone missing long before Jesse showed up in town. It doesn't make any sense at all. Where is the body, and how is it that we have her DNA on Mr. James' shoe?

"I have a few more funky pieces to add to the puzzle," Belem announced.

"Okay?" Cheri asked, not sure she liked the idea of funky.

"The tire print molds came back as a fourteen-inch car tire that sells by the thousands through Walmart."

"Hmm, that kind of eliminates Mr. James' pickup as the transport vehicle. We can't eliminate Mr. James as our prime suspect based solely on this."

"Before we come to any conclusions, we need to find this body," Belem argued.

"You have a point there."

"Did he have any plausible alibi? I wouldn't want to take this case to the DA with what we know now," Belem confided.

"We didn't get that far before he lawyered up. I'm not interested in sending this to the DA without something else," Cheri agreed. "I think I'll trot on over to lockup and see if he can give me anything else that would allow me to cut him loose in good conscience."

"I've got one more add-on," Belem said.

"Like what?"

"Well, keep in mind that we have fingerprints on the outside of the truck, but we found none on the inside. Nor did we find any other evidence that Ms. Johnston had been inside his truck at all."

"He could have wiped the inside and forgot about the outside." Cheri argued.

"Cheri, we found lots of prints all over the interior, but none matching the vic, so it couldn't be a wipe job, could it?"

"Did Mr. James hire you as his defense attorney, and I just missed it?"

"Nope, just giving you the facts, ma'am. Just the facts. I'd hate to see you with egg on your face. What's the Fed thinking?"

"He doesn't like him for Hotah's murder either."

* * * * *

"So, here's the deal," Cheri opened the conversation with Jesse as an officer brought him back to the interview room from lockup without handcuffs. She was already sitting at the table with two cups of coffee. Both red this time.

"Why don't you sit down?" Cheri offered as she pointed to a chair.

"I told you, I want a lawyer," Jesse said, cutting her off, clearly upset and fully on guard. His back was literally up against the wall, arms were folded across his chest, his jaw clenched and his face stoic.

"Please, Jesse. Just let me explain?" Cheri asked calmly without raising her voice.

Making no response, he glared back at her through narrowed and very stormy blue eyes.

"Look, I no longer believe you had anything to do with the murder," she declared.

"What?" Jesse asked, his eyes flaring. He placed both of his hands on the table, palms down. "What do you mean, exactly, when you say, *no longer?*

"Exactly that," she replied. "I no longer consider you a suspect."

"I don't believe you. More likely this is some kind of trick to get me to talk without a lawyer?"

"Does an innocent man need a lawyer?" she asked with a little exasperation of her own.

He stared at her, but once again gave no response. He simply crossed his arms over his chest and placed his back against the wall.

"Come on, why do you think you're not in handcuffs right now?"

He shrugged.

Changing tactics, Cheri tossed her hands in the air and said, "Okay, don't talk. Just listen."

Another shrug and a twitch of an eye, was all she received in response.

Cheri took that as a yes and dove right in and began methodically laying out her case against him.

"Number one. You were the last person seen talking to the victim at Maria's.

"Number two. Her fingerprints were found on your driver's window and the driver's side mirror.

"Number three. Her shoe print was found in the mud on your running board.

"Number four, and the most damning, was your DNA under her fingernails from where she scratched your neck. And, by the way," she continued, "you never fully explained that to me."

Jesse nodded in agreement.

"You see? At first blush, this looked like an open and shut case." *Link's kid or not*, she thought. "Jesse, I *knew* you were my perp, case closed." After she let it soak in for a few seconds, she then destroyed her own case. "Because we are thorough and I have the best CSI tech this side of anywhere, we kept digging."

"Number one. We only found fingerprints on the outside of your vehicle, but none on the inside, nor did we find any DNA which indicates that she was probably never inside your truck.

"Number two. The tire prints that we believe belonged to the murderer was a common brand, fourteen-inch tire sold at Walmart. Clearly not belonging to your truck.

"Number three is up to you. I'm hoping you can give me a solid alibi for your whereabouts after you left Maria's Saturday night that will allow me to cut you loose."

Jesse didn't acknowledge her last statement. He seemed to relax and take a breath just for a moment. Then his total demeanor changed. His jaw tightened and his eyes went wild all over again as he started pacing, running his fingers through his hair.

"What's the matter, Jesse? I told you I don't believe you did it."

"That's all well and good, but it still means that someone murdered that poor girl." Jesse pounded his fist into the tabletop. "If I wouldn't have left her in that parking lot, she might be alive right now."

Cheri half stood. "Do not put that on yourself." She paused briefly to let her words sink in and then continued. "Besides, it's self-indulgent and it does not help the situation."

He turned back toward Cheri. "What can I do?" he asked in earnest.

"Well, there's more," Cheri said, wondering how he was going to take the news.

Jesse took a breath. "More what?" Before Cheri could answer he blurted, "More suspects?"

"No," Cheri said. "More victims."

He leaned in towards Cheri and said in a quiet, scary voice, "What are you talking about?"

She looked Jesse in the eye. "Not only do I have at least one, maybe two murderers still on the loose, it appears that I have yet another body that we didn't even know about until today."

Leaning forward, he placed the palms of his sweaty, nervous hands on the cool top of the stainless-steel interview table. "Come again?"

"You better sit down for this one." She sighed

He sat.

"When you were still my prime suspect, I heard that you had been at the ER and had left some bloody clothes behind in the trash. I had our forensic specialist go over and pick them up. She finished running the tests on them an hour ago."

"Is that even legal?" he asked without any anger. "I never gave you permission."

"You didn't have to give permission once you threw the clothing away."

Another shrug followed by, "And?"

"Well, all the blood was definitely yours," she assured him. "But we found something totally unexpected."

"Okay? And it was…what?"

"We found human decomp tissue on the toe of your right shoe?" She ended the statement as a question.

"Come again? You found what? Exactly?"

"Forensics found decomposing human tissue on the toe of your right shoe."

"Well, how'd it get there?" Jesse nearly yelled, his guard snapping back instantly. His face went flush as his anger and mistrust regained their proper place.

"Wait, Jesse. We now know the name of the victim, and we also believe it couldn't have been you."

She quickly explained the rest of the details before he could get angrier.

"Okay," he said slowly once she finished. "In that case, what do you want from me?"

"Where could you have possibly picked up the tissue?"

"I don't know," he exclaimed, throwing his hands up in the air in frustration.

"Those shoes were brand new before I went on the run with Celia."

"Why did you pick that day to buy new shoes?"

"I wanted to hedge my bet for the run with her," he said as his cheeks turned a light shade of red. "When she appeared so confident, I decided to buy the best running shoes I could find. It just about killed me to throw them away."

"Well, the fact that they were new really kind of helps. Where did you go with them?"

"Nowhere! That's the point. They were *brand new*."

"I need you to think for a moment, Jesse. Where did you go after you put them on?"

"Like I said, nowhere. I put them on and then met Celia at the park and we ran."

"Where did you run?"

"We did five killer laps around the lake on the bike path, and then she tried to lose me by running up the hill toward the lookout. I was able to keep up with her until she turned and started running off trail back down the hill, when I—" He stopped mid-sentence and stared at Cheri for a moment.

"When you what?"

"When my right foot tripped on something in the deep grass, I tumbled the rest of the way down the hill to the bike path. I hit my head on one of those big rocks that line the trail."

"Where was that?" Cheri asked impatiently.

He looked at her, confused.

"Jesse, where did you trip?"

"Um, I'm not sure, exactly." He looked up at her. "Come to think of it, I didn't really pay much attention to where I was. But hey, if you'll find the pool of dried blood I left on the rocks, that'll be close."

"Do you remember where that was?"

"Well, I was sitting up when Celia went and got my truck... She's the one that drove me to the hospital."

Cheri nodded, waiting for him to go on, but said nothing.

"So, from the parking lot, it was past the old water wheel and about halfway to the display of the big native dugout canoe," Jesse continued. "There should be a good-sized pool of dried blood on the edge of the path, where it is closest to the hill."

Cheri nodded her head again as she frantically scribbled in her notebook.

"We were running straight down the hill, and I doubt it will be more than ten yards up the hill. Oh, look for a patch of thistles. You know the ones with nasty little burrs? I crashed through them when I first tripped."

"Celia mentioned the burrs in your face and hands," Cheri commented.

"You talked to Celia?" Jesse asked.

"Yes. I interviewed her at Maria's."

"Speaking of Celia, I tried calling her several times, but she wouldn't answer."

Cheri looked up at him for a moment. "Oh, about that." She winced before continuing. "I told her I thought you were a murderer and possibly a rapist, or maybe even a serial murderer and that she shouldn't see you or talk to you anymore."

"You what?" Jesse gasped as if the room suddenly lost all oxygen.

"Sorry." She cringed at her own pitiful tone. "I am so sorry, Jesse. But you yourself saw the evidence that was mounting against you. Would you want someone like Celia hanging out with someone like that?"

"That's just grand. I nearly get blown up earlier today, thrown in jail, and now Celia thinks I'm a murderer."

"I said I was sorry." She said lamely. "And, by the way, you still smell like burnt hair."

"Thanks,"

"Were you aware that she didn't know you were Link's son?"

"I never thought that it was important to identify myself as such," Jesse argued. "Besides, not everyone knows my dad."

"You'd be surprised." Cheri grinned as her cell rang again. "Go for Perry." She listened a moment before saying. "Standby for a moment." She looked at Jesse. "Is there any way you can go see Celia on your own and update her on what we've been through today?"

"*We've* been through?" Jesse said with just a tiny bit of sarcasm.

"You know what I mean. And if I haven't said it enough, I'm sorry to have raked you over the coals, but for a while, you must admit, you sure looked good for my perp."

"I get it," Jesse admitted reluctantly. "What about you? Aren't you coming along to back me up?"

"I'd love to, but I need to find out what you tripped on running down that hill," Cheri said. "Oh, and I asked the impound guys to bring your truck around."

"Roger that. Then, I'll be on my way."

CHAPTER TWENTY-SEVEN

On the drive over to Maria's, Jesse couldn't get Celia off his mind. Did she really think he was a murderer? Glancing in the rear-view mirror at a red light, he realized how crazy he looked with smudges on his face and burnt hair. *We just met. She really knows nothing about me. So why is she so important?* The light turned and he pushed the gas pedal hard and accelerated. *What am I going to say to her?* "Oh, it was nothing. The cops just arrested me for possibly being a serial murderer and or rapist but, hey, don't worry about it. It's no big deal." *She'll jump right back into that granite shell, and I'll never get her out.*

He punched a speed dial number on his cell phone. *She's so wary that she might not even give me the time to tell her.* The call was answered in the middle of the first ring. "Did they let you keep your phone in jail?" Link asked as a greeting.

"No, Dad. I'm out. They let me go just a few minutes ago," Jesse said with a little more emotion than he realized as the relief flowed through him yet again.

"What? That's incredible news, Jesse." Link cheered. "I've been worried sick. I've got Ty and his team flying in from Chicago in the morning."

"Thank you, Dad, but you can call them off. Deputy Perry said I was free to go." He then took Link through the entire ordeal until he got to the shoes. "You're not going to believe what they found on my shoe," Jesse exclaimed. He quickly described the last twenty-four hours, finishing with Cheri cutting him loose.

"That news could not be better, son," Link said with relief in his voice. "So how do you know Celia?"

"It's a long story, but there is something about her that I've never encountered before..." Jesse trailed off, picturing her in his mind.

"Hmmm, good or bad?" Link asked.

"I'm thinking mostly good, except that she kicked my butt on a run," Jesse replied, even now smiling to himself. "I can't keep from thinking about her, but Deputy Perry went and told her that I might be a murderer and now she won't answer my calls."

"Well, you don't hear that every day," Link commented with a chuckle. "It's not funny yet it is, now that you're no longer the accused. As for Celia, it's amazing how far she's come. What do you know about her?"

"Not much, but I'm starting to wonder what you know, or rather *how* you know her."

"That's a long story all by itself, but if I only have a minute, here it is." Link paused as if gathering his thoughts. "I first met her when she was just a ragged little girl during the Balkan wars. Her family had been murdered, and I stumbled across her, nearly starved and scared to death." Link trailed off for another moment, but Jesse knew there would be more, so he kept quiet.

"Son, some very brutal things happened to her at the hands of some vicious people before I found her." Link's jaw was set and the muscles on the side of his head were popping in and out. "From what Maria says, she's still struggling mightily with the aftermath. Even after all these years, she's still having nightmares."

Jesse's heart began to jackhammer and he had to swallow hard before he could speak. "She seems normal to me."

"Does she?" Link paused and took a deep breath. "Good or bad, she's like no one you've ever met."

The lump in Jesse's throat prevented him from answering.

"Yes, she does seem normal on the outside, but she is badly broken on the inside," Link stated cautiously. "So, tread carefully and be sure of what you're getting into, or turn and run away now."

"Are you trying to warn me off?" Jesse asked with a snarl through gritted teeth.

"Yes," Link replied firmly. "If you aren't willing to be careful with her. If you're not willing to take your time and slowly gain her trust, then yes. I'm warning you off. I don't want either one of you to get hurt. You are my son, and she's like a daughter to me."

Jesse calmed a bit before replying. "I'm not running, Dad."

"Somehow, I didn't think you would, but I needed to hear it. So, if not, would you take some advice?"

"Like what?" Came a cautious reply.

"Take it slow and be sure of your footing before taking the next step. Oh, and if you want to really impress her, say *Pivo Zolim* to ask for a beer," Link added with a chuckle.

"I'm not dumb enough to say that without knowing exactly what it means."

"Verbatim, it means, 'Beer I pray,' in Croatian."

"Okay, cool," Jesse said. "So, did you just say that the girl I can't quit thinking about is my sister?" with a relieved chuckle.

"Only in my heart," Link said. "I love you, son."

"I love you too, Dad." He ended the call as he pulled into Maria's parking lot and backed into an empty slot. After shutting down the big diesel engine, he paused for a quick moment to take a deep breath before finally opening the door.

As he stepped down from the running boards, he noticed a single white flower growing up through a crack in the cement. The light from the streetlamp was just enough to reflect off its little, pale white petals. Squatting down, he took a closer look at this little bit of life, struggling mightily, to show itself to the world.

Wow, he thought as it made him smile. It looked like it had been previously crushed, probably by another vehicle, yet it continued to survive. He looked at it and then looked at the door to Maria's. With a smile dancing on his lips, he gently and carefully plucked the flower from the crack and walked toward the entrance. Jesse stepped into the crowded restaurant and spotted Celia behind the bar. Working his way in her direction, he approached a vacant stool at the end of the busy bar. "Anyone sitting here?" he asked an old man dressed in faded overalls and a sweat-stained white cowboy hat, nursing a longneck.

"Nope, it's all yours, partner." the man said and took a pull on his beer.

Jesse sat down and waited for her to notice him, wondering if she would continue to avoid him as Cheri had instructed.

The old guy looked at the flower in his hand, chuckled, and leaned toward Jesse. "Son, That there reminds me of a woman's trust." Pointing his weathered finger at the flower he continued. "So fragile at first, and rightly so, but, if nurtured carefully, it can become strong and resilient. If you can manage that, you'd really have something special."

Jesse grinned at the wisdom and leaned toward his new neighbor. "Well, it's not really like that." *But what, exactly, was it?* he asked himself as he watched her working.

Celia finished ringing up a sale at the cash register and dropped a sizable tip into the jar. Turning back to her customers, she scanned the scattered tables, checking for empty beer bottles. She was working the bar solo, and the kitchen was already closed. Besides the bouncer, she was the only one on a Monday night. Her search eventually took her back to the long, wooden bar. She was checking for anyone there who might need another round when she spotted him sitting at the end of the bar by himself.

The smartwatch on her wrist started to beep loudly, so she quickly clamped a hand over it to muffle the tattle-tale sound. *"What is my problem?"* she thought in frustration. Not that anyone would hear her watch over the din anyway. The problem was, she didn't need a watch to tell her about her heart. The real issue was trying to figure out why her heart wasn't listening to reason.

He's Link's kid. He's arrogant. He's just like all the other spoiled Americans. He's not even good looking, she lied. *I just need to push him away and be done with it.* She made up her mind. *And besides, how am I supposed to apologize for thinking he was a murderer?* Taking a deep breath, she picked up a bar rag and nonchalantly walked toward him, calm, cool and collected.

She was still several feet from him when he looked up and grinned at her.

BEEP! BEEP! BEEP!

She stopped short as he held out a single, beautiful, little white flower. She gasped, the air suddenly went out of the room, and she grabbed the bar with both hands as if she were going to fall. Her head dropped and her eyes stung with unwanted tears. She quickly looked away, blinked her eyes for a moment and then trained her gaze back on Jesse. Composure mostly restored, a foggy memory from long ago invaded her mind.

"Are you okay?" Jesse asked, standing up, still holding the flower.

"Yes, of course," she lied. She felt totally unnerved and at great risk of losing her resolve. Celia looked away, pretending to scan the other patrons at the bar, but she wasn't seeing them. Only a hazy memory of sunshine, a bench, a flower...laughter... Taking a deep breath, she looked back at Jesse.

"What is this for?" she asked almost testily without taking it from his hand.

"I don't know." He shrugged, his confidence taking a blow. "It was growing up through a crack in the pavement and I just thought it was awesome." He placed the flower in an empty highball glass left on the bar. "It was beautiful and definitely tough, pushing up through the asphalt parking lot, and...then I thought of you...." He trailed off with another shrug, but his eyes never left hers. "I just thought you might like it."

She lost all her composure and blurted, "Jesse, I'm so sorry. Cheri called a little while ago and explained everything." Her words came tumbling out like a rapid-fire machine gun and didn't slow down. Her accent heavy. "I am so sorry. The police told me they thought you were responsible for the murder, and not to talk to you or see you." *BEEP! BEEP! BEEP!* "I wanted to answer your calls, but I couldn't. Then when I heard you had been in an explosion...I..." She stared at him, her eyes searching his. Then, reaching down, she plucked the flower from the empty glass and held it to her heart. The raw emotions wracked her mind and body as her heart thrilled and threatened to climb out of her chest. Elation and fear, no terror, in equal parts. Feelings she swore she would never allow. *No!* Tearing her eyes away from him, she spun around and faced away. *What is happening to me? I am losing all control.* She thought desperately while gripping tightly to her bar rag in one hand and the tiny little flower in the other. Blinking rapidly, refusing to let her heart do the talking, she was desperate to regain her resolve. Celia locked her eyes into the distance and deliberately set her jaw. Next she took a deep breath, held it and pressed inward. Purposefully stomping down the unwanted feelings she could ill afford. *There.* She thought calmly as she slowly let out her breath, steeling herself before turning around to face him. Once again wearing her usual porcelain facade. You must *be strong.*

Celia?" Jesse asked, holding his hands as if in prayer.

"Yes." She deliberately monotoned.

"*Pivo zolim?*" Jesse asked.

"*What?*

BEEP BEEP BEEP

Oh No!

Where did you hear that?" she asked in surprise as an unwanted smile flashed across her lips and her cheeks flushed, shattering all hope of regaining her self control.

"Um, did I say it right?" he asked, smiling at her with the prettiest blue eyes.

"Well, yes." She laughed and gave in.

"Oh good." Jesse exclaimed like a little boy.

"That is, if you want a beer." she said

"Oh, yes. Definitely."

"Um… Okay, what would you like? No wait. Let me guess. A Corona?"

"So you were paying attention the other night. Now I'm sure of it."

She gave him his answer with another blush as she turned toward the beer cooler.

"Um, I didn't think you worked Sunday and Monday?" Jesse asked as she popped the top off of his beer.

"I normally don't," she agreed, "but we are short-staffed tonight and Maria was not feeling well, so I told her I would work tonight and close up."

"What time do you close?" Jesse asked.

"We close at midnight."

Jesse checked the time on his phone. "That's only a couple of hours away. Mind if I stick around till closing and then we can talk?"

"No, Jesse. I've got a lot of work to do before closing and Maria is counting on me." she said, looking around at the other patrons still enjoying themselves before reluctantly looking back at Jesse with his lopsided smile. *I still have a chance to push him away.* she thought

"And even more work after closing, so it wouldn't be a good idea." she said as reinforcement. *There, I said it. But what if I don't want to push him away.* Her thoughts warred within her.

"With all that work to do, couldn't you use an extra hand?" he suggested. "Come on, you can't turn down free labor, can you?"

She looked down at the flower, still in her hand, and lifted it to her nose, breathing it in. More waves of faded memories rolled through her mind.

Jesse just continued to smile and wait expectantly, when he cocked his head to one side, she lost all her resolve.

"No. I mean, yes." She finally relented. "I'd like that." *I want that.*

"Good, I'm going to run home and take a quick shower. I really need it since I've been blown up, arrested, and put in jail today. I'll be right back."

"That's a good idea." Celia laughed as she wrinkled her nose.

"I'll see you in an hour." With that he headed for the exit. Celia watched him until the door closed behind him and looked at the flower once again. She looked up at the bar mirror and placed the delicate white flower in her long dark hair. *BEEP BEEP BEEP.* But this time she smiled and made no attempt to cover the sound. She didn't need her watch to tell her what she was feeling. But now, if only it could explain why?

* * * * *

It was nearing closing time and the crowd at Maria's had already started to thin out. Someone who was in the mood for 80's classics had just filled up the jukebox with quarters. Celia smiled because she knew which one of her regulars was guilty. She stood up on a beer keg, cupped her hands to her mouth and yelled, "Last Call!" over Bon Jovi's *Livin' on a Prayer*.

She quickly filled a few last drink orders just as Jesse appeared in the doorway. He smiled as he caught her eye. *BEEP! BEEP! BEEP!* She watched him as he headed for the men's room. Grabbing an empty tray and a fresh bar towel, Celia began bussing the tables that had already emptied. She had just finished wiping down the last vacated table and was lifting her heavy tray full of empty beer bottles and drink glasses into the air when she was jerked backwards. Bottles went flying as she attempted to spin around to see who had yanked her off her feet as an arm constricted around her waist.

"Hey, boys, look what just dropped onto my lap," came a thick New Jersey accent. It was mixed with a drunken slur, followed by laughter that was more like a cackle. Celia tried to turn to see his face, but a vise-like grip around her middle held her fast against his chest.

"Let me go," she stated calmly but emphatically as she continued to twist and turn.

"Easy there," came the voice again. "I ain't gonna hurt ya. I'm just looking for a little help, heh. Ya see my glass is empty." Another laugh.

A switch flipped inside Celia. "Let me go *now*," Celia growled through gritted teeth. Her long hair partially covering her face.

"Oh, you don't need to be upset. I'll be real nice to ya."

Celia dropped her chin to her chest, then pushing off with her legs, threw her head backwards, smashing into the guy's nose. She heard a satisfying crunch as her captor let out a howl. She was instantly rewarded with a hard slap to the side of her head with a big, meaty hand. The blow caused her attacker to loosen his grip just enough for her to lean her body forward again. She pivoted and sent her right elbow smashing into his temple. The fluid motion was quickly followed up by a reversal with her other elbow hammering into his left cheekbone. Without pausing, she brought down a hammer fist to his groin while stomping on his foot. He dropped his grasp entirely in order to grab at his bleeding nose and wrecked gonads, allowing her to escape. She whirled around to face her attacker head on, left foot forward, taut as a piano string and breathing heavily. The whole fight lasted less than two or three seconds and left the guy laying on the wooden plank floor, bleeding and writhing in pain.

She looked from one to the next of his buddies. "I told him to let me go," she said, brushing the long strands of hair from her face. Her voice, dark and dangerous.

His buddies looked at her while holding their hands up in the air in surrender. "Sorry, lady," one said. "He shouldn't have done what he done."

The man vomited on himself causing them all to wince.

"Uh…" his buddy hesitated for a moment.

"Can we take him and go now?" another asked.

She nodded slowly as she backed away. Just then Jesse broke through the crowd from one direction and the bouncer came from the other. Both approached Celia as if she were a provoked lioness.

"Are you all right?" Jesse asked as the bouncer took up station between Celia and the drunken crowd.

Breathing heavily, she wiped her mouth with the back of her hand and looked at the blood on it from her split lip. Then she looked at the guy on the floor and just nodded her head without saying a word. She grabbed a napkin from another table and dabbed at her lip for a moment. Then, looking around, Celia simply picked her tray up off the floor and headed behind the bar.

Jesse watched her for a moment, then turned for the man that had assaulted her. The bouncer stopped him and said, "I got this." He grabbed the drunk off the floor and escorted them all out the door. A minute later, the bouncer walked back in and announced, "Last call."

Twenty minutes later, the bar was closed, and the bouncer had said good night. As he closed the door behind him, Celia slid the lock into place, turned and put her back to the door. She leaned against it for a moment and took a deep breath. *Thank God that's over.* She thought as she surveyed the bar. *But that's my life.*

CHAPTER TWENTY-EIGHT

Without being asked, Jesse started at one end of the bar, picking up chairs and setting them upside down on the small round and square tables. Boston's *Amanda* was playing as Celia grabbed a broom and worked her way around the large room behind Jesse's progress. Jesse stopped for a moment and squatted down to the floor. She stopped what she was doing for a moment and leaned on her broom to see what he was doing. He picked something up and, cupping it in his hand, walked toward her. When he reached her, he opened his hand and there was her flower. Gently and slowly, he put it back in her hair.

BEEP! BEEP! BEEP!

Then he took her left hand in his right, held it above her head and slowly spun her around. As she came back to face him, he pulled her in, just close enough to dance.

"No, I can't dance," she explained as she held out her broom.

He took the broom from her hand and leaned against the wall. "Then let me do all the work," he whispered.

She was hesitant at first. Jesse was afraid he'd screwed up, but then she relaxed. The rhythm took over and she began to sway with the music.

As Jesse held her, he heard the unmistakable sound of tummy rumble. He looked down to Celia in surprise. "Was that you?"

She was blushing and put her hand over her stomach. "Yes, I'm sorry. I haven't eaten since lunch, and the grill is already shut down for the night."

"So, let's see what we can find for leftovers," Jesse said as he took her hand and headed toward the kitchen doors.

"Just give me ten minutes, and I'll have you feasting on my culinary delights," Jesse declared as he yanked on the handle of the stainless-steel cooler door. "Are you a carnivore?" he asked as he turned back toward Celia.

"What do you mean?"

"Do you like meat?"

"Yes, of course," Celia replied.

"Ah, most excellent." He grabbed a twenty-ounce bone-in ribeye, a basket of portobello mushrooms, an onion, a cube of butter, a sprig of rosemary, and a clove of fresh garlic and set them out on the prep table. "This ought to do it."

She hopped up onto the prep table next to the groceries, gripping the edge of the table with her hands set next to her thighs and her feet dangling off the floor. "My feet are killing me."

Stopping at the stove, he lit a burner and turned it to medium heat. "You know, that's the first complaint I've ever heard from you. And you just went toe to toe with a drunken jerk."

She smiled at his comment. Raising her hand to gently touch where he had slapped her and then the back of her head where a small lump had formed. "More like head to nose."

"It's still a little red," Jesse observed as he reached for the cast iron skillet that hung on a rack above her head. Stepping around her, he placed it on the burner, and began humming as he poured some olive oil into the skillet.

"How will Maria feel about you getting attacked that way?" Jesse asked.

"I would never tell her. She doesn't need to worry about it."

Looking around, he made a beeline to the metal pantry racks and picked out a loaf of unsliced French bread. Dropping it onto the prep table next to the rest of the ingredients, he checked on the skillet.

"How is it that you seem to know what you are doing?" Celia asked.

"All the men in my family can cook. However, I used to do this for a living once upon a time in my ill spent youth."

"Ah. A man with his own secrets," Celia said as she raised both eyebrows.

Jesse raised an eyebrow of his own. "Toothpicks?" he asked, changing the subject.

"In the bar area by the front desk," she said, pointing toward the door.

After a moment or two she heard the jukebox kick on, and in a few more moments, he reappeared through the door, holding a half dozen paper-covered toothpicks in one hand and a bottle of Merlot in the other.

She furrowed her brow but said nothing.

"Don't worry, I put twenty bucks on the bar for the wine," he offered with another grin.

"Um, that's a thirty-dollar bottle of wine."

He looked at her sideways as he pulled the cork from the bottle. "Uh oh. Then, in that case...would it be possible for me to run a tab?"

She chuckled at his attempt at innocence.

BEEP! BEEP! BEEP!

Her heartbeat thrummed just a little faster as she watched Jesse move about the kitchen. He was in his groove, cooking while listening to an old Savage Garden song.

The oil in the skillet was sizzling hot when he tossed in the cubed ribeye seasoned with cracked black pepper and sea salt. The aroma of the searing seasoned meat made her even more hungry as it filled the room.

"Who are you?" she asked. "And where is it that you have come from?"

He looked up and smiled his lopsided grin and bobbed his eyebrows up and down but said nothing.

He pulled the seared meat from the pan and tossed it into a ceramic dish. Next, he tossed the mushrooms, butter, onions, chopped garlic and rosemary into the hot pan and stirred the mixture. He looked over at her and smiled. Snatching up a toothpick, he stabbed a chunk of ribeye and said, "Open."

She did as she was told and was promptly rewarded with the delicious tidbit. "Oh, how wonderful." *This man cannot be real…can he?*

"You think that's good? Just wait till it's all put together."

"It's not possible." She moaned. "I cannot wait."

"Patience, darlin'," he said with a southern drawl. "Can you hear that vibrant sizzle of the mushrooms?" As he spoke, he held his hand above the skillet.

"Yes," she agreed impatiently.

"Well, that's called *applause*," he explained. "Just when the applause starts to die down a little, we add the wine."

After just a couple of minutes, the applause began to quiet. Jesse reached for the open bottle next to Celia.

He was so close. She wanted to reach out and touch him, but something held her back. *He's like no one I've ever met.*

"I won't need the whole bottle for the food, and I certainly don't want a thirty-dollar bottle of wine to go to waste," he said with mock deep concern in his voice.

"No, that would not be good," she agreed.

"Therefore, we must beg the very important question," he stated with authority.

"And that is…?" She asked eagerly,

"Straight from the bottle? Or…" He raised an eyebrow for effect. "Do I need to get us a couple of glasses from the bar?"

"No glasses," she said, taking the bottle from his hand.

* * * * *

Victoria looked up when Link's cell phone rang in his coat pocket. He quickly pulled it out and looked at the number and looked at Victoria and Seth. "Well, what do you know? 811. It's about time they called me back." He put the phone to his ear. "Milton, what the hell happened?" He listened for a few seconds, nodding his head. "Say that again? What exactly do you mean the locator flags were somehow re-located incorrectly?" Link asked through clenched teeth as he exited into the hallway. "How is that even possible? Milton, my guys could have died out there." He was attempting to be calm, but the conversation could easily be heard even after the door closed.

"Who is he talking to?" Victoria asked, looking at Seth. "He sounds angry."

"He's talking to the general manager of the local 811 office."

"What's that?"

"Any time we need to dig more than a few inches deep, we call 811. They in turn would have any underground services such as buried telephone, water, sewer, power, electrical and especially gas and oil pipelines marked with flags in our specific area of operation. That way you wouldn't accidentally dig up something unexpected, like what happened earlier."

"What went wrong this time?"

"That's a great question."

* * * * *

Cheri rubbed her tired eyes and took a sip of hot, fresh coffee. It was her third cup, and it wasn't working well. In fact, it was working just as well as her makeup was in covering up the dark circles around her eyes. Her husband, Dean, was her best friend and the first one to tell her she was working too hard. She loved him dearly and didn't want to put him in a position to ask her to stop. She couldn't even slow down till this concluded. She loved the job, but she loved him more. Today, she wanted to eat her cake and still have it.

She and Bravis were going over the meager evidence, looking for anything they'd missed, when Cheri's cell rang. Pulling it from her pocket, she checked the caller ID and answered. "Go for Perry. What have you got for me, Belle?"

"Good morning to you, too," Belem replied. "Have you not had your coffee this morning?"

Ignoring the jibe, she asked, "Have you found anything yet?"

Yes, we found her just a few minutes ago. Or should I say, what's *left* of her. The reason why Mr. James didn't notice what he'd tripped over was because the resident coyotes had already begun helping Mother Nature. The body was somewhat disassembled. We've recovered everything except for the right ankle and foot."

"Any obvious cause of death?"

"No, but we're still looking. I hate to say it, but don't get your hopes up."

Cheri sighed. "Thanks, Belle. Let me know when you wrap it up."

"Will do."

Cheri disconnected the call and looked up at the FBI agent.

"Well?" was Bravis' single syllable question?

"They found another...body. But it doesn't seem to connect with anything you'd be interested in."

"Who's the victim?"

"Danielle Robertson. Age twenty-three. Until recently, worked as a CNA at Trinity Hospital but went missing a few weeks ago. They found her in Spring Lake Park less than a hundred yards from our first Victim, Tiffany Johnston."

"I'm liking our theory of multiple killers more and more," Bravis agreed. "But How'd you know where to look?"

"Now that's another interesting question." Cheri walked Bravis through the episode with Jesse James.

Bravis picked up another file. "I ran Jesse's name through our databases and got nothing on him to speak of. Although his dad and his brother flagged. So I ran both Lincoln James and Joshua James through a different database. While I was waiting, I checked their military records."

"What did you find?" she asked, waving her hand in a 'gimme' fashion.

"They are about as shallow as fiction can make them."

"What do you mean?" Cheri asked, rubbing her eyes again while trying unsuccessfully to stifle a yawn.

"It means that Lincoln's record basically says he joined, went to flight school, and then it trails off to a dead end. So, I checked Joshua's record, and at first it looked normal, but then a few months ago, his record also trails off to a similar dead end."

"That does sound interesting," Cheri commented, her eyes just a bit less tired.

"That's not what's really interesting."

"If *that's* not, then what is?" Cheri felt her investigative curiosity spooling up.

"While I was reviewing the records, I got a call from the Justice department telling me to quit looking."

"At who? The dad or the son?"

"Both."

"That is *very* interesting," Cheri agreed as she quickly scribbled some notes.

CHAPTER TWENTY-NINE

I t was late afternoon as Jesse pulled into the parking lot. Celia was already waiting outside of Maria's; she waved and gave him a dazzling smile when she caught sight of him.

Damn.

Celia was wearing a pair of khaki cargo shorts, her white tennis shoes, and her dark, wavy hair tumbled loosely down the front of a simple white peasant blouse. *How is it that she never tries to dress up, but she looks so good anyway?* He swallowed hard as he brought his truck to a stop beside her and put it in Park.

"I am so glad you have the evening free," Jesse said as she hopped into his truck.

"I know, right?" she gushed. "When Maria found out about that jerk last night, she insisted I take the night off."

"From what you said last night, I'm surprised you even told her."

"I didn't," Celia said with a deeper tone. "It was the bouncer. He thinks he's my big brother or something."

"Oh, okay, that makes more sense." He grinned. "But I'm glad he did."

"I kind of agree," she said, her voice low, her accent sweet, as she looked up at him through her curtain of hair while she buckled her seatbelt. "Maria and Jake can handle it."

"You know, I'd have thought you would have some bruising where he hit you," Jesse commented. "But there isn't any that I can see."

"I am tougher than most realize, and I don't bruise that easily."

He put the truck in gear and pulled out onto the street. "So, definitely not a princess and the pea problem, huh?" He slid her a sideways glance.

She chuckled. "No, I think you are right in this."

"Well, that's a good start."

"What is?"

He grinned. "Me being right."

"I see that the cuts on your face are healing. How is the back of your head?" she asked.

"Still hard as a rock, I guess." Jesse shrugged off the question as he turned north on Highway 85. *Maybe almost as hard as a rock.*

"Tell me again, why are we going to *walk* around the lake instead of running?" she asked as Jesse drove the relatively short distance to their destination.

"Um, maybe because I'm still too sore from *first* being run to death by a mad woman and *then* nearly getting blown up. The truth is, I couldn't run today if my life depended on it," he said as they pulled into the parking lot of Spring Lake Park.

"Yeah, I think that is it…" She giggled at his confession. The sound made something inside him flutter.

"Or maybe I didn't want to get my butt kicked again by a beautiful girl." He watched her face for a reaction, testing the waters before he turned his eyes back to the road. He was on the shakiest ground he'd ever walked with a girl. She made him feel things that he'd never experienced before. Things that were both exciting and at the same time, very uncomfortable.

"Perhaps a little of both problems, I think," she offered thoughtfully.

After finding a parking spot, Jesse shut off the engine, and they both climbed out of the truck, each with a water bottle in hand. They met up by the tailgate and set off together toward the bike path.

"Should I walk slowly for you?" she offered with a teasing smile. "You *are* moving rather stiffly."

"Naw, I'll be alright. I'm almost as tough as you."

There was a festive feeling in the afternoon air even though there was no particular holiday. As they turned onto the bike path, the smell of smoke from the many charcoal grills wafted along the soft, gentle breeze.

"Well, maybe it would be better if we did walk slowly," he said as he looked down at her. "That way I might be able to sneak your hand into mine while we walked without you noticing?"

"Now that sounds interesting. But why would you not want me to notice?"

Jesse grinned, changed the water bottle into his other hand and gently took her hand in his. His heartbeat picked up dramatically. *I'm glad I don't have a smart watch.* He thought.

It was late afternoon, and the sun was leaning toward the west but still warm. The scattered white clouds were striking against the deepening blue sky. Music drifted on the breeze from scattered groups gathered at various pavilions. As they walked, one would grow louder and the last one would fade.

"How was your day at work?" she inquired. "It was well after two when you left the bar last night."

Jesse chuckled. "It was pretty ugly, but I was back up at five, showered and at work by six. We were in the morning safety briefing when my foreman took one look at me and sent me home. He thinks it had something to do with being nearly blown up, and I didn't tell him otherwise."

"What did you do with the rest of your day?" She asked

"I slept till noon and then ran some errands. All in all, it's been a fruitful day, I think."

At the beach by the swimming area, families with blankets spread out, watched their children playing in the water and squealing with delight. The old water wheel turned a little faster than normal with the runoff from the spring rains.

"No one has ever given me a flower since I was a little girl," she confided as she kept her eyes on the path. "Especially a little white one." As she finished her comment, she took a quick glance in Jesse's direction.

Jesse grinned but said nothing as he gently released her hand and wrapped his arm around her shoulder.

BEEP! BEEP! BEEP!

I love that watch. A smile spread across his lips and a tingle did a happy dance throughout his entire body.

Mother ducks with babies had waddled up from the water and were hungrily feeding on the breadcrumbs that kids from a birthday party threw to them. Wiggling their fuzzy tails, some of the ducklings couldn't have been more than a few days old. In the distance, the twinkling music of an ice cream truck could be heard circling the park in search of young customers.

As they continued to walk, a totally different smell of food cooking hit them. It wasn't long before they came to a fully setup campsite. It sported a picnic table decked out with a tablecloth and plastic eating utensils, and a beautiful, blue-eyed husky laying down on a dog bed and tethered to a tree. He was a large, furry dog, and when his mouth was closed, he looked as if he were smiling. "Where is everyone?" Jesse uttered as he looked around.

There was a wood fire crackling in the fire pit with a cast iron Dutch oven hung from a black metal tripod and nestled just above the hot coals.

"Wow, what smells so good?" Celia asked.

"I don't know, but people should not be leaving a fire unattended," Jesse said with a touch of anger in his voice. "Especially with a poor dog here."

Stepping off the path, he wandered into the campsite, first looking at the fire and then at the dog.

"Hello?" Jesse called. No answer came, but he did receive an eager set of tail wags from the smiling dog. "At least the dog seems friendly."

"Maybe they had to go use the bathroom?" Celia guessed.

"Maybe," he agreed. "What do you think about this dog?" Jesse asked as he carefully approached the dog.

"Jesse, this is not our camp. We shouldn't be here," Celia stated. Jesse noticed the pitch of her voice increase as he eased up to the big pup and carefully reached out his hand.

The huge dog had to be pushing a hundred pounds and, from the size of his empty bowl, he ate a lot. The husky stood up and sniffed his hand, and his tail began to wag even faster.

"Hey there, big guy," Jesse said as he scratched the dog behind the ears. "Where's your people?" He looked around at the camp again. "And what smells so good?"

Stepping from one foot to the other and furtively looking up and down the path, Celia begged, "Jesse, please. I think we need to get out of here before the owners come back."

"Yeah, you're probably right," Jesse admitted.

He stood back up from petting the dog and wandered over to the fire. There was a large silver serving spoon laying on top of a well-used oven mitt. He glanced up and down the path. Seeing no one, he picked up the serving spoon in his left hand and slid his right hand into the mitt.

"What are you doing?" Celia asked in a harsh whisper. "Please, let's just go before we get into trouble. Whoever owns this camp will get very angry if they catch us. They might even call the police." The alarm in her voice continued to build.

"Okay, okay. You're right," Jesse conceded. "I just want to see what's inside the pot, then we'll go."

Before she could say another word, he lifted the heavy cast iron lid off the pot. As the steam rolled up around the lid, the most amazing aroma came boiling out. "Wow, that smells so good," Jesse exclaimed in his own hushed whisper. The mixture looked like some sort of heavy stew with vegetables, potatoes, and big chunks of meat.

Celia took a step backward toward the bike path. "Jesse, please?" Nearly in tears, she wrung her hands together. "I'm going back to the truck. I'm serious."

"I know, I know. Let me just taste it and then we'll go," he promised.

"No!" she practically yelled as he dipped the big spoon into the pot and lifted a portion to his lips. She stared at him in disbelief as he blew on it and took a taste. "I'm not going to go to jail," she hissed, then she turned and headed to the path.

"Wow, Celia. You should try this," he exclaimed. "It tastes just like lamb peka."

She stopped in her tracks and spun around. "Lamb peka? How do you even know what that is?"

"I did a little research and found this great recipe," he said, grinning. Then he turned to the dog. "Hey, Larry.

This is the pretty girl I was telling you about." Larry's tail wagged like crazy.

"What…?" Open mouthed, Celia looked from Jesse to the dog and back again. "But how?" The shock was still in full force.

Jesse reached over and untethered Larry and gave him another big scratch.

"You asked me what I did after I woke up," Jesse said, grinning. "Well, this is it," he finished with outstretched hands.

"Wait. You mean this is your camp?"

"Yeah." Jesse confirmed. "Larry, too."

"You mean this was a trick?" Celia's green eyes flashed dangerously as she realized what he meant. *BEEP! BEEP! BEEP!* The sun was setting behind her, and the reddening skies reflected her growing anger.

"Whoa, there," Jesse said as the grin vanished from his face. "Celia, I just wanted to surprise you with the lamb *peka* and it was just so much fun seeing you confused, I couldn't help myself." He said in his own defense displaying the best version of his innocent, lopsided grin. She stood motionless yet vibrating, lips pursed, saying nothing.

Oh, no. His guts began to twist. *I hope I didn't blow it.*

Larry trotted over to Celia, sat down in front of her, and began licking her hand and whining. Jesse watched as Larry began to soften her anger. Her breathing slowed and her shoulders relaxed. *Oh, that's a good sign.*

Mostly keeping her eyes on Larry with only a furtive glance at Jesse as she cleared her throat. "Um, you did all this for me?" she asked, her voice quiet in disbelief.

"I wanted to do something for you that you would never expect."

She slowly raised her head, the hardness in her eyes was gone, her accent, sweet and soft. "I don't know what to say."

"Well, you could try some of my lamb peka?" he said as he lifted the lid off the pot.

"It does smell delicious." She admitted as she gave Larry a final scratch before walking towards Jesse.

"But how is it that you know about food from Croatia?" she asked as he picked up a bowl and set it on a plate, then grabbed a hunk of buttered bread and brought it back to the pot and ladled out a portion into the bowl. "I looked it up on the internet this morning and got this crazy idea." He handed her the bowl and offered her a folding camp chair by the fire. Sitting down, she looked at the bowl, stared at him a moment, and then dipped her bread and took a bite.

The look on her face said it all. *I win,* he thought. *But that was close.* She quickly picked up her spoon and took a mouthful of the stew with a big hunk of meat. Without saying anything, her face told him everything he needed to know. *I am no longer in big trouble. At least for now.*

After they ate, Larry laid down at their feet.

"Who names a dog Larry?" she asked as she scrunched up her face.

"I don't know," he said. "Larry is a rescue dog, and he came with that name. It's almost as bad as a boy named Sue." He chuckled at his own remark.

Celia looked confused for a moment. "Oh, are you referring to the Johnny Cash song?" She giggled. "Well, I like him, even if his name is Larry."

"As a matter of fact, Larry doesn't normally take to new people very well. I think he was abused when he was a pup. So, when he went up to you and licked your hand, I just about fell over."

"I think he has your blue eyes," she said teasingly with a twinkle in her own.

"Oh yeah? Well, I think he definitely has your smile."

CHAPTER THIRTY

A full five weeks had flown by since the twins were born. After Jenny was more or less discharged and healed from her C-section, she still had a room at the hospital to stay with the twins. Today was the day they were all coming home. Seth struggled with the new car seats in the back seat of his four-door pickup. After twenty minutes of fruitless attempts, he finally lifted the cover on the back of his truck and searched the empty car seat boxes for the instructions. He was pressed for time as Jenny and the girls were due to check out any minute, and he wasn't ready. He stood there, instructions in hand, staring, but he wasn't really looking at them. His mind's eye was distracted by the doubt creeping in from around the edges. Doubt? Or was it fear he felt in his gut? *Fear of what though?* Fear of not being a good dad? Fear of not being good at taking care of them? Fear of having someone so precious in his life, once again? Fear of losing them…once again.

"Excuse me, Seth, would you like some help?" A voice broke into his mental anxiety.

"What?" Seth looked up and saw Brooke standing there, looking good even in her scrubs. "Oh, uh. Hi, Brooke."

"You poor thing. You look totally confused," Brooke said as she put her hand on his arm. "I'd love to help you with those car seats if you want."

"Uh, yeah," Seth said. "I didn't realize how difficult they are to install."

"You men." She laughed sweetly as she climbed into his truck. "You are always trying to make it harder than it really is. It would be much easier on everyone if you could only see what's right in front of you." She paused but Seth just stared at all the straps. "But, in fact, they are actually quite easy once you figure it out. When I worked for Doctor Griffin, we gave classes on this stuff."

Seth watched intently as she went to work pulling straps and buckles, then a couple of clicks. "There you are," she said with satisfaction as she climbed out of the truck. "We must keep those sweet little babies of yours safe, now don't we?" Her dazzling smile fell off her face and was replaced by something cold and dark as her eyes looked past Seth.

"Are you okay?" he asked as he turned to see what she was staring at. Taylor was pushing Jenny in her wheelchair through the double doors with Ivy right behind them, pushing a cart with the twins.

"Hey, I've got to get to work," Brooke stated curtly. She stood very close to Seth, looking up at him, then looking back toward Jenny.

"Uh, yeah. Thanks for the help." *What was that all about?* Seth wondered.

"Anything for you and those adorable babies," Brooke said, the smile back on her face. Without warning, she went up on her toes to kiss him on the cheek, looked straight at Jenny, and headed into the hospital without another word.

"What was that all about?" Jenny asked with a little extra zing in her voice.

"What? Brooke?" Seth replied, pointing his thumb in Brooke's direction. "She was just showing me how these new kinds of car seats work." He leaned in for a quick kiss, but she tilted her head the other way and dodged him.

"Seth, I don't like her." Jenny's eyes narrowed as she watched Brooke disappear through the entryway.

"Let's get these kiddos in the truck, shall we?" Ivy asked, interrupting whatever was happening.

"Uh, yeah. That would be great," Seth agreed but his mind was considering the innocent kiss...followed by a deliberate... *what was that... a challenge?* Seth knew it wasn't good.

Taylor looked from Jenny to Seth, then back over her shoulder toward the hospital door but said nothing as they began loading.

After everyone was in and buckled up, Taylor stood outside Jenny's open window. "I'll follow you out. I used the key you gave me and brought most of my stuff over last night. I found an empty room downstairs that looked like a cowgirl's dream. I hope that's okay."

"Absolutely," Jenny said. "Where are you parked?"

"That little red Ford Fusion over there is mine." She pointed with her index finger. "It's totally packed with the rest of my things from the dorm. I had no idea how much stuff I'd collected in such a short time."

"It looks like my car when I first arrived here from Chicago," Jenny admitted. "And before you take the twins out for any reason, we are going to find you something with a little more metal," Jenny sent a knowing glance at Seth.

* * * * *

Taylor and Jenny were in the newly remodeled nursery, changing the twins after they arrived at the cabin. The two women were less than four years apart and similar in build as well as personality. Taylor was fun to be around, and Jenny had begun feeling a connection. She had never had a friend close to her own age before. At least, not since she was a little girl, before her parents were killed.

Jenny began to speak without looking up, instead, concentrating on dressing Faith into her onesie. "Taylor, I have a confession to make."

"What's that?" Taylor asked

"I must admit to you that I really didn't like the idea of having an au pair when Seth brought up the idea. In fact, I fought it as best I could. But after getting to know you, I am so glad you're here and truly grateful to Seth for insisting."

"I was so nervous walking into that hospital room that day," Taylor admitted.

"Why?" Jenny asked in surprise.

"Because it wasn't until I arrived that I found out that he hadn't told you about me yet. I was worried that you would fire me before I even got started.

Jenny laughed. "I can imagine how intimidating it must have felt."

"I considered leaving while I was waiting outside the door."

Jenny laughed again. "When it comes to Seth and Link, they can be intimidating, but they are both big teddy bears inside."

"It wasn't them that scared me, it was that CNA Brooke," Taylor explained. "She kept staring at me like she was burning me with laser eyes."

"Yeah, well, Brooke is in a class all her own," Jenny agreed. "As for me, I am glad you kept your courage up enough to stick around."

"After the wedding, you can have my room if you want it," Jenny said, changing the subject. "It's got the best shower you've ever seen in your life."

"Don't you sleep in the master bedroom?" Taylor asked curiously.

"No, that's Seth's room."

"You mean you bore his children, twins even, and yet you don't sleep together?"

"Isn't that funny? I know it sounds kind of weird, especially if you don't understand the context," Jenny admitted with a chuckle. "But, the truth of the matter is, we decided to wait until we're married."

"If you love each other, what difference does it make?"

"Exactly," Came Jenny's reply, leaving Taylor to work it out for herself.

"Hello in the nursery?" Victoria said as she stepped through the door.

"Oh, hi, Victoria," Jenny greeted.

"How are the two most precious little babies in the whole wide world?" Victoria asked.

"Just getting their first fresh diapers in their new home. Would you like to hold baby Faith?" Jenny offered.

"Does Link drink coffee?" Victoria answered with a 'duh' tone followed by a chuckle as she held out her arms.

Jenny smiled as she handed the baby over to Auntie Victoria. "Speaking of coffee, where's Link?"

"He's out pouring himself a cup and talking to Seth in the Kitchen."

"Great," Jenny said a bit breathlessly, her face flushed. "I have something very important to ask him."

"Like what?" Victoria asked.

"If you and Taylor would follow me, you are sure to find out," Jenny said cryptically.

Taylor and Victoria followed her out the door and down the hall toward the kitchen.

Link was sitting at the granite kitchen island, and Seth was leaning up against the counter next to the coffee maker.

"Seth, I've got to admit it."

"Admit what?" Seth asked. "That you finally realize that I'm better looking than you?"

"No, smart ass, but you did hit a home run when you found this Black Rifle Coffee." Link took a sip.

Jenny cleared her throat in an attempt to get Link's attention as she slipped up onto the stool next to him.

"How is the prettiest new mom in Williston?" Link asked.

"The prettiest new mom in the whole state of North Dakota," Seth corrected with a smile.

Jenny blushed for a moment and slipped her arm through the crook in Link's elbow and stared up at him with her big blue eyes.

"Uh-oh," Link said. "Somethings up and I should probably be very afraid right now."

"Don't you go all scaredy-cat on me now," Jenny said. "At least give me a chance."

"What wouldst my lady liketh of me?" Link asked in a mock Shakespearean accent.

"Would you give me away at my wedding?" Jenny asked.

Link just stared and blinked, but no words came out.

Seth burst out laughing. "He's speechless! Link is actually speechless."

Link's own blue eyes became very shiny, and he rubbed them with his free hand. "Damn allergies."

"Is that a yes?" Jenny asked.

"Honey," Link began after composing himself. "It would be my greatest honor and privilege to give you a way at your wedding."

"Thank you," Jenny exclaimed and stood up and kissed him on the cheek.

"But under one condition," Link quickly added.

Jenny stepped back in surprise. "What's that?"

"That I get to give you away to somebody else besides that big jerk over there."

Jenny giggled a little girl giggle.

"Fat chance," Seth said.

"We are getting married at the New Hope Church," Jenny explained. "However, we are going to wait till the twins are at least six months old."

"Yeah, and then we get to go on our honeymoon," Seth added with a smile as he raised his eyebrows mischievously.

"Honeymoon?" Link asked. "Where are you going on your honeymoon?

Seth looked at Jenny and nodded.

"We are going for a full month to Greece and Italy!" Jenny screamed in excitement as she hopped up and down on her toes.

"Nice," Link said. "Great food, amazing weather, good people, plus the best ouzo."

"Uh, Link, there is one other thing we need to ask you." It was Seth's turn now to look solemn.

"Yes?" Link asked as he looked for the nearest exit.

"We'd like your permission to set up a 'Missing Man' table at the reception in honor of Jason."

The mist instantly returned to Link's eyes. Again, in as many minutes, he couldn't speak. Victoria came around behind him and hugged him, then Jenny slid over and wrapped her arms around him too. Link wiped his eyes on his sleeve, but words still would not come so he just nodded his head in approval.

"So, Link," Seth said obnoxiously loud. "Do you suppose you could manage the operations at Reagan while I'm out of the net for a whole month?"

Link burst out laughing, shattering the emotional moment and saving what little dignity he had left. "Are you kidding me? You've been out of the net ever since Jenny showed up at the cabin."

CHAPTER THIRTY-ONE

Reagan's office manager, Susan, heard the ringing phone as she hurried down the hall to her office. She carried her cup of coffee, and a stack of papers that she'd brought home with her. Doing her best at balancing it all in her left hand, while she fumbled with her keys in her right, as she turned the knob and hit the door with her hip and headed toward her desk. Just as she picked up the phone, her coffee dropped and splashed hot liquid all over her shoes and carpet.

"Damn," she exclaimed with the phone halfway to her mouth. "Uh, Reagan Oilfield Services, this is Susan, how may I help you?" It was her standard professional opinion to answer the phone the same way every time.

"Susan? This is Dale here with Bakken Lease Management. It sounds like you're having the same kind of morning as I have."

"Hey, Dale. I just managed to spill my coffee all over myself and my office."

"You have? Well, funny you should say that as I've got an oil spill here at the Laura Long Lease, and I need you guys out here as soon as possible."

Dale Lupton was a fourth-generation oilfield pumper. His great grandfather started in oil at the turn of the twentieth century in Wyoming and it just seemed to stay in the blood line. The cowboy hat, boots and jeans he wore wasn't his western outfit. It was who he was. Good under pressure and not easily ruffled, he was always calm, cool and efficient, no matter what the circumstances. His demeanor, easy confidence and simple way of speaking plainly, often reminded folks of Matthew Quigley.

"How big is the spill?" Susan asked.

"None that got past the berm, but you'll need your biggest truck and probably a tanker to offload into."

"What happened?" Susan asked. "Did a gathering pipe or tank rupture?"

"No, it's the strangest thing. I showed up this morning and the well pump was going crazy and pumping at twice the rate it should have been. Consequently, the oil storage tanks overflowed. I've got it all shut down now, so the problem won't be getting worse."

While he was talking, Susan looked up the location of the spill on her wall map and estimated the time enroute. "Tell you what Dale, I can have a crew on your spill site in about an hour if that'll work for you."

"That'll do just fine," Dale replied in his typical easy drawl.

"Are there any particular instructions to get out there?"

"Tell 'em to turn left at the T intersection, take the bridge over Dry Creek and they'll see my truck on the pad. They can't miss it."

"Thanks, Dale. We'll see you in an hour."

"See ya then," he replied and hung up.

Susan went to the electronic work board and dispatched the Boyington brothers for the cleanup. Once they arrived, if they needed more manpower or trucks, they would send more. The work board would automatically send the dispatch, by cellphone, to the brothers and their supervisor, Dave. With the urgency of this 'Pop-up' she decided to give the brothers a call just to confirm they saw the dispatch. She tried Dave first, but it went straight to voicemail, so next she tried Jeffrey.

"Howdy, Miss Susan," Jeffrey said in his southern Mississippi drawl.

"Hey, Jeffrey, did you see the dispatch I just sent?"

"Sure did, Miss Susan. Kody and I should be rolling in ten minutes."

"Thank you, Jeffrey. I tried to call Dave, but he didn't pick up."

"Link, Jesse and Dave took the drone out to check on the flagging markers before we re-start on the pipeline."

* * * * *

Jesse skillfully lifted the drone into the air and made a 360-degree turn.

"I can't get over how quiet it is," Dave commented.

"Yeah, I know. Right?" Jesse responded, smiling ear to ear. "I can't believe I get paid to do this."

"Nice hover too," Link added. He and Dave watched as Jesse maneuvered out of the hover and effortlessly began flying figure eight patterns.

"Son, can you get enough altitude to see the gas line marker flags on both sides of that hill at the same time? I want to make sure we don't have any more misplaced markers."

"I think so," Jesse acknowledged. "We'll know for sure in a minute or two."

The task at hand for the day was to examine the rest of the pipeline project from the air. They had two more miles to check out, and they could do the rest from this final vantage point.

"Okay," Link observed as he looked through a set of binoculars. "You can see the straight lines of the flagging all the way up the hill. Back where you hit the gas line, someone had shifted the flag line over exactly twenty feet, just as it came across the last hill so no one would notice."

"Hey, Dad, remember that white truck we saw the other day?" Jesse asked.

"Yeah," Link replied. "What about it?"

"I think we've got another bandit."

"Show me," Link said as he shifted his gaze from his binoculars to the video feed of the drone. It showed a white work truck in the wood line.

"Where is that?" Link asked.

Jesse pointed toward the north along a windrow. "He's parked near that tree line."

"Okay, that's very interesting, isn't it?" Link asked as he trained his binoculars on the tree line.

"What do you want to do, Boss?" Dave asked.

Handing the binoculars to Dave, Link pulled the cell phone out of his pocket and put his ear buds in. "Well, right now, he is just a bogey. We don't know for sure if he's a good guy or bad guy. But it's time to find out."

"Do you want me to take a closer look-see?" Dave asked.

"No. Jesse, keep him in sight but not so close that he notices you," Link commanded. "I want to get this all recorded on video."

"I can still go," Dave insisted.

"I don't think so, Dave. I've just got a feeling, so I'll go take a look-see for myself, and I want you and Jesse to give me a play by play of where he is and what he's doing while I'm enroute."

"Are you sure?" Dave asked.

"With any luck, I can catch up to him, ask him a few questions, and maybe find out who he's working for."

"Copy that, Dad. Be careful."

"Of course. I just want to find out what he's doing out here now, but even more important, who is he working for," Link explained again. "Corporate espionage will not be tolerated." With that, Link jumped in his truck and headed back out to the main road.

"I've seen that look before," Dave stated as he watched Link drive away.

"You have?" Jesse asked.

"Yeah, when these guys tried to pick a fight with him and Seth over at Maria's. It didn't end well for them."

Five minutes later, Dave's cell rang. "Go, Boss. I've got you on speaker."

"Hey, Dad," Jesse hollered.

"Sounds good," came Link's voice. "I'm coming up behind the line of trees on the far side of the ridge."

Jesse rotated the drone camera toward Link's location. "Okay. We can see you now and it looks like you're less than a hundred yards from his truck."

Link slowed his truck and pulled off into the trees. "Okay, can you get a good enough shot of the truck to figure out who owns it?" Link asked. "If this is corporate espionage, I want to know who we're dealing with."

"I can't see any logo," Dave said, still looking over Jesse's shoulder at the video feed. "It's just a plain white truck without any signs."

"What's he doing now?" Link asked as his own engine went quiet.

"He grabbed a yellow and black tool bag and carried it down to that bridge crossing the dry creek bed," Dave responded.

"Dave, you know this area better than me, what's on the other side of that bridge?" Link asked with concern.

"Boss, that particular bridge is the only land link to more than fifty oil wells and their tank farms. Dale over at Bakken Oil Lease Management is one of our customers. Until the pipeline gets finished, that's the only way his crude oil tankers can transport the oil. Without it, they would have to shut in the wells, at least temporarily."

"So, an average of forty barrels per well, per day, huh? That equates to what…?" Link paused. "At least two thousand barrels of oil a day?"

"We're using the same math, Boss," Dave agreed. "Not a huge dent in total Bakken production, but a dent nonetheless."

"We sure have had plenty of seemingly *random* dents lately," Link observed dryly as he rubbed his chin in thought. After a brief minute, he grabbed the heavy wad of truck keys, hefted them in his hand for a moment and dropped them into his jacket pocket and slid out of the truck onto the damp earth.

"Yeah," Dave responded. "Have you ever heard of death by a thousand cuts?"

"Yes, I have," Link agreed with a wry chuckle. "I sure have." He was already moving through the trees as his speech transitioned from talking to a whisper. Squatting down in the bushes, he caught a glimpse of the white truck and began easing quietly through the leaves and grass, still wet from last night's rain. His *spidey sense* on full alert as his heart rate increased accordingly.

"Okay, I'm within twenty yards of the truck," Link whispered. "Where's my guy now, in relation *to* the truck?"

Dave looked over Jesse's shoulder at the video feed. "He's currently down by the bridge, but he's been moving back and forth for the last five minutes or so. If you wait by the truck, my bet is that he'll come to you."

"That sounds like a very good plan," Link whispered. "Way better than me looking for him and he accidentally finds me first." *What are you up to?* Link thought as he planned his next move.

"Link, this doesn't look like your first rodeo," Dave observed. The statement was more of a question, but his comment received no response from his boss.

Dave and Jesse shared a look as they watched Link work his way over to the back right of the bogey work truck.

Link gave the truck a quick examination. It had all the tools and equipment he would expect to find on any oil field truck except that everything was clean. Not one drop of crude oil or drilling mud smudge to be found anywhere. *Whoever you are, you don't get much work done.*

"Dave, take down this license plate number," Link whispered as he peered at the blue North Dakota plate.

"Ready to copy."

"Eight two eight Bravo Charlie Bravo."

"Eight two eight Bravo Charlie Bravo," Dave repeated. "Is that a commercial plate?"

"You'd think so, but it does not appear to be," Link responded. He was hunkered down by the right rear tire and realized that his squat position was not sustainable for very long.

"Link, he's coming back up to the truck and it looks like he's talking on his cell phone." Dave added excitedly, "It looks like he has one of those battery powered grinders in his hand.

"Copy," Link whispered as he peeked underneath the truck to get a location on the guy. "I'll not be talking anymore. He's getting too close." Link whispered as he could now only see the guys boots and pant legs under the truck.

"He keeps pointing at the battery pack," Dave observed. "I'll betcha he's got a dead battery."

"You are now less than eight feet apart," Dave whispered into Link's ear.

CHAPTER THIRTY-TWO

Link could hear him talking with great animation into the phone but couldn't understand the words, so he quickly popped out one ear bud and attempted to hear the rapid-fire conversation. He quickly realized the guy was speaking in Spanish. However, the speed of the one-sided discussion still left him without a clear picture.

One word Link recognized clearly and heard over again was "Coño." Link was fully aware of what that word meant and smiled to himself. *This guy must be really pissed off about something.*

"Dave, can you hear that conversation enough to record it?" Jesse asked.

"Not sure, but I'll try," Dave said

Good idea, son, Link thought. *This is just getting interesting.*

Link slowly maneuvered around the back of the truck, and then just stood up right behind the guy. The two men now stood about six feet apart.

"Can I help you?" Jesse and Dave heard Link's voice loud and clear through the cell connection and at the same time, they saw the man spin around in the video.

"*Un hombre aqui,*" the man said into the cell and quickly hung up.

"Just exactly what are you doing here?" Link asked.

"Who do you work for?

The man's eye twitched, but then he held up his hands and said, "*No hablo ingles*," as he moved toward the truck door.

This Coño *has got me by forty pounds and twenty years, but he doesn't move like he has any real balance or training. Hopefully.* "Your mother is a big, fat, stinking pig that likes goats," Link intoned calmly, without any emotion as if he was talking about the weather.

The guy turned back to Link with fire in his eyes.

"Easy, Boss," Dave said into Link's ear. "I think he just officially transitioned to bandit. Do you want me to catch up?"

"No. Stay there," Link said calmly. "This is going to be over rather quickly, I think."

"No *hablo*? Huh?" Link said as he cocked his head with his hands down by his sides, palms out. "You're a liar, *Coño*. That's your name, isn't it? *Coño*?" Link said with a great deal of derisive emotion.

"What did you say?" *Coño* asked.

"I said, who do you work for?"

"Mind your own business, old man."

Definitely South American, not Mexican. "Exactly my thoughts, too," Link exclaimed. "This *is* my business."

In the blink of an eye, the yellow and black grinder in the man's left hand came flying at Link's face. He ducked, the projectile passing past his head harmlessly as the guy reached for the truck door.

Link leapt at the door and kicked it closed just as *Coño* was pulling it open, his eyes wide with surprise.

"You, my friend, are not going anywhere, and the cops are on the way," Link bluffed.

The man eyed the truck door again and appeared to make a different decision. He quickly reached behind him, pulled out a big knife from some hidden sheath, and waved it back and forth, flashing his white teeth through an evil smile.

"Come on, *Coño*. We don't need to do this," Link complained. "Don't be stupid."

"Shit, Dad, he's got a knife," Jesse whispered as the man began to move to Link's right.

"I can see that, son," Link said calmly as he circled to his left.

"It's time to die, old man," *Coño* said through his leer. "You should have minded your own business and stayed in bed today."

"Hey now, what's with the '*old man*' shit?" Link spoke calmly as he took the heavy wad of truck keys back out of his jacket pocket.

"Come a little closer, old man. I'll make it real quick. I promise."

"Oh, I don't know," Link said almost casually. Sliding two middle fingers through the heavy brass key ring, he took hold of the longest key and fixed it between his index and thumb as if he were ready to start his truck. "You see, only my friends are allowed to insult me. But you and me? We only just met."

Coño eyeballed Link. His gaze darted around for an advantage as he licked his lips.

"Look, man, we really don't have to do this. All I want to know is who you work for," Link coaxed as he estimated the man's reach and speed from when he threw the grinder. "Just tell me that, and you're free to go." Link suggested as he continued to move to the left. *So, he's right-handed.*

Coño began closing the distance between them. "Come to *papi*," he said with a little *come-to-me* wave of his left hand.

Link took a deep breath and threw his hands up in the air. "Okay, okay. I give up trying."

Coño paused in a brief moment of confusion.

"I'll just have to wait and ask you again afterwards," Link finished.

"Oh shit," Link heard Dave whisper under his breath.

"Exactly what I was thinking," Link agreed.

The man lunged with surprising speed. Link had just a split second to react. The knife came down in a slashing move toward Link's left shoulder. Jumping back, the blade narrowly missed him, as the momentum carried the heavy knife in a broad arc. Stepping back in, Link used the truck key and stabbed into the back of *Coño's* forearm, bicep and shoulder in lightning-fast succession. *Coño* Pivoted and this time swung the knife down towards Link's right shoulder. Using his left hand, Link grabbed *Coño's* knife hand at the wrist. Slamming the weakened arm down to *Coño's* own thigh. Rotating hard, Link hit *Coño* with his right elbow, driving it deep into the man's solar plexus.

Coño came back with a powerful left punch to the side of Link's head, but Link didn't release the dangerous knife hand. Instead, he pulled it up and away from the man's leg. *Coño* instinctively resisted Link's movement and pulled the knife hand back toward his leg. Link used the reverse momentum to drive the blade deep into his attacker's leg, just above the knee.

Howling, the attacker let go of the knife and shoved Link back enough to swing a punch toward Link's forehead. Just as the blow approached, Link dropped his face enough for the blow to land on the top of his thick skull. Hearing popping sounds as some of the hand bones broke, Link knew the right hander just became a left hander as he delivered a snap front kick to the man's chest. The blow sent him flying back against the side of the truck.

The kick created more distance between the two fighters and gave Link the advantage by keeping the big guy from rushing him. Close battle was not Link's first choice, especially with the size difference.

Coño reached into the bed of the truck and pulled out a metal pipe wrench. Instead of rushing Link, he foolishly chucked it as Link easily avoided the wrench and it went sailing well behind him.

"Look, *amigo*," Link suggested, breathing heavily. "Just tell me what I want to know, and I'll take you to the hospital."

Coño looked down at his knee and the puddle of blood rapidly building around his boot spilling down from his pant leg. His gaze darted back toward the knife, but it was laying in the dirt, too far for either of them to grab.

"You are bleeding pretty badly," Link tried again. "Who the hell are you working for?"

Link straightened a bit from his fighting crouch. "*Damn*, Dave," Link whispered between gulps of air. "His right hand has got to be broken, and his right arm hanging at his side won't be working very well for a while. But this guy doesn't seem quite ready to give up and I'm about out of juice." He continued breathing heavily.

"Boss, I can be there in five minutes," Dave eagerly offered.

"Jesse, keep filming everything you can, just in case I can't keep him here. I'm not worried about him seeing the drone anymore."

"Wilco, Dad. I'm moving in closer now."

"Dave, I'm taking you up on your offer. If I can just keep my distance without letting him go, that might give you time to reach me."

"On my way, Boss." Dave said, "Hang on."

Link heard the truck door slam, the engine start, and the seatbelt alarm all in a matter of seconds. *Backup's on the way*, he thought as he turned his full attention back to the bleeding man.

Just then *Coño* made a break for the truck.

"No, you don't," Link yelled as he rushed toward the truck.

Coño had the door open and was halfway inside by the time Link hit the door with everything he had, crushing *Coño's* lower body and legs between the door and frame. Looking through the window, Link saw a gun in *Coño's* hand just as a bullet smashed through the window. The aim was off but was close enough so that the concussion blew out the earbud in Link's ear, throwing little shards of safety glass everywhere.

Coño pulled the trigger again as Link ducked his head lower still, pushing on the door, trying to pin him in tight and keep him from getting a better shot. Then, changing tactics, this time pulling the door open, Link successfully slammed it back into *Coño's* head and body, but it still wasn't stopping the bullets from flying, some going wild but others getting closer and closer.

Link knew he couldn't properly aim the gun but still... Now the gun was pointing out of the window, *Coño* twisted his wrist for another blind shot, but this one would be point-blank. Link had nowhere to go, and nowhere to hide. Just when Link couldn't make himself any flatter against the door, Jesse's drone came rocketing out of nowhere, smashing through the truck door window and slamming right into *Coño's* gun hand.

One more shot rang out, but the bullet went wild. *Coño* turned his head to look for the gun just as Link reached around the door and aimed his fist for the only viable target. He drove the truck key, still in his right hand, deep into the man's left temple. The weight of his hand combined with the brass key ring buried the blade of the key all the way to the hilt, easily penetrating the soft tissue. Not waiting a second, Link pulled it out and aimed for his left eye when the man suddenly went limp.

Link halted the blow in midair as he felt the body sag. Exhausted, he examined the man's face for a moment before releasing pressure on the door and watched carefully as the body slid lifelessly to the ground. A steady stream of blood continued to exit the wound where the key penetrated. With his chest heaving, Link took hold of the arms and dragged the body a short distance away from the truck and laid it flat. Dropping to one knee, he checked his assailant's pulse to confirm what he already knew. He wouldn't be getting up again. Ever. *Maybe I really am getting too old for this shit.* He forced himself to his feet before staggering backwards against the pickup and gasping for air.

"Dad! Dad! Are you okay? Dad!" Link heard a weak voice coming from his pocket. He pulled out his cell phone and hit the speaker.

"Jesse?" Link said in surprise.

"I'm here, Dad."

"I didn't know you were still there." Link let out an exhausted chuckle. "Son, I got to tell you, that was the highest and best use of a four-thousand-dollar drone when you knocked down his gun hand. I don't think I could have gotten out of the way of that last bullet."

"The phones never hung up during the whole fight. I think Dave's got the entire audio recorded," Jesse explained. "The only problem was that I lost video when the drone flew through the window, and I didn't know if you were okay or not. The only thing Dave or I could hear is a little more fighting and then a whole lot of heavy breathing."

"Yeah, the breathing part was me, not him," Link explained as he looked down at the body. "Speaking of Dave, what happened to the damn cavalry?"

"I'm inbound Link." Dave's voice was tense. "I just passed your truck."

"Did you bring any coffee?" Link asked between breaths. "No, take that back. I think I need something much stronger."

* * * * *

The place was covered in police cars, fire trucks, Reagan trucks, and an ambulance by the time Deputy Perry arrived, coffee in hand.

"Dustin, please tell me this is a nightmare I'll wake up from," Cheri demanded.

"I would, but I'd be lying," the patrolman said with a shrug as he approached.

"How is it possible that everyone has forgotten the sacred commandment?" Cheri asked in exasperation.

"Which sacred commandment would that be? Thou shalt not kill?"

"No, but close." Cheri took a sip before continuing. "Thou shalt not commit any serious crime in Williams County on Cheri's day off."

"Oh, that one," he said tongue in cheek. "I seem to recall that from my training."

"Okay, okay," Cheri acknowledged with an attempt at a smile. "I was filled in on the basics already, during my drive out, so tell me what's new in the last forty minutes."

"I've already viewed the drone video and the audio from one of Reagan's cell phones, now the CSI guys have it. They both back up Link's story."

"You should see the video," Dustin said with a little awe in his voice. "You'll never look at Link the same way again."

"What's that supposed to mean?"

"It means that Link is a really good guy to have as a friend and not an enemy."

Hmm, I'm not shocked.

"Who's the perp?" she asked, changing the subject.

"No ID and so far, his fingerprints are not in the system."

"What about the truck?" Cheri asked. "Who owns it?"

"Stolen several weeks ago, and the plates were reported stolen a few days ago."

So, he was just trading in for fresh plates, huh? "Anything we could use in the truck itself."

"The only thing telling is that there were half a dozen magnetic signs from different companies here in the Bakken. It appears that the perp was cutting into the I-Beam under the bridge down there with a battery powered cut off grinder but, according to Link, the battery must have died, and he was talking to someone on the cell up by the truck when he confronted him."

"Have you checked the cell?"

"Burn phone calling a burn phone."

"So, we've got what?" Cheri asked.

"Not much."

"Out of curiosity, who reported the truck stolen and when, exactly?"

"The registered owner is Global Endeavor Alliance, but it was reported stolen three weeks ago."

"Hmm, that's interesting. Who reported it?"

"It says that Natalie Hotah filed the report for the company." He looked up from his notes. "Isn't that the name of one of our vics?"

"Yes, it is," she replied. *Poor girl, so that's why they killed you? You knew something was off, didn't you?* Anger brewed in her heart.

Cheri took the lid off her coffee cup and blew the steam away as she thought about the new development. "It looks like our friend at the FBI can add this to his investigation." Cheri said.

CHAPTER THIRTY-THREE

"Mr. Erickson. What, exactly, are we paying you for?" came the terse yet familiar and very unfriendly voice over the secure line. Mr. Erickson felt sick to his stomach. He swallowed hard and looked over at Jack Martin, his chief of security, and mouthed the words, *It's him.*

Jack was tenderly massaging a bandage of gauze over his right eye. Mr. Erickson's chief of security spoke with a similar accent as himself, as they were both citizens of the United Kingdom. The Chief Of Security was quite capable, but not as an expert in the oil business. He received his education in the British SAS. Trained in sabotage & guerilla warfare.

"Sir, I'm not sure I understand," Mr. Erickson replied in his clipped, British accent. A hint of perspiration appeared on his upper lip as he put the phone on speaker.

"For years we have bankrolled your entire company. We have bought your way into every inner circle in the Bakken, and still no measurable results."

"We've been very busy, sir, I can assure you," Mr. Erickson replied. "Why, in fact, they just shut down all operations in the Bakken for an entire day for a safety stand down due to all the *accidents* that have happened lately. Our efforts have not been entirely fruitless."

"Mr. Erickson, did the oil wells shut down too? Did they close the valves on the gathering pipelines during their stand down?"

"Well, no, not exactly."

"The Bakken is producing over one million barrels of oil per day, flooding the international oil market and driving down our profits. One little slow down for a day is not adequate for the money we have spent on you."

"Sir, I promise you we are making headway and our saboteur operation will continue to slow and disrupt the flow of oil."

"Well, Mr. Erickson, not to worry. We have another plan in the works that will definitely shut down the entire Bakken oil production."

"Ah, that sounds excellent, sir. What exactly is the new plan?"

"The plan? The plan is for you to anticipate a significant increase in the number of your security personnel. Expect their arrival in the next few weeks. The head of your new security team will arrive in a few days to coordinate. His name is Mr. Andrus, and let me assure you, he'll get the job done. You will comply with anything he wishes."

"Yessir," Mr. Erickson agreed. "We are looking forward to his arrival."

* * * * *

The early morning was cool and still nearly dark as Jesse and Celia pulled off the highway overlooking lake Sakakawea, located on the headwaters of the Mighty Missouri River. From their vantage point above the river, they could just catch a glimpse of the one hundred- and eighty-mile-long reservoir.

"How do you say the name again?" Celia asked between sips of coffee.

"Sak-ak-Uh way Uh," Jesse said slowly.

She looked at him funny and giggled.

You're going to want to breathe soon, Jesse told himself before he passed out. There was no sound like it.

He cleared his throat. "It was named after the female Shoshone Indian guide that, along with her newborn son, escorted the Lewis and Clark expedition from here, all the way to the Pacific Ocean."

"Wow, what a strong woman she must have been," Celia marveled. "I can't imagine doing that, especially with a baby."

"They don't make 'em like they used to," Jesse teased.

Celia smiled. "The men either, I think." she said, tilting her head just a bit.

"Ouch. And touché," Jesse replied while grinning into his coffee cup. The gouge on the back of his head was healing nicely.

"You're not from around here, so how do you know all this?" Celia asked.

"My dad and the internet." He eased the truck onto a dirt road.

"Impressive," she said as she took another sip. "You can read?" *Oh, this girl is good.*

Larry whined in the back seat as Jesse navigated the rough terrain. "Won't be long buddy."

The long driveway to the Reagan lake house wound down a hill from the highway and included a couple of switchbacks. The clapboard style cabin itself was nestled into a draw that ended just above the high-water level of the lake in a little plateau, nicely blocking the wind from both up and down the lake.

There was a light fog floating lazily on top of the dark water with the thin blue line of dawn barely visible against the horizon.

"Our timing is perfect." Jesse commented as he placed the truck in park and smiled at Celia.

Larry wagged his tail as he impatiently waited for someone to let him out. Looking from one human to the other, he finally nuzzled Celia's neck and licked her ear.

"How do you mean?" Celia asked, giggling at Larry's affections.

"The fish should be looking for breakfast just about the time we get on the water."

"I see, and you are an internet expert on this also?" she teased.

"Nope, I grew up fishing. In fact, I think I was born with a fishing pole in my hand."

"Your poor mother," Celia exclaimed with feigned horror.

"Admittedly, each lake is different, but we've got all day to figure it out," he said, totally ignoring her comment.

"Oh, what a confident man."

He grinned at her. "Let's leave the cooler and backpacks here until we get the boat dropped in the water and the engines warmed up."

Larry ran ahead as Jesse and Celia sipped their coffees and strolled toward the cabin's wrap around deck.

"So, you've *never* been boating or fishing?" Jesse asked.

"No. I haven't." Celia chuckled. "Why do you find it so hard to believe?"

She was dressed in the khaki cargo shorts, a black Jack Daniels hoodie and her long, perfectly toned legs disappeared into the same white sneakers she wore at the bar, but without socks this time.

"Weren't you raised next to the Adriatic Sea?" Jesse inquired, trying not to linger too long.

"Oh, so you know your geography?" Celia teased.

"I make it my business to know who I am going fishing with," Jesse lightly countered.

"During the war, there was no time for play, and after the war it was all about rebuilding our lives. Maria, Sophia and I worked very hard every day to make a new life out of so much death."

Her answer had a depth of honesty that sobered Jesse's mind. "I'm sorry for asking."

"Do not worry." She dismissed the thought with a wave of her hand and started walking.

Jesse hesitated for a moment, angry with himself for bringing up the subject. He caught up to her as she left the upper deck by the cabin and walked down the sloped wooden gangway to the floating docks below. The slight breeze off the water brought the scent of freshly washed hair gliding past Jesse's senses. It made him smile as he felt the gentlest of tickles in his chest.

Larry was already at the bottom, wagging his tail impatiently. Suddenly, Celia let out a little yelp as her shoes skidded on the heavy dew from the night before. The slip sent her coffee flying and her arms flailing as she fell backwards. Jesse dropped his own coffee and caught her before she tumbled into the water. She wrapped her arm around his neck and clung tightly to him, eyes wide in shock.

"Woah, there." He held her for a brief moment, his heart thumping in his chest, and he could feel her heart doing the same. "Are you okay?" he asked without making any attempt to release her.

"Yes," she said. "A little embarrassed, but I am fine." She tensed her body as she struggled to stand.

"Don't be," Jesse commented as he eased the girl back onto her feet. "You saved me when I busted my head and today, I got to save a beautiful girl from getting wet." He finished with a grin. "I'm a winner both ways."

She looked at him and started to respond, but her words got lost for a moment. *BEEP BEEP BEEP.*

* * * * *

The boat was not really set up for working an oil spill. It looked a lot more like a luxury craft. Outfitted with twin three hundred horsepower engines and enough white and maroon couches and chairs to comfortably seat ten or twelve people.

It didn't take long to get the pontoon boat lowered into the water and the engines started warming up. They brought the gear and coolers down from the truck and were on the water as the first rays of the sun splashed across the lake.

"You might want to take off your white shoes before we start fishing," Jesse suggested.

"Why?"

"Well, if we get lucky and catch something today, you might get fish slime all over them."

"What do you mean *if?* I thought you said you were an amazing fisherman?" She chided, but the smile she wore did something to his insides.

She's giving me a hard time. How cool.

"There's no guarantee we'll get anything," he said. "That's why it's called fishing and not catching."

"Oh, I see," she said with a knowing smile. "Hmm, that is a definite change from your brochure."

As they exited the little harbor, a pair of tundra swans swam out with six fluffy yellow cygnets in trail, paddling their little webbed feet like crazy to keep up with mom and dad.

Larry licked his chops as he watched them intently. Suddenly, he looked to Celia and whined, then looked back at the delicious looking swans.

"No, no, Larry," Celia said as she wrapped her arm around his neck. "Those are not for eating today."

"Nice hoodie," Jesse said to change the subject.

"Oh, thanks," she replied as she looked down at herself. "It was a giveaway during a promotion at the bar." Her dark hair was arranged in a large, loose braid that tumbled down her back, like water flowing over large stones. There were some slightly lighter tones that he hadn't noticed before. She was smiling like a little girl, hugging Larry, as the boat began to gain speed. A squadron of white pelicans were skimming along the morning wave tops, seemingly flying formation with the boat.

"Never went to Disneyland or any of those places?" Jesse asked after a few minutes. She was sitting across from him on a couch with her now bare feet resting on the edge of his seat.

"No."

"Not even a water park?"

"No. Well, maybe yes, if you count the beach."

"Tell me about that?" Jesse asked as the bow wave tossed white frothy water into the morning sunlight.

"Maria, Sophia and I would go down to the water sometimes. There wasn't much sandy beach like you see in the movies. It was mostly kind of rocky and tiny seashells made up the sand. I'd play in the water and sometimes step on these black sea urchins that would stab their little spines into my feet. I'd cry a little, Maria would pick them out, and five minutes later I'd be back in the water." She paused for a moment staring out over the water. The tranquil, easy smile, let Jesse know she was re-living a good memory.

"I don't believe it," Jesse blurted, displaying his own teasing smile.

"You don't believe what?"

"That *you* would cry when the sea urchins would stab your feet. You didn't even cry when that guy hit you the other night in the bar. That still pisses me off to no end."

"That was different. He was an asshole." Her eyes narrowed and her face went dark for a moment. "I don't cry for assholes."

Larry whined and cocked his head to the side. His blue eyes locked on Celia with concern.

Uh oh, bad idea. Change the subject. "I've heard the Adriatic Sea is really clear."

"Oh, it is. I remember the water, it was so clear that even at twenty feet deep, you could see the bottom like it was only a foot down.

"I remember one summer... I went to an English bible camp on the coast put on by a group from America. We didn't have much money, but this one was free, so I got to go. The theme was Pirates of the Adriatic," she said, gazing out over the water. "We built a pretend pirate ship complete with a ship's wheel and everything. That was the first time I met regular Americans. They were so kind." Celia chuckled again. "Maria, in her toughness, couldn't understand why these people would come halfway around the world to help us learn English and ask for nothing in return."

"That sounds wonderful."

"It was. It truly was," She agreed. "Especially to a little girl like me."

Jesse cocked his head and paused for a moment, considering her words. "So, tell me something else that is good about Croatia."

"That's easy. Gelato," she said with a grin combined with a *duh* tone.

"Gelato, huh?"

"Yes, heaven in a cone," she cooed. "My two most favorite things in life are Italian Ice Cream and American chocolate. *Especially* the Hershey bar. You know the one with lots of little squares. There is something different and wonderful about them and no other chocolate is quite as good."

Jesse just watched her talk, how her face lit up as she was obviously re-living a very special time. The rest of the world faded into the background and the only thing he could see was a little girl with a chocolate bar in one hand, an ice cream cone in the other, and maybe a messy face wearing a big smile.

"...what's yours?" he heard Celia say. The image faded.

Jesse's eyes refocused on the here and now. "What did you say?"

"Jesse, I asked what your favorite kind of ice cream is."

"Oh, um…" Jesse paused again. "Uh, Cookies and Cream."

CHAPTER THIRTY-FOUR

"**D**o you lay out and sunbathe a lot?" Jesse asked as he tried not to admire her olive toned legs and feet resting next to his own leg. He wanted to reach over and place his hand on her ankle but was unsure. *Take your time, don't mess this up.* Jesse warned himself.

"No. Other than running," she admitted, "I don't spend much time in the sun at all. Bartending is kind of a night thing. So, my day thing is reserved for mostly sleeping."

"Yeah, but you look so tan," Jesse said with raised eyebrows and a quick glance up and down.

"No, this is the tan I was born with." She laughed as she lifted one of her long, toned legs off of his seat and rubbed a spot just above her knee. Jesse began pulling the throttles to idle and bringing the boat to a stop.

"Oh yeah?" Jesse said. "Then, in that case, you'd better put on some of this." He reached his hand into a small compartment and pulled out a blue tube of sunblock.

"I don't normally use such cream but, being all day in the sun, it might be a good idea."

As Celia began to apply the sun block, Jesse busied himself with setting up the trolling rigs, dropping the lures into the water while making a futile attempt at not looking forward as she slowly applied the coconut-scented cream. *Is she doing that on purpose? Why does she have this power over me?* He wondered. *Loads of beautiful women have come and gone and yet, he never felt this confused.*

"What are we fishing for?" she asked as she smoothed the cream into her legs and bare feet.

"Uh, walleye mostly, but anything that'll bite." He turned back to his task, forcing himself not to even glance in her direction. After setting up the GPS-controlled trolling motor, he shut down the boat's big engines and the boat began to move. At first imperceptibly, then slowly the rod tips bent, and the boat steadied out in a direction and speed.

"Have you caught this kind before?"

"No, but I have caught a lot of Northern Pike, and they are similar." He played out more of the fishing line and tested the tension of the drag on each reel.

With the GPS motor in full control, the two took seats at the rear of the boat for a better view of the coming action.

The sun had slowly warmed up and burned off the rest of the fog from the water. A warm, gentle breeze created by their forward movement kept the day from becoming stifling. It didn't take long before Celia peeled off her hoodie, revealing a simple black bikini top, well defined arms, toned abs, and just enough cleavage to make his heart skip a beat. Or two.

Jesse swallowed hard. He'd seen plenty of bikini-clad women, but this one did something strange to him. *"Uh, she'll probably need more of that sunblock..."* he hoped.

After an hour or so, with no fish, the warm sun began to take its toll. Celia's eyelids grew heavy, and it wasn't long before she began to nod off. Jesse kept one eye on her and the other on the rods that were slightly bent at the tips and moving to the motion of the gentle waves.

What is with this girl? She was unlike any other girl he'd ever met. *Why is she so utterly captivating?* She was *stunning*; tall and with an incredible body, but he'd dated loads of beautiful women before. *Maybe it's her green eyes?* Now, that was new. He'd never dated a girl with green eyes before. *What about her accent?* Yeah, that is super sexy too, but even before he heard her speak, when she was helping Jenny clean up the spilled groceries... He chucked to himself. The hand slap? *No, but it was funny. She's got some sort of fire inside her. There was a kind of steel behind her beauty.*

He watched her now, fully asleep with her face turned slightly to the side, with just a wisp of a smile on her lips. *Wow.* His heartbeat started to climb. *I wonder if she has on black bikini bottoms under her khaki shorts. Shut up!*

Jesse James, knock it off or you are going to get yourself in serious trouble. Again, As the sun rose higher in the sky, The temperature was also rising causing a thin sheen of perspiration gathering on her midriff and upper lip.

Maybe it was because she was so beautiful but didn't act like it. Hell, she probably has no idea. She didn't even try to dress sexy, but she was the epitome of gorgeous.

I'm sure glad I'm not wearing her watch right now.

She could probably wear a flour sack and still look amazing. But there's more to her than that. She's mature, yet almost child-like. Could it be true that she's never dated before now?"

He watched as her chest rose and fell in the deep rhythm of sleep.

Wait a minute. Reaching into the same compartment as the sun block, he retrieved a bottle of kid's soap bubbles he'd seen earlier. Positioning himself upwind from her, he began blowing bubbles, trying to get them to land on her. After a few experimental tries, he managed to land one on her tummy before it popped. Just a tiny little twitch was her only reaction. *Okay, let's send some bigger ones.* As they began reaching their target, she continued to shift around but not come fully awake. When she'd become too restless, he'd stop and wait long enough for her to settle back down before sending another barrage of the biggest bubbles he could manage.

He watched intently as the next salvo approached her middle section. As they began touching down, one after another, her eyes fluttered open. *Oh, dang!* His heart left the building.

Suddenly one of the fishing poles slapped down hard, the tip going all the way into the water. The reel zinged, and the fishing line started feeding out behind the boat so fast that it would soon run out.

"Shit! We hit a snag," Jesse said as he reached for the motor controller.

Celia was coming awake with all the noise. "What's happening?" she asked groggily. "Do we have a fish?"

"No, I think it's a sna—"

"Look!" Celia shrieked as she jumped up and pointed aft.

He spun his head around just in time to see a monster fish jump clean out of the water behind the boat. The pole started to slide out of the holder when Jesse yelled, "Quick, grab the pole! Celia, grab the pole fast before we lose it!

Celia jumped over and grabbed the pole, but the fish yanked hard against the line, preventing it from clearing the holder. As she heaved with both hands, the pole popped out and the fish began pulling her toward the water as she let out a squeal. "It's getting away!"

"No, no, it's still there, honey! Keep the rod up and let him run." Jesse quickly adjusted the drag on the reel. He could see the muscles in her arms flex as she braced her feet on the AstroTurf floor.

"I wish I had a fighting belt, but who'd ever think we'd need one out here?" Jesse said.

The look of determination on her face was that of pure concentration.

The fish jumped again, pulling her toward the rear of the boat, causing another little shriek as her bare foot neared the edge. Just as she started to go over, Jesse reached out and grabbed the back of her shorts as she lost her balance. *She didn't let go of the rod.*

"Whoa, babe," Jesse pulled her deeper into the boat and wrapped his left arm around her waist. For just the briefest moment he felt her entire body tense in a totally different way. She looked down at his arm and then directly at Jesse, her eyes bright and excited, before turning back to her task. *Was that what I think it was...*

The line started to go slack as the fish now swam toward the boat as Celia squealed.

"Reel, reel, reel!" Jesse cheered and let out an unintentional whoop.

She glanced down and smiled. Her arms and hands worked feverishly to retrieve several feet of line when the pole tugged hard again toward the water. Jesse's arm was the only thing that kept her on board. She gritted her teeth and quickly returned the favor and gave the fish a mighty pull of her own.

"Jesse, is this a walleye?" She asked breathlessly.

"No, I don't think so. If it is, it's bigger than any walleye that I've ever seen."

Celia fought the fish for several more minutes, secured in Jesse's arm. Her own toned, athletic arms and taught abs, straining against the power of the fish. Pumping the rod up and down and reeling frantically, she slowly dragged the big fish toward the boat.

As the fish got closer, Jesse realized he needed to get the landing net prepared. Looking around, he spotted it clamped along the gunwale but couldn't reach it without releasing her. "Celia, I've got to let you go so I can grab the net." For an instant, a shadow of what looked like disappointment clouded her eyes but then her smile returned.

"Okay, what do I need to do?" She asked.

"Keep pumping and reeling but brace your right foot on the rail." Jesse said as he reluctantly released her. "Don't give him my slack but be careful, your fish is much too big for this fishing rod."

She turned to him in alarm. "What are you saying?"

"I'm saying that it is possible for that monster to break your fishing rod if you pull too hard."

"That fish is mine!" She exclaimed but eased up a little on the pressure.

He briefly touched her shoulders and said, "I'll only be a second." He dashed to the front of the boat and grabbed the net out of its holder. He returned to Celia just as the fish came completely out of the water less than forty feet away and tail-walked across the sun-sparkled surface.

"Oh no!" Jesse exclaimed. "That's a king salmon!"

"What's the matter with that?" Celia asked through gritted teeth as she pulled with all her might.

"The net!" Jesse yelled. "It's not going to be big enough!"

She flashed him a look that could've killed someone. "I'm not losing my fish!" She howled as she pulled. Even the muscles in her face were chipping in. Celia was in full competition mode. *God help anyone who got between her and that fish.*

After several more minutes fighting the salmon, she finally wrangled it alongside the boat.

Jesse carefully placed the undersized net under the fish and, saying a little prayer, gently lifted him out of the water and onto the flat deck of the boat. The fish spit the hook as Celia dropped her pole and began hopping up and down and screaming with delight. Larry barked and hopped up and down, sharing in her excitement.

How could it get better than this?

"Open the fish hold?" Jesse asked. As he lifted the net off once again, the fish tore through the webbing and began flapping freely across the boat deck. When the strain on Jesse's arms was suddenly released, he fell backwards into the water and the fish began flopping toward freedom.

Jesse was under water for just a second but when he popped to the surface, Celia was straddling the fish trying to trap it with her hands, knees and bare feet, as it slapped, flipped and flopped despite her weight on it. "No, you don't!" she declared, her accent on full display.

Larry barked as if saying, *'Don't lose it.'*

Jesse couldn't help it and began to laugh uncontrollably at the sight and swam back to the boat and climbed up on the swim step.

"Jesse, help me," she demanded as the fish slapped her in the face with a slimy tail fin. He stepped around her and quickly grabbed the giant fish by the gills and dragged it to the fish hold and plopped it in, leaving a trail of slime on the carpet.

They both crumbled to the floor in laughter.

"That was awesome," Celia clapped her hands together and gave out a whoop of her own between gasps of breath.

"You were awesome," he said. "I can't believe the fight you put up."

"I can't believe we caught such a big fish."

"*You* caught the fish, and if you're only going to catch one, that's the kind you want." Jesse looked over at her and started laughing all over again as he reached out and gently rubbed her jaw with his thumb.

"What?" she asked a little indignantly.

"Honey, you are covered in fish slime," he said as he stood up to grab a clean hand towel from a fishing compartment. First handing her the towel, he then held his hands out to help her up off the floor. She glanced up at him, briefly hesitating, then raised her hands up and he pulled her upright and nearly into his arms. *BEEP BEEP BEEP* She quickly turned away from him and began to wipe her face, chest and arms. She suddenly chuckled as she looked down and saw her clean white shoes tucked under a couch.

"Hey, Jesse."

"Yeah?"

"You were right. At least my shoes are still clean."

CHAPTER THIRTY-FIVE

"I've got an idea," Jesse said. "Are you up for a little more adventure?"

With a cautious smile and a cock of her head, she asked, "What do you have in mind?"

"Well, it depends on how hungry you are…"

"Oh, that's easy. I'm starved."

"Good."

Without explanation, he started both big motors and pointed the bow of the boat toward an island on the far side of the lake. The sun was leaning a bit into the western sky, and the temperature was continuing to rise.

As they approached the island, Jesse aimed for a little cove on the upper end that collected driftwood when the lake was high with spring snow melt. He idled the engines and slowly came to a stop several yards from the beach.

"Time to get a little wet," he said with a grin as he shut down the engines. Walking to the bow, he picked up the anchor and tossed it overboard. Once he ensured the anchor had set, he in one quick move he pulled off his T-shirt and dove off the boat into the deep, cold water. "Whew," Jesse hollered as he popped to the surface several yards from the boat and shook the water from his hair. "Yeah, that's what I'm talking about."

After a moment, he waded back to the boat and looked up at Celia. "Are you coming in?"

"Not just yet," she replied uneasily.

"Well okay, can you hand me the backpacks?"

"Sure. I packed a couple of sandwiches and two bottles of beer. They are in a cold pack in the bottom section of mine." She said as she set the backpacks down at the edge of the boat.

A mischievous grin spread across his face. "Cool," he said as he grabbed them and brought them to the beach.

"What was that look for? she thought as she watched him return to the boat.

"Can you hand me my red and white cooler?" Jesse asked as he approached.

Celia reached down to grab the handles. "What is in here?" she asked. "It weighs a ton."

"You'll see," he said with another grin as he lifted the cooler onto the top of his head. He turned and headed back to shore. Celia watched him climb out of the water, his muscles flexing under the load as water ran off his toned back muscles. BEEP BEEP BEEP

He turned and briefly sat on the cooler, taking a quick breather, looking back toward the boat at Celia. "The sand is like powdered sugar. You're going to love it," he hollered.

Larry was whining and pacing, looking back and forth from Celia to the water and over to Jesse.

"Come on, ya big chicken," Jesse hollered to the big husky.

Celia reached down to pet the dog and Larry leaned into the attention.

"Okay, suit yourself." Jesse said as he started to walk up the beach, past the scattered piles of driftwood and disappeared into a copse of willows. It didn't take long before Larry couldn't stand it anymore and launched himself off the boat. He managed to get halfway to the sand before making a huge splash and swimming the last few yards.

"Good boy," Jesse called as he ran back toward the cooler. Just as Larry's paws touched solid ground, he leapt out of the water as if being chased by a polar bear. As he ran toward Jesse, Jesse hollered, "No, Larry, don't shake!" But it was too late. Stopping only after he was next to his master, he promptly gave a mighty shake, spraying water in great arcs in all directions.

Celia couldn't help but laugh as she covered her mouth. *Is he real? Is it possible? BEEP BEEP BEEP*

"Well, come on now. Don't tell me you're going to be like Larry."

"But I'll get all wet," she said with an involuntary shudder as she looked down into the water.

"That's true, but you need to wash the fish slime off of you anyway so, it's a kind of win-win."

"Is the water cold? I can't see the bottom." She hugged herself as she looked at the distance from the boat to the beach.

"Really? You pick now to be all girly?"

"I hate not being able to see the bottom of the water, and I don't like the cold very much." There was a hint of whine in her voice.

"Hmm, are you aware that you live in North Dakota?"

"That's different," she said defiantly. "Maria is here."

"Tell you what... I've got some big beach towels in my backpack, so after you get all wet, we'll build a fire, and you can dry off."

She stood on the bow of the boat looking just as Larry did. Back and forth. "Um, I really don't think it's a good idea."

Looking down at Larry, Jesse exclaimed, "Finally we find out that there is something that she *is* afraid of."

"I think I'll just stay on the boat," she didn't even try to defend herself from his remark. She just stared down at the water, her arms crossed tightly across her chest.

"Suit yourself," he said with a shrug.

She watched as Jesse turned his back and began picking up firewood with an occasional backward glance in her direction. She was watching intently and wringing her hands. He grinned and started whistling as he continued to pick up armloads of driftwood.

He piled up the kindling and larger wood about a yard from a large gray drift log. In just a few minutes more, he had a blazing fire with flames that leapt toward the late afternoon sky. Celia watched from the cold boat as the fire burned brightly. It was an agonizing wait before he glanced her way again as he went about organizing the makeshift camp site.

"Time to filet your catch." Jesse said, still in the water as he approached the boat. Celia reached out her hand and helped him aboard.

"Thanks. You're stronger than I realized."

Celia smiled at the complement.

"Damn, this is a big fish," Jesse said, as he stared down at it in the hold. He grunted as he lifted it up by the gills. "We really need to get a picture of this big boy before I clean it. It's got to be forty pounds."

"Yes?" Celia exclaimed with a clap of her hands and a little hop. Quickly turning, she set out, excitedly, in search of her cell phone. When she came back, Jesse was busy tying some clear fishing string onto the fish's mouth.

"What are you doing?" she asked, eyes bright and excited.

"I am setting up your epic photoshoot."

"My what?" she asked with a giggle.

"Just watch and learn," he replied, grinning.

She laughed but watched without argument. *Is it okay to think he's beautiful? She asked herself.* As Jesse picked up the fish and held it at chest height while he lashed the other end of the clear fishing line to a cleat mounted on the roof of the boat, leaving the appearance that the fish was hanging in midair.

When he was finished, he said, "Stand right about here, behind your Monster." He pointed to a spot on the deck of the boat next to the hanging fish.

"Here?" she asked as she moved into position.

"Yes. Now put your hand in its gills like you are holding it up by one arm, and I'll take your picture."

Instead of standing in front of her to take the photo, he casually wrapped his arm around her shoulder and took a selfie of the two of them.

She excitedly took the cell phone from his hand and opened the photo as though she were opening a Christmas present.

As the photo appeared on the cell phone, she realized that they both had tilted their heads in toward each other with his arm around her. *BEEP BEEP BEEP.* She didn't even notice the fish.

To her amazement, Jesse made quick work of preparing the fresh salmon, making two beautiful filets with the skin still attached.

"I'm going back ashore to put these on the fire and get them cooking. Are you coming?"

Her smile dropped to a worried frown as she looked down at the water.

"Well?" he asked.

She just shook her head without saying a word.

"Suit yourself," he answered with a shrug, as if he didn't care either way.

Sitting down, her knees drawn up and her chin resting on them, her mind wandered. *He sure is beautiful*, she admitted reluctantly. And kind. He acts as if it is no big deal about the war. As if everything could be normal. He treated *her* as if she were normal. The thought was utterly inconceivable in her own mind.

After he waded back to shore, she watched as Jesse busied himself with tending the fire and spreading out a beach towel on the sand.

What was with this guy? He could have anyone he wanted. Since that first night in Maria's, she knew that. *So why is he wasting his time on me?* She wondered as her eyes followed his every move.

Next, he reached inside the cooler and pulled out half a dozen seasoning containers and placed them on the gnarled base of driftwood he used as a makeshift table. After making his selection, he began to apply them, one by one, to the filets before weaving them onto a web of willow sticks like some sort of caveman.

I can't have a life, she thought. But she'd already accepted that. *Why can't he just leave me alone?*

Jesse reached his hand into the cooler once again and pulled out a couple of potatoes and two ears of corn. He rubbed a little butter on the potato skins, sprinkled some salt on them, and wrapped them in tin foil. He stuffed the potatoes beneath the coals in the fire and nestled the corn, still in the husks, on top.

She chuckled, breaking her own train of thought. A caveman that has a magician's hat for a cooler. He seemed to reach inside and pull out anything he needed.

When the fire died down just enough and was perfect for cooking, Jesse held his hand over the fire for just a moment, then set the filets a few inches above the hot coals, skin side down, and placed a sheet of aluminum foil over the top.

I can't even have children, she thought, her mind focusing back on her previous line of thinking. She couldn't even give him that. She had nothing to offer. Absolutely nothing.

Her heart began to ache as she watched him move around the little camp. He'd be great with kids…

Stop that, she scolded herself.

It wasn't long before the aroma of cooking fish and wood smoke filled the air and wafted over the water to the boat. Even from the boat, she could hear the crackle and pop from the sparks, as Jesse was continuously turning the corn over the fire. The air was still warm, with a gentle breeze coming off the water, even though the sun was beginning to slip low in the western sky.

Oh, get real, Celia. What would he think the first time she woke up screaming, soaking wet with sweat?

Her hand moved down to her tummy as it rumbled. She looked down at her middle and then across the few yards of water to where Jesse sat by the fire with his arms wrapped around his own knees. He lifted the tin foil and prodded a sharpened willow stick into the fish.

But…why not me? Just for right now? her mind begged. *So what if it lasts only a little while? That is, until he realizes how broken and messed up I am.*

CHAPTER THIRTY-SIX

The sun was getting low, and Larry laid on the sand next to Jesse, quietly dozing. The food was nearly done when suddenly, he heard a scream. He looked up, just in time to see Celia splashing as she hit the water.

Jumping up and grabbing a towel, he ran down to greet her, but when she gained her feet and stood up in the waist-deep water, she had a look of relief on her face. Larry beat Jesse to the water's edge, barking excitedly and bouncing on all fours.

She laughed at Larry's antics and splashed water at him.

"That wasn't so bad," she said with surprise.

"Oh? What wasn't so bad?"

"The water. It's not really that cold, and the bottom feels good on my feet. I was afraid there would be stuff down there, maybe grabbing at me." She finished with a quick breath. "But it is actually quite nice."

"I told you so," Jesse said with satisfaction as he held up the towel.

"Now that I am wet, I may as well get cleaned up," she concluded as she began to splash water on her body, scrubbing the dried fish slime from her arms, tummy, shorts and bare legs.

"Um, are you in need of any assistance?" Jesse offered.

"No." She laughed again. "But thank you. Your offer is too kind." There was no mistaking the sarcasm in her tone, but it also had warmth.

"What made you change your mind?" Jesse asked.

"It was hunger. No, actually, it was starvation, plus the smell of the food, the sight of a warm fire, and finally realizing I was being stupid."

"Then, what was the scream for?"

"Oh, that?" She shrugged. "That was me not being quite convinced it was a good idea just *after* I jumped but before I hit the water."

Jesse chuckled as he waited on the beach for her to finish her little bath. It seemed so innocent, but it was stirring his insides like crazy. To get his mind off things, he played with Larry while he waited.

"You must be freezing now," he said as he held open the towel. As she approached him, Celia searched his eyes, before she turned a bit so he could wrap the towel around her. He was sorely tempted to wrap his arms around her as well, but something told him to be patient. As she accepted the towel, she felt his warmth in her cold hands.

"Come up to the fire, Madame. Your table is waiting. The catch of the day is almost ready."

Assuming her role she replied, "Oh, thank you, sir," with a touch of shiver in her accent.

She sat down cross legged on the beach towel to the sound of water squishing from her khakis. "Oh." She looked around and deftly removed them while Jesse was checking on the potatoes and placed the soaked shorts on a branch sticking out at an odd angle from the log. Now dressed in her plain black bikini, she wrapped the blanket around herself once again. Jesse looked up and smiled. Without a word, he fashioned a clothes drying rack from a few of the leftover sticks he'd gathered and set her shorts to dry near the fire.

"There, that's much better," he said, standing back and looking at his handiwork.

"Is there anything that you cannot do?" She asked

"Of course, but I cannot divulge such secrets." He replied as he gave a final adjustment to the makeshift dryer. Then turning to Celia, he asked, "Would you like an appetizer? Our dinner won't be ready for another twenty minutes."

"Oh, yes. We could eat those sandwiches," she offered.

"No, no, no," Jesse said as he turned away from her and reached into his magic cooler once again. Retrieving two bottles, he turned back to Celia.

"Ah, želite pivo ili vino?" Jesse asked while holding a bottle of red Croatian wine in one hand and a bottle of Croatian beer in the other.

Celia laughed. "I can't believe it. Where did you find these?"

"That is another secret I shall take to my grave," he said with a haughty air. "Madame, which shall I pour?"

"You mean we're not drinking straight from the bottle this time?" She asked, tucking a loose strand of long hair behind her ear as she let out a shiver.

"Not at all."

"Well then, in that case, I'd like a glass of the wine, please."

Jesse set the bottle on the blanket and returned with two glasses and a corkscrew. "Would you mind opening the bottle?" he asked. "After all, you are the bartender."

"Of course," Celia gushed. While she was busy removing the cork, Jesse again reached into the magic cooler and pulled out a plate covered with plastic wrap and filled with thick slices of mozzarella cheese, sliced tomatoes and basil. Peeling off the plastic wrap, he fixed the slightly lopsided arrangement neatly on the plate with his thumb and forefinger, then he drizzled a small amount of olive oil and balsamic over the appetizer. Picking up a loaf of fresh bread, he returned to the blanket with the food and sat down cross legged. Looking at the aperitif hungrily, Celia smiled and held out a glass of wine to him while taking a sip of her own. The motion caused the blanket covering her shoulders to slip down around her waist. Celia's damp hair was beginning to dry enough for the curls to take form as they trailed down her shoulders, laying softly on her olive toned skin.

Jesse swallowed hard, trying not to stare but suddenly, his sight was the only sense that was getting through to his brain.

"Jesse?" Celia asked, her brow slightly furrowed.

The vision had overwhelmed all of his other senses as he nearly dropped the plate.

"Jesse, are you okay?" Celia asked for the second time, with genuine concern in her voice as she quickly took the plate from his hand.

"Uh, I uh…" Jesse stopped speaking and shook his head with a dire look about him. "I have a confession to make."

"Oh?" Celia's face dropped further, she swallowed hard and set her glass down, holding her breath.

"Somehow, I uh…," Jesse looked her in the eyes. "Celia, I forgot all the silverware."

Celia's laughter could have been heard a mile away and it was better than music.

"Well, I guess we'll just have to eat with our fingers?" she replied after regaining her composure and dove into the plate of food.

Not long after, Jesse served up the main meal, partially burning his fingers while breaking open the potatoes.

"This salmon is so good," Celia stated between mouthfuls. "I've never eaten anything like this before." She sipped the wine and dove her fingers in for another morsel.

"The two most important secrets are ultra-fresh fish and cooking it over a wood fire," Jesse explained with great satisfaction. They continued to eat in silence until they had no more room. Larry kept licking his chops until Celia fed him her last bit of dinner.

"Oh, now you're going to spoil him," Jesse complained with a grin.

As the fire burned down, Celia leaned into Jesse as if it were the most natural thing in the world. They both stared into the flames in silence. Jesse shifted and accidentally tipped the wine glasses over into the sand. Without a word, Celia giggled and reached for the wine bottle and handed it to Jesse.

"I guess we're just straight from the bottle people after all."

Jesse took a swig and handed it back to her. After she took a pull from the bottle, she wiped her mouth. Looking up at Jesse, she asked, "What about you? Who are you, really?"

Jesse grinned looking down at her. "What about me?"

"Well," Celia started tentatively as she drew circles in the sand with her finger. "What was it like growing up with Link?" She asked, almost afraid to look in his eyes.

"It was great, when he was home, but he was also deployed way too much. So, whenever he was home, we'd do a lot of hunting and fishing where he grew up in the Alaskan bush."

She relaxed when he answered the question so easily. She propped her head in her hand. "It sounds like an interesting place to grow up."

"It was," Jesse agreed. "What do you remember about my dad?"

Suddenly, a shadow passed over her soul. She didn't answer for a long moment, just gazed past the fire and out over the lake. *It doesn't have to be that way anymore.* She thought as she watched a squadron of white pelicans skimming the wave tops on their way home. The sun continued its slide.

"Are you okay?" he asked gently. "I didn't mean to ask anything to hurt you."

"No. I mean yes, I am okay. Now. That is. It's just that before a few days ago, I only remembered him in vague dreams and fleeting, foggy memories. It seems that Maria kept a lot from me because of other things that happened. But now, after seeing a photograph and hearing the stories, I am having many memories come back vividly."

"Good ones?" Jesse asked.

"With Link, yes. Good ones." She responded with a smile. And maybe one that wasn't. "He was the one in my dreams that would give me a little white flower and chocolate when I was a little girl." She looked up to Jesse. "I suppose that's why I adore them so much." Then she looked away and continued. "When you brought me that little flower from the parking lot, that old memory, it hit me very strongly." She paused again, then looked deeply in his eyes. "It was the first time I'd ever been given a flower since I was a little girl."

"It won't be the last," he said as he softly stroked her hair. "I promise you that."

She smiled and seemed to enjoy his touch.

"What happened?" Jesse asked quietly. "What was the bad memory?"

"Didn't Link tell you?"

"No. The only thing he told me was that you suffered through some terrible times during the war, but he would not elaborate. He said it was your story to tell if you wanted to."

"Can I trust you?" she asked, searching his eyes.

"Yes, of course."

"I'm afraid that you will see me differently. If I tell you, then you will realize I am damaged. I am broken inside."

"No, I won't."

"But I am," she said quietly, but inside, the little girl was screaming.

"It doesn't matter."

"Jesse, why do you want to be with me? You could have had any girl in the bar that night. Any night, anywhere." She asked with such desperation her chin began to tremble.

Jesse swallowed hard and took a deep breath before he answered. "I don't know for sure, but Dad always said God has a plan and a path for each of us, and it was the fortunate man who finds it. I'm beginning to think that God had blinders on me all this time because he meant me to see only you. Find only you. I've spent a lifetime running from the plan because I was afraid of what it might be, and it doesn't seem to matter now because I believe that I ran right into it."

She gazed into his eyes, looking for the truth. Praying it was the truth.

"I already see you as the most wonderful, beautiful girl in the world who has survived so much because she is strong. Please believe me Celia, you can trust me."

She pulled back from him and sat up straight. Grabbing a stick, she poked the fire with it. "Okay, here goes." *Please don't run away.* she pleaded silently before she spoke. "Your dad saved my life in many different ways." She stared into the fire but really, she was staring past the fire into her dark and painful past.

"I was just a young girl, and I was held as a prisoner with my mother and my older sister, in a place we called rape hotel. There were many of these places during the war. We were starved with little to eat or drink. My mother was murdered before my eyes because she would not give me to a soldier. My sister disappeared a few days later after she tried to protect me. I believe that she was murdered also. From the window of our room, I could see the men throwing bodies into the river." Her voice cracked. She looked at Jesse, his face was drawn and the muscles at his jaws were popping in and out, his fists curled. She took his hand in hers and uncoiled his fingers. "I wanted to die, Jesse. I intended to kill myself, but I didn't have the courage. Yet. Then one day, your dad came in wearing a flight suit and holding a rifle. He saw me being raped by a soldier. Your dad killed him and dragged his body off of me. I was so scared." Her chin began to tremble, and her hands began to shake all over again, as she continued to speak. Her voice became even lower and broken. She looked from the flames back to Jesse for a moment, tears brimming in her eyes. Jesse wrapped his arm around her and pulled her into him and just held her. She laid her head on his shoulder, took a deep breath and continued, still gazing past the fire. "I thought he would hurt me too, but instead, he gave me some chocolate." She let out a short chuckle and looked up at him. "You know the kind with lots of squares?"

Jesse nodded without speaking. She noticed a tiny crack of a smile found its way to the surface.

"He ate the first little piece and I thought that he was going to be cruel like all the rest and eat it in front of me, but instead, after showing me how good it tasted, he gave me the rest to eat all by myself."

"That would be so much like my dad."

She started again, this time, her voice filled with desperation. "Jesse, I was so hungry." Her voice broke, and Jesse could feel her body shake in silence. "Then..." She sniffed. "...he held out his arms and I crawled into them. He wrapped me in a warm and smelly blanket..." Her nose wrinkled at the memory. "...and took me to a helicopter. He spoke to another man dressed like him, who buckled me into a seat and gave me another chocolate bar to eat from his own hidden pocket. He wrapped me in his arms and took care of me while your dad flew the helicopter. I couldn't speak English at the time, but I knew." She paused.

"Knew what?"

"That I was finally safe. The man I came to know as Link saved me."

Jesse's throat tightened up and his eyes began to smart.

"When we landed, he took me to Maria's." Then her expression changed, it went cold as she looked Jesse dead in the eye once again. "You must know something. I have terrible nightmares. I wake up screaming, soaking wet with sweat and I can't make them stop. You don't want to be with me, Jesse." She pulled back from him. "I'm lost, I'm broken, and I can't seem to fix it."

Jesse swallowed hard, trying to clear the lump in his throat. She was verbally pushing him away and daring him not to go. "Maybe...uh... Maybe it will be better when you wake up next to someone who loves you and cares deeply for you?"

"What?" Leaning forward, she turned to face him. "How can you say that?"

"Do you mean, how can I say I love you? It's easy." He fell silent for a moment, taking in the whirlwind. He knew it as if it had always been a fact. "The problem is, I think I fell in love with you the moment I saw you jump in and help Jenny clean up. Or maybe it was when you slapped my hand. No, I've got it. When you said you liked my cooking." He smiled.

Celia placed her hand on his chest. "Don't you see? I am terrified of loving you."

"So, does that mean you *do* love me?" He asked with an arched eyebrow. "Are you admitting to loving me back?"

"Jesse, you don't understand. I can't even have children."

"Okay," he said with a shrug.

"What do you mean, okay?" she asked, anger and frustration building in her voice. "You don't understand. You can't just say okay."

"Well, what I mean is, that it doesn't scare me. And besides, if you've never dated anyone, how do you know for sure?"

She sat back at the question. "I don't." She admitted. " I overheard the doctors tell that to Maria when she first took me to hospital. I was bleeding, and I was so scared. I don't think they realized I was listening."

Jesse pulled her to him and squeezed tighter while kissing the top of her head.

"Are you real?" she asked, looking up at him.

"Is your tummy full?"

"Yes."

"Then I guess that makes me real." he said, pulling her back to his chest and wrapping his arms around her once again. They stayed in that position for several minutes in silence.

Jesse took the bottle from her hand and tipped it to his lips. It was already empty. "Damn bottle must have a leak in it," he said as he tossed it towards the cooler where it made a thud when it hit the sand.

"I wish today would never end," she whispered softly as she laid her head on his chest. Larry was resting his chin on her thigh, dozing once again as she stroked his furry head and ears. "I'm afraid that I'll wake up tomorrow and this will be nothing but a dream," she whispered, as if speaking only to herself.

The tempo of Jesse's heartbeat started to rise. He kissed the top of her head as she leaned into him.

"I don't believe this," she said with her accent becoming stronger. "I cannot believe this."

"This... what? Exactly?" Jesse asked.

"You. That's what." she replied.

"What you see is what you get, baby. I'm a terrible actor."

"You are too good to be true." she insisted.

"That's funny." He paused to chuckle at her comment. "Let me get this straight. I'm sitting here on a blanket next to a stunningly beautiful girl. And," He paused again, "we are in front of an amazing fire after a beautiful day after a great meal and some fine wine. Do the math, honey, It's not me that's too good to be true, it's *you*."

"No, of course not. I am just me," Celia replied with a self-deprecating tone. Her accent just a little stronger.

"And, as crazy as it sounds, that's exactly what's so great about you," Jesse said as he wrapped his arms around her. "No pretenses. No games. Just you." He paused for effect. "With me, of course."

Suddenly, in one fluid motion, she turned to him, and fervently pressed her lips to his. Her first kiss, and it was everything she'd dreamed of and nothing she'd feared. His lips were warm and soft and sweet. He didn't force or fight his way into her mouth, but softly, so softly, touched his lips to hers. He teased her with his tongue, gently but at the same time, making her world spin and the fires that had been dormant for so long seemed to erupt inside her. *Oh no,* She wasn't ready to face that heat, and she pulled back before it was too late. Her breaths were ragged and her chest heaved as she turned her eyes once again to stare into the fire, trying to collect her thoughts, to pull her mind and body back together. She took his hand and interlaced her fingers between his as the fire crackled and popped, sending sparks like fireflies into the darkening sky, mimicking the way she felt inside.

"I love you too, Jesse." she confessed.

"Well, that was certainly worth the wait." Jesse whispered huskily.

"Jesse, I don't want this night to end…" She blurted, turning her head to look up in his eyes. Pleading. He stroked her cheek. Then, turning back to stare into the flames once again she asked, "Can we stay here forever?" The question came from a frightened little girl searching for love, safety and sanctuary. *Is it possible?* She hoped it was. Before now, she would have never even dreamed, let alone believed that something as wonderful as this could happen… to her.

"Sure, who needs civilization?" Jesse exclaimed. "I could build you a cabin right on this little island of ours. There's plenty of logs. We could call it…Jesse's Island."

"Why not Celia's Island?"

"Because I jumped off the boat first, so technically it's mine." Jesse explained as she held his hand.

"Oh yeah? Is that how it really works?"

"Sure is." Jesse replied with a wave of his hand.

"Well then, we could live off the land like Sacagawea and her little baby. Catch some more fish." She giggled as the vision they were creating formed in her head.

"That's right, baby. We'd knock off a couple of deer and maybe a pheasant or two from time to time. Heck, a moose would last us a whole year." He chortled.

Leaning back against his chest she was quiet for a moment, then whispered. "I think I would love that. Especially if you are cooking."

She smiled up at him and laughed a laugh that started from her toes as she snuggled deeper into his arms.

Tired of being left out, Larry began to whine and wag his tail. His blue eyes looking from Celia to Jesse and back again.

"Awe, come here Larry, We love you too."

CHAPTER THIRTY-SEVEN

As Link walked toward the entrance to Zorba's restaurant, the scent of Mediterranean food wafted out to greet him. The aroma took him back to times in his distant past. Places that were both wonderful and terrible, depending on the particular moment in time. To a people he loved and sometimes loathed, depending on which side they were on.

From the doorway, he could see the roasting lamb and beef as the vertical rotisserie went round and round. The smell of which was permeating the air throughout the small and somewhat intimate restaurant. Link smiled again, even the bouzouki music coming from the overhead speakers brought him back to a restaurant just like this, only a half a world away.

The lunch crowd had already gone back to work, and the dinner crowd hadn't begun to show up yet, so he pretty much had his pick and he decided on a table. Link grabbed a chair that gave him a view of both the front door and the kitchen door and hailed the waitress. Tall and thin, she had long dark hair, well defined brows, and large brown eyes.

"Welcome. Would you like something to drink?"

"*Evet, bir bira lütfen,*" Link replied with a grin.

"You speak a little Turkish?" she asked with a surprised smile, showing bright white teeth.

"*Evet, ama sadece biraz ve korkarım çok kötü,*" Link said slowly, with his hands in the air in way of apology.

She laughed out loud this time. "Yes, I agree, your Turkish *is* very bad, but I can still understand you."

"Hey, it's been a couple of years since I was back there," Link said as a lame excuse.

"So, what kind of beer would you like?" she asked, still smiling.

"Do you have *Efes?*"

"No, we don't have any Turkish beer here, but we do have most everything else."

"Well…" He looked at his watch. "For starters, can you bring me a Blue Moon? Oh, and that's with two slices of orange. I need it to keep up on my vitamin C."

The waitress smiled again, this time flashing a beautiful set of white teeth. "I'll get that poured for you right away."

"Hey, after that, I need you to go in the back and tell Moose that there's an ugly bald guy who speaks terrible Turkish and wants to see him.

"Uh…right away sir," she said a bit hesitantly.

Link smiled at the look on her face. "Also, tell him that I said my *donkey* makes better food than he does."

"Uh…I…I'd rather not. He's been kind of grumpy today."

Chuckling, Link said, "Good. Tell him anyway."

The waitress sighed a bit and said, "Okay." And started for the kitchen door. "It's your funeral," Link heard her say under her breath as she disappeared into the kitchen.

"Uh, what about my beer first?" Link asked to the closing kitchen door.

"Who?"

Link heard the question come from the kitchen. The waitress must have been speaking quietly because Link could only hear the responses.

"He said *what*?"

The familiar voice yelling made Link smile.

"He did, did he? I'll ring his skinny little neck," came a roar as the kitchen doors burst open.

Link saw him coming like a freight train and decided to stand up, just in case this wasn't working out the way he thought it would.

"What do you mean your donkey makes better food?" he bellowed. Wearing a white collared shirt and his white apron, he was big and burly with a huge black mustache and wild curly black hair topped off by a traditional red Fez hat. "My donkey tasted way better than your donkey ever did." His laugh was so deep and contagious that it shook the building. "Jiff, you never use enough spices, so your donkey had no flavor."

"Where was I going to get any spices in that place?" Link yelled back, his laughter contradicting the feigned anger.

Link found himself lifted off the floor in a bear hug by the giant, his feet dangling, and his arms crushed to his side.

Setting him back down on the floor, he held him at arm's length and asked, "How are you, Jiff? How is your family?

"We're all good," Link replied. "In fact, my youngest son just joined the company. And you? How is Zehra and little Mira?"

"Thanks to you, we are all doing terribly wonderful."

"I am truly glad to hear it," Link replied.

"Are you hungry? I have your favorite."

"Doner-babs?" Link asked as he licked his lips.

"Of course," he exclaimed. "Would I offer you anything but the best?"

"Yes, you would," Link declared.

"No more talk of the times when we could only eat donkeys. Come, I have a table in the kitchen for special guests. We can talk there."

Link followed Moose into the kitchen, the waitress was busy setting the special guest table and to Link's surprise, his Blue Moon was already waiting for him, complete with two slices of orange.

"So, to what, do I owe your visit?" Moose asked just as Link stuffed a fork full of roasted lamb and tzatziki sauce in his mouth. "It must be important if you are visiting me. When I first arrived, I thought we agreed that we would not be seen together. Do you remember little Mira?"

Link nodded his head and said, "Of course," while savoring another bite.

"The waitress you talked to *is* little Mira."

Link stopped chewing and stared in disbelief at the doorway into the restaurant. "No way." Link exclaimed with a mouth full of food. "She's beautiful. Good thing she doesn't take after you."

Link swallowed his food and then looked around before he spoke. "Let me ask you, my friend, why would I need to come see the best operative I ever had in Aleppo?"

"Link, that was a lifetime ago, for both of us. We both have a new life here."

"Unfortunately, that lifetime seems to be catching up with me," Link admitted.

Moose took a deep breath and slowly let it out. "Tell me more, my friend. I can never repay you enough for finding my family when they were kidnapped. Every day that I am allowed to look into Zhera's eyes is another day in my own little paradise."

"You don't owe me anything. I didn't do anything special."

"You lie, my friend, but we can argue about that later. What can I do for you now?"

"For starters," Link launched in a new direction. "Have you noticed anything out of the ordinary around here or heard anything?"

"Yes, of course," Moose replied in a hushed tone. "That is why we came here, because nothing is ordinary, and anyone can make a new start here. Thanks to you."

Link smiled but had another mouthful.

"The beauty is in the chaos of this place," Moose continued. "Normally, it might be difficult to start fresh, but you were right. Anyone can come here and be successful. Become anonymous, just part of the backdrop."

"I'm not talking about your business. I'm asking if you've seen or heard anything that might have caught your attention."

"Like what? Why are you asking me this?"

"Haven't you noticed an exceptional number of *accidents* and random problems lately in the news?"

"Yes, come to think of it, there have been quite a few in the past few weeks."

"I'm beginning to think it's not a coincidence."

"How do you mean?"

"If it was just one accident, or maybe two random accidents, I might buy it. But the sheer volume of absolutely random accidents makes it something else entirely. It makes it feel intentional."

"I see," Moose considered. "Everyone has heard of the explosion that Reagan was involved in. A tremendous blessing that no one was hurt."

"So, I was hoping that a man of your particular talents may have noticed any tidbits that might point me in some direction."

"No, nothing at this point. But now that you have awakened those talents you speak of, let me think." Moose stroked his bushy mustache as he considered Link's request. "You know, there have been many close calls that don't even get reported, as well as the many that are."

"Go on," Link encouraged after washing down a mouthful with beer.

"There seems to me a new crowd coming in. Spanish speakers. They mistook Mira for a Latina and seemed quite confused that she did not speak their language. What makes them stand out is that they were not wearing work clothing of oil workers."

"What were they wearing?" Link asked as he carefully put his fork down on his half empty plate.

"Combat boots and cargo pants," Moose answered. "And Jiff, they didn't move like tired roughnecks either."

* * * * *

Cheri had been going over every little fragment of evidence with no new direction to move to. She yawned and picked up her cell and pushed the button for Special Agent Bravis Brown. *Maybe he's come up with something."* she thought. *Anything.*

"Brown here."

"Bravis, it's me Cheri."

"Hello, Cheri. I was just reviewing all the notes you had sent over. I agree with your conclusions on Natalie Hotah. There is no way she was killed at home, which makes it highly likely that she was killed on Federal land. I've already received the go-ahead to run with it full steam.

"I'm glad you're on board with it, because we just got another injection of weird."

"Okay, shoot."

"Point number one. Natalie worked as a security guard for GEA."

"Yes, we've already established that."

"Point number two. We had an attempted homicide on Lincoln James out on a job site. According to Mr. James, he turned the tables on our murderer and the suspect is now in the morgue. Captured it all on a drone camera."

"Who is the guy in the morgue? Anyone you know?"

"No, we've run his prints and photo through multiple databases with no hits so far. I'm hoping that you might be able to run it up your channels."

"No offense, but why would I be interested in this one?"

"Glad you asked. The truck he was driving was reported stolen from GEA."

"Now that *is* interesting."

"And it was Natalie Hotah that filed the report."

"Send me what you've got. Anything else?"

"Yes, if you hadn't been interested before, I saved the best one for last to set the hook in your mouth."

"Okay, I'll bite. What is it?"

"We just found Jack Martin, dead outside of a strip joint this morning." She trailed off knowing he'd asked.

"Who is Jack Martin and why do I care?" he asked, knowing there'd be a reason.

"Because he is the Chief of Security for GEA." She baited.

"Yup. You're right. I'm hooked. Cause of death?"

"Garrote, from the back seat. From what this small-town cowgirl can see, it looks like a pro.

"Hook, line and sinker. Where are you?"

"I'm at the station."

"Got any decent coffee or should I bring my own."

"We've got plenty."

"Okay." He replied. "See you in twenty."

338

CHAPTER THIRTY-EIGHT

As Jesse pulled up to his dad's house, he noticed Link's truck wasn't in the driveway yet, but Victoria's was. Surprised, he checked the time. "Looks like Dad's going to be in trouble," Jesse said in a sing-song voice to Larry. Victoria had called to invite him over for dinner and emphasized, *Please don't be late.*

Even though Victoria wasn't his mom, he always had great respect for her because of the way she treated Link, and despite the difficulties that come with a man like him, she obviously loved him deeply.

"At least *we're* on time," he said to Larry, his canine sidekick. "Like Dad always says: Don't piss off the redhead." He parked his company truck behind Victoria's rig, leaving room for Link to pull into his normal spot. The garage was only used in the wintertime but no matter what, Link always parked on the right side and the redhead parked on the left. Jesse chuckled at the comments he'd get if he parked in his dad's spot. "You know what, Larry? It would almost be worth the ass chewing." Jesse hopped out of his truck, Larry right behind him, and the two headed for the front door. As his hand reached for the doorbell, he looked through the glass and saw a big pile of military issue stuff dumped on the living room floor. Just then, Josh, his older brother appeared in the window, smiling like big brothers do when they are thinking of doing something mean to their younger brother.

"What's the password?" Josh yelled through the heavy glass.

"How the hell should I know, butthead?" Jesse yelled back, smiling as Josh unlocked the door and let him in. Larry went bounding past them to the kitchen, obviously thinking Victoria might have a morsel for him. She did.

The two brothers bear-hugged each other, in an unspoken contest to see who could hug harder.

"Oh, it's so good to see you little brother," Josh said as he attempted to crush Jesse.

Larry began to whine as he watched.

"It's great to see you too, big brother." Jesse said through gritted teeth though still holding his own. They released each other and took a step back to look at one another. They were the same height, same color of hair, but Josh's was mostly straight and short, and Jesse's was wavy, if not curly. Still dressed in camouflage trousers and a military under-armor T-shirt, Josh was broad at the shoulders and powerfully built.

"You filled out, little brother. You're a man," Josh exclaimed.

"Yes, I have been for quite some time," Jesse said sarcastically then changed the subject. "Does Dad know you're here?"

"Nope," Josh said conspiratorially as he looked back over his shoulder into the kitchen where Victoria was cooking. "I enlisted Victoria's help to surprise the old man."

"I can't wait to see his face," Jesse said. "You know, since he's late, I should move my truck into his parking spot so when he comes in, he'll already be at a high hover."

"Why risk death, just for a little fun?" Josh asked. "Or has he recently mellowed out and I'm just unaware." The smartass look of the James family DNA was spread all over his face.

Jesse leaned in toward Josh while glancing toward the kitchen. "Uh, I've got some drone footage you need to see."

"Oh yeah? What of? Wait, don't tell me. Some unsuspecting bikini-clad girls on a beach somewhere?"

"No," Jesse said seriously. "It's a video of Dad."

"Dad's in a bikini?" Josh exclaimed. "Brother, that's just wrong."

Jesse didn't blink. "Do you know what Dad did in the military?" he asked as he pulled out his cell phone.

"Of course," Josh replied. "He was a pilot. You know that as well as I do."

"Yeah, I know that. But what else?" He scrolled through his phone before looking up. "I've selected the more interesting parts of this video." He hit play on his cell and held it up for Josh to watch. "I synced the audio from the cell phone conversation to the drone video."

"Damn," Josh blurted out as the scene began to unfold.

"I know, right?" Jesse asked.

Josh took the cell from Jesse's hand and stared, wide-eyed as he watched his father fight for his life. When the bullets started flying, he was so transfixed on the scene it didn't occur to him that the drone was getting closer until it slammed into the gun.

"When did this happen?" Josh asked.

"A few days ago. He's still pretty sore. So, I ask again. What exactly did Dad do in the Army besides fly?"

"I don't know, but what I do know is that ain't no plain ol' Army helicopter pilot," Josh exclaimed.

"Even I know that a fight like that takes some special skills," Jesse admitted.

"I know, right?" Josh agreed. "That dude was way bigger and younger than Dad."

"I was starting to freak out as that gun barrel was pointing closer and closer to Dad's face," Jesse added. "I could hear everything through the cell phone. I could especially hear Dad getting winded."

"That was some great flying though, little brother," Josh added. "If you wouldn't have hit his gun hand, that pistol was pointing right at his forehead. One more second and it would have been too late."

"Late? Late for what?" Link asked a moment before he stepped through the open doorway.

Josh quickly dropped the cell into his pocket and grinned.

As Link looked up from his cell phone, his jaw dropped momentarily and then a huge grin of his own spread across his face. "Joshua," Link exclaimed while the two men moved toward each other for a similar embrace. "Oh, man, it's good to see you, Son." Link said as he held Josh at arm's length. "Your hair is getting kind of long, isn't it?"

"Yeah," Josh said as he ran his fingers through his relatively short, blond hair. "I've been meaning to get it cut, but it's been really crazy PCSing to my new station."

"Oh, yeah? Where are you going?"

"I've got orders back to Bragg, but I had a few days in between and thought it would be fun to surprise you guys."

"Who was your co-conspirator to pull this off?" Link asked as Victoria approached the three men.

"The only one here that can keep a secret," Josh replied with a grin.

"Wait, slow down for us lowly civilians," Jesse said. "Earlier, you said you were PCSing. What exactly is PCSing?"

"It stands for Permanent Change of Station," Josh replied. "When the Army moves me to a new base."

"What unit are you working for at Bragg?" Link asked.

"I don't know. I'll find out when I report next week."

"What's your orders say?"

"Just to report to the Special Operations Group for assignment."

Link glanced sideways for a long moment. Then finally said, "Hmm. Well, nothing like leaving you in the dark. When you find out, let me know, will ya?"

"Sure thing, Dad."

"Is that unusual?" Jesse asked out loud.

"No, I guess not." Link said. "But having you both under one roof calls for a celebration libation," Link stated authoritatively. "Who's up for some Jameson?"

The boys followed Link into the living room, where he stepped behind the small wet bar and reached for a half bottle of Jameson Stout while placing three hi ball glasses on the white pine bar before removing the cap from the bottle. With his left hand he pushed the glasses together so that they all were lined up, with rims touching and with his right, he poured a continuous stream across all three, splashing the amber liquid, two fingers high in each. Then he handed glasses to his sons and raised his own.

Link: "To those who know me best and, for some strange reason, still love me."

Josh: "If you're lucky enough to be Irish, you're lucky enough."

Jesse: "May we be loved by those we love."

Link and Josh look at each other. "Huh?"

Link: "A shot of Jameson for the sons of James. May we all be reunited one day in heaven where the whisky tap is stuck open."

All together: "To us and those like us, damn few left." They tapped their drinks on the table. "To Jason." they all declared and then drank their whisky.

As they placed their empty glasses back on the bar, Link turned to Jesse. "So Jesse, speaking of being loved by those we love… How is Celia?"

Jesse's ears flushed red before a word came out of his mouth. "uh…"

"Who's Celia?" Josh asked, looking at his baby brother.

"Just one of Dad's daughters," Jesse replied with his best attempt at being nonchalant.

"What?" Josh spun his glance toward his dad. "You mean DeNedra?"

"No, it's a different daughter," Victoria confirmed.

Josh looked over at his dad with an eyebrow raised.

"Hey now. It's been kind of busy around here lately," Link explained as he shrugged his shoulders.

Then Josh looked at Victoria for help.

"Don't look at me. Your dad managed to do this without any of my help."

Jesse smiled at Josh's confusion. "She's a girl I am seeing."

"Hold on. You're dating Dad's daughter?" Josh asked with surprise. "A daughter that I don't even know about?"

"No, not his real daughter."

"Then his fake one?" Josh asked incredulously and without pausing said, "Oh, brother, we need to have a talk."

"It's not like that," Jesse exclaimed, his frustration growing along with the red in his cheeks.

"*You* are in love with her," Josh stated matter-of-factly. "So that's what your toast was all about."

"Yes. I am," he said with a big sigh as he felt the blush continue to creep mercilessly across his face.

"I didn't think anyone could ever capture your heart. I know there's no one that could ever tie down my wings. She must be something special."

"She was a little girl that Dad found during the war in the Balkans," Jesse explained.

"Wow, that's heavy," Josh admitted soberly. "Wait. Are we talking about the same Celia that works as a bartender at Maria's?"

Jesse nodded with a smile. "Whoa, good job, little brother. She's hot, but I had heard she wouldn't date anyone."

"It's a long story," Link interjected. "And you'll probably need a full beer to keep your anger doused when you hear it," Link said with a sigh of his own as he dropped himself into an ugly but comfortable, overstuffed chair.

* * * * *

Cheri awoke to her cell ringing on the nightstand, the darkened room illuminated by the flashing light coinciding with each ring. She fumbled for the light switch before picking up the phone. The caller ID read: Watch supervisor. *What the?* She reached over and spun the alarm clock face toward her. *2:30 in the morning?*

Dean, her husband, sat up in bed, rubbing his eyes. "This can't be good."

"Go for Perry, and this better be something really good or really bad."

"It's Dustin, Ma'am, for the supervisor. Sorry to wake you, but we have an apparent carjacking to include a dead body."

"Is the dead body the victim or the carjacker?" Cheri asked as she sat up in bed.

"It looks like the body is the victim, Ma'am."

"Why did you call it a carjacking?" Cheri asked

"A witness saw someone holding a gun climb into the passenger side in the south lot, and then the vehicle drove away.

"What is going on in this town?" Cheri asked without expecting an answer. She took a deep breath. "Where's the crime scene?"

"In the north parking lot of the university."

"Got an ID on the vic?"

"The vehicle is registered to a Taylor Hansen."

"Oh shit. Taylor?" Cheri gasped. "That's Seth and Jenny's Au Pair. They're my neighbors."

"Crime scene team is already on site."

"Copy that. I'm on my way. Uh, I'll be there in like... twenty minutes. Perry out."

Cheri jumped out of bed and reached for her ear pods on the charger and popped one into her right ear. She punched the number for Seth and started throwing on clothes while she waited for him to answer.

"Hello, Cheri," Seth said in a sleep-deepened voice. "It's kind of early. Uh, lost your cows again?"

"Seth, I'm sorry, but no time for jokes. Is Taylor there at the house?"

"No, she left after dinner," Seth answered warily. "Said she was going to the university to turn in some papers. Has something happened?"

"Her car was jacked, and when they found the car there was a body in it at the university parking lot." Cheri said bluntly.

"What? Wait. No!" Seth shouted.

"Look, Seth," Cheri said as she opened the door to her SUV. "I'm on my way over there now, and I'll call you as soon as I know any more.

"Okay, Cheri. Thanks for the head's up."

CHAPTER THIRTY-NINE

"What?" Link's voice was terse and grumpy as he answered his cell.

"Link? It's Seth, and I am really worried." Seth spelled out what Cheri had told him over the phone as he hurriedly got dressed.

"Have you double checked her room to make sure she's not there?" Link asked

"No, I'm sure I would have heard her come in, but I'm checking her room and the garage now, just to be certain."

"This is crazy," Link said. "My spidey sense is going off the charts."

"Wake up, honey," Link said as he roughly tapped Victoria's cheek.

"Link, her bed's made. She hasn't been home."

"Tell you what," Link said as he pulled on his pants. "Victoria and I are on our way out. Call me if you find out anything else."

"Will do," Seth said. "And Link? Thanks."

"Not a problem." He hung up.

Link went to his nightstand, flicked a hidden switch, and out popped his Glock 17. He dropped the mag, checked the weapon, and re-inserted the mag and slid the .45 caliber pistol into a concealed carry holster. Then he turned around and spotted Victoria's purse. He reached in and pulled out her little pink-handled nine-millimeter pistol and conducted the same procedure for it before dropping it back into her purse.

Next, he snatched up his cell from the bed and dialed a number from memory.

"Hello, Link," Maria answered. "We just closed the bar, and I was heading to bed."

Link filled Maria in as he and Victoria walked out the door. Tossing the truck keys to his wife, he continued to explain the situation to Maria.

"I've got a bad feeling about this, Maria."

"Your gut has kept you and other's alive a long time," Maria suggested. "I think we need to listen closely to it."

"If Celia is okay with it, can I borrow her from you as an interim au pair?"

"I've got you on speaker phone and Celia's nodding her head."

"Great," Link said. "Celia, I owe you one."

"No, you don't, Tata," Celia stated matter-of-factly. "We'll be right behind you."

"I'll see if I can get Sophia up from Bismarck in the morning to help at the bar," Maria said as an afterthought.

* * * * *

Victoria's mind was racing. She, Jenny, Maria and Celia were all sitting in the living room at the cabin, talking in hushed tones. *Who would want to kill Taylor,* she thought desperately. Or was it just a coincidence? Simply a case of the wrong place at the wrong time. Seth and Link had gone to the crime scene to see what they could find out.

Faith was peacefully asleep in Victoria's arms, but Hope was becoming a bit fussy.

Jenny had just handed her to Celia and went into the kitchen to warm up a bottle of milk when the doorbell rang. "Who could that be at this time of the night?" Jenny asked.

"Don't answer the door, Jenny," Celia yelled from the living room.

Jenny didn't respond.

Alarm bells went off in Victoria's head. A sudden burst of adrenaline instantly followed as she looked for her purse.

"Jenny?" Maria called as she got up to see who was at the door, but it was too late. Jenny walked around the corner white as a sheet. Brooke was right behind her with a revolver stuck in Jenny's back.

"Sit down over there," Brooke commanded Jenny. She pointed to the empty place next to Victoria on the couch.

"You sit back down right where you were, Maria." She waved her gun at the spot Maria had just vacated next to Celia.

"If any one of you moves a muscle, I'll have to kill precious little Faith, or maybe heavenly Hope." She tittered at her own words. "There'd still be one left. Got it?"

"What are you doing, Brooke?" Victoria demanded, handing Faith back to Jenny.

"I'm here to fix the only problem I have left."

"What's that?" Victoria asked, her voice just above a growl.

"*This* is not my fault," Brooke began. "If only Seth had loved me properly, if only he had told *me* he needed a surrogate first, we wouldn't be here. And if Danielle would have left willingly, and if Tiffany hadn't got in the way that night, they too, would still be alive. How could Jenny possibly be better than me? I'm a Certified Nursing Assistant. Who better to be a surrogate? Those babies were rightfully mine! She grew silent for a moment just looking at all the faces watching her. *Yeah, watching me. I'm in charge.*

"You know, it's not really that hard to kill someone," Brooke broke the silence with a wry chuckle as she began to pace back and forth. "In fact, I was kind of disappointed that there wasn't much excitement to it. At all."

She stopped pacing for a moment and looked at her hostages. "It feels so good to finally tell someone who cares," Brooke said as she chuckled happily. "You have no idea what it's like to keep this secret all to myself."

"Why are you here?" Jenny asked.

Ignoring her question, Brooke launched back into her subject. "Back to killing people. Let's take Danielle for instance, she was my first… She drank the rest of my bottle of Jack Daniels that might have been *slightly* tainted with a roofie mixture, and she went out like a light. Not even a struggle. I thought there would be more thrill to it, but sadly, there wasn't."

Victoria watched as Brooke seemed to savor the moment.

"I know right? Shocking, isn't it?" Brooke said with another giggle before continuing. "Now Tiffany, she was a little different story. I gave her enough rohypnol in her Jack Daniels to put a horse to sleep, so she should have been out like a light as well, but she just kept talking and talking. She just wouldn't shut up, so I finally had to just jump on her in the car and do it. The end result was the same. A pretty corpse.

"Brooke, I've got to use the bathroom." Victoria claimed, with a look of urgency on her face.

"Don't move, Victoria." Brooke said as she swung the gun in her direction. "You can hold it."

"Your gun looks kind of old and rusty," Celia observed. "Are you sure it works?"

350

"It sure does. Just ask your precious little Taylor." She sniggered a little. "In fact, this is the same gun that killed my mother too." She looked around at her captive audience. "Yup. Betcha didn't know that, did ya? Same one. Of course, I didn't do it. My grandma did because Momma wouldn't behave. But I was seven years old and saw the whole thing. You know she's still buried in the basement of that old house? I even helped.

"Taylor, however, I truly felt sorry for her. Not because I was going to kill her, but because I *had* to shoot her. I tried to get her to take a drink or two of Jack, but she was a little *miss-goody-two-shoes* and said she couldn't. She said that she had to get back to her precious little babies and didn't want to get loaded." Her mocking tone turned toward anger. "*She would not listen!*" she concluded with set teeth. Her anger then subsided with a slow breath, and she calmly continued. "So, I had to shoot her. I decided not to shoot her in the face though, because it really wasn't her fault, and I didn't want to mess up her pretty face, especially that *cute* little dimple of hers." She paused as if she were waiting for an "*aww*" from her captive audience." When none came, she continued undaunted. "Unfortunately, it took three bullets because she kept looking at me and I *didn't like it.*"

Turning to Celia, she demanded, "What are *you* doing here?"

"I was called to help with the twins when they found out that Taylor was killed."

"Why you? You're just a lousy bartender."

"I offered to do it for free," Celia said calmly. "Just room and board. I was getting sick and tired of living with Maria behind the bar."

"What? I would have done it for free too!" Her indignation renewed. She swung the gun back to the left toward Jenny. "What is wrong with you people? Can't you take a hint? Don't you understand that if Seth would have asked me to have his babies instead of you, no one would have had to die? It's all *your* fault."

"No one else has to die now," Victoria said calmly as she looked at her purse sitting, out of reach, on the kitchen island.

Ignoring the comment, Brooke continued. "Or, if Jenny would have hired me instead of that college girl as the au pair, at least *she* wouldn't have died." She lowered the gun momentarily to her side. "So, her death would be Jenny's fault after all," she stated casually while addressing Victoria.

"And you!" Her anger began to swell once again as she pointed the gun at Jenny. "You're too stupid to know what to do with a man, even when you have one right in front of you. Why are you still sleeping in your own room when you have a stud like that down the hall?"

"Brooke, Jenny didn't hire Taylor. It was Seth and Link," Victoria said, trying to buy some time. "They are the ones that have caused you all this pain. You really should take it out on them."

"I know. You're right." She paused for just a second as if she was mulling it over. "I would but, ya know, Seth is so good looking," she gushed, and then added, looking thoughtful, "And... I'd really hate to lose the relationship that we already have."

She turned to Victoria. "And Link." She paused for a long moment, then, pointing the gun in Victoria's direction, said, "If I'm being completely honest, he's really too much man for just one woman." Another thoughtful pause. "If the timing was better, I might could help you out in that department." She finished with a little wave of her gun and a shrug of her shoulders.

"Brooke, what do you hope to gain? What exactly are you planning?" Victoria asked with narrowed eyes and gritted teeth.

"Oh, don't you worry, *Vicky*. I've got it all figured out. You see little miss green-eyed bartender here, they're gonna find this bag of roofies and heroin on her body." She pulled a baggie out of her coat pocket and tossed it onto the coffee table. "Did you know that heroin is really cheap to buy? Who knew, right? You see, unfortunately she killed all y'all in a fit of stoner rage before I arrived, and then I just happened along and had to kill her. In self-defense of course." A sardonic smile spread across her face. "And here's the best part." She said, raising her eyebrows and making a surprise face. "I save the babies and because of that, finally, Seth falls in love with me." She threw her hands wide as if saying, *Ta da!* pistol still in her hand.

Celia passed Hope back to Jenny. Maria watched as she eased imperceptibly forward in her seat. Muscles taut, a compressed spring ready to lunge.

"It doesn't make any sense." Celia's accent was heavy, her gaze fixed and determined as she began to stand. Maria's eyes glanced in Celia's direction then back at Brooke.

"*It makes perfect sense!*" Brooke screamed as she spun toward Celia, raising her gun.

Just then Maria pushed Celia sideways and launched her own body at Brooke just as the gun fired. Maria was pinning Brooke's arms to her sides as Celia kicked the gun out of her hand and landed a blow to Brooke's temple, causing her to drop into unconsciousness.

Maria slowly released Brooke and let her slide to the floor. "I'm glad that's over." she said calmly as she looked down at the serial killer on the floor. Slipping back into her old command voice from long ago, "Somebody call the police. Celia, find something to tie her hands in case she regains consciousness before they get here. When Celia didn't move, she turned in her direction to restate her request. Celia quickly moved to Maria. "Tetka, you've been shot."

Maria looked down at her tummy where there was blood flooding from somewhere near her belly button. She grabbed at the bloody spot with her hand.

"Oh, damn." she said, as calmly as if she was talking about a stain in her blouse. "That's not good." Maria's breaths began to come quick and shallow and where she held her hand over her belly, blood flowed unrestrained between her fingers. She staggered a bit and looked into Celia's eyes. "It's okay," she said. "I just need to lay down for a moment."

"No, Maria. No!" Celia cried as she gently guided Maria to lie on the floor.

Victoria returned from the kitchen island after grabbing the cell phone from her purse and tossed it to Jenny. "Call 911." She grabbed towels from a drawer in the kitchen and rushed back to Maria's side

"Why did you do that?" Celia cried.

"I realized what you were planning, and I couldn't take the chance of you being hurt. She replied, coughing a bit of blood onto her chin. "I used to be faster, you know." Maria said with a wan smile, "I must be slowing down." her breathing became more labored. Victoria knelt on the floor and pressed the towels to the wound in an attempt to stop the massive flow as Celia held Maria's hand.

"I could have stopped her," Celia explained through tears. "The stupid girl only had one bullet left in her gun. I could see the empty shells in the cylinders when she pointed it at me."

"*Duzo*, your life is just now beginning with Jesse, and my life is now complete for I have seen you happy."

"I can be happy and have you at the same time." Celia insisted.

"I don't think so, *Duzo. Not this time.*"

"I don't want to be alone." Celia cried.

"You have never been alone, *Duzo.* Jesus brought you to me and Jesus will see you through." And with that, she coughed once again and became still.

"No! Don't leave me, *Tetke.* I need you." Celia cried as she pressed Maria's hand to her cheek. "Please don't go." Celia's sobs wracked her entire body as she rocked back and forth.

Victoria sat next to Celia on the floor, holding her. Jenny, with both girls in her arms, stood over them, tears streaming down her face. After a while, Celia reached down and closed Maria's eyes.

Celia sniffed and wiped her eyes. "Go with God, *Tetke,* Go with God."

CHAPTER FORTY

"How does it feel to be the first serial killer in Williston, North Dakota?" Cheri asked Brooke in the interview room. *Just what kind of a wack-job are you?* Is what she was thinking but it wasn't the professional way to ask the question.

Brooke was handcuffed to a bolt sticking out of the table. They were not taking any chances with her.

"The first that you *know* of," Brooke corrected with an arched eyebrow.

"Fair enough. Even so, seven bodies are a lot of bodies." Cheri interjected. "Why don't you tell me your secret? How did you manage them all?"

"Seven? I only killed three—well four—if you count Maria, but she kind of helped." Brooke shrugged. "That bullet should have been for the bartender."

"What was your plan with the rest of them at the cabin?"

"Well, in the end, I needed to kill Victoria, Jenny and Maria anyway." She stopped for a moment as if she was thinking. "Oh, wait. I just realized that Maria was on the list anyway, so I guess you can count her. But as for the others, I don't know who killed them. I always thought it was kind of funny and had hoped that those would take you off my trail, so to speak, but I never really thought about it much."

Even though the interview was being videotaped, Cheri frantically scribbled in her notepad as Brooke spoke. *SOCIOPATH.* Cheri scribbled the word in large letters. *This girl is totally devoid of a conscience. Worse yet, I think she's telling the truth about the other victims.*

Cheri looked up from her writing to find Brooke politely waiting, lips closed in a prim smile. "Oh, sorry, please continue."

"What prison do you think they will send me to?" Brooke asked, changing the subject. "When I get settled, would you ask Seth if he'd come visit me? Just for old times' sake, of course. I know he still loves me, and it'll be hard at first for him, but these things take time."

Brooke leaned in toward Cheri and whispered. "You don't think they would let us do anything during his visits do you?" Brooke actually turned a little red as she asked the question. "Oh, and tell him to bring pictures of little Faith and Hope. I fell head over heels in love with them at the hospital, and I'm going to miss them so much." Brooke said as she adjusted her chair causing the chain to rattle a little.

Cheri stopped writing and simply stared, blinking at Brooke for a moment, and then slowly turned toward the one-way mirror where Bravis was observing from the other side.

They had another killer to track down…

* * * * *

Doctor Scott was driving past the hospital on his way to the wedding when his cell alert system went off. "What the…?" The Alert was only used when there was some sort of mass casualty event such as the massive wreck that happened a few months before. He hit the brakes and spun the wheel, and in less than four minutes he was striding through the doors of the ER.

Abby was talking frantically with the new CNA that replaced Brooke. Before he got close, he heard Abby say, "Jackie, this big blue button is only pushed when we have a massive emergency. Please don't lean against this panel again." As Doctor Scott turned the corner of the nurses' station, he locked on to the prettiest set of soft brown eyes he'd ever seen. Her hair was pinned back with the exception of one escaped lock dangling in her eyes and her Latina skin was shadowed with the deepest burning blush on her face.

* * * * *

Link sat at the head table, thinking about the past year since Jenny came into their lives. "Wow," he said under his breath. He smiled when he thought of her, stuck in the snowbank, panicking that he'd tell Seth. He took another sip of his Jameson's and set the glass back down. *Olivia must be happy. No. She's got to be absolutely overjoyed.* He thought with another easy smile. The music the DJ was playing wasn't quite to his taste, but every now and then they played something he recognized and enjoyed. Jenny was stunning in her wedding dress. But was it just the dress? Jenny was certainly a beautiful girl, but maybe there was more. Maybe, because happiness creates its own radiance and when a soul has been through as much darkness as she has, it's much easier to appreciate happiness, the light, when it finally arrives. *Maria*- the thought of her came unbidden. *She too knew more hardship, more pain, more adversity than most people could know in three lifetimes… gone but never forgotten.* He picked up his glass, tapped it on the table and took a long swig of the amber liquid. "To you, old friend. I wish I had some of your plum schnapps."

Both the bride and groom held a special place in his heart. They were every bit his own. *Family. And the twins...* He swished the remaining whisky around in his glass. The twins had him wrapped tightly around their tiny little fingers, too. *I can't wait to take them fishing*, he thought. Then smiled as he dug out his memories of taking his own kids fishing. Not nearly often enough. His gaze swept across the room and settled on the Missing Man table, a lump instantly formed in his throat. An ache that will never cease, a hole in his heart that will never be filled. Link took a deep breath and held up his glass in a silent toast. "Miss you, Jason. Till the day I see you again, son." Then he quietly tapped his glass again on the table and took another pull of the slightly smoky whisky. Just then a pair of arms encircled his neck from behind and long dark hair tumbled down his bald head and past his cheeks.

"Tata?" Celia whispered in his ear. "I think you would look funny with hair."

Link looked up and smiled, grasped both of her hands and briefly held them in his own hand before kissing each one. "Hello my little mouse."

Celia took the seat next to him, wrapped her arms around his bicep and silently put her head on his shoulder.

"I miss her too." Link said softly.

They sat quietly together and watched the bride and groom dancing. "You couldn't knock the smiles off their faces with a brick." Link said with a chuckle. Seth still had a barely perceptible limp and some icing on his nose from where Jenny had stuffed it when they cut the cake. Link chuckled again. *I'm so proud of that girl.*

Ray, the DJ, called for time to throw the bouquet. Celia stood up suddenly and, without a word, headed out to where all the single girls gathered in front of Jenny causing Link's eyebrows to shoot up in surprise.

The DJ called out, "3...2...1..."

When Jenny tossed her bouquet, it was Celia who caught it. As high as she jumped, no other girl stood a chance. *Hmm... What does that mean?* Link asked himself. Scanning the audience, he didn't have to wait long for his answer. Jesse worked his way through the crowd and planted the biggest kiss on Celia's lips, to which she seemed to respond quite well. Then he scooped her up in his arms... and she let him. "I'll be damned." He said with satisfaction. *My son is in love with my daughter. Wait. Is that weird?* A secret and mysterious joy filled his heart. "Ah, life is good today."

His mind drifted around the room before it locked on a scene that played out earlier. Link and Victoria had parked a good distance from the reception hall. In typical fashion, Link reached out and took Victoria's hand as they walked down the sidewalk. They stopped to cross the street when Link caught sight of a man out of the corner of his eye. It was just for a moment, but Link knew exactly who it was. Willie. A former protégé from his past. "What was he doing here?" Link pondered.

"Don't be stupid," Link said aloud to the once again, empty table. *You know exactly why he's here and you know exactly what it means. It means that my IOU is about to be processed for collection and it just might get expensive.*

EPILOGUE

A well-tanned man with a movie star smile and short, jet-black hair pulled a cell phone from his pocket. He was leaning on the doorpost to a little bookstore where he could survey the downtown wedding festivities in Williston without being too obvious. The cell in his hand looked like any other cell phone to the casual observer, but to the user, it was always a bit heavier than the old one due to its *extra* features. Looking around first to make sure no one was close, he pressed a button, and waited. After a few seconds of beeps and hisses in his ear pod, the secure connection was finally made.

Tyson's Corner, VA

A curt female voice answered. "Jefferson-Franklin."

"Maggie? It's Willie. Is Mark about?" he said in a hurried, rushed voice, with a strong hint of a Kiwi accent.

"Hello, Willie." Maggie's voice brightened. "No, he's still at an appointment for his neck and he's been in a very bad mood today. Are you still in North Dakota?"

"Yeah," he replied. "But I'll be flying out this afternoon to keep an eye on the newlyweds. Tell me again why I've

361

been assigned to watch them and even more importantly, who gave them the call signs Fred & Wilma?"

"That decision was made above my paygrade but Mark says they are high value even though they don't know it yet.

"Well, I haven't been to Greece in a while, it ought to be fun.

"Speaking of Greece, Mark is sending a new analyst to Greece with you. You two will connect at JFK. She's developing some strong theories that Mark wants you two to kick around, plus he thinks some international field experience would give her some perspective outside the sterile world of analysis."

"Maggie, I am not in the business of babysitting."

"The boss says otherwise so you're just going to have to suck it up buttercup." Maggie said matter-of-factly.

"I can't believe this." Willie said, gripping the cell tightly. "Alright, which one is it? Do I know him?"

"It's not a him, it's a *her*, Stacy McFarland." Maggie said as she read it off of a roster.

"McFarland? Oh yeah, uh. Okay." Willie said, his attitude changing suddenly. " I saw her at the range, during my last qual. That girl can really shoot." Willie said, but it wasn't her gun handling that left the biggest impression. Even with her shooting glasses on, he remembered her eyes and her smile. Among other things. *I'll just have to suck it up and deal with it.* He thought to himself with a smile.

Maggie lowered her voice. "How does *he* look?" She asked, changing the subject.

"Link looks like he's never left Dagger," Willie replied with just a touch of awe in his voice. "He's quite fit, and still moves like a bloody cat."

"He trained you, didn't he?" Maggie reminded him.

"Yeah," Willie agreed. "But I thought he would have slowed down at least a little bit. To be honest, I was being careful, but I think he might have spotted me."

"Now Willie Toataua, is the Mighty Maori warrior losing his touch?" Maggie chided a bit.

"No, Maggie," he replied a little defensively. "But, I just may have underestimated Jiff in retirement and allowed myself to be a bit sloppy. I promise you, it won't happen again."

LINCOLN JAMES LEGACY
THE DAGGER'S OWN

PROLOGUE

It was a little after seven on a cold and windy North Dakota Friday night. As usual, Ashira was alone, at work, in the brand-new lab. The facility and equipment were state-of-the-art at a cost that climbed into the millions. She had fully dimmed the LED lighting in the rest of the lab and kept the lights semi bright just over her current workspace. The lab's bluetooth Bose Speakers were cranked up loud playing Pandora's classic rock channel. Currently, AC/DC's Thunderstruck throbbed throughout the room.

Working late again by choice, her new boss had told her she could have all the overtime she could handle so she'd probably be working straight through the weekend. *The extra money will really help my poor, starving bank account.* She thought. *What did dad always say?* Make hay while the sun shines and right now the sun is shining bright.

It wasn't just the overtime in her sights, she was attempting to get caught up on the huge backlog of shale oil samples. Mr. Whitman, or John, as he told her to call him, had been working side by side with her since she started. However, after receiving a phone call, he suddenly left work early to go home and pack. Whoever was on the other end of the phone wanted him on the next flight to Washington. He yelled over his shoulder on his way out that he wouldn't be back till Monday and not to work too hard. *Yeah, right.*

At five-foot two, she preferred to stand at the lab tables instead of sitting on the round lab stools scattered around the space. She was a twenty something brunette, with long straight, chestnut hair that came from her father's side of the DNA. It flowed down the back of her white lab coat all the way to the small of her back. Her large hazel eyes were currently fixed on the sample under the microscope. Each blink brushed her long eyelashes on the eyepiece as she scrutinized the crude oil soaked, shale rock. Busily taking notes, she moved from sample to sample.

Suddenly she looked up and pressed pause on her music, then pressed a large red button on the console that was labeled REC then said in a loud, clear, almost staccato voice. "Core sample 6177-91364. Tight shale, forty percent porous with significant hydrocarbons and Paraffins. Recommend Verde Frac solution 125." And pressed the button again.

She was a brand-new geologist, earning her degree from George Washington University. It had only been a month since she had started working for Global Endeavor Alliance, a relative newcomer in the oil industry known simply as GEA. The job was in their oil exploration operation in the Bakken oil fields located in Williston, North Dakota. Her Uncle Link had used his connections to get her an interview, but she got the job on her own merits.

Even with the music playing loudly, somehow, she was able to move smoothly to the beat as she concentrated on the new shale core sample under the microscope. With her back turned, she didn't notice that her silenced cell phone was vibrating on the desk behind her. The caller ID read Uncle Link. She didn't know it, but it was the fourth time in three minutes he'd tried to call.

The other ten missed calls were from her father, Mark.

She hit the red record button again, when, without warning, she was jerked backwards off of her feet and her lab speakers went flying. Two black-gloved hands grabbed her from behind. One hand over her mouth and the other around her chest. Bewildered for only a moment, her instinct for fight or flight kicked in and flight was not an option. Yet.

* * * * *

Made in the USA
Monee, IL
27 May 2022